Everything
We Ever Wanted

ALSO BY SARA SHEPARD

Everything
We Ever Wanted

A Novel

SARA SHEPARD

HARPER

NEW YORK • LONDON • TORONTO • SYDNEY

HARPER

This is a work of fiction. The characters, incidents, and dialogues are products of the author's imagination and are not to be construed as real. Any resemblance to actual persons, living or dead, is entirely coincidental.

Originally published in slightly different form in 2010 in Great Britain by HarperCollins UK.

HarperCollins books may be purchased for educational, business, or sales promotional use. For information please write: Special Markets Department, HarperCollins Publishers, 10 East 53rd Street, New York, NY 10022.

FIRST EDITION

Designed by Justin Dodd

Library of Congress Cataloging-in-Publication Data has been applied for.

ISBN 978-0-06-208006-6

11 12 13 14 15   OV/RRD   10 9 8 7 6 5 4 3 2 1

For Joel

Prologue

The man introduced himself on the phone as Michael Tayson, the new Swithin headmaster. "We haven't had the pleasure of meeting yet," he said.

"Ah, yes, of course," Sylvie said quickly, sitting up straighter. It was almost 9 p.m. on a Sunday night. *A strangely intimate time*, she thought, *for a chat*. "What can I do for you?"

"We have a bit of a situation," Michael Tayson said.

For a moment, Sylvie wondered if she'd fallen through a pocket in time. Her sons, Charles and Scott, were still teenagers. They were upstairs in their rooms, doing their homework—or, in Scott's case, *not* doing his homework—and it was Jerome Cunningham, the old headmaster, on the phone instead. He hadn't retired yet, the boys hadn't graduated yet, and James . . . well, James was still here, too, upstairs behind his closed office door. He could walk downstairs and she could still talk to him.

"One of our students passed away this morning," Michael Tayson went on, bringing her back to the present. "We're not sure how, but there are suspicions it might have been a suicide. His name was Christian Givens, a freshman. One of the scholarship boys."

Sylvie murmured how terrible that was, how sorry she felt for the family. All her years on the board, they'd had a few deaths—some car accidents, a case of Hodgkin's lymphoma—but never a suicide, thank God. Was he looking for suggestions about memorial services?

The church clock down at the end of Sylvie's drive bonged out the hour. "He was a wrestler," Michael finally said. "Your son coached him."

"Oh," Sylvie whispered.

"This is a delicate situation, obviously. We know how much you and your family . . . we know what you've done for us. But there might be questions. We'll try as best we can to keep things out of the spotlight, but you have to understand that it might not be possible." He took a deep breath. "Scott's job is all right for now. The season's finished. Next season, we'll have to see. This might blow over."

Sylvie stood up. "I'm sorry, what does this have to do with Scott?"

She heard a chair creaking and imagined that the man on the other end, a man she hadn't yet met, was leaning back. Sylvie had been in the office the school reserved for the headmaster plenty of times, especially when Scott was a student. Jerome had never suspended Scott for anything, even though Sylvie assured him that he should treat Scott the same as any other student. She knew why he let Scott's transgressions slide.

"There's a rumor going around," Michael Tayson said. "Apparently, there's a lot of pressure among the wrestlers. Some of the boys couldn't handle it."

"The weight-loss pressure," Sylvie ventured, "to make their weight class. But doesn't that happen on all wrestling teams?"

"This wasn't the typical weight-loss stuff, no."

"Okay . . ."

He coughed weakly. "I'm not saying it's true. I'll say that up front. But I've heard that if a boy doesn't perform well in the match, the boys . . . I'm not sure exactly what they do. There are beatings. Sometimes brutal, though you know boys—they hide these things if they can. No one wants to be the snitch; no one wants to look pathetic. There's humiliation as well. I've heard . . . well, I've heard all kinds of things. It's hard to say who's doing it. It may be just a few boys, but we suspect the others stand around and, well, watch. It's definitely bullying. Some may even call it hazing."

Sylvie felt dizzy. "Hazing," she repeated slowly.

"I also heard that Christian was one of the boys who . . . didn't perform well," the headmaster said. "I doubt you would remember him from the matches—he was awfully small, didn't get to compete much. Kept to himself. Maybe he wasn't cut out for the wrestling team, but as you know, we encourage our boys to participate in sports . . ."

Outside, the porch light made the wet tree branches glitter. "How many people know about this?" She thought of this getting out, the community talking—people outside the Swithin family. Some would grab onto a story like this and hold tight. The school's reputation suddenly felt delicate and precarious.

"We've tried to keep it quiet," he answered. "Bullying is such a sensitive topic right now . . ."

Suddenly, Sylvie scoffed. "Who told you this crazy idea?" It couldn't be true. Not at Swithin.

"I . . . I can't say."

There was a tingling sensation in her stomach. "And are you implying Scott encouraged these boys to . . . ?" She trailed off, touching the mantelpiece.

"Of course not," Michael said. "That's not—"

"What about the head coach? Mr. Fontaine? What does he have to say?"

"He's in England, visiting his mother. He left after the season ended. We're trying to reach him."

"And how many boys on the team have corroborated this story?"

"I didn't hear it from any of them, Mrs. Bates-McAllister."

"Well, there you go." Sylvie's heart was beating fast. "Someone made this up. You know how teenagers get with rumors. You know how they embellish things. Something is whispered to one person and by lunch it's a huge scandal."

There was a long pause. "I'm not suggesting I believe it," the head-master said. "I'm just explaining what I've heard. We take everything seriously, as you know. For now, I'm arranging for a few people to meet with Scott. It will be an independent council of teachers, none of your colleagues on the board. I don't want this to get out of hand, either for us or for you. Your family has done so much for the school, after all. And I know there have been some attempts at . . . how shall I put this? Some attempts at character assassination, I suppose, regarding certain members of your family in the past. I assure you that I intend to be discreet."

Sylvie ground her nails into the fabric of the sofa. *Character assassination. Discreet.* He had a way of making the words sound so dirty. "This is unprofessional." She paced around the room. "You can't call a coach in to talk to them about a ridiculous rumor. And you shouldn't come to me with something like this unless you *know.*"

"Calling Scott in to talk seems fair. If there was a rumor going around about someone else on the staff, another teacher, another coach, you would want us to feel that person out about it, wouldn't you, Mrs. Bates-McAllister?"

When Sylvie pressed her hand to her forehead, she felt a muscle in her temple throb, a tiny flutter under her skin. She glanced out the window in the kitchen; Scott's car wasn't in the driveway. She dared to think of what he was doing: lifting weights at the gym, playing video games, driving the Mercedes too fast, whipping around the turns and grinding the gears. She thought of the jobs he'd held: the stint as an auto mechanic, mostly learning the ropes so he could soup up his own car, which he'd since crashed. Pouring concrete, coming home covered in gray film. Even that time he caddied at James's golf club, though that had lasted only a day; he'd said the golfers were racist, giving him accusing looks as if he was going to walk off with their clubs. She'd felt urgently optimistic with each job he took, praying that this one would be his true path, the thing that set him straight. He quit each job after only a matter of weeks.

Something else appeared in her mind, too. When Scott was ten or eleven, she had come upon him in the basement. He was crouched in the corner, watching something. A mouse was trapped under a large glass vase, slowly suffocating. It clawed the sides of the vase, its little paws scrambling. How had it gotten there? It took her a few moments to understand. "Scott!" she'd cried out, but her voice was so weak, so ineffectual. *Always* so ineffectual. When he didn't do anything, she'd pushed him aside, lifted the vase, and let the mouse go. Scott had looked at her like she was crazy. She complained about mice in the basement all the time—didn't she want them dead? But it was Scott's expression, as he'd watched the mouse flail under the dome that had made her set it free. The look on his face was one of iron-cold indifference, as if he'd almost enjoyed the poor creature's suffering.

Oh God, she thought now, a rushing feeling between her ears. *Oh God*.

"Mrs. Bates-McAllister?" the new headmaster said softly into the phone. "Are you still there?"

"Thank you for calling," she said in the strongest voice she could muster. "But I think what you're suggesting—"

"I'm not suggesting anything," he broke in. "You've misunderstood—"

"—is a mistake," she finished and hung up.

The living room was foolishly quiet. The antique armchair was tilted toward the bookshelf at a rakish angle. The old etchings of the Swithin School, commissioned by Sylvie's grandfather and handed down to her when she had inherited this house, were at perfect right angles on the walls. Sylvie looked at the framed photograph of her grandparents that sat on the top of the sideboard. Her grandfather's cunning, sepia-toned eyes seemed more narrowed than usual, as though he'd heard both sides of the phone conversation.

Oh, how she'd cared for everything in this house. How she'd taken pride in all its details, preserved it to the letter, thinking that keeping everything exactly the same would embalm the spirit and ideals of her grandfather forever. After all, this house essentially *was* her grandfather—the local press had dubbed it Roderick, the middle name he often went by. But the resemblance didn't stop there. The old leather books on the shelves were like the wrinkled tops of her grandfather's hands. The curled vines that climbed the stone walls were his thick mass of hair. The scalloped cornices on the porch resembled his mustache. Sometimes when Sylvie walked through certain rooms, she could still smell her grandfather—spicy yet clean, like tobacco and books and linen. She sometimes glimpsed a flicker out of the corner of her eye, a glimmer in a mirror, the wattage in a lightbulb adjusting— all signs, maybe, that he was watching.

Hazing. She couldn't quite connect it to the meaning the new headmaster had given. She saw a fogged window instead, fresh with dew. A method used by pastry chefs to brown the top of a crème brûlée. *Hazing.* It was too artful a word to have such a connotation.

"Well," she said aloud, and brushed her already-clean hands on her pants.

She climbed up the staircase and stood in front of James's office door. It had become her ritual to linger there for a moment before going in. Sometimes she even knocked, as if he were still inside. The room was colder and darker than the rest of the house. James had only been gone for two months, but the office had lost his essence—the general chaos of his papers, the constantly illuminated message light on his office line's phone. All the books had been put away on the old bookshelves. James's desk—a clean, modern thing of glass and metal that had long ago replaced Sylvie's grandfather's old, mahogany mammoth—had been wiped down weeks ago, not a fingerprint marring its surface.

A month ago, Sylvie finally found the key to James's filing cabinet nestled behind one of the books on the shelves. It now rested at the base of the lamp, waiting. Sylvie could easily imagine sliding it into the lock on the filing cabinet. She could almost hear the *click* of the barrel releasing, the metallic hiss of the drawer opening. Knowing James, she guessed that he saved the most significant documents of his life in paper hard copy, not stored on his computer's hard drive. All she had to do was unlock the drawer, riffle through a folder, and finally have a name to connect with her hurt. That would be all it took to know.

She remained in the office for a minute or so, daring herself. Then, as always, when things began to seem too close, she turned around and left the room, leaving the key behind.

Part I

one

Joanna Bates-McAllister—née Farrow—had heard from the very start that her husband Charles's adopted brother, Scott, was an asshole. *An ungrateful asshole*, were the precise words. Needless to say, they'd never been close.

According to her husband, Charles's delivery had been so painful and dangerous that the doctors had told the Bates-McAllisters that it wouldn't be safe to conceive again, so they had chosen to adopt. They'd gone through all kinds of hoops to bring Scott into their home. *And look how* that *turned out*, was what the entire family seemed to think, though no one ever said it aloud.

Recently, the Bates-McAllisters had willingly converted a whole section of their estate into a bachelor pad for Scott, furnishing it with high-tech electronics, a kitchenette, and even a separate entrance, never encouraging him to leave, even though he was twenty-nine years old. Charles told Joanna that Scott didn't hang out with a single student that went to their private school, Swithin, but instead with kids from public school. And not the public schools in the suburbs, either; Scott gravitated toward kids without parents, kids whose fathers were in jail, kids whose siblings dealt meth.

By the end of high school, Mr. and Mrs. Bates-McAllister's standards for Scott had fallen so laughably low that they were relieved Scott had made it the whole way through Swithin without getting expelled, developing a drug addiction, or going to prison. Joanna had known lots of Scotts in her day. He was the kind of guy who somehow always had something pithy and painfully intuitive to say, even though he did miserably in school. *What a pity*, adults would whisper, crossing to the other side of the street when he came near. *Wonder what went wrong?* Joanna had dated a few watered-down versions of Scott in the past, their self-absorption impossible to crack, their indifference heartbreaking, and their roughness touching something deep inside her. Perhaps that was why she found herself defending him to her husband whenever he complained. Perhaps that was why she blushed whenever Scott came near, her heart drumming like a metronome cranked up to *molto allegro*.

Despite Scott's tough exterior, when Charles told her that his brother had been implicated in a boy's death at school, Joanna could not believe that he would have anything to do with someone's suicide. Much less encourage . . . well, whatever had happened.

What could have been going on? She tried to picture a fluorescent-lit, ripe-smelling wrestling room. The boys in a huddle, having lost their match. Scott approaching, the anticipation of a pep talk about how they were going to practice harder and do better next time.

And then, what? Sure, a lot of people had it in them to say, *You, you, and you. In the center there. Practice isn't working, but maybe this will.* And then beatings. Horrible humiliations, like the ones Joanna had seen so many times on television. Scars that would never heal. Maybe all that had happened, but Joanna had her doubts about whether Scott cared enough to be that involved. It was high-school wrestling, for Christ sake. Scott didn't seem to care about anything else; why start with that?

It was possible, she supposed, that he'd heard the boys were performing silly hazing rituals but hadn't witnessed it firsthand, and so let it slip his mind, figuring the boys would just work it out themselves. Really, who wasn't guilty of letting things happen without doing the appropriate things to stop them? Once, when Joanna lived in Philadelphia after college, she'd watched out her apartment window as a young guy robbed an old woman. The man knocked the woman to the ground and ran away with her purse—it was black patent leather, with an old-fashioned chain strap—and Joanna just stood stock-still against the kitchen counter, her hand to her mouth. Lately, more and more, Joanna felt as though she was watching her own life pass by without intervening. It was as if, she sometimes thought, her true self was becoming smaller and dimmer, and all she could do was stand there, her hand at her mouth, simply staring.

Joanna and Charles had been in bed when Sylvie called with the news. Joanna picked up the phone, saw Sylvie's name on the caller ID, and quickly passed it to Charles without picking up first, feeling too shy and intrusive to talk to Sylvie herself. Charles took the phone, waited, and then pushed back the covers, slid on his slippers, and padded out of the room. "Now wait, Mom," he said as he walked down the hall. "Just a second. He said *what?* And that has to do with us . . . *how?*"

Charles came back to the bedroom a little later, his face ashen. The phone was in his limp right hand; his left hand raked through his hair. Joanna knew right away something was wrong. She also felt a twinge of annoyance that he'd gotten up from the bed to have the conversation away from her. Why didn't he feel comfortable with her listening?

They'd been married for six months; when would these boundaries between them go away?

"There's some sort of trouble with my brother at school" was all Charles had said. He'd climbed back into bed and turned the television to a tennis match, cranking the volume high. She'd pressed him for information, but he hadn't told her much else, staring glazed-eyed at the screen. Most of the details were still tangled in Joanna's mind. She didn't understand whether there *was* any evidence that hazing had happened, or whether the school could point fingers at Scott and, by association, Sylvie, or what would happen if they did. Nor did she know if Charles believed, deep down, that Scott was capable of such a thing. He hadn't said one way or the other.

It was the next day, as they were on their way to Charles's childhood home, when Joanna dared to bring it up again. "So, is your mom worried about her place on the board?" she asked.

Charles gave her a sidelong glance. "Why would she be worried?"

Joanna sighed. Fine, he was going to make her spell this out. "Because of that boy's suicide. Because of—you know—what people are saying. I thought you said the school was superjudgmental. If one family member's bad, they're all blacklisted."

"Why would you think that?" Charles said.

"I don't know," she said, adding, "I didn't go to that school, Charles. Remember? I don't know *what* to think about it."

"Well, you should know better than to think *that*."

Charles had recently had his hair cut, the ends now hung bluntly just above his ears, reminding her of the crisp bristles of a broom. He still went to the same barber who'd cut his hair when he was a boy. He was fiercely loyal in that way, patronizing the same business establishments for years, diligently keeping in touch with old prep-school friends, and even remaining faithful to inanimate, unresponsive things, such as old jogging routes and brands of breakfast cereals.

"And anyway, I don't think it's going to go very far. It's just a stupid rumor," Charles said as they swept past a large vacant lot that sold Christmas trees in December. "You know how kids talk."

They turned up the winding street that eventually led to Sylvie's house. She had invited them over for dessert that evening. Charles had announced the invitation only an hour ago upon coming home from work: a sharp contrast to the protocol by which Sylvie usually summoned them for visits—e-mailing them days ahead of time, negotiating both their schedules to see when was best for all. Sylvie wasn't the type to demand they come only when it suited her. That was Joanna's mother's territory. If Joanna had to make a guess—and she always had to guess because none of the Bates-McAllisters would ever tell her directly—she'd say that today's invitation was a response to whatever the situation was with the wrestlers.

Joanna sat back in the passenger seat, letting the iPod she'd been fiddling with fall to her lap. "So what happened, anyway? How'd the boy kill himself?"

"I don't know," Charles answered.

"Your mom didn't tell you?"

"I don't think she knows, either."

"Was there a suicide note?"

"No. They don't even know if it's a suicide. They're doing an autopsy to find out."

Joanna paused, considering this. "My mother says Scott should talk to a lawyer."

"You talked to your *mother* about this?" His face registered annoyance.

"It just slipped out on the phone today," she admitted.

"You had to run and tell her, didn't you?"

"It just slipped out," she repeated defensively, adjusting her seat belt. "So, do you have any idea who's supplying these hazing rumors?"

"No." He took one hand off the steering wheel and ran it over his head.

"Who could it be?"

"Joanna, I don't know."

"Why aren't you curious?"

"Why are *you*?" But he said it quietly, almost tepidly.

The trees formed a canopy over the road. Small green buds dotted some of them, but others were bare. "I just worry, that's all," Joanna said. "Your poor mom. After your dad and all . . . she doesn't need this."

Charles pulled the lever for the wiper fluid. The windshield wipers made a honking sound and slid the liquid across the glass. "Probably not."

"And I think you should help Scott. You're his brother, after all. Don't you think you should?"

"Well, he hasn't asked for help."

"People don't always ask," she reminded him.

"We don't know that he's done anything wrong."

Joanna touched the smooth, slick buttons on her jacket. She was tempted to ask Charles if he really believed that.

"Don't worry about it, okay?" Charles said, putting on his turn signal. "It's not a big deal."

They were at the turnoff to his parents' house. It was so ensconced by trees it was easy to miss. Charles pulled up the long, winding drive. A pine near one of the turns had fallen against a few other trees, reminding Joanna of a drunken girl propped up by her friends at the end of a long night. They pulled into the circular drive behind Sylvie's car, the barely used Mercedes she often parked outside, and Scott's car, the slightly older Mercedes that Sylvie had given to him, which was always outside. Scott's Mercedes had dings on the side, worn tires, and a speckled half-moon of rust across the front bumper. The back bumper was plastered with stickers, many of them angry. One bumper sticker near the window read FREE MUMIA; it featured a picture of a black man with a beard and dreadlocks who'd been wrongfully imprisoned. According to an article Joanna read on Wikipedia after first seeing the sticker, this Mumia guy had been accused of committing a crime because of preconceived notions about his past, his looks.

The house loomed ahead of them, a grand estate more than a hundred years old that Charles's great-grandfather had passed on to Sylvie. It was made entirely of stone with a low wall around it, a little balcony on the upper floor surrounded by a wrought-iron terrace, and a six-car detached garage across the driveway. The house had several chimneys for the four fireplaces inside, three gables that demarcated the separate wings, and a brass weather vane in the shape of a rooster at the very highest point. There were three patios, a sunroom, and a pool out back, and the whole thing was surrounded by thick, shapely pines and an elegant garden. Whenever Joanna beheld the estate, she got reverent chills; she always felt that she needed to be on her best behavior here. It was like what her mother used to say to her when they went to Mass at the drafty, icon-filled, stained-glass Catholic church in

Lionville, Pennsylvania, where she'd grown up: *Don't make any noise. Don't touch anything. God's looking at you.*

Sylvie was already waiting for them on the large brick side porch, her hands clasped at her waist, a brave smile on her face. As always, she was impeccably dressed in an ironed lavender skirt and a perfectly tucked-in eyelet blouse. She even wore heels, lavender, to match the skirt, and pearls looped twice around her throat. She always dressed this way—to go to the grocery store, to go for a walk. The ring Charles's father had given her a few months before he died glimmered under the porch light.

"I made banana bread, Charlie," she said after everyone hugged. "Your favorite."

They entered the house through the kitchen. Dim, golden light filtered through the stained-glass window, dappling the white wooden cabinets, the ancient, rounded Sub-Zero refrigerator, and the stout, space-age MasterChef stove. The smell of banana bread drifted comfortingly through the air. Sylvie had put on an old classical record, presumably plucked from the collection that belonged to her grandfather.

"Sit, sit," Sylvie urged, gesturing toward the kitchen table. A bunch of vacation property brochures were spread out on the surface. As Joanna and Charles sat down, a very different sort of song thumped through the walls to their left. Joanna cocked her head, listening to the thumping beat, the muddy bass, the muffled shouting. Scott's suite shared a wall with the kitchen. She tried to meet Charles's eye.

"So listen—we're so behind!" Sylvie said, fluttering from the oven to the cupboards to the sink and then repeating the cycle all over again, though bringing nothing to the table. "We haven't picked out a vacation house for this summer! But I think I found a good one. It's on the water in Cape May. July seventh to the twenty-first."

She plucked a magazine from the pile on the table and leafed to a marked page. "Here. It has seven bedrooms, which seems like a lot, but you know those houses—they're all huge. Really, I wonder if we should just buy a place instead of rent. Then we could decorate it the way we want."

Charles shifted in his seat. Joanna wondered if he was thinking what she was thinking: planning a vacation in the middle of a scandal seemed inappropriate. Only, *was* that what was going on? A scandal?

"And it's brand new," Sylvie went on, pointing at the tiny pictures of the house's interior: a country kitchen with white bead board on the walls, a master bedroom with lavender striped curtains, and a shed filled with beach balls, bicycles, plastic kayaks, and kites. "It won't have that smell—you know that old beach smell? Even the nicest houses get it sometimes." She flipped through the catalog to another page. "Though this one's nice, too; it's closer to town. It's hard to decide." She looked up at Charles, her face softening as if a thought had just struck her. "Honey, don't feel like you have to come for the whole time. I know you have to work. But at least for a week, right? And then for the weekends?"

The volume on the other side of the wall rose higher. Joanna glanced at Charles again, but his eyes were stubbornly fixed on the rental magazine.

"And we'll need so many supplies," Sylvie added. She grabbed a Land's End catalog from the bottom of the pile. "I've marked lots of things." She turned to a page that displayed flashlights, travel mugs, a fondue pot. "We could make s'mores on the beach," she crowed gaily. "Wouldn't that be fun?"

"Huh," Charles murmured vaguely.

Sylvie folded her hands over the magazine. "How *is* work, by the way?"

Charles shrugged. "You know, busy."

"Dealing with any interesting clients?"

There was an abrupt, fuzzy *thud* next door, and then a faster-paced song. Joanna flinched, but she didn't bother glancing at Charles again. He was obviously ignoring it, and her.

"Not really," Charles spoke over the noise. "Same ones."

"And Joanna?" Sylvie turned politely to face her daughter-in-law. "How's the new house coming along?"

Joanna smiled. "Good. Lots of boxes to unpack still, though."

"Have you met any of your neighbors?"

She looked down. "Uh, no one yet. But I'm sure we will soon."

Sylvie nodded. Joanna could tell she was searching for something more specific she could ask her about—a hobby, maybe—but was coming up with nothing. "Excellent," she finally said. And then, "Goodness. The bread."

She scampered to the oven, slid on two mitts, and pulled the banana bread pan from the tray. Steam curled around her face, fogging her small, wire-framed glasses. She carried the pan over to the table, removed one of her oven mitts with her teeth, and set the mitt on the table below the bread pan. The knife slid easily against the sides of the pan, and more steam gushed out. She pushed the pan over to Charles, who cut himself a thick slice and put it on his plate. He used the side of his fork to cut off a bite.

Joanna waited and waited. Just as he was about to put the bite in his mouth, she touched his arm and said in a voice far whinier than she intended, "*Charles?*"

He looked up; she nudged her chin toward the pan. He lowered his fork. "Oh. Sorry."

He began cutting her a piece, but she changed her mind and waved him away. "I'll be back," she muttered, standing.

"Joanna," Charles protested. "I didn't know you wanted any. You don't usually eat dessert."

"It's fine," she said loudly, backing out of the room. "I just . . . the bathroom." She rounded the corner into the hall.

It was probably silly to feel slighted over banana bread. More than that, Joanna just felt too weird sitting there, looking at vacation houses, chatting about work, ignoring the obvious, especially with Scott fiddling with the stereo one wall away. Nothing seemed to ever get to the Bates-McAllisters, though. Joanna certainly hadn't been raised like this. If Scott was her brother and her parents were faced with such a scandal—and if her parents were still together—they would confront the problem head-on. Her mother would be a hurricane of panic, making sweeping what-will-the-neighbors-think-of-us statements. Her father would be smacking his fist into an open palm, declaring he'd never wanted to live in such an arrogant, stick-up-your-ass part of Pennsylvania in the first place. He was from the western part of the state, where what one drove and where one shopped and the way one pronounced certain vowels didn't matter nearly as much. His anger would just incite her mother's panic—*If only you would've tried harder to fit in, Craig, this might not have happened*, she would say—and that, in turn, would stoke his fury, and they'd circle each other like two worked-up dogs, their bad energies becoming so toxic that a massive fight was inevitable.

Joanna walked down Roderick's grand hall, which was lined on both sides with heavy, gold-framed oil paintings of foxhunts on scenic vistas, Scottish moors, and generals on horseback. Charles had first brought her here to meet his family two Julys ago, and though she'd been building up the Bates-McAllisters and their estate in her mind long before she and Charles met—though Charles didn't know anything about that—the house had lived up to every one of her expectations. Sylvie's meticulously tended garden had been abloom, the tiki lamps by the pool cast soft shadows across the slate patio, and there was a full moon over the roof, so perfectly centered that it was as though Sylvie and James had commissioned it to hang there for them alone.

She'd been blind to the house's imperfections for a long time. She didn't notice the wet wood smell. She didn't see the chips in the leaded glass, the stains on the intricate woodwork, or the large brown patch on the ceiling from a previous leak. It didn't occur to her that the Chippendale highboy chest of drawers was water-warped, that the oil paintings needed a professional cleaning, or that the chandeliers were missing several of their crystals. So what if one of the rooms was filled with nothing but piles of papers, old, cloth-wrapped paintings, and a piano with chipped, yellowed ivory keys? So what if the library had a mouse hole the size of Joanna's fist? So what if the oil painting of Charles Roderick Bates, Charles's great-grandfather, which hung over the stairs, freaked Joanna out every time she passed by it? All old aristocratic homes had charming idiosyncrasies. And this was *Roderick*.

But lately, something had changed, and she'd begun to see the house as, well . . . *old*. Unkempt, even. The rooms were always too cold, especially the bathrooms. The cushions on the living room couch were uncomfortable: a sharp spring managed to press into her butt no matter which position she tried. Some of the unused rooms smelled overwhelmingly like mothballs, others like sour milk, and there were visible gaps amid many of the bathroom floor tiles, desperate for grout.

The most unsettling thing, though, was that when Joanna walked into certain rooms, it was as if someone—or something—was following her. The house and everything in it seemed *human*, if she really got down to it. And not like a sprightly young girl, either, but a crotchety, elderly man. The pipes rattled like creaky bones and joints. When she sat down in a chair, any chair, there was an abrupt huffing sound, like someone collapsing from a long day's work. The radiators wheezed, coughed, and even spat out strange hints of smells that seemed to be coming from the house's human core. A whisper of soapy jasmine seeped from its plaster skin. An odor of ham and cloves belched out of an esophageal vent.

She stepped down the hall now, gazing at the black-and-white photographs that lined the walls. Sylvie had taken the pictures during a trip to the beach when the children were young. In some of them, Charles and Scott, probably about eight and six, were flying a kite. Charles had an intense look of concentration as he held the kite's string, as if a judging committee was watching, while Scott looked disdainfully off toward the waves. In the pictures of them in the ocean, Scott ran happily toward the waves, his arms and legs outstretched like a starfish. It was startling to see a photo of Scott so young and carefree, enjoying life. James skipped out to the ocean, too, equally exuberant, but Charles hung back, his expression timid and penitent. The last photo in the row was a close-up of the three of them. Scott and their father were soaked, but Charles's hair was still neatly combed, bone-dry. Two genuine smiles, the third seemed forced.

"See anything interesting?"

Joanna jumped. Scott stood at the bottom of the stairs, his hands hidden in his sweatshirt pouch. His eyes glowed, as if she'd turned a flashlight on some wild animal in the woods.

Joanna pressed her hand to her breastbone. She could feel her heart through her thin sweater. "H–How did you get here?"

Scott gestured with his thumb toward the front door. The easiest way to get to the main house from his quarters was to exit through the door of his suite, walk all of four steps, and enter the house through the mud room, which led to the kitchen. Instead, Scott had walked the whole way around the outside of the house to this door, the front door. He had to know that Joanna and Sylvie and Charles were convened in the kitchen. The smell of banana bread was overpowering, penetrating the thick walls.

So he'd avoided them. Of course he didn't want to see them. Was it because he didn't want to answer their questions about the incident? Although that was laughable; they wouldn't *ask* him questions. *No one* ever asked Scott questions. Sylvie would flutter about, shove a piece of bread at Scott, and hover over him obsequiously until he ate it. Joanna would make small talk, busying her hands with the bread knife or the catalogs. And Charles would sit silent, seething. Scott wouldn't have to face anything. Everyone always tiptoed around him, even when he hadn't done anything wrong.

Scott raised his chin, gazing at her unflinchingly. Perhaps he knew what was going through her mind, what she was trying to figure out. She dared to peek back. He looked the same as he always did—disheveled and self-assured, lazily handsome. He obviously looked nothing like the other Bates-McAllisters, with their wide eyes and thin lips and ears that stuck out slightly. While Charles and Sylvie's skin were pale, Scott's was more of an olive tone, easily tanned and never blotchy. His facial features a curious, intriguing mix of cultures. It was one of the many things the family never talked about—that Scott wasn't white. It both was and wasn't an issue for them. They acted as though it didn't matter, yet Joanna wondered if, subconsciously, it affected their every reaction.

Scott didn't *seem* any different in the wake of the boy's death. Certainly not weighed down or guilty about anything. If he was hiding something, the shame would be written all over his face, wouldn't it?

Joanna lowered her eyes, realizing she'd been staring at him too long. "I should . . ." she said, ducking her head and teetering, idiotically, toward the kitchen.

"Leaving because of me?" he teased. When he smiled, he showed off long, wolflike teeth.

"Um, no. No!" Joanna sputtered. Her face felt hot. She scrambled for a pressing reason to be back in the kitchen but came up with nothing.

Scott stepped forward until he was just inches from her. He remained there, appraising Joanna, making up his mind about something. He was close enough that Joanna could smell cigarettes and soap on him, so close he might kiss her. She could see the V-shaped fibers in his sweatshirt and that the drawstring for his hood was tipped with silvery metal. He breathed in and out. She barely breathed at all. She felt so small and vulnerable next to him. Hummingbird-frail.

"Boo," Scott whispered.

"Ha!" Joanna exclaimed, as if she thought it was a joke, jumping a little.

Scott quickly receded. In seconds, he was at the front door. Once his back was to her, he held a dismissive hand over his head. "Later."

The door banged shut. Joanna listened to his footsteps walking down the flagstone path. A car door slammed, the tires screeched. The heat kicked on, and an unsavory mix of dust, clove cigarettes, and varnish wafted through the vents. She remained in the hallway for a moment, raking her fingernails up and down her bare arms. There was a wet prickle of sweat on the back of her neck. Her skin felt flushed.

Boo.

When Joanna returned to the kitchen, she expected Charles and Sylvie to look up, instantly aware that something about her was askew. But their heads were pressed together close, whispering.

"But, Mom," Charles was saying. "The call. Don't you think—"

"There's nothing to talk about," Sylvie interrupted.

Joanna took a step back and slid behind the wall. They hadn't seen her.

"Still. You should call a lawyer. Just in case," Charles hissed.

Joanna widened her eyes. So he *did* think a lawyer idea was a good idea.

There was the sound of rustling papers. "What would be the point of that?" Sylvie asked.

"Protection, obviously. It could mitigate things."

Sylvie murmured something Joanna couldn't hear. Then Charles sighed. "But what about what happened at the graduation party?" he whispered. "Remember? The fight in front of Bronwyn? Do you think that could be a link to this thing with Scott and the boys?"

"No," his mother interrupted fast. "There's no link between this and that."

"How can you be so sure?" he pressed. Sylvie didn't answer.

Joanna couldn't stand it anymore. She tiptoed back to the bathroom, flushed the toilet, opened the sink taps the whole way so that Charles and Sylvie would hear them gushing. She stared at herself in the mirror. Her mouth was a small, crinkled O. Her skin was pallid, almost yellowish.

What had happened at the graduation party? Did Scott attack Charles? He'd never told her that.

She shut off the taps. And then she clomped across the living room, shaking the tension out of her hands. She even feigned a cough, as if all those other sounds weren't enough. Sylvie and Charles were already snapped back to their cheerful selves by the time she walked through the doorway. They were waiting for her, smiling welcomingly.

"Everything all right?" Sylvie asked.

"Of course." Joanna sat down, pulled an L.L. Bean catalog toward her, and whipped through the pages. Travel alarm clocks! Monogrammed tote bags! Pictures of vacationing families, all of them guileless and trouble-free!

So Charles and his mother *were* worried about Scott, but they were leaving Joanna out of it. Maybe because she wasn't family, maybe because she wouldn't understand, or maybe because she wasn't important enough to know. There were so many possibilities. Joanna tried to conceal the mix of hurt and disappointment she felt as best she could, leaning over the pages, chuckling when they got to the travel section for pets. The manufacturer made a dog travel bed that could fold up to the size of a hackey sack. Imagine that.

two

Fischer Custom Editorial had been planned out carefully by designers and architects, perhaps even sociologists and psychiatrists. Individual workstations were private and quiet, whereas the meeting rooms were bright, vivid, and provocative, overlooking Philadelphia's City Hall. All the bathrooms were equidistant from where everyone sat. Even the items in the vending machines had probably been chosen after months of careful research—enough low-calorie treats for dieters, enough Snickers and Milky Ways for bingers. Things with nuts and things without nuts. An assortment of teas and gourmet coffees. There was always wine and beer in the full-size fridge, and they had parties at 4 p.m. every Friday to boost morale.

Charles Bates-McAllister sat in his boss's office with a few others, staring at a pamphlet which lay on the glass table. The photo on the front was of a couple standing in a field, the man with a long beard and wild hair, the fresh-faced woman in a long dress and an apron. It reminded Charles of the famous *American Gothic* painting, except that the man had an earring and a tattoo on his neck that peeked out from under his plaid shirt, and the woman looked way too refreshed and delighted to have spent all her life working the fields. "Back to the Land," said the caption, in large yellow block letters.

"So this is the idea," his boss, Jake, said. "For one year, people give up their lives. They quit their jobs, they leave their homes—maybe they sell their homes—they come to central Pennsylvania and build a house from scratch, out of logs, moss, and whatever else. While they're building their house, they have to live in a tent. Even if it's winter. They build their own furniture and grow their own food. If they eat meat, they shoot and prepare it. They're mostly given some livestock and sheep, and they make their own clothes. They can choose to be in a community and have a specialized job, or they can live in the wilderness. Of course, the wilderness isn't really that far from civilization. A hospital is only twenty minutes away. If they need a telephone, they can find one."

The whole table stared at him. "And people *do* this?" Jessica, the photo editor, finally asked.

"A lot of people," Jake answered. "You wouldn't believe how many people."

"It sounds like a cult," Steven from the art department murmured.

Jake shrugged. "Some people see it as a vacation, I guess. I know, *I* don't get it, either."

"And you have to *pay* for this?" Steven asked.

Jake nodded. "You pay for the land you live on. I think it's thirty thousand dollars a year. And they provide training so that you won't die out there."

"Thirty thousand dollars?" Jessica whispered.

"And some people stay for more than a year," Jake said. "They see it as an escape. Freedom."

Everyone was silent. "Maybe in this day and age, with the economy tanking, terrorists blowing up hotels, and the housing market crashing, this is what people want," Becky, a fellow editor, suggested.

Charles looked at the photo again. The couple *did* look happy. But he figured it was a kooky kind of happiness reserved for the same kinds of people who meditated and spoke to plants.

"They want us to do a magazine feature about their community," Jake explained, "to drum up business. I know it's a little unusual and not the normal kind of account we typically accept, but we're hurting for money. And maybe this will be an opportunity for all of you to stretch your skills a little."

Charles shifted. *Stretching their skills* was a euphemism for putting aside all judgments about this kind of endeavor and making the best possible product he could. Then again, it wasn't that different from the slightly contradictory messages he was encouraged to ignore about Fischer's other clients. Like the car manufacturer that asked him to write an article about their brand-new SUV and just "tone down" the fact that the car got terrible highway and city gas mileage. Or the credit card company that suggested Charles write a story encouraging shoestring-budget families to charge thousands of dollars more on their Visa, so that they would accrue enough rewards points to buy a handheld shoulder massager or an iPod docking system.

Perhaps Jake had selected Charles and the rest of his colleagues for this particular project because they were all the least likely to say no. Steven was unabashedly Christian; spiritual songs were always floating out from his office, and at last year's Christmas party, he'd earnestly asked one of the junior designers to check out his church. He never refused anything that was given to him, as if it wouldn't be Jesus-like to do so. Jessica was at risk for being fired—she had been egregiously late with shots for another magazine, and another photo editor had to step in and bail her out. Becky always did whatever anyone asked of her, without complaint. Charles was somewhat the same—he never voiced a moral objection to anything they wrote about or stood behind. Whenever he felt tempted to whine, he saw himself at eight years old, running frantically behind his brother into the ocean. When a wave took him down and tossed him back to shore, his father stood over him on the beach. *What's the matter with you? You're alive. You're fine. Your brother can do it, and he's two years younger. Stop crying.*

Charles had been fresh out of journalism school when he was hired by Jake three years ago. His dad had gotten Charles the interview without asking him if he wanted it—Finn, a colleague at the investment firm, had a wife who was high up at Fischer, and if Charles wanted a job as an editor, he could have one. At first Charles blurted out that it didn't sound like the type of job he was looking for; it seemed an awful lot like advertising. His dad's face had clouded. "Finn didn't have to talk to his wife, you know," he said. "Not every job can be the *New York Times*."

Realizing his mistake, Charles had backpedaled and thanked his dad for thinking of him. The night before the interview he had dinner with his parents and his father asked him when the interview was and spoke about how it was a decent company, how Charles would probably get further working for a company like Fischer than slaving as a beat reporter at a fledgling local newspaper. "You and your dad could meet up for lunch!" his mother added wistfully, because Charles's office would only be four blocks from his father's. Charles had nodded along, simply trying to keep the peace. Scott had sat at the table, too, snickering. No one asked him what was funny. All their father did was glance benignly at Scott, a hopeful smile on his face, desperate to amend whatever he'd done wrong. Eventually, Scott laid down his fork and scraped back his chair and left the table, as if he'd suddenly realized they all thought he was willingly participating in a family event.

After the interview, Charles drove back to his parents' house and triumphantly told them that he got the job. His father looked at him blankly, and then guffawed. "Well of course you got it. Finn promised me you would. That interview was just a formality." And then he went back to his newspaper.

That was three years ago. Charles always thought he'd be at a different point in his career by this age. Traveling the world, reporting on famines, bombings, and assassinations. Sneaking into trials and interviewing the wrongfully accused. Possibly ghostwriting a book about a senator with secrets. His mother had told him that by the time his great-grandfather was thirty-one, he'd had a private meeting with Nelson Rockefeller. The most influential person Charles had ever met was a hostess of a television quiz show whose program was being converted into a game that a certain cell phone provider's customers could play on their BlackBerries. And though Jake promised that Charles would get a lot of opportunities to write, usually he passed Charles over for assignments, giving them to his freelancer friends instead.

Every so often Charles would glance through the paper for entry-level newspaper jobs, but they didn't seem to exist. Newspapers were disappearing across the country and with all the bloggers, Twitterers, and iReporters, journalists were becoming extinct as well. Though starting over seemed exhausting, and he had to stand on his own two feet. It was bad enough that he'd had to draw from his trust fund for the house's down payment. His mother had always told him not to feel bad about using money from the trust. It was *his*, there was no use feeling ashamed. But Charles couldn't help it—everything made him feel ashamed. Every choice seemed incorrect. What would his life have been like if he'd gone to law school? Where would he be now if he'd taken that job at the local newspaper in that little town in Montana? The one he'd applied for on a whim and been hired for, sight unseen?

And there were other choices, ones that quietly dogged him. Where would he be now if he and Scott hadn't gotten into that fight the day of his graduation? What would be happening now if he could take back what he had said? Would he still be with his high-school girlfriend, Bronwyn? Would she still be *speaking* to him at least? And would this business with Scott and the wrestlers have even happened?

Maybe it was foolish to think like that. One episode couldn't have altered Scott's entire trajectory. Scott was who he was before Charles had said what he said. The past was the past, and the best thing Charles could do was put it out of his mind.

By the time the meeting ended, the editorial team had decided the story lineup for the Back to the Land promotional feature. There would be a short piece about the land the organization had annexed for the community in central Pennsylvania, a valley rife with deer and rabbits for shooting, streams for drinking, and hearty trees for log cabins. Charles had no idea how a plot of land in the middle of Pennsylvania could be desolate and remote enough to trick people into thinking they were truly alone. Sure, parts of the state were quieter than others, but evidence of modern civilization was everywhere. It was in the smell of a factory, the roar of a truck, the itchy tag on the back of a T-shirt. Or would the people of Back to the Land make their own T-shirts? Would they mix up their own medication, resort to Native American–style poultices and inhalants?

And yet, the literature said people thrived living this way, even chronically sick people with cancer and diabetes and autoimmune diseases. That was another story for the lineup: an interview with a doctor who had treated several people before they moved to Back to the Land and then tested them again once they'd been living there for a year. The improvements were amazing. Allegedly the lifestyle's simplicity and lack of commercial pollutants had remarkable healing powers. *But it had to be a placebo effect*, Charles thought. They got better because they *wanted* to. He didn't believe in any of that New Age nonsense. The power of positive thought couldn't save you. Circumstance was circumstance, and you had to make do with what you were dealt.

After the meeting, Charles went outside to get some air. He took the elevator eleven flights down and walked through the marble lobby, exiting onto Market Street. There was a traffic jam outside the building, the cars wedged at odd angles, honking. Suburban Station loomed across the avenue. Hot dog and pretzel carts lined the sidewalk. Two cleaning women in pink smocks and white athletic shoes paused at the corner, talking animatedly with their hands.

The meeting had been especially difficult to sit through and not just because he found the concept ridiculous; his mind couldn't stay focused on work. He kept returning to what was happening, what might be happening, what his brother might have done. All he could think of were the worst case scenarios: a secret society of sorts, a band of boys abusing one another for kicks, for power, with Scott at the helm. Not that he had any proof that this was happening—he hadn't been able to get any details out of his mother, and it was possible that even she didn't know. It was unclear whether Scott even understood the magnitude of the situation. It only took a few bad decisions to ruin everything. But reputation meant nothing to Scott. Neither did history nor tradition. Or, well, *family*. Charles recalled how, long ago, he'd been ordered to look after Scott at one of their parents' Fourth of July parties.

Scott, then about six, grabbed a pack of matches teetering on the side of the grill and struck one. He waved it near the old trellises, threatening to set them on fire. "You can't do that to the *house*," Charles hissed, appalled. It was the equivalent of harming an old relative.

Scott struck the match anyway, a cruel smile on his face. The trellises were rotted, their brittle timber just waiting for an excuse to burn. Their father blamed Charles for not watching his brother more carefully, and Charles, frustrated and confused, said, "I tried to stop him, but he didn't care." And then, after a moment, "It's because he's adopted, right? Because he's not one of us?"

His father flinched. Even today, at thirty-one years old, Charles could still conjure up his dad's red, looming face in his mind. "Don't you ever say that again," his father growled.

And now, almost certainly because of the conversation he'd had with his mother last night, Charles's old girlfriend, Bronwyn, was on his mind, too. Various images of her had been flashing through his mind all morning—Bronwyn on the living room couch, outlining the type of cummerbund Charles must wear with his tux so it would match her prom dress. Bronwyn standing on the patio next to the grill, trying to make small talk with Scott when his brother had unwittingly arrived home while Charles was entertaining a group of friends. Diplomatic and eager for everyone to get along, Bronwyn always tried to invite Scott into the conversation. *It's not going to get you anywhere,* Charles tried to tell her. *He chooses to be an outcast.*

And, of course, Charles envisioned Bronwyn in the mud room, standing behind Charles as he held Scott by the throat, all those hideous things spewing from his mouth. He would hear her gasp until the end of his days.

"Charles?"

He raised his head now. "Charles?" the voice said again. Caroline Silver was striding across the courtyard. She worked in the marketing department of Jefferson Hospital, and Charles edited their promotional magazine for donors. The magazine only came out biannually, so Charles hadn't seen her or talked to her in a while.

He watched as Caroline crossed the square, trying to smile. "I'm here to see Jake," she explained, shaking his hand. "For a late lunch meeting. Goodness, it's been a while, huh?"

"It has," he answered.

And then she cocked her head, her expression shifting. Charles could tell she was reaching back to recall just how long it *had* been since she'd seen him, remembering what had happened between then and now. And then, as though Charles really *did* have an inside view of her head, Caroline shifted her weight and covered her eyes. "Oh, Charles. Your father. Oh my goodness. I'm so, so sorry."

"It's all right," Charles said automatically.

"We read about it in the paper. How awful."

"Yeah."

"I meant to call. I didn't know what was appropriate, though."

"It's fine. Really." He smiled at her. "Thank you."

"What a shame." She clucked her tongue. "He wasn't even very old, was he?"

He shook his head. "Healthy every day of his life before it happened."

"You must miss him."

The vendor on the corner slammed the metal lid that housed the hot dogs unnecessarily hard. Charles stared across the street at a budding dogwood tree. Farther down that block was the Italian restaurant his father sometimes visited for lunch. Once, when Charles had walked down this block to a lunch place on Walnut, he'd glanced into the Italian restaurant's front window and seen James alone at the bar, with his tie flung over his shoulder and a glass of amber liquid in his hand. There was a ball game on TV, and the waiter was leaning on the bar, watching. Charles's dad had looked so comfortable being alone, a posture Charles had never mastered himself. Charles had panicked, crossing furtively to the other side of the street so his father wouldn't see him. He had no idea what James would have done if he'd noticed Charles walking by. Ignore him? Grow furious that Charles was walking down *his* block, invading *his* space? One thing was certain, his father certainly wouldn't have invited Charles into the bar—despite his mother's Pollyannaish suggestion the day before his interview, Charles and his father never met for lunch. What would they have talked about?

Caroline shifted onto her left leg, waiting for Charles's answer. *Did he miss his father?* He didn't really know. "I—I should be going," he said, turning blindly toward the street.

"Of course," Caroline said, her voice dripping with foolhardy sympathy. Maybe she thought he was too overcome with grief to properly respond. Charles still said nothing, focusing instead on the shiny spots of mica in the sidewalk, the xylophone part of a Rolling Stones song he'd heard on his iPod that morning thrumming absurdly in his head. Finally, Caroline patted his arm and told him to hang in there. Charles watched her push through the revolving door, cross the lobby, accept a badge from security, and disappear around the corner toward the elevator bank.

Charles leaned against the cold slate of his building, wishing he could nap beneath one of the big stone benches. The burbling fountain smelled pungently of chlorine. There was a sharp pain at his right temple, maybe the beginning of a migraine. The cleaning ladies were still standing on the corner, chatting. Was one of them her? The security guard who'd called the ambulance for Charles's father had met the family in the ER lobby later that same night. "A cleaning lady found him," the guard had said. "She called down to the front desk, and I called 911." About a week later, after Charles's dad had died, Charles tracked down the agency that employed the building's cleaning staff and asked for the woman's name. The agency was evasive, saying that the woman had quit and they didn't have a forwarding number.

Maybe she was in this country illegally. Maybe she felt guilty and embarrassed that she had come upon such a thing—an executive limp and lifeless on a bathroom floor, soaked in his own urine. But the woman was out there, certainly, and she had information Charles wanted. If only he could see her and ask her about his father's final moments of consciousness. Had he said anything? Regrets, maybe? A sudden confession of love?

The hand on his watch slid to the three. Charles peeled his body from the wall, straightened his shirt, and prepared to go back to work. The sun came out for a moment, turning the marble fountain base in front of his building amber. An exact match, Charles realized, to his dad's headstone.

three

Normally Sylvie looked forward to the biweekly Tuesday board meetings at Swithin. She loved sitting in the library, drinking tea, plotting, and gossiping, with the Philadelphia classical station on quietly in the background. It was less a board meeting and more a nice cozy get-together with people she'd known for years. But she dreaded this one, staying in the shower until the last possible moment. She found herself wishing the weather would abruptly turn biblically catastrophic, raining down frogs or locusts or bumblebees, forcing the Department of Transportation to close the roads. She longed for a sudden high fever, nothing dangerous, just a passing flu. She even took her temperature as she sat at the kitchen table drinking her coffee.

It was just that she needed a few more days. A little while longer to collect herself, to get her bearings. If only the biweekly board meeting was scheduled for next week instead. In a week, she'd be organized; everything would be in its place. She would have planned out everything she needed to say, a clever response to every prying, insolent, loutish question.

James would know how to deal with this situation. He'd talk to Scott, or he'd at least try. He had been the one to encourage Scott to

take the coaching position in the first place. At a fund-raiser last fall, a
Swithin teacher and activities organizer approached Sylvie and James.
"The wrestling team needs an assistant coach," he said. "Would that
be something your son might be interested in?" James stepped in, saying he was sure Scott would be happy to take it. Sylvie gawked at him.
How did he know? That night, when James went into Scott's apartment and shut the door, she heard them arguing through the wall.
"Where do you get off, making decisions for me?" Scott roared. "How
can you assume that's what I want to do with my life?"

Sylvie sighed, but she wasn't surprised. Of course Scott was putting up a fight; James should have known better than to speak for him.
James and Scott had been close when Scott was young, building things
in the garage together, playing in the waves at the beach houses they
rented every summer, sharing stories about wrestling matches, which
they both had experience with, but then, around the time Scott was in
high school—around the time of the Swithin awards ceremony Charles
had referred to the night before—Scott abruptly stopped speaking to
his father. Sylvie guessed James knew why Scott was angry at him, for
he always seemed so contritely attentive to Scott, forever trying to clear
the stale air between them, but it was yet another thing James and Sylvie
never discussed. Maybe it was just that Scott was uninterested in all of
them. And maybe, deep down, Sylvie felt a tiny bit grateful that her husband was suddenly as disconnected from their son as she was.

But then, without explanation, Scott took the job. When James's
schedule allowed, he and Sylvie climbed up Swithin's bright blue
bleachers and watched the matches, just as they'd watched Scott
wrestle when he was younger. Scott stood next to the wrestlers, clad
in a burgundy Swithin blazer. After the last match, Sylvie and James
overheard Scott speaking to Patrick Fontaine, the head coach and the

school's phys ed teacher. "You wouldn't have any interest in subbing for me for a few of my gym classes one of these days, would you?" Patrick asked. "Sometimes I think these kids need someone closer to their own age to get them moving." Scott's eyes lit up. "I have lots of ideas about how to make gym more fun," he said excitedly, pressing his right fist into his open left palm. "Obstacle courses, real Marine Corps training kind of stuff." Fontaine smiled and said that sounded great. It might even lead to a permanent position.

James took Sylvie's hand and squeezed. *You see*, the squeeze said. *Convincing him to take the coaching job was a good thing.* And Sylvie had felt that same swooping, desperate optimism. Yes, this was a good thing. Maybe even the answer to helping Scott.

Sylvie's mind wandered back to James. Even if James couldn't penetrate Scott, he'd known how to talk to everyone else. James was *good* at things like that—he had a way of making his opinions sound like inscrutable facts. *Global warming is a myth, a regular earthly cycle. Capital markets are best left unregulated and free. Unions are always unwieldy and corrupt.* He made declarations about more personal things, too. Sylvie *had* to go out to dinner with him when they first met, no questions asked, as though something horrible might happen to her if she didn't. And the day after Charles announced his engagement to Joanna, when Sylvie remarked offhandedly that she was surprised Charles hadn't chosen to marry someone more like Bronwyn, James's eyebrows melded together, his chin tucked into his neck, and little puckers of skin appeared at each corner of his down-turned mouth. "Oh *no*," he'd said. "Charles and Bronwyn weren't right for each other *at all*." Sylvie couldn't recall James saying one word to Bronwyn when she and Charles were dating, but perhaps James was right. Maybe the two of them *hadn't* been right for one another. James had a way of appearing very wise, while simultaneously making everyone else seem very childish.

Sylvie could see James making a grand, sweeping statement about Scott now. All he'd have to do was unequivocally and righteously say that Scott wasn't responsible for the boy's death, and just like that, he would eliminate the foolish thought of consulting a lawyer. He would reverse everyone's suspicions.

The side door to the kitchen opened and shut, startling Sylvie from her chair. Scott loped through the mud room and into the kitchen, talking on his cell phone. He opened the fridge and stuck his head inside, not even glancing in her direction.

She stared, feeling visible and obtrusive in her own home. When had she last seen him? When had they last spoken? He looked sloppy, unshowered, his mess of dark hair thick around his face. His tattoos peeked out from under his clothes, the ones on his wrists, the one creeping up his neck, another peering out under the T-shirt sleeve on his bicep. Before Swithin gave Scott the assistant coaching job, they'd balked at his tattoos, ordering him to cover them up. It was difficult to imagine Scott at Swithin as an adult figure, a quasi-authority. Certain teachers, all prim and neat in their burgundy blazers and tortoiseshell glasses, probably gave him wide berth in the hallways and conversations probably halted when Scott entered a room.

Scott barked a few more words into his phone and hung up without saying good-bye. Sylvie cleared her throat, and he looked over. His eyes were dark, unresponsive. She had no idea what to say. Every ice-breaker seemed clumsy, inappropriate.

Scott shut the fridge, shuffled to the coffeemaker, and lifted the carafe. "The coffee's cold," Sylvie said quickly, rushing over to him. "Here. I'll make some more."

Scott held the carafe in midair. "I'll just microwave it."

"No, you should have fresh coffee. It's terrible microwaved. Skunky."

"I don't care."

"It's no trouble." She already had the grinder out and was dumping the cold grounds into the trash.

Scott stepped away, folding his arms over his chest. Even though he was fairly thin, he filled up a room. Sylvie spooned the fresh grounds into the filter and cleared her throat. "So. What's new with you?"

He didn't answer, instead opened and closed cabinet drawers, looking for something to eat.

The coffeemaker began to burble and hiss. Sylvie licked her lips, staring at a slight water blemish on the stainless-steel toaster. Her heart drummed fast. "Wrestling team going well?"

Scott snickered. Sylvie was glad she wasn't holding a coffee cup; if she had been, it would be rattling in her hand, the liquid sloshing over the side. He knew that she knew. He knew what was being said. And now he was enjoying watching Sylvie scramble to figure out a way to talk to him about it. How could he *chuckle*? A boy had died under his watch.

She turned to him, a vein at her temple suddenly throbbing. "They said you have to meet with some of the teachers." There. That was her way in.

He assessed her, leaning against the counter. One eyebrow arched. "Yep. That's what they say."

She stared at him, trying her best not to blink. Would it be better or worse to just flat-out ask him what had happened? Did she want to know, or was she happier remaining in the dark? Even if she did ask, would he tell her? "Do you know when your meeting is?" she blurted out.

"Next week, I think." He inspected his nails.

"Ah." It was as though they were having a conversation about the weather or if she should put regular or premium gas in her car. Sylvie ran her finger over a chipped spot on the countertop, wishing she could crack something against it. "And . . . do you know who the meeting is with?"

"Nope."

She stared at the slowly filling coffeepot and took a breath. "Well, maybe you could dress up for the meeting. Wear a jacket."

Scott made a noise at the back of his throat. "A *jacket?*"

"Or at least a shirt and tie." *Just don't wear those ridiculous pants that hang around your ankles and show your underwear. Just don't wear the sweatshirt with that word I can't even repeat on it. Just comb your hair.*

Scott said nothing. He turned and took the lid off the old earthenware cookie jar, the very same one that held homemade sugar cookies when Sylvie was a girl. Scott reached for a chocolate chip cookie, took a big bite, and then held the uneaten part outstretched reflectively. "Mmmm," he decided. Crumbs fell to the floor.

He finished his cookie, laced his hands together and turned them inside out, giving each knuckle a crack. "I thought you were, like, a powerful force at that school. You can make it go away."

She blinked at him, trembling inside. *Is that what you think?* she wanted to say. But now Scott had walked into the mud room—the conversation was over. A few moments later, he returned with his sneakers, loud orange and white high-tops. She watched as he sat down at the table, propped one foot up on his knee, and began to leisurely lace the shoes up. It was as if he was another creature entirely, one whose actions she couldn't begin to predict. One of those sea creatures that lived in the sunless depths of the ocean. Or maybe a carnivorous plant that ate gnats.

"Going somewhere?" she asked.

"To the city. Just for the morning."

"How come?"

He gave her a pained look. "I'm helping out at Kevin's shop. Someone can't come in until one, so I said I'd cover."

"Kevin was at the funeral, right?" Scott had come with three friends, two girls and a guy, all of them like Scott—wild, waiting for confrontation.

"Uh-huh." Scott threaded the other shoe but left the laces untied and dangling.

"What kind of shop does he own?"

"Shoes."

"Oh!" She knew she sounded relieved, but shoes were so . . . *innocuous.* "Well. Tell him 'Hi' for me."

He sniffed. "You didn't even *speak* to him that day."

At that, Sylvie shrank. She strode out of the room, found her handbag near the laundry, and walked across the driveway to her own car. She still parked outside, not yet wanting to disrupt the half of the garage that housed James's jigsaw, lathe, and woodworking rasps. She slammed the car door hard. It felt good. Once belted in, she shut her eyes, listening to the birds and the gentle swishing sounds of the tree branches. She lifted her ring finger to her mouth, cupped her lips around the big yellow stone on the ring James had given her, and sucked.

That first night, when she just thought James wasn't coming home in retaliation for what she'd brought up the night before, she had taken off this ring and buried it at the bottom of her jewelry box, hating what it meant. Then she'd gone into James's office and looked carefully around the room. James's infuriatingly clean desk, the stack of blank computer paper next to the printer, the Lucite plaques on the bookshelf. She'd walked in and touched the bare spot on the bookshelf where she'd found the little box that held the bracelet. A film of pale gray dust stuck to the pad on her finger.

The ring tasted like cold metal. Maybe it was primal, like a child sucking on a pacifier. Because only after Sylvie let the stone click against her teeth and press on her tongue did her pulse begin to settle down.

In no time Sylvie found herself pulling up the hill to Swithin, the school resplendent at the top. The guard at the gate recognized her right away. "Good afternoon, Mrs. Bates-McAllister!" he cried. "So nice to see you!" He waved her right through.

Sylvie loved this drive up the Swithin lane, how the school rose up before her, all stone and brick, with its spires and bell tower and flags and dazzling green fields beyond. There wasn't a tree branch out of place. The steps, windowsills, and sidewalks were all swept twice a day. One of Sylvie's earliest memories was of her grandfather bringing her into the library and showing her the rare book collection. "These were almost lost forever," he told her. And then he wove the tale of the fire; how it had caught in the east-wing classrooms and spread furiously into the gymnasium, burning half the school to the ground before the firefighters even arrived at the scene. When her grandfather surveyed the damage the day after, he sobbed. "It was just so *sad*," he told Sylvie. "I felt like the school was calling out to me, *Please don't let me go*." Whenever he got to that part of the story, tears always welled in Sylvie's eyes.

Since it was the Depression and no one had any money to spare, Charlie Roderick Bates financed rebuilding Swithin with his own

money and resources. He used materials from the countless lime-
stone quarries and brick foundries he owned to pour the new foun-
dation and rebrick the walls. Rebuilding the school from scratch
provided a lot of jobs, so he was a hero several times over, hiring
Polish and Italian crews to do the construction, even providing jobs
for people in the black neighborhoods. "But we had to make great
sacrifices during that time," he told Sylvie. "I paid everyone's wages.
I bought all the materials."

"Did you have to move out of your house, Charlie Roderick?" Sylvie asked—her grandfather got a kick out of her calling him by both
his names. He shook his head and told her that no, they were able to
remain in the house, but his wife, Sylvie's grandmother, couldn't travel
to Paris, and Sylvie's father, who was a young child at the time, wasn't
allowed new riding gear. They didn't even have their annual Christmas
party. "Did you still have a tree?" Sylvie asked. He nodded, patting her
head. "Yes, of course. We still had a tree."

Those afternoons with her grandfather were filled with pepper-
mint tea and chocolate chip cookies on the estate's enormous back
porch. They watched the swans in the pond, which were probably the
grandparents or great-grandparents of the swans that lived there now.
They sat at the Steinway baby grand piano that is still in the music
room. He played Chopin for her, his fingers kissing the keys.

When Sylvie saw her mother's car wending up the driveway, her
heart would plummet. Her own house was dark, the blinds pulled
tight. Doors in different wings eased quietly shut; her parents rarely
spent any time together except for meals. Sylvie hated eating with her
parents most of all—they never spoke during those taut dinners, the
only sounds were of the clinking forks, the scraping plates, and the
chewing. When Sylvie couldn't stand another second of silence, she'd

burst out with something her grandfather told her that day, even though her parents had heard the stories plenty of times before. "Did you know Charlie Roderick let some of the people who worked on Swithin stay at his house?" she'd crow. "Did you know he worked even on his birthday?" But this just angered her mother, Clara, even more, and she often wearily snapped, "Your grandfather isn't the messiah you think he is. Those people who rebuilt the school? The ones he let stay at his house? Fat chance he let their children go to Swithin. Even if they'd scrimped and saved all their money, he would never let them in."

And then Clara would glance at Sylvie's father, Theodore, as if daring him to scold her for saying such things about his family. But Sylvie's father never took the bait; his eyes remained fixed on his *Wall Street Journal*, his jaw working his food.

Sylvie didn't understand what her mother meant by those comments. It wasn't until she was in middle school and heard similar rumors that she finally worked out what her mother was implying. But by then she refused to believe it. Everyone was jealous of the Bates family, including Sylvie's mother, who had come from a good family, but not *as* good. And anyway, her mother was bitter and mean-spirited about everything and everyone. It was obvious why Sylvie's father was around less and less, conducting most of his business out of New York. Sylvie would have escaped to New York, too, forever avoiding those crypt-quiet dinners, her mother's inimical remarks, and those heaving sighs through her nose. Her mother had once been involved in Sylvie's life. Sylvie still remembered the dollhouse she'd gotten for Christmas when she was six. Clara had even helped Sylvie to select furniture for it from a big, glossy dollhouse catalog. And Sylvie used to slip her hand into her mother's when they walked through the revolving doors at the Strawbridge & Clothier department store in Philadelphia, snug and secure in her mother's grip. But something had happened to her mother in the years between, something that seemingly couldn't be reversed.

When she was thirteen, Sylvie called her father at the hotel he usually stayed at in New York, wanting to know if she could take the train up and visit him. She thought that once outside their dour house, her father would be more like *his* father, the great Charlie Roderick Bates. The hotel concierge connected Sylvie to her father's room and a woman answered. Sylvie said she must have dialed the wrong room and went to hang up. "Are you looking for Teddy?" the woman asked. "Who?" Sylvie said. "Theodore," the woman corrected. "He's in the shower."

Sylvie slammed the phone back into its cradle, her heart beating fast. *Teddy*. She couldn't imagine her father being called that. It seemed childish, a stuffed bear flung on a bed.

After that, Sylvie drifted away from both her parents. Whenever anyone teased her at school, she sobbed into her grandfather's lap, feeling that he was the only person in the world who loved her, who made time for her. "Don't worry about any of them," he said softly. "You're different than everyone. You're better. Someday, all this will be yours."

"All what?" Sylvie had asked. But he hadn't elaborated. Perhaps he meant the house, knowing even then that he would bequeath it to her, skipping right over his only son. Or maybe Charlie meant the school. Maybe he meant the whole world.

Now, Sylvie parked her car and turned off the engine. Her heels clicked across the parking lot. The flag in the middle of the lot was at half-staff, and there was a small, red ribbon tied around the pole, although she wasn't sure what it signified. She looked around for other evidence of the boy's death—a picture on one of the glass-paned doors that led to the lobby, for instance, or a collection plate in his memory on the arched, wooden sign-in desk. But there was nothing. Photographs of the class officers hung next to the flag. A large stuffed hawk, the school mascot, sat on top of the secretary's desk. There was a big poster for an upcoming school play, *A Midsummer Night's Dream*. Inside the auditorium, she heard a piano, then someone singing, probably a late choir practice. The song in the auditorium didn't sound somber, either, but something Sylvie vaguely recognized from a Rogers and Hammerstein musical.

The others were already in the library. They were sitting on the leather couches, a pot of tea on the large, low coffee table. When they saw her, they stood.

"Sylvie." Daniel Girard held out his arms. He was good-looking, tall with silver hair. He had come from work, presumably, still in his suit. Geoff Whitney stood, too, jowly and blustering, smelling a little like cigars. The other two stood as well. Jonathan Clyde, bookish and nervous-fingered, and Martha Wittig, plump and matronly, always wearing a different colored pair of glasses. Today's frames were a warm pumpkin shade.

Sylvie kissed them all on the cheeks. She knew intricate details about each of their lives—Jonathan had bought an eighteenth-century historic Quaker meetinghouse that had allegedly once belonged to William Penn. He and Stewart, a man he always referred to as his *friend*, restored it themselves. The house had been featured in a splashy magazine, highlighting just one photo of Jonathan sitting on the couch, his hand clenched nervously in his lap. Last year, Dan's father had unexpectedly willed all his money to charity, forcing Dan to find his first job at forty-four. Geoff and his wife had divorced, and he'd married a much younger woman named Melinda two months later.

Of course they knew about Sylvie, too. That her children had gone to school here, that Charles had attended Cornell, that he'd married Joanna, and that Joanna . . . well, Sylvie knew that Joanna had held some sort of job before they moved out to the suburbs a few weeks ago, but she could never remember what that job had been; nor did she know what Joanna was planning to do with herself now.

They knew about Scott, too, though they never asked about him, as if it would be intrusive to do so. And they were around for James's death. They'd paid their respects at his funeral and gone to the luncheon afterward.

They had all attended Swithin and so had their children. They'd worked together for years now, planning and debating and deciding. When they considered adding an extra member to the board, they pored over each potential candidate as if they were running for political office, examining tax records, properties owned, and extramarital affairs. They didn't help vote for teachers or staff—which meant, thankfully, they hadn't had to discuss Scott's position as an assistant coach—although they did help to choose Michael Tayson as headmaster two months ago after Jerome announced his retirement. That meeting had been only one week after James had died, and Sylvie had felt too shell-shocked to come. Now, she wished she had.

They sat down and Martha pressed PLAY on the mini-recorder. It taped the meetings from start to finish, and afterward Martha's husband, who was adept at all things technological, would plug the recorder into his computer, press a few buttons to launch the software that could translate the contents of the audio file into a Word document, and *voilà*, they had minutes without any of them having to feverishly write or transcribe.

Martha started talking about the numbers and research on the school-wide laptop program, which issued laptops to every student to use to take notes and do homework. "The thing is, they're all using them to do non-school-related activities," she said. "Apparently, the network goes down at least once a week because everyone's on their laptops, using all those Facebook sites. And they're not very careful with them. Seventeen machines have gone in for repairs just this month."

"Are they encouraging the kids to learn?" Dan asked.

"It's hard to say." Martha flipped a page. "The way kids learn isn't the same anymore. But the teachers are also a problem. A lot of them aren't nearly as technologically savvy. They're still making their students write their papers in longhand."

"Oh, God, especially that Agnes," Geoff said, rolling his eyes. "How old is she now, eighty?"

Martha pressed PAUSE on the tape recorder. "And still spry as a fox," she whispered giddily. "There are rumors that she's dating Harold." Harold was one of the guidance counselors. He was quite a bit younger than Agnes, the doyenne of the English teachers.

"Speaking of Harold," Dan said while raising a finger. "That daughter of his is back at home. I heard somewhere that she was kicked out of Brown."

Martha's eyes widened. "Another one?"

"She's all out of Ivies," Geoff said.

"Cheating again?" Jonathan asked, shaking his head.

"I thought she was kicked out of school because of prescription drugs." Martha blew her bangs into the air. "Poor Harold."

Sylvie stared at her fingernails. Nothing seemed amiss. None of them was looking at her pointedly, indicating they had heard about

Scott. Maybe Michael Tayson had kept his word, not telling them about the rumors or Scott's upcoming meeting.

Martha pressed PLAY on the recorder again. "Anyway. Back to the laptops. Should we take them away?"

"Laptops do look good, though," Dan said. "Parents are impressed by that kind of stuff."

Geoff stroked his chin. "But it's a big expense. I've heard some complaints from the art department. Their supplies are getting more and more expensive, and they can't buy what they need with what they've been allotted. A few of the sports coaches have also come to me, talking about replacing old uniforms and equipment."

"Which teams?" Martha straightened her papers.

Geoff shrugged. "It was the basketball coach who spoke to me. And Carla from gymnastics registered a request in the office."

"We still *have* a gymnastics team?" Martha sniffed. The others snickered, and just like that, the suggestion was dropped. Basketball and gymnastics weren't steeped in history and scholarship money the way, say, girls' soccer was—the team was top in the state, and many girls were recruited by Division I schools—or the way the boys' crew was. Crew was Swithin's first official sport, and the school had sent several boys on to row for Yale and Penn, and from there on to the Olympics. Those were the teams that got the money.

Sylvie often wondered why her fellow board members invested so much of their time in Swithin. What made them come back, year after year, budget after budget, graduating class after graduating class? Did they feel they were part of something? Did it *define* them, as it did her, or did they simply do it because, as people of means, it was their obligation? Take Martha, for example. Sylvie remembered Martha from when they were in school together, though Martha had been a few grades behind her. Back then, Martha had been a bossy, controlling field hockey player, always preening herself, always surrounded by a group of cackling girls. When a representative from the New York Public Library Conservator's office spoke at an assembly about Swithin's rare book collection, Martha whispered with the girl next to her the whole time, completely uninterested.

But as a board member, Martha had gotten involved in just as many school projects as Sylvie had. There had been some discussion that Martha had become so involved because of trouble at home—she and her husband had wanted another baby, but then she unexpectedly started her menopause. "Maybe their marriage is falling apart," Sylvie once whispered to James only a few months before he died, after she'd found out everything about him, "maybe the school is Martha's oasis." "So the only possible reason Martha could be so heavily involved at the school is because she's miserable at home?" James had replied, raising an eyebrow. "Of course not!" Sylvie said quickly. "I mean, *I'm* involved. *I'm* not miserable." James looked at her challengingly. Sylvie looked back. Neither said anything.

"Next up?" Jonathan said. He leaned over the table and glanced at the list. "Hmm. This."

Martha tipped forward, now curious. "The boy's death."

Sylvie's heart started to pound. She glanced at the recorder, thinking that Martha might hit PAUSE again. She didn't.

Geoff leaned back in his chair, the springs squeaking. Dan riffled through a few papers on the desk and found a photo of the dead boy, Christian Givens. Sylvie leaned forward. He had elfin features and freckles across his cheeks. His hair was bright green. Acid green, really, a color not found in nature.

Sylvie's stomach fluttered. She recognized him.

"What do you suppose they call that color? Antifreeze?" Martha murmured. She covered her mouth. "Goodness. Sorry."

"What happened?" Dan asked.

"We don't know." Martha admitted. "They're doing an autopsy. That's all Michael Tayson would tell me. The boy's father has been very private about everything."

Jonathan glanced at his watch. "I wonder where Michael is. He said he would come to this."

Sylvie's heart rate picked up. She hadn't considered that the new headmaster might show up. She didn't want to see him.

"Has counseling been made available?" Geoff asked.

"They're using Judith." Jonathan laced his hands together. "She really helped out when those girls on the crew team died in the car accident last year. And during that school shooting at Virginia Tech. A lot of kids saw her after that."

"Judith is so good," Martha cooed.

"Which one's Judith?" Geoff scratched his head.

"The one with the long hair," Dan said.

"She's so gentle," Jonathan added. "But firm."

Everyone looked again at the boy's photo. Unnatural hair colors weren't allowed at Swithin; teachers were required to immediately send home anyone who wasn't adhering to the dress code. So how had Christian's hair gone unnoticed long enough for him to sit for his picture? Maybe Christian was the type of boy who fell between the cracks, even with acid-green hair. Sylvie thought about what Michael Tayson had said on the phone: *You probably wouldn't remember him from the matches.* But Sylvie did remember him, an image of him with the wrestling team flashing through her mind.

"So what about the boy's mother?" Geoff looked at Martha. "You only mentioned the dad. Are they divorced?"

"Out of the picture for some reason or other, I guess," Martha said. She looked at the piece of paper, presumably some kind of dossier on Christian. "He's a scholarship boy. *Was.* The address we have on file has him living over at Feverview Dwellings." She flipped a page. "It doesn't list an employer for the father."

"Maybe he's unemployed," Jonathan suggested.

"Or on disability," Martha said.

"Do we remember admitting this boy?" Dan asked. "What's the father's name?"

"Warren," Martha read.

"Warren . . . Givens," Dan repeated. "Doesn't ring a bell."

Everyone looked around, sheepish. Sometimes they had a say in admitting students, especially those receiving scholarships. But there was a separate committee for that, people with actual credentials to judge one candidate from another.

"If we wanted to set up a scholarship in his name, what could it be for?" Geoff said quietly.

Martha picked at her cuticles. "Well, we'd do the standard scholarship, of course. Needs-based, I would imagine. How does that sound?"

"Or we could make it kind of specific," Dan suggested. "You know, according to what he was interested in. Do we know if he liked particular subjects in school? Art? Music?"

"He doesn't look like he'd be too involved in anything," Jonathan said, holding up Christian's photo. "I suppose we could look for his transcript . . ." He started to leaf through the papers.

"Good Lord, stop," Sylvie blurted out.

They all paused, raising their heads.

"I mean, the poor boy died only days ago." Sylvie's voice was a tautly held string. "We should have some respect."

The grandfather clock in the corner bonged seven times. Sylvie *had* to stop them. If they looked through his transcript, they'd see that he'd wrestled. Then the conversation would turn to Scott, the tape recorder still rotating, still capturing everything. She could picture their faces. *Did Scott* know *this boy? Funny he was on the wrestling team . . . he doesn't look like the type.* She had no idea what would come after that. She had no idea what she might say after that, either. She kept thinking about the look on Scott's face when he'd tried to suffocate that mouse in the basement. And all the times he'd dressed up as slashers from horror movies for Halloween. And his aversion to children—especially babies. Once when a teenager, he had even chuckled over a news story about a pit bull mauling a toddler. *Jesus, what a mess,* he'd said, as though he was commenting on an unkempt room, a ramshackle house.

Geoff sat back. "Goodness, Sylvie. You're right."

Martha coughed quietly. "Of course."

The others hung their heads. *They don't know,* she thought. She wondered instead if they thought she was sensitive about them talking behind this boy's back because so many people had talked behind hers. It was what Michael Tayson meant by *character assassination*—all those rumors about how her grandfather selectively chose who did and didn't get to attend Swithin. All that tut-tutting that Scott was so unruly and *different. And what was with that ring Sylvie had started wearing,* they might have hissed more recently. *What do you think* that *means?* They probably even gossiped about how James died—on the floor soaked in urine. It had gotten out, she knew it had. So many things had gotten out.

Dan leaned over and patted Sylvie's hand. Jonathan brought her a box of tissues from the librarian's desk. Or maybe they thought that with James's passing so recent, Sylvie couldn't talk about death right now. If that was the case, it was wrong to accept their pity.

The topic moved off Christian immediately, and the rest of the meeting bumped along. They made decisions and doled out who should do what. As they were finally leaving, Geoff reminded them of the cocktail party at his house next week for his wife's birthday. "The party's on a Monday," he warned. "But she insisted on having it on the day." He rolled his eyes as if to say *ah, youth*. This was Geoff's second wife; she was twenty years younger than he, than all of them.

From there Martha caught up to Jonathan, and they walked out of the library together, rehashing the laptop details. Geoff and Dan were already on their cell phones. Sylvie lingered behind, gazing after them. All of her colleagues walked with such assured entitlement. *But my grandfather told me all this was mine*, she wanted to tell them. *I'm the rightful owner of this place, not you.*

And she wanted to say something else, too. She wanted to yell out to them to be careful—their good fortunes might be more precarious than they thought. It could blow away in the blink of an eye, especially when they weren't paying attention.

four

The first time Joanna heard about the Bates-McAllister family, she had been a few weeks shy of eleven years old. She and her mother, Catherine, were waiting at the orthodontist's office for an appointment to see whether or not Joanna would need braces—unfortunately, she would—when Catherine noticed a Main Line newspaper that was wedged between a *Highlights for Children* and *Woman's Day*. It was the kind of paper that announced community activities, openings of new local restaurants, and road construction. In the back, it featured a society page.

Catherine folded back the page and passed it to Joanna. She pointed to a picture of a woman wearing a long velvet gown, sporting a nest of diamonds on her head. Two young boys stood next to the woman, both of them about Joanna's age, wearing suit jackets and ties. "Sylvie Bates-McAllister and family, attending the annual gala for the Swithin School," said the caption.

The waiting room was empty, Joanna remembered, save for the team of receptionists behind the desk, women who were made to wear matching purple sweaters and floral-print turtlenecks. Joanna's mother had specifically chosen this orthodontist because he was *the best*. All the women in the grocery store or at the PTA meetings or

at Catherine's health club said that he was the only reputable guy
to send one's children to, and because the hygienists and receptionists were featured in a local newspaper not long ago for their brisk
cheerfulness, their annual all-patients-invited Fourth of July parties,
and their matching uniforms. In Joanna's slowly forming consciousness about money and class, she had begun to realize that Catherine
often sought out the best of things, even if they couldn't always afford them. Catherine chose to plant Japanese maples in their front
yard, instead of run-of-the-mill sequoias or pines, trying to make
their little split-level just on the outskirts of the Main Line stand out.
She insisted that the family go on vacation to Avalon or Cape May,
where the people in the bigger, newer, cleaner houses went—and,
incidentally, where the Bates-McAllisters went—instead of Ocean
City or Wildwood, where the people in the shabbier ranch houses
gravitated. And then, after returning from the only beach house they
were able to afford in Avalon or Cape May, which inevitably bordered a house shared by no less than twenty sorority sisters, Catherine made sure to paste an Avalon sticker on their Volvo so everyone
would know where they'd gone.

The summers they didn't go away, Catherine enrolled the family
at the local country club, which, in spite of not having a golf course or
a bar, was pretentious and exclusive all the same. Catherine dragged
Joanna to the country club every day those summers, seating them on
Adirondack chairs near the tanned, pinched-faced women who lived
a few train stops closer to the Main Line, hanging on their every sen-
tence, desperate for any scrap of conversation. The country club was a
sticking point between Joanna's mother and her father. He wanted to
know why they couldn't just join the Y instead, which had two outdoor
pools and more kids Joanna's age, at a quarter of the cost. But Cath-

erine never relinquished the country-club membership. She went, she sat in that Adirondack chair, and she *belonged*.

And so when Catherine saw the photo of Sylvie Bates-McAllister and her boys in the *Main Line Times* at the orthodontist's office, her eyes glistened with envy. "Would you look at them," she gushed. She placed her thumb under Charles and Scott's faces. Their hair was slicked; their bow ties were neat and straight. She zeroed in on Scott, who even then was strikingly handsome, with big, round eyes, enviable cheekbones, and thick black hair. "Lovely."

"What's a gala?" Joanna asked, reading the caption.

"A big party," Catherine said knowingly. "Probably to raise money." As if she'd been to plenty of galas herself.

After that first mention of Sylvie Bates-McAllister, Catherine would bring her up again and again. At a jewelry store at the mall, eyeing the displays: "I bet Sylvie Bates-McAllister buys diamonds like that and thinks nothing of it." Passing by a stable: "Do you think Sylvie Bates-McAllister takes riding lessons there? Goodness, I'd love to learn how to jump; I should inquire about lessons." When spotting a stretch limo paused at a traffic light next to them: "Perhaps Sylvie's in there." She would say, peering longingly into the tinted windows.

She started to spend like Sylvie Bates-McAllister, too. Every time Joanna's father received the monthly credit card bill in the mail, her parents would have the same, tired argument. "*This* is where the money goes?" her father would boom to Catherine, who would be sitting at the kitchen table, doing her nails. "I just want things to be nice," she'd holler back. "Is that too much to ask? I deserve this." "If you want all this shit, get a job," he'd say. To which Catherine would say that she absolutely would not get a job, no self-respecting Main Line woman had a job, at which Joanna's father would stomp down to the basement, where he kept a weight bench and a few free barbells. Bruce Springsteen would start blaring, and Joanna would listen to the sound of metal against metal, the grunt of heavy weights being thrust over her father's head. Catherine would put down her nail file and little bottle of polish, look at Joanna, and say, "This isn't right. This isn't right at all."

Nothing was *ever* right for Catherine. Nothing was ever good enough. When her health problems developed—episodes that made her writhe and faint and spend hours in the ER, begging to be examined—Joanna was certain it was because of her crippling dissatisfaction. It had metastasized through her body, Joanna figured, in precisely the same way her friend Chelsea's mother's breast tumor had metastasized to her lungs and liver. If one could die from cancer, then one could certainly die from unhappiness and unfulfilled dreams.

For a long time, Joanna didn't notice the looks the ER nurses gave one another when Catherine was wheeled in yet again. Nor did she question why her mother was never really given a diagnosis, or why she was never properly admitted to the hospital, or why her father only dropped the two of them off at the ER entrance, wanting nothing to do with them. She'd just assumed that her father was mean and insensitive, burdening Joanna with all the responsibility so he could spend more time lifting weights or tinkering with his Ham radio. On Joanna's eleventh birthday, just as Joanna was welcoming the first of her friends to their house—she was having a sleepover party in the finished part of the basement—her mother got that pale, vague look again, and Joanna knew what was coming. Joanna hustled her friends downstairs, watching with trepidation as her mother yet again collected her things to go to the ER. "I can't go with you this time," Joanna said.

Catherine's eyes widened. "Why?"

Joanna was suddenly near tears. "My friends are here," she answered. And then, more indignantly: "It's my birthday. Maybe Dad could go."

Catherine looked terrified. "No! It has to be you!"

And then Joanna's father had stepped in, forming a barricade between mother and daughter. "It's her fucking birthday, Catherine," he reiterated. Before Catherine could react, Joanna's father grabbed her by the arm, announcing that he was taking her and her friends out for birthday pizza. If Catherine needed to go to the ER, she would have to drive herself. Instead of going to the ER, Catherine had stormed up to the bedroom and slammed the door. Which confused Joanna—didn't her mother *need* the ER? Wouldn't she die if she didn't go? And then she realized how foolish she'd been. The discovery hit her hard, rippling through her whole body. Though she uncovered her mother's secret that night, she kept it to herself, never admitting to anyone she knew.

After that birthday, Joanna started to also daydream about the Bates-McAllister family. She brought the magazine home from the dentist one visit and stashed it in her nightstand drawer, looking every so often at Sylvie's smiling face, so poised, so serene. Sylvie wasn't a striver; she was already *there*. Could a life like hers solve everything? As time passed, she collected more photos of the Bates-McAllister family, following their lives the way other girls followed the goings-on of popular bands. She kept a photo of Charles at Swithin, a photo of James and Sylvie at a ball for the Philadelphia Museum of Art, a photo of Charles and Scott standing outside a new running trail on the east side of the county, and a clipping of Sylvie alone, holding a plaque indicating she was being honored at a Swithin charity event. Joanna dug out a worn map from the junk drawer in the kitchen and found the Swithin grounds, which were a few towns away, and then Roderick, nestled in the woods of Devon. The more trips her mother took to the hospital, the more complex Joanna's fantasies grew. She envisioned herself and her mother going over to Roderick for a family dinner, though the interior of the house looked very different in Joanna's imagination than it did in reality. Whenever her father was kind enough to drive Joanna and her mother to the hospital, Joanna would shut her eyes and imagine them in the Bates-McAllisters' car instead. It would be a very fancy car, of course—a Rolls-Royce. They would listen to the classical radio station, not the angry, evangelical talk radio her father preferred. In reality, after her mom had been discharged and they waited at the curb for Joanna's dad to pick them up, she would imagine that Sylvie Bates-McAllister would pull up to the curb instead. Maybe Sylvie and Catherine would become friends. Maybe Sylvie Bates-McAllister would die young and include Catherine in her will.

After fantasizing through her high-school years, Joanna earned a scholarship to Temple that allowed her to move out of her family's house and into the school's dorms in Philadelphia. After that, there was a string of jobs and boyfriends, and her parents' inevitable divorce. Out of the suburbs and that house, the cloud over Joanna's head finally began to clear. Her mother would call with reports of yet more ER visits, and though Joanna would sometimes accompany her, she no longer felt responsible for pulling Catherine out of her misery. She lived her own life. She had all but forgotten about the Bates-McAllisters until the day she saw Charles in a bar in Philadelphia, standing across the big, square room, a beer in his hand.

She'd nearly dropped her glass of wine. It was startling that Charles was *real*, standing a mere twenty feet away. His posture wasn't as upright as she'd imagined, and his pants were a little high-waisted. He had razor burn on his jawline, and his leather jacket fit like a poncho. And his voice, which she could hear across the mostly empty room, was wholly different than she had imagined—a bit flat and gravelly, without any accent at all. For some reason, Joanna had always assumed he would sound like John F. Kennedy.

Seeing Charles filled Joanna with bittersweet nostalgia—*Oh, there's that boy whose family I used to be obsessed with!* And she could have left it as a sad, funny, odd little moment and gone home, closing that chapter of her life, except that Charles walked over to her. He bent over at the bar right next to her and ordered another beer, even though there were other empty spots at the counter closer to his friends.

So Joanna said something to him. Maybe something about his complicated platinum watch, maybe something about what he was drinking, she couldn't remember now. Charles said something back, looking her over and smiling. It was surreal, Charles Bates-McAllister smiling at *her*, like a character from a book coming off the page and asking her to dance. After about a half hour of talking, Joanna dared to take him by the hand, lean over the bar, and kiss him. Charles's eyes popped in surprise, but then he kissed her back. *Charles Bates-McAllister kissed her back.* She pulled away and sat back on the stool, grinning, and noticed he was grinning, too. Later that night, when she left with her roommate, Faith, she asked why Joanna had thrown herself at the short guy with the ugly tie and terrible shoes. "He's an old friend" was the only way Joanna could explain.

Charles called later that week. After they had been dating for three months, Joanna decided to finally break the news to Catherine that she had a new boyfriend—someone whose name she might recognize. It felt like the biggest moment in her life. After she made her announcement, there was a long pause. Catherine stared at her, a nail file in one hand. Finally, she set the file on the table. "Why in God's name would he be interested in *you*?" she cried.

Joanna was taken aback. "What?"

"You don't know how to hang pants on a hanger. You don't know how to set a table. You always put the knives on the wrong side of the plate."

Joanna had stood up, walked to the bathroom, and inspected her reflection, looking for . . . well, she wasn't sure what. A blemish? Some visible ugliness? She looked the same as she always did: her thick dark hair past her shoulders, her gray, almond-shaped eyes bright and alert, and straight teeth from years of treatments from the *right* orthodontist. For a moment she thought worriedly about Charles's old girlfriend, Bronwyn, whom he'd told her about by then. The thought of Bronwyn had made Joanna very nervous and cagey, but Charles assured her that Bronwyn didn't matter and that he wouldn't bring her up again. But Bronwyn *would* know how to put knives on the right side of the plate, certainly. She sounded so perfect, the daughter of a brilliant physician and a professor, the girl whose parents gave her every opportunity in the world. In fact, Joanna could easily imagine Bronwyn standing beside Charles in those old, dusty *Main Line Times* photographs that were still in a box at her mother's house. Was her mother on to something? Should Charles be with someone like Bronwyn instead?

And then she'd snapped out of it. Who the hell cared about knives and plates? She emerged from the bathroom, her composure regained. "Charles likes me," she insisted.

"Okay," her mother said suspiciously, not letting down her guard. Why wasn't she happy? Wasn't this what Catherine was attempting to groom her for?

"He *does*," Joanna protested. "And I like him, too." She hated how hard she was trying.

She *did* like Charles. He was just what she'd imagined he'd be and much more. He took her to great places in the city for dinner. He had season tickets, courtesy of his parents, to the Philadelphia Orchestra. He enjoyed going to plays and museums. When they went shopping, he didn't sit sullenly on the couches put out for bored husbands and boyfriends but instead helped Joanna pick out items that fit her best. Whatever she liked, he bought for her. Whenever they went out to dinner, he paid. His apartment in Rittenhouse Square was clean but not generic. He read Civil War biographies and *Vanity Fair*. He had square ceramic plates and a collection of old *Star Wars* toys. He saved his old baseball and concert ticket stubs in a leather-bound black book. Once, when he was taking a shower, she'd found a lined notebook full of original poetry. In that same book, she'd found a creased flyer that said, *Redemption Is Near. Repent!* A man had shoved it at them on their first date; they'd laughed about it in the restaurant, making a jokey second date to attend the prepare-for-the-apocalypse meeting advertised. They'd gone to a bar instead of that meeting and then back to Joanna's apartment. But Charles had saved that flyer. It meant something to him.

After Joanna found that flyer, she gave herself over to Charles. He became more than just the boy in the magazines she had saved; he became someone real. The first time she cried in front of him—recounting an old argument her parents had had that culminated in her dad throwing a plate and her mom sobbing on the kitchen floor—she felt safe and protected. Charles unburdened himself to her, too, telling her about his stilted relationships with his father and brother, recounting memories of being ostracized at summer camps, and sadly wishing he was better with his hands. He had flaws, which she liked. It drew her closer to him, made him more attractive. When he came over, she would tear off his clothes. She liked the way he kissed her all over, and she liked the way he stared at her as if she was beautiful and unique. When Charles asked her to marry him at their favorite Italian restaurant in Philadelphia, the one with the homemade pastas and the exuberantly touchy-feely proprietor, Joanna had been rendered speechless. All those pictures she'd saved of Charles's family, all that *wanting*. But what made it even sweeter was that where Charles came from didn't matter anymore. She would have chosen him out of anyone. And she'd thought he'd chosen her out of everyone, too.

Now, though, she wasn't entirely sure how the choosing had happened.

It was ten in the morning on Wednesday, two days after Joanna and Charles went to Sylvie's for dessert. There had been no more talk about Scott since then, and although Joanna wanted to bring up what she'd heard Charles and his mother talking about in the kitchen, she didn't know how. What was this fight Charles had referred to at his high-school graduation? Why hadn't he ever told her about it, and what did Bronwyn have to do with it? How much did he think about Bronwyn, anyway? Charles had said he hadn't spoken to Bronwyn in twelve years, but he'd never explained why they'd broken up. Joanna suspected that Charles had not been the one who had cut it off. She couldn't exactly say why she felt this way—perhaps because of the far-away look Charles got on his face when he spoke of her. Or how when Joanna had made a snippy, jealous comment about Bronwyn one of the first times Charles had mentioned her name, Charles had immediately become defensive, as though Bronwyn was someone to protect, as though he felt unresolved about how they'd left things. Perhaps the strongest case was that Charles hadn't dated seriously after Bronwyn until Joanna had come along. But she tried not to think about that.

She lay in bed now, staring up at the clean, smoothly plastered ceiling, willing herself to get up. Out the window, she saw the rest of the houses lined up along the streets. Their development was called Centennial. There was a stone sign at its entrance, crowing the name in curly "We the People" font. The streets' names had something to do with American ideals. There was the cluster named after great American leaders: Washington, Franklin, Hancock; there was Valor Drive, Integrity Circle, and Freedom Court. Joanna and Charles lived on Democracy, just past the dog park and the jogging path and the playground.

It was nothing like Joanna's old neighborhood in Lionville, with its hodgepodge of houses linked together by a gate at either end, her own house slightly on the bedraggled, lower-class side. Each house in Centennial was big, beautiful, and perfectly maintained in exactly the same way. The only flaw was the line of houses on Spirit, two streets down. They were originally models, but the developers had decided to try to sell them off. Charles had put a down payment on this plot before he and Joanna had seriously begun dating—a fact that he'd announced only after they'd gotten engaged and a fact that had disappointed Joanna a little, knowing that they wouldn't be choosing a house together. But no matter. By the time the construction on their house had been completed, the market had taken a steep downturn, and the developer hadn't started any new projects since. All the houses on Spirit were still empty. Quite a few of the "for sale" signs in the yards—LOW FINANCING! UPGRADES! REDUCTION!—had fallen over. One was missing entirely. A tree in front of one of the houses had become so overgrown it looked as if it was doing damage to the siding.

There was a rumor teenagers had broken into one of the homes and were using the closets to grow pot. Maybe it was naive, but Joanna had thought life in the suburbs—suburbs like *this*—would be untouched by the recession. More than that, Spirit houses seemed so expendable. Without people inside them, they were without identity, mere structures of concrete and siding and faux stone.

She sighed, rolled out of bed, and stumbled toward the bathroom, forgetting for the millionth time that it wasn't in the hall but to the left, part of the master suite. Though they'd lived in this house for two weeks, she still felt lost. She felt a little aimless, too. She'd quit her job in the city two weeks ago, her position at a nonprofit not lucrative enough to justify the commute into the city, and it was the first time in years she'd woken up without somewhere to go, without something concrete to do. There were rooms to paint, she supposed. There were new fixtures to buy for the kitchen, patio furniture to scope out. And there were all the unpacked boxes to attend to, including the ones stacked in the living room containing items from Joanna's old apartment in Philly.

She walked downstairs and looked warily in the boxes. She hadn't seen any of the contents in almost a year, since she'd put the stuff into storage when she first moved in with Charles. Only one box had been opened, its flaps gaping free. All of its contents were still packed inside: a stack of old foreign films on VHS, a pair of seventies-style sunglasses she had bought at a thrift shop and worn incessantly one summer, an industrial-size backpack she'd used on a trip to Europe, all funded on a ridiculously tiny amount of money. These items from the past smelled a bit moldy and unclean, instantly conjuring up a long-suppressed memory of a house party she and her roommate had about five years ago that had culminated in a bunch of strangers kissing. The time when she'd used any of it felt like three Joannas ago, and she couldn't quite remember who that Joanna had been. She also wondered what the Joanna who'd used those items, who'd kissed strangers at a party, would think of the Joanna now in her bright, clean house.

She turned away from the box toward the kitchen, focusing her gaze on a Crate & Barrel box by the fridge. Inside was the Cuisinart mixer she and Charles had been given as a wedding gift. She lifted it out of the Styrofoam packing material and put it on the counter. Maybe she'd make cookies to lighten her mood.

A sound in the backyard made her turn. The women from the neighboring houses were standing outside in their yards. Two little kids sat in an enormous sandbox that straddled the neighboring lawns, feeding sand into a wheeled and levered contraption and sifting it out in a neat, pyramid-shaped pile.

Joanna sprang into action, running her hands through her hair and racing upstairs to put on a bra, a clean T-shirt, and a pair of jeans. She walked down the stairs, turned right instead of left for the kitchen, stopped, reversed directions, and padded around the island and the table and the pile of broken-down boxes near the laundry room. Sun dappled across the back deck, and the one birdhouse they'd installed twisted on its chain. When the women heard Joanna's sliding glass door open, they turned their heads for just a moment and gave her a passing, uninterested glance, as though she was just another Canada goose slowly meandering across their lawn. Undeterred, Joanna walked over.

"Hi," she said. Her heart beat quickly, although she wasn't quite sure why. She was usually good at making plenty of new friends. "I'm Joanna Bates-McAllister. My husband and I just moved in. I've been meaning to say hello for a few days, but I've been so busy."

The brunette woman nodded. "I thought I saw a van." She was the type of woman who wore matching velour sweat suits and shimmering athletic sneakers, ready to exercise at a moment's notice. She lived on the left side of Joanna, and Joanna had watched yesterday as she'd hung a silk flag decorated with an Easter basket outside her front door in honor of the upcoming holiday.

"I'm Teresa Cox," the woman added as an afterthought. "And this is Mariel Batten."

Joanna turned to Mariel, who had blunt-cut blonde hair, a slender, down-sloped nose, and very white teeth. There was a lipstick imprint on her white coffee cup. She appraised Joanna without much enthusiasm. "Is your husband related to Timothy McAllister?" she asked blandly. "From Chadds Ford?"

"Oh." Joanna tugged self-consciously on her earlobe. "No, my husband's last name is Bates-McAllister. His father was from Boston. He didn't have family from around here. His mother did, though. Sylvie Bates?"

Mariel shrugged noncommittally. There was no recognition of Sylvie's name. No swift change of expression, no grabbing Joanna's arms and saying it was *so* nice to meet her. No begging that she and her husband had to come over for dinner sometime. No huge grin and confession that when they'd heard Joanna and Charles were coming to this neighborhood they'd gotten so excited, for it's truly an *honor* to have them.

Joanna rubbed her hands up her bare arms, struck dumb. "Anyway," she fumbled. "Cute kids."

Teresa Cox smiled. "The girl is Forrest. She's mine. Hollis is Mariel's. Do you have any children?"

Joanna shook her head. And then there was that dead air again.

But my mother-in-law is on the board of directors at the Swithin School,
Joanna wanted to say. *The best school in the county.* Didn't that matter?

"Anyway," Joanna said, not able to stand the pointed, exclusionary
silence any longer. "It was nice to meet both of you. I have things to do
inside. So . . ."

"Nice to meet you, too," the women said in unison, as they tilted
their bodies away. Joanna took faster steps than normal back to her
house, suddenly painfully aware of how cold it was outside. Goose
bumps rose on her arms and her whole body shook with shivers. There
was a peal of laughter behind her, followed by a gasp. She whipped
around to see one of the children turning a crank of a sandbox toy.

She shut the screen door quietly and placed her palms flat on the
cluttered kitchen table. The house was judgmentally quiet. She longed
for the noise of the city—traffic screeches and subway rumblings and
buzzing chaos to drown out what had just happened. She snatched
her cell phone from the island and pressed the speed dial for Charles's
office. When he answered, she let out a whimper.

"What is it?" he gasped.

"I just tried to meet the neighbors," she blurted out in a scratchy
whisper. "The ones I told you about? With the shared sandbox? The
ones that just stand there and talk all day?"

There was a three- or four-second pause. "Okay . . ."

"They were so . . . cold. I felt like I was the new girl at school not
wearing the right clothes."

There were voices in the background, someone else's phone exten-
sion ringing. "I'm sure they're very nice, Joanna."

"Oh." She sat down on the couch, not anticipating this answer.

"I don't remember you being this way about people in the city."

"I wasn't. It didn't matter."

"Why does it matter now?"

She stared up at the ceiling. "I don't *know*," she whispered. There was something about these people peering out from their identical houses that made her want to conform and belong. Sadly, it reminded her of her mother sitting on that Adirondack chair at the country club, in the right place but so, so wrong. Joanna had always assumed it would be so much easier for her.

"Is that all?" Charles asked.

She swallowed, now almost in tears. "Are you okay?" she blurted out.

"Me? Yeah. Why?"

"You've been . . . quiet."

"No I haven't."

She squeezed the red throw pillow on the couch. *Give me something,* she thought. *Anything.* "Are you and your mother worried about Scott? Is there anything I can do?"

He paused for a long time. *Let me in,* she willed, staring at her reflection in the blank television screen. *You have to know I heard you two talking.*

Charles sighed. "Joanna, I'm actually in the middle of something. Can I call you later?"

The receiver was limp in her hands. She tugged on her sweater sleeve so suddenly and with such force that she heard a seam rip. "Don't bother," she snapped.

And then he hung up. Joanna sat upright on the couch, her back pressed into the cushions, her calves at right angles to her thighs, waiting for him to call back, but he didn't. She felt silly for wasting his time. To Charles, *she* was the one at fault, *she* was the one who'd broken some kind of social contract and was now being whiny and impatient.

Where was the sympathy for her? Again she thought of Bronwyn and tried to imagine what Charles was referring to two nights ago, but it was like trying to bake a cake without any of the ingredients.

She stared blankly at the mantel across the room. The only thing they'd put up there so far was a framed photo from their wedding, Joanna in her long and simple strapless gown and Charles holding her waist just as the photographer ordered. They stood in Roderick's garden, where the wedding had taken place, grinning at one another. Joanna squinted at the photo until their faces blurred.

On the day of their wedding, Catherine had arrived at Roderick in a long red dress that dragged on the floor, almost like a wedding train. Her posture was very poised and upright; Joanna could tell she was trying very, very hard to act as though she'd visited Roderick many times. But whenever Catherine thought no one was looking, she stole long glances at the stained glass on the second floor, or at the labyrinth and wading fountain over at the other side of the grounds, or at the opulent yellow diamond Sylvie had recently begun wearing. It was early fall, the air growing crisp, and some of the guests wore furs. Catherine gaped at those, too.

"A garden wedding," Catherine had sighed romantically. She spied a man with a camera over her shoulder and gripped Joanna's arm. "Who do you think he is?" she whispered. Her breath already smelled like gin; she'd been making good use of the open bar, probably due to nerves. "Maybe from the *Inquirer*? Or the *Main Line Times*? This is just the kind of thing that would make it into that."

"He's just the wedding photographer," Joanna said, shrugging.

"Nonsense," Catherine said, craning her neck at other guests. "I'm sure he's from the *Main Line Times*. I think I recognize him. And oh! I just met Charles's brother, Scott. So unusually *handsome*. And such a flirt!"

Joanna craned her neck to see where Scott was. Charles had cho-sen not to include him in his small wedding party—"It's not like he'd do it, anyway," he'd said defensively—and so Scott had been a ghost at the ceremony. Joanna had definitely taken notice of the thin, beauti-ful, dark-skinned girl he'd brought as his date—Queenie, or Quincy, something with a *Q*. As she walked through the crowd earlier, taking a look at the cocktail-hour appetizers, everyone quickly parted. It was as if the other guests were slightly afraid of her.

Catherine inspected Joanna carefully. She reached out and brushed a few strands of hair from Joanna's eyes. "Why do you look so pissed off? You should see yourself. It's like you've swallowed a wasp. Your pictures in the *Main Line Times* are going to be terrible."

"Mom, the *Main Line Times* isn't here, okay?" Joanna snapped. And then her mother's face fell, and Joanna clenched inside. Okay, so she *was* pissed off. A sour, irksome feeling had infected her in the last hour, crawling under her skin, though she couldn't quite put her finger on the cause. Catherine, most definitely, was a contributing factor, but that wasn't all of it. Was she irritated about the band not showing up on time? Was it because the bustier beneath her dress was digging into her ribs? Certainly, but she was also just the tiniest bit rueful about a particular entry in an old journal she'd kept when living alone in Philly, which she'd come upon a few days before while cleaning out her things. The entry described Joanna's ideal wedding—barefoot on a beach on a midsummer night with only a handful of guests, culminating in a clam-bake on a patio and a lot of dance songs like "Come On, Eileen." It was a silly idea, one she never would've shared with Charles, but that was the thing, she was never able to share *any* ideas with Charles. The details for the wedding at Roderick had more than likely been in place before they'd gotten engaged, probably before Charles was even born.

"You'd better start smiling," Catherine whispered through clenched teeth, nudging Joanna's elbow. "Don't screw this up. You probably don't even realize what you have here."

Joanna took stock of Catherine's words and finally understood. Her mother's reservations weren't about Joanna not knowing how to hang pants on a hanger or how to properly set a table. Catherine thought Joanna didn't deserve this marriage—*Catherine* did. She was the one who had wanted, who had worked, but Joanna had swooped in and taken.

Joanna walked away from her mother, not dignifying her with a response. As she headed back toward Charles, who was sitting with his groomsman, having danced his one and only dance of the wedding and therefore fulfilled his duties, a sharp pain pierced her side. She suddenly felt dizzy and thirsty and on display. When the photographer grinned at her from behind his camera, she was afraid he was secretly laughing. What if Catherine was right? What if she didn't deserve Charles? Was *that* what was eating away at her?

It wasn't possible. She was just feeling wedding jitters and, underneath that, a fizz of excitement. Excitement that her life was about to change into all she'd anticipated it would be. In fact, no, more than that, excitement that it was going to be better than she'd ever imagined.

five

A horrible idea had begun to form in Sylvie's mind.

It was a torturous idea, an enticing idea. Yesterday her fellow board members had mentioned where the boy had lived. They'd dangled it out there, a worm on a fishing line. She knew where that apartment complex was—everyone knew where it was, even though they pretended places like that didn't exist. She could remain anonymous and just go and see.

No, she told herself, as though she was a bad dog. *No.* She tried to garden, to do a crossword puzzle. She read the first few pages of her grandfather's copy of *The House of Mirth,* one of his favorite guilty-pleasure books. He wrote notes in the margins, chicken-scratched nonsense she could barely decipher. She went into James's office and stared at the filing cabinet. It was so infuriatingly unchanged. She looked again at the blank spot on the bookcase where the jewelry box had been. She turned her diamond ring around and around on her finger.

To stave off the idea, she called Hector, the lawyer who had handled James's will. She described the situation at the school to him in dainty, unworried tones. *Just if you have a couple minutes to chat. In case you have an opinion.* Hector passed her to another lawyer, one who "handled cases like this." Sylvie wanted to ask what he meant by that, but he quickly added, "I just handle tax law and estate planning, Mrs. Bates-McAllister."

The second lawyer's name was Ace. He sounded about nineteen years old. Uncomfortably, Sylvie explained what she knew all over again—that Scott had coached this boy, that there was a rumor floating around that the coaches might've been negligent or even encouraged the hazing. "Though I can't imagine how," she added. "Certainly the coaches wouldn't be stupid enough to whisper terrible things into boys' ears just to see if they'd do them. Boys look up to their coaches, sometimes even more than their parents."

But then she looked down at her hands. She'd picked the skin on the side of her thumb clean off. Scott hadn't used his power as a coach to turn these boys into monsters. Scott hadn't put the hazing ideas into their malleable heads. She refused to believe it.

Ace the lawyer let out a long sigh and waited almost ten whole seconds before speaking again. "Well, if his parents choose to fault the school for negligence, your son might be called to answer questions since he works for the school. It seems like a hard thing to prove, unless, of course, one of the other boys confirms the rumor. If they discover evidence, they may be able to build a case against your son—that his influence led to this happening, that sort of thing."

"There's no evidence," Sylvie said quickly. "Someone's making this all up."

Ace cleared his throat. "The boy that died . . . he was on scholarship, right?"

"Yes."

"And Hector mentioned you're the chairman of the school's board of directors."

"Yes," she said slowly. "I've been on the board for years."

"And Scott still lives at home. I understand both your grandfathers left quite the estates when they died. I'm so sorry about your husband, too, by the way."

She sniffed out a thank you. Then, "Where are you going with this?"

"Well, when some people lose a loved one, they look for someone—or something—to blame," Ace said. "Worse than that, they lose sight of what's important. I've seen it more times than I want to admit. They just see dollar signs, especially if they think you'll do anything to preserve your reputation."

"I'm not asking these questions out of concern for money or for my reputation," Sylvie spat. "I've called you because I don't want my son to be implicated in something he had nothing to do with."

"Come now, Mrs. Bates-McAllister," Ace said softly. "There's nothing wrong with wanting to protect what's yours."

She bristled. What could some fresh-out-of-law-school upstart know about protecting what was hers? What could he possibly understand about reputation? He certainly spoke as if he was some kind of authority, and what kind of name was *Ace*, anyway? It was a cruel affront that Hector had passed her to someone like this.

"Have you spoken to Scott directly about this?" Ace asked.

"No," she said automatically.

"Maybe you should."

Sylvie wanted to laugh. *Talk* to Scott? When was the last time she'd done that? She felt their relationship was cursed before they even met. Even before the paperwork was finalized for Scott's adoption, Sylvie's mother, Clara, had shaken her bony finger from her cancer deathbed and asked Sylvie why on earth she wanted another boy. *You'll never be a good mother to two boys*, she scolded. *You're too delicate. You take everything too personally.* And she'd propped herself up on the mattress and added, *And he's mixed race?* She made a pinched, worried face. *Are you trying to be political or something?*

Politics were the furthest motivation from Sylvie's mind when they got the news that a young mother from the Southwest who could no longer take care of an eighteen-month-old toddler had chosen Sylvie and James as new parents. Adopting an American child was far more difficult than Sylvie had imagined, and she and James had jumped through all kinds of hoops to even get this far; it seemed ungrateful to turn the child down. Still, when the adoption agency broke the news about Scott's background, she felt a push and pull inside her. It didn't matter; it did matter. There would be a whole separate culture to consider, a world she knew little about. There would be talks they'd have to have, a painful explanation about the woman who'd given him up, a woman they knew nothing about. But maybe that wouldn't matter. Couldn't they just raise him as theirs? Couldn't their culture be his culture?

You're doing a wonderful thing, you know, the adoption coordinator mentioned during one of their private conversations, when James wasn't around. Sylvie found the statement churlish and crass. Did the coordinator sense her uneasiness? Was it because she'd asked her if adoptive parents sent out some sort of I-just-brought-home-my-child announcements to friends, similar to a baby picture with weight and length and tiny footprints and handprints? Could the coordinator pinpoint the ambivalence that welled so deeply inside her, the fear that she might never be able to bond with this child as she'd instantly bonded with her biological son?

James, of course, didn't care one way or another. *A baby is a baby,* he'd said. He longed for another boy and didn't care where he was from.

After a while, Sylvie warmed to the idea of having a second boy in the house. She imagined looking out her window and seeing her two sons hauling red sleds up the hill in the winter. It could be the image on her Christmas cards.

Sylvie meticulously planned how she would break the news to Charles, nearly four, that he was going to have a brand-new brother. It was going to involve an ice-cream cake, a trip to the zoo, and maybe a walk around the Swithin grounds. The day before the news, Charles arrived home from a play date, eager to show his parents an origami crane that his friend's mother had taught him to make. When he proudly placed it in James's hands, a perfect folded bird out of shiny pink paper, James frowned. "What are you, a fruit?"

Charles looked confused. "Like . . . a banana?"

James held the crane by its beak, scoffing at its pinkness. "This is gay, Charles."

James had that obstinate, self-righteous look on his face again—it wasn't an opinion, it was *law*. Charles's face took on a worried, guilty, self-conscious expression that Sylvie would never get used to seeing. His gaze swiveled from James to Sylvie. "What does *gay* mean?" he asked worriedly, his eyes already filling with tears.

"It means happy," Sylvie said quickly.

Charles looked relieved and James snorted. "Thank God we're going to have another boy around here, Syl. Maybe he'll teach this one not to act like such a pussy."

Sylvie held her breath. Her son seemed to stop breathing. It was hard to know whether Charles understood the individual words, but he understood their thrust. He whirled around and ran out of the room.

Sylvie glared at James, who was busy pouring himself another drink. "What?" He raised his hands defensively. "What did I do?"

"I had plans for how I was going to tell him about the baby," Sylvie said.

"How was *I* supposed to know that?"

"Because I told you!"

She ran out of the house and found Charles in the garden, sitting on a rock, sticking a twig into the dirt. She crouched down next to him and told him his father was just teasing him. But there *was* a surprise—Charles really *was* going to have a new brother. They were adopting a new little boy for him to play with, two years younger than him. They were picking him up and bringing him home next week. Charles would get to teach this little boy everything he knew.

"Now, he may look a little different than you," she added. "But it doesn't mean he's different inside. He'll be your brother. A boy just like you."

Charles nodded, not really understanding what she meant. After fiddling with his toes for a while, he raised his head. "What does 'adopting' mean?" he asked.

"Well, it means he's coming from another family. But once we adopt him, he'll belong to *our* family."

Charles wrinkled his nose, confused. "Why?"

"Why what?" Sylvie cursed James for forcing this on her a day early. She felt unprepared for questions.

"Why can't he stay with his own family?" Charles clarified.

Sylvie sat back. "Well, sometimes mommies can't take care of their babies in the way they should be taken care of."

Charles's eyes widened. "Why?"

"Well, sometimes the mommy is . . . sick. Or too young. Or maybe poor."

"Or *bad?*" He sounded thrilled.

"Well . . . yes. Maybe."

Why had she said it? She should have said *No, mothers are never bad, mothers are always good!* But she was still so raw from what had just happened in the house. She couldn't bear the thought that Charles might believe what James had just implied. What James *often* implied. *That's not the way you throw a baseball. Do it like this. Like* this. *It's not like it's hard. What are you thinking about, just sitting there? You're day-dreaming? Men don't daydream, Charlie. That's girly.* And, *Why do you need a night-light? Being afraid of the dark is for babies.* She saw Charles's face crumble every time James corrected him. She didn't want Charles to ever think he was inferior, that he was anything less than perfect.

A look of intrigue sparkled through Charles's eyes, and the idea took hold. The first few times she caught Charles stating matter-of-factly that Scott's real parents were poor poop-heads who'd given him up, she tried to correct him, but Charles would always look at Sylvie quizzically—*she* was the one who had told him this. And then James would cluck his tongue as if he understood that she had perpetuated it. Sometimes she felt like Scott knew she'd planted the idea, too. Even as a little boy, she'd noticed how he stared at her sometimes, his dark, round little eyes derisive, his pink mouth a flat line. Judging, seething. Sylvie thought Charles would eventually forget what she'd told him and accept Scott as his brother, but as the boys grew older, their relationship deteriorated. That Christmas card of them pulling sleds up the hill never came to fruition.

Sylvie told Ace the lawyer thank you and good-bye. She couldn't ask Scott outright; nor could she ask the lawyer if what she wanted to do—the idea that had begun to grow—was wise. She already knew his answer. But there was so much she'd lost this year, so much she'd given up. The lawyer had said it himself: *When some people lose a loved* one, *they look for someone—or something—to blame. They lose sight of everything important.* Imagining her life without the school seemed inconceivable. It was a second heart beating inside her; she wasn't sure who she was without it.

Resigned, she opened the closet and pulled out James's tan trench coat. The last time he'd worn it was on a trip they'd taken to France, when the boys were little. It was too big on her, the sleeves hung well past her hands, but she'd taken to wearing it often, pushing her hands into the deep—and empty, she'd checked—pockets, feeling the smooth, large buttons, knotting the belt tighter and tighter. But when she looked at her reflection in the mirror, she didn't see a glimmer of James, as she'd hoped. All she saw was a middle-aged woman in a man's coat that didn't remotely fit.

The apartment complex was in one of the unimproved parts of the county. It loomed behind a shopping mall that housed a dollar store, a Salvation Army, and a facility called Payday Advance. FEVERVIEW DWELLINGS, an old tan sign said at the entrance. A faded starburst in the corner crowed RENTALS AVAILABLE! The complex consisted of a cluster of buildings joined by crumbling walkways. Some of the cars in the parking lots had the beginnings of rust and unrepaired dents. One of the apartment windows was covered with a trash bag. The strip mall's enormous parking lights towered over the trees; it never got truly dark here at night.

As Sylvie pulled into a parking space, she looked around. A curtain fluttered behind a window. A shadow shifted behind a tree. Even though Tayson said everything would remain hushed up, this *could* have gotten out somehow—and maybe Sylvie wasn't as anonymous as she thought she was. She'd watched enough news programs to know how ruthless the press could be when they got hold of a story, especially one that featured an injustice between the rich and the poor. When she walked to her car to drive here, she thought the flowerbeds in the garden looked unusually tamped-down, as if someone had been standing in them, peering through the kitchen window. And a lid to one of the garbage cans she kept outside the garage had blown off. Or maybe it had been *removed*. The garbage bags were still intact, though, the trash not rooted through. And when she turned off her car in the Feverview lot, she wondered if an investigative unit might be crouched in the bushes near the entrance. Maybe a reporter was rehearsing his script right now, ready to go in front of the camera and speculate why she was here and what she was doing. Paying her respects? Striking some kind of deal? Admitting that she knew something?

She cocked her head, trying to coax whispers from the silence. A young black man ambled out one of the complex doors; clearly neither Sylvie nor a school scandal weighed heavily on his mind. The man's pants hung nearly to his knees, and he had one hand in his pocket, the other hand sort of at his hip, clenched. He walked right past Sylvie's car with that same kind of aggressive yet apathetic swagger that Scott had. Sylvie shrank into the seat and stared down at her lap, not wanting to make eye contact. The man walked right by.

The aura of Feverview reminded her of the first time she'd been to Philadelphia—*really* went to Philadelphia, not one of those chaperoned trips with her grandfather to art retrospectives or symphony performances. She and James had gone when they were still dating, walking around Old City and wandering down Independence Mall. Even in the nicest parts of town, homeless people staggered up to them. A bicycle messenger nearly knocked Sylvie over; a lanky, unattractive man wearing a business suit and carrying a briefcase muttered as he passed; and a bunch of tall black men with soft hair laughed aggressively at a joke Sylvie was certain was about her.

Sylvie had grasped James's hand tightly, but he'd just laughed. "You're acting like you've never been here before."

"I never came by myself," she explained.

James poked her side. "You're so sheltered. We need to get you out in the world a little more."

He had felt this way about her from the day they'd met. She'd first seen him on the grounds of Swarthmore when Sylvie was a college freshman. It had been a crisp fall day, and James, ten years older than she was, had been walking around and admiring the campus, killing time before meeting with an old family friend in Haverford. Sylvie had been sitting on a bench, trying to come to grips with college life, which was unsettlingly alien. So many of the boys there had long, scruffy hair and didn't bathe. So many of the girls didn't wear bras or makeup and had so many ideas about America and capitalism and God, things Sylvie had always thought of as fixed, revered institutions. Even the girls who'd grown up privileged like Sylvie were standoffish. Many of them were already engaged to be married; others were always gone on weekend jaunts with boyfriends or families; and others were far too worldly for her, into experimental poetry and women's rights protests and experimenting with drugs. Where had they *heard* of such things?

Sylvie had chosen to dorm at Swarthmore instead of commuting from home, feeling too much like a ghost in her parents' gloomy, impassive house, but every night after class, when the other girls in the dorm were gathering in the dining halls or smoking joints in someone's room, Sylvie shut herself in one of the dorm's shower stalls and sobbed. She was so alone. Everything scared her, and what was she supposed to do now that her grandfather was gone? He had died unexpectedly of a heart attack two weeks before she'd started college. She'd almost considered not coming, but she kept hearing her grandfather's raspy voice, telling her to stop being so foolish. And then there was the gift her grandfather had given her. During the reading of the will, the lawyer announced that her grandfather had passed his home on to her, not her parents. Why had he shouldered her with such an immense responsibility? It was something that finally made her parents sit up and notice her, but not in the right way.

James had stopped at Sylvie's bench. *He was in town from Boston*, he said. *He didn't know this area at all. Did she know of somewhere around here he could get lunch?* Sylvie looked him over. He had thick, dark hair, pale skin, thin lips. His wing-tip shoes reminded her of the ones her grandfather had worn. He looked like more of a professor than a student. As she fumbled for a pen to write down the names of some nearby restaurants and close approximations of their addresses, James asked if she'd like to join him. Sylvie paled, blurting out that she hadn't meant to imply herself in his plans. "I know," James said, smiling sweetly at her. "But it's what I'm asking."

And then, much to her embarrassment, Sylvie began to cry. It felt like he was the first person besides her grandfather who'd shown her kindness. "Hey," James said nervously, tentatively touching her shoulder. "Come on now." He didn't shrink away, he didn't flee, which only made Sylvie cry harder. This was the most attention anyone had given her since her grandfather's death.

He never made it to see his family friend that day. Sylvie skipped class, ate lunch with him, and then asked him if he'd like to go on a drive in her car down the Pennsylvania country roads. He agreed. Sylvie took him by Roderick, confessing the huge and terrifying responsibility that had just been foisted upon her. "What would you do with a house like this?" she asked him. "Why would he choose me?" she went on. "I certainly don't deserve it." James looked at her and said, "If he gave it to you, he must have thought you deserved it."

She was grateful to have an eager listener. Even more grateful, in a way, that he was someone she barely knew, someone who had no stake in her life; for that day she'd assumed she would never see him again. But James made sure that they did. Sylvie had never had a boyfriend before James, so she had nothing to compare him to, but she enjoyed the comforting, protective attention he gave her—doting without being grabby, respectful without being cold. After that first day's drive, he took the train down from Boston regularly, and she sometimes went up to visit him. She met his family, a successful group, who lived in a big, rambling house in Concord that had lacy curtains in every window, rattling baseboard heat, and a dollhouse-size guest room that was always made up for Sylvie. At the time, James was helping his father run the family's burgeoning plastering business. The hope was for James to take over once his dad retired, but James was trying to unwind himself from the responsibility. "It's too fussy," he said. "And messy." Furthermore, his world would remain maddeningly small if he took over the business, as he would be buying materials from suppliers he'd known since he was little, employing the same guys or their sons, and probably repairing and restoring houses in the same smattering of neighborhoods his father had relied on for years. James wanted to be something else, something bigger and more important; he just didn't know what that was yet.

As they got to know each other, James became increasingly enamored by Bates lore. He grilled her about Swithin, about her grandfather's quarries, which her father now ran, and about the estate she'd inherited. A few months into dating, James told Sylvie that it seemed like a shame to have inherited that big, beautiful house and not live in it. His father had relieved him of the family business duties; he could find a different kind of job in Philadelphia . . . if Sylvie would answer one question first. And then he slid a small, velvet ring box across the table.

It was a relief to be engaged—Sylvie finally felt like everyone else. James doted on her joyfully and asked if she wanted children. Sylvie remembered her grandfather prodding her to have kids someday, saying that the world needed more people like her. *Yes*, she decided, *she would live in his house; she would fulfill his wishes.*

She told James she couldn't bear to change anything at Roderick. "At least not for a while," she backtracked, wondering if wanting to preserve a house with the exact specifications of its previous owner sounded a bit crazy, kind of like the stories she'd heard of penniless, once-aristocratic spinsters who remained for decades in filthy, unkempt estates—the clutter piling up, the cats multiplying, and the house deteriorating devastatingly fast. But James stroked her hair. "It's okay. We won't ever change it if you don't want to. We'll keep it up to the letter." *He understood*, she thought. Finally, someone understood.

The next step, of course, was for James to meet Sylvie's family. On Thanksgiving, she and James drove to Roderick, where the family had held Thanksgiving dinner for fifty years and had no intention of holding it anywhere else, despite the fact that Sylvie wasn't yet living there. On the way there, James kept relining his lips with Chapstick, looking again and again at the label inside his suit jacket, as if there was some sort of cheat sheet inscribed there that would tell him exactly what he should say. For the most part, he got along with everyone just fine. Sylvie's extended family shook James's hand and talked to him about sports and cars and Boston. Sylvie's great-uncle Clayton asked James what he did for a living, and James paused, looking expectant, and then said he was waiting for the right opportunity to come along. Sylvie's cousin Paul, who was almost twenty years her senior, clapped James on the shoulder and told him to try finance: there was a lot of money to be made in the stock market.

Sylvie's mother cornered her in the pantry right before dinner, the ice in her gimlet rattling. "I guess congratulations are in order," she said coolly. "But really, *he's* the one I should congratulate. I bet he thinks he hit the jackpot."

Sylvie tried not to take it personally. Her mother had been drinking all day; she had said nasty things to everyone. The second after the last bite of pumpkin pie had been swallowed, Sylvie's dad—who by then was living almost exclusively in New York but had made an appearance at the old house for tradition's sake—promptly stood up and announced he had a big meeting in the morning, telling everyone good-bye except his wife. Her mother screamed out, "You don't have a meeting, you dumb shit. You're going back to the city to fuck that whore in the ass and everyone here knows it." Years later, Sylvie would learn that her mother had found out about the metastatic lump in her breast the day before, which might have explained her behavior. Her mother would keep the lump a secret from the rest of the family, though, even long after the disease had spread to her bones.

Later, when Sylvie and James were driving back to Swarthmore, they stopped for gas. When Sylvie looked over, she saw her father's Lincoln across the parking lot, its lights off. Her father was just sitting there in the car, staring straight ahead. After filling up the tank, James got back into the car and followed her anxious gaze. His eyes lit up. "Would you mind if I went over and talked to him for a minute?"

Sylvie let out a nervous chuckle, certain James was kidding, but James shrugged, his face open, earnest, and hopeful. Sylvie realized then how little she knew him.

"I don't think now's a good time," she said slowly.

James's gaze lingered on her father for a little longer, and then he hunched his shoulders. Sylvie still didn't know what he was thinking, and her heart began to beat faster. After a while, he turned to her. "It's just, I thought he'd offer me a job tonight. You know, since we're getting married and all."

"He runs my grandfather's quarries and brickyards," she cried out. "You certainly don't want to do that. It's worse than plaster."

"No, I meant . . . something else. Like an executive job."

Sylvie's family business was far out of her control, something she'd never been involved in. And she had no pull over her father; she hadn't for some time. More than that, her father might flat-out refuse. He was bitter, she knew, that she'd gotten the house instead of him—why should he toss her new fiancé a cushy job?

"I think Cousin Paul's idea was a better one," she said finally. "Finance. That sounds exciting."

A look of embarrassment crossed James's face. "Well," he said. "Forget I said anything."

He started the car, drove her back to Swarthmore, and pecked her good-bye impersonally on the cheek. Days passed and he didn't call. She tried reaching him in Boston, but he didn't answer. What had gone wrong? What had he expected of her? Had her mother been right—*I bet he thinks he hit the jackpot?*

Then, eight days after Thanksgiving, she found a message slipped under her door saying he was on his way down to the city and could she please meet him at 30th Street Station. She found him standing in front of a flower stand, holding a single pink rose. He'd found a job at Janney Montgomery Scott, he said. He was moving to Philly the following week. He'd rented an apartment on Pine Street, and he would live there until they were married.

Authority had been restored in him. The crackling, unstable insecurity she'd seen in the car on Thanksgiving night was gone. Sylvie was so relieved that she didn't bring up her annoyance over his weeklong chilly silence . . . or what it meant.

Now Sylvie squared her shoulders and got out of the car. The air was cool and soggy, and dew had collected on the grass. Wind blew the edges of her hair. She'd picked up a cup of coffee at a drive-through Burger King a few miles back, and steam swirled around her face. She would be a woman out for a leisurely stroll with a cup of coffee, a woman alone with her thoughts.

Far away she heard a car alarm and then two people screaming at each other. There was an upended garbage can across the path; McDonald's hamburger wrappers, bottles of beer, and a soiled diaper spilled out onto the scrubby grass. On second thought, the idea of her coming here to be meditative was ridiculous. This wasn't an idyllic park, a nature trail. People didn't perambulate around places like this.

And then Sylvie saw it, under a tree just twenty feet away: a bunch of flowers, a lit candle, a photo. It was the same photo of Christian they'd had at the board meeting, his sour expression, those innocent freckles, that green hair. The photo was eight by ten, cut out from a contact sheet. When Sylvie circled the tree—looking over her shoulder again, pricking up her ears to listen for snaps of cameras or gasps of onlookers—she saw that someone had stuck the photo to the tree trunk with a wad of fluorescent-yellow gum.

She stared at Christian's picture. She'd recognized him instantly the other day; she always noticed boys like him. Not long before James died, Sylvie had been driving home from the mall one weekend and noticed two boys standing at the edge of a yard near an intersection. One boy looked normal enough; Sylvie barely noticed him. But the boy next to him had that green hair. He'd painted his face white. There was heavy eye shadow around his eyes and red lipstick sloppily applied to his mouth, so one corner of his mouth was an exaggerated grin, stretching up to his cheekbone. His face had almost caused her to crash. But he was talking to the other boy as if he looked perfectly acceptable, almost as if he was daring people to think otherwise.

The Joker, she'd realized later. From *Batman*. *That's who he was dressed as.* But it had been nowhere near Halloween.

She next saw him marching with the Swithin team at one of Scott's wrestling meets. Someone must have made Christian wash the hair dye out, though tinges of green still showed on his scalp. This time he wore a cape. Or perhaps *cloak* was a better word; the thing was brown, possibly made of a potato sack. A ripple went through the crowd, followed by a few giggles and jeers. Christian was trying to dress like someone or something this time, too—a character from a Tolkien book or a creature from a sci-fi movie. Sylvie quickly searched for Scott, who was standing by the line of chairs set up for the wrestlers, watching them march in. Scott clearly saw Christian, but his expression hadn't changed. He seemed neither intrigued nor annoyed by the boy. It was almost as though he didn't see him at all.

In a funny way, Christian reminded her of Scott. Not that Scott dressed in costumes, but he had his way of challenging who and what he was expected to be. At the match, Sylvie wished she knew who Christian's parents were. She wanted to ask if it was hard for them to have a son who didn't act like everyone else. *You give them so much, you send them to the best school, and they just spit it all back in your face,* she would say. *Do you feel that way, too?*

Sylvie gazed at Feverview's square, dirty windows, trying to imagine Warren Givens waking up this morning, the reality of his son's death raw and unrelenting. Passing by the bathroom where he found him. Or perhaps it had been in the bedroom or maybe at the bottom of a dingy stairwell. Wherever it had happened, it was probably somewhere Mr. Givens had to see every day.

Maybe he still held conversations with his son. Maybe he was able to forget the negative things about Christian, all of that irrelevant after death. Maybe he could now say all the things to Christian he hadn't been able to get out when the boy was alive. Maybe he made all the wrongs right, misunderstandings understood. Maybe the father's leaden heart lifted when he found something personal of Christian's—a torn-off note wedged inside a book he was reading or an inscription on a mix CD left in the downstairs stereo. Maybe he would find warning signs, too, indications of deep, unspoken torment. A quickly scribbled poem mentioning names of all those who hurt him, including the name of a consenting adult. A name that was recognizable, hyphenated.

A door to the apartment complex opened, and a man paused under the awning. He wore a gray Windbreaker and shabby blue pants. When he noticed the collection of items by the tree, he winced but then settled down on a bench nearby.

At once, Sylvie knew. She didn't know how, she just did. She had nothing to go by except instinct. No pictures, no memory of him at any of the school functions, where she and the other board members were supposed to say hello to all the parents but usually concentrated on a select, deep-pocketed few, and yet, she was sure. It was in the way he slowly trudged along. It was in how his fingers nervously played with the lapel of his jacket.

Warren Givens leaned against the back of the bench, his face jowly and creased. Sylvie oscillated between wanting to hide and wanting to inspect him closer. She tried to imagine this man taking green-haired Christian out to dinner, balking as everyone stared at his son's cloak, his clown-white skin, his lipstick. She *got* it, she could tell him. She could recount the times she'd entertained people in the dining room, and although—or maybe because—she always begged Scott to stay in his bedroom, he inevitably rolled past, not saying hello, not being even remotely polite to her guests, looking like such a hoodlum.

It was that he exchanged *was* for *were*, despite the fact that they'd sent him to private school and where she knew, definitely, that he'd *learned* simple grammar and tense, despite the fact that they'd gotten him a tutor for ninth-grade English and tenth-grade geometry and eleventh-grade history, English again, and economics, and in twelfth grade just throwing in the towel and crossing their fingers and toes that he did well enough to squeak by and graduate. It was the fact that he sucked his teeth and walked like a gorilla, all hunched over with his arms swinging low, his eyes flickering here and there, as if looking for—what? An assailant? Someone in a different gang? But *was* he in a gang? What drugs was he using? There had been marijuana, she knew; she smelled it on his jackets when he used to come in from hanging out with his nameless, faceless, empty-voices-on-the-answering-machine friends. She'd sent James to talk with him about it, but nothing had been achieved. She read books about how marijuana was a *gateway drug*; the terminology made her think of Scott boarding a train made of hemp leaves, riding it express to a carved-out tunnel full of crack pipes. And yet what could she do? She wasn't equipped to talk to him.

All she knew how to do was to huddle—anxious and obsessive, rifling through the possibilities and what-ifs.

"Are you doing this to make a statement?" Sylvie had asked Scott after a dinner party. "Am I doing *what?*" Scott retorted. "*Acting* the way you do," she tried. She felt so clumsy. Nothing was coming out right. "Acting like *what?*" he said. "Dressing like, like . . . *that*," she fumbled, pointing to his oversize, untucked T-shirt. "*This?*" He pointed. "There's nothing wrong with dressing like this. This is who I *am*. Sorry I don't wear *loafers* and *rugby shirts* and I don't shop at *Brooks Brothers*." His face pinched with each word, as if the store and attire were curses.

There was a sharp flicking sound across the courtyard, snapping Sylvie from her thoughts. Warren Givens's fingers trembled as he lit a cigarette. He sat there with it, not smoking, just letting it burn down. He glanced at Sylvie and then looked away. Sylvie's fingers twitched. Maybe he knew who she was—her picture was in most of the Swithin bulletins. And he had to know about the rumors—surely someone had told him. It wouldn't be hard to make the connection that her son had coached his son and had possibly *caused this*. He probably wasn't like Sylvie, either. He didn't push things under; he faced things. He was probably so full of rage and blame that he wouldn't accept her apology; nor would he understand her bumbling explanation for why Scott might have done it.

But *was* that what she believed—that Scott had done it? She didn't know.

Then Warren looked straight across the courtyard at Sylvie. "Afternoon."

Sylvie froze. "Hello," she mouthed.

The wind made the loose edges of Christian's photo flap. The candle someone had placed underneath it had long blown out. There were a few stray wildflowers thrown down on the grass. This was Sylvie's chance to say something, to ask a question. That was why she'd come, wasn't it? To see what she was working with?

Abruptly Warren twisted at the waist, turning away from her. His cigarette shook in his fingers. His shoulders heaved. A thin wail escaped from his throat.

Sylvie's hand slowly rose to her mouth. *There. That was what she was working with.*

He continued to shake. Sylvie pressed her nails into her thighs and stood up. Her heart pounded. It was only twenty or so steps to him.

"Here," she said, handing him the unopened packet of tissues she always carried.

He turned back, his blue eyes glassy. He examined the package blankly, as if he wasn't quite sure what it was.

"They're scented," Sylvie said, as though this explained everything.

He opened the packet very slowly, and then put a tissue to his nose. His eyes smiled. "Thank you."

She remained next to him, not wanting to leave just yet.

He breathed in raggedly, his face contorting with embarrassment. "I apologize. I shouldn't be like this."

"It's okay," she whispered.

A game had started on the basketball court. A cluster of girls stood by the gate, talking in Spanish. All at once, Sylvie felt very visible. She quickly backed away from the bench, barely feeling her legs, not saying good-bye. She didn't remember the walk back around the corner to her car, and she was halfway to the bypass before she realized she'd left her cup of coffee on the roof. She had made so many turns already; it was most definitely gone. She pictured it careening to the ground, the lid popping off, the remaining liquid splattering all over the road.

six

Another Thursday full of conference calls, action boxes about websites to visit, 1-800 numbers to call, and discussions about whether the word *effusive* was too highbrow for the "regular American readers" of the financial services magazine printed on thin matte paper that made it look like less of a magazine and more of a coupon circular. Another day of fiddling with the itchy wool band of his pants and smelling other people's lunches, of talking to the clients on the phone and watching Jake bullshit to the publisher.

Charles stepped outside a few minutes before the people from Back to the Land were due in the office, coming to look at the lineup they'd put together. He sat down on the bench in front of his building and watched the regular string of the lunchtime crowd walk by. Men in suits, women in suits, teenagers in Phillies caps, workers in jumpsuits, and a tall, beautiful woman who looked a little like Joanna. The Back to the Land people would be easily identifiable, he figured. They'd look like mountain men, ungroomed and burly. They'd have the same smug, serene look on their faces that Buddhists did—their lives fixed to a very different set of priorities than the rest of the world, their minds and bodies trained to withstand things mere mortals couldn't bear.

Was that what possessed someone to join Back to the Land—a righteous quest for purity? Did they laugh at all the regular folks who functioned on high fructose corn syrup, twenty-four-hour-news outlets, and allergy medications? Would they snicker at Charles when he walked into the room, sensing that he had never built a fire or pitched a tent? Would they know that he was a little *afraid* to pitch a tent, certain he would do it wrong?

He'd tried, once. When Charles was in eighth grade and Scott was in sixth, their father proposed a camping trip in the Poconos. It was the first trip of its kind, and their father had bought an industrial tent, big enough for three people. He wanted to practice assembling it in the backyard before they set out, and he had asked Charles to help. Charles was delighted to be included, but as hard as he puzzled over the instructions, it just made no sense. He couldn't figure out which posts went where. "Come on," Charles's father goaded. "What do we do first?"

The directions shook in Charles's hands. The pole he held slipped from his grip, clattering loudly to the ground.

"Just give it here," his father said, his voice ice. He yanked the instructions from him and picked up the post. When he glanced at Charles again, there were blotches of red on his cheeks and his neck. Charles backed away slowly, his heart a jackhammer. It was ten steps to the side door of the house.

His father didn't summon him back. After a few minutes, Scott emerged up the driveway—he'd been playing basketball with friends. The two of them built the tent together; Scott understood the schematic right away. The worst part was that Scott, the younger brother, stepped inside halfway through to see if Charles wanted to help, which Charles saw as pedantic and condescending. Scott didn't want Charles to help any more than his father did. As Charles peered out the window at the two of them easily building, their rapport light and easy, he knew exactly what the camping trip would be like.

The next morning he told his mother he had a fever. She reached out to feel his forehead, but he caught her eye. Understanding flooded her face fast, and she patted his hand and turned. "Charles is sick," she announced at the breakfast table. "You boys will have to go camping by yourselves."

Their father stared at Charles for a few long beats, his mouth taut, one eyebrow slightly raised. Then he shrugged, turned, and hefted his backpack over his shoulder. And off they went, loading the tent and supplies into the back of the car. Charles spent the weekend reading and watching TV with his mother. She didn't mention that he seemed to have miraculously recovered.

Charles wondered if, in a way, that was what made him really fall in love with Joanna. He'd begun dating her because she was beautiful and because she'd struck up a conversation with him at a bar near his office, capping off the night with an open-mouthed kiss. She was so different from Bronwyn: not as rigorously mannered, not as prudish. What really sealed the deal, though, was when Charles brought her to meet his parents. Though Joanna seemed antsy with his mom, freaking out as if she'd done some great damage to the house when a paper towel she'd thrown into the trash missed the can and landed on the floor, she seemed at ease with his dad. James struck up a conversation about Scotch with Joanna after she admitted that she'd tended bar during college at Temple. She told him about a beer-making course she'd taken at Temple, bored with philosophy electives. Her final beer project was pretty decent; she'd like to try making it again sometime. "Bring it over with you if you do," Charles's father had said. "I'd like to give it a try."

Charles had been flabbergasted. His father hadn't paid a mote of attention to any other girl he'd ever brought home, though of course, they weren't serious. At one point, his dad even met Charles's eye and gave him a terse, approving nod. Charles felt a little lift inside him, as if he was eight years old again, showing his father his report card. On the drive home from the house that day, he'd asked Joanna if she wanted to go on a trip with him. They went to Jamaica, lying on the sand, eating goat and organic vegetables, watching movies under mosquito netting. Joanna was the type of girl who plunged right off the cliff into the ocean without looking down. She didn't tell Charles what shirt to wear for dinner. She didn't mind when he got a little loud after drinking too many Red Stripes. She made friends with the wait staff and the bartender but not in a slightly condescending sort of way, as Bronwyn might have done, and one of the bartenders invited them to an after-hours, staff-only party in one of the caves. On that trip, Charles fell more and more in love with Joanna. She was refreshing and intoxicating, a cool gin and tonic after years of heavy red wine. He still had dreams about them in Jamaica, swimming in that clear water, their legs entwined in that small, hot room. They were their ideal selves there. Funny how remoteness could do that.

A bus huffed from the curb, giving way to a fleshy, apple-shaped cleaning woman in a pink cleaning uniform leaning against the glassed-in elevator that led to Suburban Station. Her face was red, as if scoured with steel wool. Her smock stretched across her breasts and stomach, the skirt stopping just above her square, blockish knees. Now that Charles was on a search for cleaning women, they were suddenly everywhere.

He could hear her barking into her cell phone in Russian. There was something utterly capable about the way she stood, the way she spoke, the manner in which she glared across the street, daring someone to make fun of her outfit. She definitely wasn't the woman who'd found his father in the bathroom, who held captive the secret of those final intimate moments. For if this woman would have found him, Charles knew, his dad would have lived.

When he got back to the office, they were all in the conference room: Jake, Jessica, Becky, and Steven. The Back to the Land woman was in there, too. Just a woman. Not a large mountain man, not a small Indian elder, not a small girl walking a deer on a leash. The woman wore a tweed business suit and leather pumps and carried a brown suede bag.

"Sorry I'm late," Charles said. Everyone had their notebooks out, and there were business cards strewn across the table like confetti. "I had to run out for something, and . . ."

"This is Charles Bates-McAllister," Jake interrupted, a bit wearily. "Another editor on the team."

The woman stood up and introduced herself as Mirabelle DeLong. She was barely five feet tall, with a pointy chin and bright eyes that reminded Charles of a fox. Sitting back down, she said how happy she was to be working with them and how she admired their other projects and was certain they could do wonders for Back to the Land, which had been a brainchild of two businessmen in the eighties. Their hope was to build Back to the Land communities in all fifty states, providing a sort of anti–housing development—an alternative way of living.

Charles bit back his skepticism, picking at a dry piece of skin on the inside of his palm. Looking over, he noticed that Steven was doodling crosses in his notebook.

Jake took Mirabelle through the lineup they'd developed. When he finished, Mirabelle said she'd like to add a final story: a profile of one of the current Back to the Land pioneers. "I have a few candidates in mind," she said. "There's a couple you could speak to who moved there very recently. They're both very sweet, really excited to be there. Just got their house up and running."

"We'll use your discretion," Jake said quickly.

"Do you have a writer in mind for that?" Charles asked Jake. "I could call them after the meeting, make sure they're free."

"Why don't you write it?" Jake said.

"Me?" Charles thumbed his chest.

"You're always asking to write things. Plus, you live out that way. A lot closer to where the community is."

Mirabelle smiled and pushed a pamphlet across the table to Charles. It was different from the one he'd seen yesterday, with only a simple log cabin on the cover. "The directions to the homesteads are there," Mirabelle explained, turning the shiny pages and pointing. "That's probably where we'll set up the interview, and then they'll take you to their cabin and show you around."

Not knowing what else to do, Charles opened the pamphlet. On the first page was a group of adults sitting in a circle, talking. It must have been pre–Back to the Land, for they were all wearing Ralph Lauren polo shirts and sneakers and lipstick. "Life can be simpler than this," said the caption.

He flipped to the next page, which described the training process of becoming an intrepid frontiersman. Now the same people were sitting outside on logs and tree stumps, dressed in rags. A woman was holding a long, wobbly saw, examining a tree trunk. Someone else was hovering over a smoldering fire, grinning.

Charles turned to the next photo, his eyes skidding over it. Then he turned back; a chilly hand squeezed his heart. A woman was leaning over a square of soil, pulling at a stalk. She wore a long skirt, frayed at the ends, and an oversize cotton shirt. Her mouth was half open, and there was a smudge of dirt on her cheek. Charles blinked at her oval face, her slender nose, and her full lips. The photo was in black and white, but if it had been color, Charles was sure her eyes would be blue.

He tapped the photo; the words dried up in his throat. He read the caption. Her name.

Mirabelle leaned forward. "Oh, she's *wonderful*."

Her name was Bronwyn Pembroke.

"I didn't even think of her," Mirabelle went on, "but she'd be a great person to profile. Young, intelligent, articulate, and *really* exemplary of what we're trying to accomplish."

"Done," Jake said, brushing his hands together. "Let's use her."

Charles pressed his lips together, trying to conceal his panic. It was *her*. Bronwyn. *His* Bronwyn.

"Are you all right?" Mirabelle said.

Charles looked up. Everyone was staring at him, and he wondered if he'd made some sort of sound. He nodded and reached for his water glass but missed it, tipping the whole thing over. Everyone leaped up and grabbed their papers. "I'll get a paper towel," one of the assistants cried and ran out of the conference room. Charles mopped up the water with napkins as best he could, apologizing. His hands felt so clammy.

The assistant returned with a roll of paper towels. The conversation rushed on without him. It had been settled; Mirabelle told Charles that she would contact Bronwyn—*Bronwyn!*—and they'd set up an interview for early next week. In no time, Mirabelle was standing to leave. She shook everyone's hands. Jake held the conference room door for her, and Charles followed them out.

When the elevator doors closed, Mirabelle safely gone, Charles turned back to the conference room. The pamphlet was still there in the middle of the table. He rushed back in and practically pounced on it, whipping to the photo again, eager to scrutinize it without restraint. Bronwyn looked so plain. Older, too, and she'd gained some weight. Her hair was pulled back in a sloppy ponytail, a few pieces hanging in her eyes, and there was a pile of what looked like carrots next to her, dirty, teardrop-shaped things just lying there on the filthy ground.

He closed his eyes and saw Bronwyn softly talking to Scott on the patio at his parents' house, trying so desperately to draw him into their world. He remembered the last day they'd ever spoken, how she'd pulled his hand to get him to sit back down, nudged him to clap at the Swithin awards ceremony. He recalled the horror in her eyes when he'd said all those foul, putrid things to Scott, the pain on her face when she broke it off with him a blink later.

There was a knock on the glass, causing Charles to jump and look up. Jake opened the door and poked his head inside. "Everything all right?"

Charles swallowed, running his fingers along the sides of his pants. "Uh-huh."

Jake hesitated, then walked in and put his hands on the back of one of the swivel chairs. "What's up?"

Charles's throat felt tight. "It's just that . . . I'm not sure I'm the right person to write this story."

"Why not?"

For a moment Charles considered confiding in Jake. But they'd never had anything close to a personal relationship. Charles fiddled with his shirt collar. "I just . . . I think it's weird, that's all. I think a different kind of person should write this. Someone who hunts, maybe. Someone who's more . . . eco."

Jake laughed. "You said you wanted to write more." He shifted his weight. "What—do you know that girl or something?" He pointed at the picture of Bronwyn.

Charles sucked in his stomach, horrified that Jake had guessed. "No. Of course not."

"Then what is it? Because I don't think they care about whether you're eco or not. All that matters is that you make Back to the Land look good."

Charles shrugged.

"You said you wanted to write a piece. This is your chance. We'll pay you, of course, and you'll get a byline, for what it's worth." Jake pressed his palm against the glass wall that separated the conference room from the reception area. "But if you don't want to do it, there are plenty of other people who would jump at the money."

Charles bristled and looked away. "No, it's all right. I'm sorry; I'll do it."

Jake rubbed his hands together. "Okay then."

The door swished shut, and Charles put his head in his hands. Why had he said anything? He could handle Bronwyn, couldn't he? He was older, married, his life had changed. He would go and it would mean nothing. He would watch her garden and chop wood. He would be professional and polite, interviewing her about what life is like without real toilets. Bronwyn who could do complicated math problems in her head, the girl whom everyone envied because she was beautiful *and* smart *and* had amazing parents who gave her every opportunity imaginable, now stomping on her good genes and upbringing, traipsing off to live at Walden Pond.

Good Lord, what *did* her parents think about this? Mr. and Mrs. Pembroke had given their children, Bronwyn and her older brother, Roman, every opportunity in the world, encouraging them all the time that it was their duty to become something great. So why had she become a farmer? Was there something *wrong* with having chances? Wasn't she supposed to use the gifts she'd been lucky enough to receive instead of wasting them? Or did something from her previous life leave a sour taste in her mouth? A certain some*one* she'd dated, perhaps, a boy who was similarly privileged, who had said certain scathing things she wanted absolutely no ties to?

But no, that was projecting. It was both naive and arrogant for him to think *he* had something to do with the person she'd become. Still. It felt as though the rules of the universe were suddenly thrown into doubt.

Charles stood up and walked to the conference-room window, rapidly blinking over and over again. A bunch of guys in yellow hard hats were jackhammering a hole in the ground. Eleven flights up, behind all this glass, it was only a muffled groan.

seven

Just as she didn't yet have her bearings in her new house, Joanna had no sense of direction in her new community. Even though she'd grown up fifteen miles from here, it might as well have been Egypt, things seemed so alien. Every bright, massive shopping center looked the same. The Revolutionary-era stone house on one corner was identical to the Revolutionary-era stone house a half-mile down. It seemed as though there was a one-lane bridge on every side street, treacherously narrow and seemingly not spanning any water, as far as she could see.

Even before Joanna and Charles had moved here, Sylvie told them that their town was getting a La Marquette grocery store. Although Joanna had no idea what this really meant—for the last ten years, she'd been shopping at either cramped Philadelphia groceries or outdoor farmers' markets—her curiosity was piqued. So on Thursday afternoon, she printed out directions to the new store and got in the car. Mrs. Cox and Mrs. Batten were talking in the yard as usual, but she didn't look over. She'd started calling both of them *Mrs.* in her head—if she couldn't know them intimately, then she would think of them as formal schoolmarms or as strict, scary piano teachers.

The grand opening banner was still hanging over the grocery store's automatic doors, which opened accordion style into a bakery. From there, Joanna could see a separate room for cheese, a whole aisle of salad dressings, and a large sign in the back that shouted ORGANIC, although she wasn't sure *what* was organic. An older, stylishly thin woman stood at a table, handing out mini tomato-and-mozzarella tarts. "The recipe is in my book," she crowed at Joanna as she passed, gesturing to a glossy cookbook at her side.

Joanna did a lap of the place, marveling at how many types of barley there were to choose from, ogling the flowers in the extensive plant nursery tucked away in the corner of the store, perusing the pottery, handblown glass, and folk-art weather vanes that were displayed near the fruits and vegetables. She sampled everything: all the cheese on toothpicks, little slices of right-out-of-the-rotisserie-oven rosemary chicken, crackers accompanied by thimble-size dipping cups of olive oil. On her second lap, she began to notice something. The aisles were clogged with women in pairs, their carts side by side, and baskets swinging on their arms. Women her age, in yoga pants and T-shirts, laughing together. Women Sylvie's age, cluttered at the wait-staffed café tables, picking at Cobb salads. Clusters of women at the bakery counter, clucking at the cheesecake and the chocolate-chunk muffins and the lemon-mousse tartlets. There were too many baby carriages to count.

Suddenly, Joanna felt overtly singular. She began to make a game of it, finding someone like her, someone who was simply here for the utilitarian purpose of shopping for food, not to hang out. No luck. Was there an unwritten subtext about La Marquette, like the old adage about gay men and highway rest stops? She pushed her hair out of her eyes, pretending to concentrate on her list. How did these

women know one another? How did one make friends here? She'd had
a growing snowball of friends in the city, gathering them as she rolled,
but now it felt impossible to even talk to anyone. She looked down at
her unpolished fingernails, her ripped jeans, and Charles's parka that
she'd plucked out of the closet because it was the only other coat besides his good work trench that had been unpacked. She should have
showered, put on makeup, blow-dried her hair, and ironed her clothes.

"Help you?"

She realized she was standing in front of the meat counter. A kind-
eyed older man with ham-hock biceps and a droopy mustache gave her
a pitying glance. *Why aren't you with anyone?*

She perused the meats, trying to seem occupied. But then, desperate to talk to someone, she asked him what he thought was good today.
"Cornish game hens," he suggested. She nodded, asking if he could
wrap up two. She'd made them once before and they'd turned out all
right. As the butcher ripped off a section of paper, he said, "You ever
have lamb? This shipment we got in is great. From a local farm." And
so Joanna said he could wrap up some lamb for her, too. She went for
two steaks as well, some hamburger patties—she could freeze it all,
she figured—and was even considering ordering a whole goose before
her phone rang. It was her mother. Joanna gave the butcher an apologetic smile and picked up her phone.

"So have you heard?" Catherine said. No hello.

"Heard . . . ?"

"Heard about me, of course."

Joanna walked up the condiments aisle. "No . . ."

Catherine exhaled and paused dramatically. "I'm going into the
hospital on Friday."

"For what?"

"I thought they might have called you. I thought they called emergency contacts for things like this."

Joanna leaned on her cart. "Why are you going to the hospital?"

"Oh, honey. It's too depressing to talk about, really." Her voice was frail.

"Mom . . ."

Catherine swallowed hard. "Treacher found a lump in my breast. *I* couldn't feel it, but who knows. They're going to start with a biopsy. I'm sure it's stage three. They're going to have to do a mastectomy."

"Oh," Joanna breathed out.

"I can feel the cancer growing," Catherine continued. "It's probably in my lungs. Yesterday I woke up with such a headache, and I just know it's in my brain. We probably don't have much time left. There are so many things I need to tell you before I go."

Joanna pinched the bridge of her nose, murmuring more notes of worry. Her mother was still going to the hospital regularly, though now she went to a hospital in Maryland. It had been a surprise when Catherine moved to Maryland six months ago, not long after Joanna's wedding. Joanna's dad had left promptly after the divorce, relocating to Maine, but Catherine had continued on in the little house on the outskirts of the Main Line, though Joanna had no idea how she kept up with mortgage payments. Joanna reckoned the only way she'd ever leave was if she somehow miraculously managed to find a suitable property in the Main Line proper, but when a great-aunt had died and left her a house in Maryland, Catherine had announced rather matter-of-factly that she was going to take occupancy. Joanna had helped Catherine move in and had visited almost monthly since then to accompany Catherine to her bigger medical procedures. The house wasn't very remarkable, a brick ranch with a carport, an unused,

aboveground swimming pool out back, and a foul-smelling mix between a stream and a swamp beyond that.

In moving there, however, Catherine had acquired a new doctor,
Phinneas Treacher, who eagerly supported every crazy self-diagnosis
she'd dreamed up, ordering Catherine test after test, plying her with
medication after medication. During the past six months, Catherine
had had screenings for lupus, fibromyalgia, and restless leg syndrome.
This winter she was certain she had mesothelioma—"It's from *asbestos*," she whispered, "and we had asbestos siding on our house when I
was a kid. The lawyer on TV said that sometimes *you don't even know
you have it*." She'd also undergone countless tests for colon, lung, ovar-
ian, cervical, pancreatic, and throat cancers, though they were all benign, and she took meds for type 2 diabetes, osteoporosis, early-onset
Alzheimer's, and chronic pain. It was unclear whether she really suf-
fered from any of those things, though Joanna doubted it. She was
too cowardly to ask her mom why she was still orchestrating all these
trips to the ER. Maybe Catherine was so used to having Munchausen's
syndrome that it was now routine, in the same way some people got
up every morning and went jogging. The closest Joanna ever got to
broaching the subject was when she suggested Catherine might seek
a second opinion, but Catherine said that was out of the question.
Treacher was the *best*. By whose standards, Joanna wasn't sure.

"When's the biopsy?" Joanna asked now.

"Tuesday."

"Well, I can be there Monday night."

"Oh honey! Are you sure?"

"Yeah, of course."

"You're not busy?"

"I can manage."

"Charles won't mind?"

"He'll understand."

Her mother let out a sigh. "That's wonderful! And perhaps you can come to the sail club with me after."

"The sail club?" Joanna repeated, wincing. Leave it to her mother. She pictured men in seersucker suits, with thin, foreign paramours on their arms. She pictured yachts in the marina with names like *My Marilyn* and *Fantasia II*.

Then switching gears, her mother asked her how she was doing. Joanna stood up straighter. "Fine!" she chirped. "Great!" She smoothed down her hair. "I'm at the market right now, looking for something to make for dinner. We have the greatest grocery store near us. Everything is gourmet."

"Well, that's good," Catherine said slowly, as if yet again she didn't quite believe her daughter. Then again, maybe she shouldn't. Not that Joanna could get into it with her mother. She couldn't say, *Charles didn't respond the right way when I freaked out about my bitchy neighbors. Charles and Sylvie don't include me in their family discussions. Charles brought up an old girlfriend in a conversation I wasn't supposed to hear.* It sounded petty and maybe even insane. If she did say anything, anything at all, Catherine would just repeat what she said at her wedding: *Don't screw it up. Don't you dare.*

"Have you heard anything else about Scott?" Catherine asked.

Joanna said no, he was meeting with a group of teachers next week to talk about the situation. Just to ask him about the wrestling team in general.

"Oh dear," Catherine sighed.

"I thought you said you didn't think Scott had anything to do with it," Joanna inquired, turning down the frozen-food aisle.

"I don't. But I don't doubt those boys were doing something. There was this special on CNN recently about how this group of girls banded together and tormented another girl on—what's that site? Friendbook?"

"Facebook."

"That's right," Catherine said. "Well, that poor girl they were picking on killed herself, can you believe it? Just like this boy at Scott's school! And I saw this crime program the other day where a boy was sent to prison because his interrogators wore him down until he was so confused he admitted to something he didn't do."

Joanna stopped in front of a freezer containing organic pancakes and waffles. "Well, let's hope that doesn't happen."

After she hung up, Joanna stared at the little screen of her phone, feeling the same emptiness and despair that overwhelmed her whenever she and Catherine got off the phone. And she felt as if she'd voiced her silly frustrations with Charles out loud.

She dialed Charles's office to tell him she was going to Maryland again, but before she could complete the call, she heard someone calling her name. When she looked up, Scott was standing at the end of the aisle, his hands in his jeans pockets.

Joanna dropped her phone into her bag, her heart thumping. "H–hi," she stammered. *Had he heard her talking about him to her mother? What had she just said?*

"I thought that was you," he said, strutting down the aisle. A red grocery basket was hooked in the bend of his elbow.

"What are you *doing* here?" she blurted out.

Scott smirked and gestured to his basket.

"But . . . *here?*" She waved her arms at La Marquette's splendor. Scott seemed like the type who would buy everything he needed from the nearest gas station mini-mart.

Scott wore an enormous red hooded sweatshirt with a drawing of a boom box on it and stood with his shoulders hunched. Two women carrying coffee cups passed. They glanced at both of them for a second and then moved on. Joanna wondered if any Swithin mothers were shopping here today. Certainly they came here—this was just the kind of place they would shop. She wondered who had told the headmaster about the possibility of hazing. A student . . . or a parent? A teenager would risk excommunication if he told. It seemed more the work of an adult.

"So," Joanna said. They continued to stand in the middle of the frozen-food aisle. She didn't want to start walking because he might not follow her, and then she would be walking away from him. Nor did she want to look inside his grocery cart—it felt like an invasion of his privacy. "H—how are you?" she fumbled.

"Eh," Scott answered.

A woman with a cart cleared her throat, and Joanna and Scott stepped out of her way. Joanna looked at Scott. "Um, do you want to . . . get coffee or something? Sit for a minute?"

Scott paused for a moment, and Joanna winced. Of course he was going to say no. Of course he was going to snort and say, *What, like we're friends?* This was a man who loomed over her and said, *Boo.*

But then he shrugged. "Okay. Whatever."

He turned toward the coffee counter. She started pushing her cart to follow but noticed the carefully wrapped parcels of meat at the bottom of her cart. They were the only items in there so far, but when she added up the prices on the labels it totaled more than eighty dollars.

She backed away from her cart as if it were a territorial dog. Scott turned and looked at her. "What?"

Her eyes were still on the wrapped packages. Scott walked over and peered into the cart. "Lamb?" He chuckled, though not unkindly.

"I don't know what got into me."

He shrugged. "Just leave it."

"*Leave* it?"

"Yeah. I worked at a grocery store when I was in high school. They make the workers put it back." He gestured to the front of La Marquette where there were a bunch of kids manning the checkout counters. They weren't the usual pimply, gangly, surly grocery-store workers; the girls had glowing skin and ballerina posture, and the boys, with their tucked-in shirts and combed, neatly cut hair, looked like student council presidents. Joanna found herself wondering where Scott had worked.

She glanced at her cart again. "I feel bad."

"Jesus." Scott rolled his eyes and gestured for her to follow him to the coffee bar. She stepped away from the cart, feeling as though she was fleeing the scene of a crime. When she flopped down at a table, her cart no longer in view, her heart was racing with excitement. She felt as if she'd gotten back at La Marquette for all its snobbish beauty, for all its cliquey women and baby carriages.

Scott asked what she wanted. Joanna gave him money, which he took and stood in line to order. When he came back, he sat down and took the lid off his coffee but didn't add milk or sugar. Joanna stared at the faux-antique French posters on the wall, having no idea what to say.

"I'm so fucking bored," he exploded, lacing his hands behind his head. "I'm helping out at my friend's sneaker shop in Philly, but it doesn't take up that much time."

"Like, running sneakers?" Joanna asked.

Scott drummed his fingers on the table. "Designer sneakers. You wouldn't get it."

She squinted, thinking. "Is this the store that just opened near South Street in an alleyway? It used to be part of an old cheesesteak place?"

He raised an eyebrow accusingly.

"I read about it in *City Paper*," she explained, almost as if she was making an excuse.

He pointed at her. "Well look at you. You get an A-plus."

She shoved her tongue into her cheek. To him, she was a brown-noser at the front of the classroom, calling out the answer.

Scott raised his eyebrows. "Oh. I guess I should ask you about your new house, huh?"

"It's all right." She waved him away. "I'm sick of talking about it."

He cocked his head.

"It's just exhausting to unpack, that's all."

He was still watching her, not buying it. She sighed and leaned forward, aware of the crowds around her. "Are people out here typically . . . cold?" she whispered.

Scott's eyes widened. He rested his chin on his palm, intrigued. "Cold?"

She rubbed her hand on the back of her neck. The overhead lights seemed to burn like ultraviolet. "I just mean . . . women in this neighborhood. Suburban women." She gestured around them. The women she was referring to were on all sides. "How does one get accepted by them? Is there a password?"

He snorted. "How about, 'You're a bitch, and so am I'?"

She hid a smile.

Scott leaned forward. "Are you talking about those ladies that live next door to you?"

She looked up, startled.

"After Charles bought the house, but before you guys moved in, I drove by. I saw them standing in the yard."

Her cheeks burned. "Well, yeah. I'm talking about them, I guess."

Scott balled up a paper napkin and aimed it for the trash can. It went in. "They're fucking Stepford wives."

She stirred her coffee. *There*—that was the answer she'd longed for when she called Charles yesterday. That was what she'd wanted him to say.

A woman passed, carrying four bouquets of tiger lilies in her arms. And then something else tumbled unwittingly out of Joanna's mouth. "How about . . . Bronwyn?" She squinted, as though groping for Charles's ex-girlfriend's name. "Was she cold, too?"

Behind them, a man working at the bakery counter called the next number, and a woman strutted up and asked for a box of croissants. "Probably," Scott replied, his tone suddenly hard.

"I've never met her. I guess she moved or whatever."

"Couldn't tell you."

She rotated her ankle, feeling the joint pop. "Do you know why they broke up?"

He raised his eyebrows, creasing his forehead. "Like *I* would know?"

"Well, Charles hasn't really given me an answer, so . . ."

He pointed at her. "I never pegged you for that kind of chick."

She sat back, self-consciously touching her chin. "What kind of chick?"

"The kind that cares."

"N–no," she answered. Her pulse raced, throbbing at the insides of her elbows, the backs of her knees. *I didn't used to be,* she almost said.

She sat back, having said way, way too much. "No, I'm not," she said more firmly, more certainly.

This was by far the longest, most intimate conversation she'd ever had with Scott. It was wearing her out, but at the same time, she didn't want to move. "I'm going to see my mother next week," she said. "I was talking to her when you came up."

Scott smiled. "I remember your mom from your wedding. She wore that red dress."

Joanna hid a smirk. After a few cocktails, that red dress had slipped off Catherine's shoulders, exposing the lacy edges of her strapless bra.

"What?" Scott asked, noting her look.

"Nothing." She stared down at the checkerboard floor. It was shiny, so clean one could probably eat off it. "She's having some kind of breast biopsy."

"That's *funny?*"

"No . . ." She waved her hand. "I mean, it won't be anything. It never is. But I always have to go and be with her."

"Why do you have to go?"

"Because . . ."

"Doesn't she have friends who live closer? Other family members?"

Joanna stared at the barista behind the coffee counter as she industriously wiped down the steamed-milk nozzles. She wasn't about to try and explain her issues with her mom to Scott of all people. "It has to be me," she finally said.

"That's pretty shitty."

"It's . . . complicated."

Joanna's eyes finally wandered to Scott's shopping basket. There were a few items in it—peanut butter, a jar of olives, Klondike bars, an industrial-size bag of beef jerky. It didn't exactly add up to a meal. Then she noticed a purple box tucked into the corner. "You like Sleepytime tea?" she exclaimed, pointing at the bear mascot on the label.

Scott paled and quickly turned the box of tea over. But that just made it worse—the bear mascot was now tucked into bed, a striped sleeping cap on his head, little holes cut out for his ears, his eyes two closed half-moons. Little z's floated above his head, and a cup of tea sat on his nightstand, steam rising from the cup.

"Aww, that's you," Joanna said, pointing to the bear.

Scott winced. But his face was still open. He hadn't shut down, amazingly.

"Does it help you sleep?" Joanna pressed.

"Maybe."

"Do you have trouble sleeping?"

"Only when I'm thinking about you."

Joanna flushed and looked away. But when she glanced at him again, he was chuckling. It was a joke. Of course it was a joke.

The automatic doors wheezed open again. Cold wind blew in, and as Scott raised his eyes, his face went gray. Joanna turned around to see what he was looking at. A few people had stopped to gather baskets or carts: a guy talking on his cell phone, a college-age couple, a forty-something woman in a tan trench coat and gray pants.

"What?" Joanna asked as Scott's face tightened.

"I think I know that bitch."

"Which one? In the trench coat?" Joanna wondered how often Scott went around calling people *bitches*.

Scott nodded and shrank against the wall. "She won't recognize me or anything. She never came to the matches."

Joanna struggled to understand. "Her son wrestled?"

"I saw her picking him up a few times. She never came to watch, though, just waited outside in her car. And even if the kid had had the shit kicked out of him, she never helped him with his bags or anything."

Joanna glanced at the woman again. She had short, no-nonsense sandy hair and wore pearl earrings. A white oxford collar peeked over the neckline of her sweater. She smiled at the elderly woman handing out toothpicked samples of Gruyère.

"What about the father?" Joanna asked in a low voice. "Did he come to the matches?"

Scott shrugged. "Never saw him."

Joanna raised an eyebrow.

"That mother, though. She'd wait at the curb, talking on her cell phone the whole time. She wouldn't even say hello to the kid when he threw his stuff into the car, just look at him like he was this huge burden. This one time she was pissed because his shoes were dirty—we'd been running laps on the track outside, and it was muddy—and she was worried it would get all over her precious car floor mats. I heard her screaming at him."

They both watched the boy's mother, who was now perusing the baked goods. After a moment, she cocked her head and reached into her jacket pocket. Her cell phone blinked, silently ringing. They watched as she cradled it between her ear and her shoulder.

"I used to tell them to visualize things," Scott murmured. "Like, reasons to fight, I guess. People's faces, Satan, Jesus, I didn't really care. I never asked any of them what they visualized, but I wondered sometimes, with a few of them. If I were that woman's kid, I would've visualized her."

Joanna remained very still. It felt as though she was close to finding something out about Scott, but she had no idea how to forge the rest of the way there.

Scott leaned back, put his arms behind his head, and whistled through his teeth. "This place. Sometimes I wonder why I'm still here.

It's so fucking *stifling*, don't you think? I've thought about getting the hell away."

"Where would you go?"

"I don't know. Drive across the country. Settle in . . . who knows . . . New Mexico? Arizona? I could, like, be a rancher." He glanced at her. "Would you miss me?"

She startled, jostling her coffee cup. "I . . ."

"Maybe a little?"

Her mouth felt gummy. "Sure. We all would."

"Charles wouldn't."

Joanna rushed to correct him, but then stopped—it might be true.

"I probably won't go." Scott stared out the window into the parking lot.

Joanna had a thought, breathed in, but then changed her mind and clamped her mouth shut. Scott stared at her, sensing she'd been about to speak. "It's just, if you need to get out of town, you could come with me to visit my mom," she said.

A little smile blossomed on Scott's face. Wrinkles formed at the corners of his eyes when he smiled. His teeth were white and straight. "Really?"

Joanna touched her earlobe. Her stomach hurt; now she just wanted to get out of there. "Well, no. I mean, I was kidding. I don't know why I said that. I mean, why would you want to visit my mom?"

He waited, that same smile hovering.

"I was just kidding," she repeated.

"Well" —he balled up a napkin in his palm— "if you change your mind, I'd be happy to come."

Joanna stood up to throw away her cup of coffee, eager to create some space between them. A few feet away, the wrestler's mother finished her phone call and was heading to the back of the store toward the wine section. A college-age girl was heading in the opposite direction, and both were caught in a narrow strait between two cheese tables. The mother stepped aside, letting the girl pass first. She even smiled graciously.

It was amazing how appearances could so easily fool everyone. A clean, well-made trench coat, a nice necklace, decent manners, it all said this woman was a good parent, a respectable person. As Joanna dropped her half-empty coffee cup in the trash, she wondered what else she didn't know about the polished, preppy people around her. Maybe the man in the three-piece suit lived in his car. Maybe the poised, stately woman with the butter-blonde hair, wearing the pink Lilly Pulitzer dress was so dreadfully unhappy she could barely drag herself to the store.

Then she peeked at Scott, who was still sitting at the little bistro table, fiddling with his cell phone and swimming in his sweatshirt, with his coffee-colored skin and thick, almost dreadlocked tufts of hair. What did people assume about him? How did it contrast with what was going on inside him? It was so hard to know.

She pivoted on her heel, gazing into the wide expanse of the store. Then she remembered her grocery cart. She'd abandoned it by a Jenga-tower display of organic biscotti cookies, but now it was gone. The store hummed, the price scanners made small, polite *beeps*, the butcher called the next person in line. Joanna could just see the well-scrubbed grocery boy who had rescued her cart, now removing the butcher paper from her purchased meats and slapping them back behind the glass. Two Cornish hens. Slabs of lamb. Gnarled hamburger. Everything back in its right place.

eight

At the end of the day Jake stuck his hand between the closing elevator doors. "We have an interview set up for next Tuesday with the little woman on the prairie," he said. "Bronwyn . . . Pemberley? Paddington? Something like that."

Pembroke, Charles wanted to correct him. "Okay," he answered.

Jake held the doors open. He'd been watching Charles all day with a perverse curiosity. He was right to watch, of course—something was bothering Charles, something that was directly linked to work. Not that Charles was about to explain himself.

They stared at each other for a few seconds more. Then the elevator buzzer sounded, indicating that the door had been held open for too long. "So, see ya," Jake finally said, releasing his hand.

"Yep," Charles answered. The elevator doors slid closed.

So this was where Bronwyn had turned up after twelve years. Charles didn't see her the summer after senior year. In fact, none of his circle did. She didn't attend the parties people held when they were all home on breaks from their respective colleges the following Thanksgiving and Christmas, and no one heard from her the next summer, when they were all home for three months. Bronwyn's dad was still a member of the local country club, and a few of Charles's friends asked him if Bronwyn was okay. Bronwyn was doing wonderfully, he reported. She'd aced her first year at Dartmouth, just as everyone thought she would. Mr. Pembroke had gotten her a prestigious internship in Europe for the entire three-month summer break. The same thing happened the summer after sophomore year and junior year—more far-flung internships, all orchestrated by her father. By the time everyone finished senior year, many weren't coming home for summers anymore. They'd found jobs elsewhere. Their strong ties to their Swithin friends were forgotten, at least until the five-year reunion. But Charles, well, Charles didn't know how to move on.

Charles couldn't see Bronwyn now. There was no way, not after all this time, not after what he'd done, what she'd heard, which he was sure was why she'd stayed away. Or maybe he could face her: How bad could it be? And really, wasn't he kind of curious? But then he pictured her with that pitying look on her face, the one she'd given Scott when she cornered him on the patio, probably asking him to come and sit with Charles and the rest of his friends. The same one she'd given Charles the very last moment they were together.

She'd still feel sorry for Charles. She'd see him as a powerless consumer, a slave to modernity. Not brave enough to build a tent, for he'd told her that story of how he'd failed miserably at camping with his dad. He'd told her lots of things about his father in moments of weakness. He'd even slipped out a few resentful words about Scott. Charles always took back everything he said about anyone quickly and repentantly, and Bronwyn understood he didn't mean it—"Family can be so awful sometimes," she'd say—but that only made what Charles eventually screamed to Scott in the mud room all the more shameful. It proved to Bronwyn once and for all that he really *did* mean all those things he'd said. His father and brother affected him far more than he let on.

And then Charles was right back to where he started—he *couldn't* see her. He had to get out of this. He could pretend he was sick, maybe, the day of the interview. Or he could just blow it off altogether. Which would get him fired.

If only he could ask Joanna what he should do. But he also knew that hearing about Bronwyn made her uncomfortable—it was a sensitive spot when they first started dating, and he feared raising it again. Soon after they'd become serious, they'd revealed their past relationships. Joanna had had several: some boyfriends in high school, casual flings in college, someone with whom she was serious about shortly after she graduated. It had surprised Joanna when Charles admitted he'd only dated Bronwyn; he'd gone on dates after that, but nothing had panned out. Her eyes had widened. A look of intimidation had crossed her face. "Was she the one who got away?" she'd teased, trying to sound playful. Charles hadn't offered up a satisfying explanation— everything sounded like a halfhearted excuse. It wasn't really that no one could measure up to Bronwyn. It was more that he wasn't sure he deserved anyone after she broke it off.

But it was more than just wanting to spare Joanna's feelings that held him back from telling her. The longer he and Joanna were together as a married couple, the more she made him uneasy. He sensed something was a little off in her; she was a little restless. There was something on the tip of her tongue she wanted to say but never did, and this hesitancy had multiplied since they'd moved out of the city. Several possibilities floated through his mind—was she resentful of family obligations, especially since they lived much closer to Roderick now? Did she hate living in the suburbs altogether? When Charles had walked her through their current house, she'd passed through the rooms silently, woodenly. Then when she was done, she gave him a yearning, pleading look. "What?" Charles had snapped.

"Nothing," she answered quickly, opening a cabinet and peering inside.

"You don't like it."

"No, I do. It's . . . nice."

"Then *what?*"

"Nothing."

Was there something wrong with the suburbs? Joanna had lived here before, though; she'd known what to expect. She *said* she wanted to move out here with him. Why was she making him feel so wrong-footed, as if he'd forced her into it?

The looks came so often these days. He'd gotten one when he rearranged some of his books she'd unpacked on the bookshelf. He'd gotten another one when he corrected her on the correct pronunciation of *Kandahar* and another when he came home with window curtains he'd ordered from Horchow. Hadn't she *wanted* window coverings? Hadn't she said she hated how people could look in and see everything they were doing? She'd looked at the curtains and said, in a baffling, crushed voice, "I've never even *heard* of Horchow." Charles had no idea how he was supposed to respond. In apology?

Those looks got to him in ways he couldn't articulate. And then not long ago, it had clicked: they were the same exasperated, disappointed looks his father used to give him. Joanna raised the same questions in him, too. *What am I doing wrong? What do you want from me?* Perhaps that was why Charles's father liked her. Perhaps he saw himself in this girl. It both drew Charles to Joanna and repelled him from her at times.

If he told her about the Bronwyn conundrum, he might also get that disappointed look. *How dare you? How* could *you?* More than that, Charles wasn't sure if he could get into the nuts and bolts of it with Joanna. He wasn't sure he could tell her what he'd said to Scott and why Bronwyn had broken up with him. If he did, Joanna might think differently about him altogether.

It began to pour as he boarded the westbound SEPTA train. He watched the rain drip down the windows, flooding the streets. At his station, he bought a bouquet from the flower seller by Starbucks and sprinted to his car. When he got home, he sat in the driveway, wind-shield wipers squeaking, and took in his own house's brick facade—the newly growing grass, the red flag on their mailbox. The house was on a hill, and in the rearview mirror he could see the rest of the development splayed out in the valley. Lights were on in the windows. TVs flickered. A woman stood at a kitchen sink, rinsing dishes. There was the perfectly circular cul-de-sac, the flat, well-sodded dog park, the softly lit sign at the development's entrance. Down the hill to the left was Spirit, the street of unsold homes. There no lights were on. Every window was bare.

Somewhere beyond the trees was Swithin. Charles hadn't been there in a while, but he knew that right in the middle of the grand lobby was a bronzed relief of Charles's great-grandfather's face. The first time Charles visited the school was when he was about four years old, not long after his parents adopted Scott. His mother let him walk up to the plaque and run his hands over the mold of his grandfather's nose, the sharp etchings of his eyebrows, the cross-hatchings of his mustache.

"This school wouldn't be here if it weren't for great-grandpa," she whispered, squeezing his hand. "He made all this possible. And you're part of this story, too. You have his name."

"What about Scott?" Charles asked. "He's not part of the story, is he? He's not one of us."

His mother looked conflicted. "You shouldn't say things like that," she said after a moment.

When Scott was in second grade at Swithin and Charles was in fourth, Scott came home and announced a rumor he'd heard: Great-grandpa Charlie Bates once paid a wealthy black family a lot of money *not* to go to Swithin. "Is that *true*?" Scott gasped. "Did he not like black people?"

Scott understood by then that *black* was part of his identity, too. He stood out from the rest of them, so their parents couldn't keep his adoption a secret. They'd taught him that his difference was *good*, special. To Charles, it just felt like another thing Scott had and he didn't—it seemed like that list of things was getting bigger by the day. And although Scott hadn't become connected with black culture yet—that would come later—he was certainly curious about black people.

Charles had heard the rumors Scott was referring to, but Sylvie had quickly dispelled them. He stood up and faced his brother, feeling that he needed to set this straight. "You shouldn't say that," he said to Scott. He repeated what their mother said to him: "He was a good man. He rebuilt the school."

"But . . ." Scott looked confused. "Why would someone say it if it's not true?"

"It's not true." Charles looked at Sylvie for assistance. She sat there, stunned, her fork at her plate. "He's the reason you're here," he said to Scott. "You should be grateful."

"Enough," James said, rising to his feet. His face was red again. He pointed to the door, sending Charles to his room.

"James!" their mother pleaded.

"I don't want him saying things like that," James boomed, turning to her. He looked at Charles again, who had shrunk against the wall, tears in his eyes. "Just go," James said.

Charles ran upstairs as fast as he could. His bedroom was configured in such a way that a moment later he could hear his parents whispering through the vents. They must have been in the dining room, putting some distance between themselves and Scott.

"Are you *trying* to turn him against my family?" Sylvie hissed.

"Am I supposed to lie?" James lobbed back.

"It's not a *lie*," she answered.

"Don't be naive."

Then there were harsher, stilted whispers Charles couldn't discern.

That same night while Scott was taking a bath, Charles stood outside the bathroom doorway, clenching his fists. Why did Scott have to push buttons? Why was Charles always the one getting punished for it? Maybe Scott *didn't* deserve the privilege he'd been given, the life they'd rescued him from.

Charles wanted to make his brother understand what he had. Charles fantasized about bursting into the bathroom and telling Scott that their parents had come to a decision: they were sending him back to his real family. He would have to leave tomorrow on a Greyhound bus, alone. That would show him.

Then he'd felt a hand on his shoulder and turned. Sylvie stood above him, a questioning look on her face. "Do you need something in the bathroom, sweetie?" she asked. Charles wavered, wanting to explain to her why he'd defended Charlie Roderick Bates at dinner. The only thing that mattered was defending her honor, their family's honor.

"I made pudding cake," she said to him, guiding him downstairs. "You can have an extra-big piece since you didn't get to eat all your dinner." And there was nothing else he could do but follow her, swallowing his pain. His frustration continuing to build and build.

Charles found Joanna sitting on the couch, flipping through the channels from one reality show to another. There were still tons of unpacked boxes all around her. "It's really coming down out there," he said.

"Is it?" She didn't look away from the TV. There was a glass of wine balanced between her knees. "I haven't been out."

Charles thrust the flowers at her. "Here."

She looked baffled. "What are these for?"

"I thought you'd like them."

She blinked fast. The cellophane crinkled as she touched it. "Huh."

She held the flowers outstretched, as if they were wilting. He sat down next to her and looked at the television. A dark-haired news anchor was announcing that some economists were predicting that housing prices might drop another fifty percent by next fall. "Jesus," Charles said. "Maybe we should have rented."

Joanna looked at him, startled. "That doesn't apply to *us*."

"It doesn't?" He gestured out the back window. "Those houses on Spirit? The longer they sit there unoccupied, the lower our value will go. We won't have any equity anymore. I won't get the down payment money back."

Joanna stood up, walked to the kitchen, and found a vase for the flowers. "Yes, but I mean, it's not the *same*." When he stared back at her, not understanding what she was getting at, she added, "It's not down-payment money from *your* salary, is it? It's from your trust. It's not like you slaved away for it."

Charles winced. Something about that hurt. "It's still my money."

Joanna tucked her chin into her chest. "Well, I bet Mrs. Cox and Mrs. Batten aren't worried about *their* deposits," she said over the running water.

"Mrs. Cox and Mrs. Batten?" Charles squinted. "Our . . . neighbors? The ones you called me about yesterday?"

She turned her head toward the fridge, giving him her crooked ponytail.

He laughed. "Do you really call them by their last names? They're our age."

She placed the vase of flowers on the island. Several of them drooped over immediately, nearly kissing the marble surface. "They don't seem our age," Joanna said. "They seem . . . different."

"Maybe you're not giving them enough of a chance."

Her expression became wounded, then beseeching. The *look*.

"What?" Charles implored, suddenly exhausted.

She turned her head toward the refrigerator and said something very softly. It sounded like, "So I'm the pathetic one then." And then, after inaudible mutters, something like, "Banana bread."

"Huh?" Charles said, growing more and more perturbed.

She walked back to the couch, reached for her wine, and took another sip. "Nothing. Forget it."

He waited. The television flickered against her face. It showed a commercial for Gatorade, three long-limbed basketball players spinning and dunking. "Scott's working at a sneaker shop," Joanna said.

Charles cocked his head. This conversation was making him a little nauseous. "Scott . . . my brother?"

"Uh-huh. Helping out a friend or something."

"How do you know that?"

She picked at her nails. "I saw him at the grocery store, La Marquette. We had coffee."

Charles shifted his weight. "Well, aren't you two buddy-buddy."

Joanna folded her hands, matching his stare. What was she driving at? *Look at me. I can have a civilized conversation with your brother and you can't?*

"So is this sneaker store he's working at like a Sports Authority?" Charles asked after a while.

"Not exactly," Joanna answered. "It sells limited edition stuff. Everything's high end."

"Sneakers can be *high end?*"

"Sure. It's kind of a city thing."

"Ah." *City.* This basically shut Charles out of knowing or understanding anything about it. "And how do *you* know so much?" he asked her.

She let out a huffy, indignant smirk. "It's not like it's a *secret.*"

He bristled and turned away. Joanna always had an inside track to things that had flown straight over his head—music, old foreign films, indie artists, fashion trends. "You've never seen *Kill Pussycat, Kill!?*" she'd say, and off they'd go to the video store to rent it. "You've never heard *anything* by the Velvet Underground?" she'd exclaim, and she would pull out her large, zippered case of old CDs and play *What Goes On.* But as time passed, the exclamations sounded more like disgusted accusations. Once, Charles even groaned and said, "No, I've never seen any of the *Dirty Harry* movies. It's amazing I've got testosterone in my veins. It's incredible that my brain hasn't exploded." She had stared at him, stunned—it had probably been the first time he'd raised his voice at her—and then shrugged and backed off. Those kinds of comments waned after that.

He turned back. "It could be a drug front, you know."

She pushed her hair out of her eyes. "What could?"

"The sneaker store Scott's friend owns. It's in an *alley*? They sell high-end *sneakers*? Come on. They're probably selling meth in the back room."

A wrinkle formed on the bridge of Joanna's nose. Now it was her turn to look naive. Charles held her gaze, hoping she wouldn't call his bluff. She turned away and stared at the television. Now it was a commercial for a company that paid cash for old gold jewelry. "Nice," she whispered sarcastically, looking at Charles out of the corner of her eye.

Charles placed his hands on his head and swiveled around to face the kitchen. What the hell was happening? Why were they arguing? And why were they talking about Scott? There was no way he could mention Bronwyn now, not in this tense room.

"We should go out," he announced.

She didn't take her eyes off the television. "Out?"

"Let's go get a drink."

"A drink?"

"Sure," he said. "There's that Italian place a couple miles from here we've never tried. I think they have a bar."

She gestured toward the window. "It's pouring."

"So? You told me before we never go out. And that *you* didn't want to be the one to always suggest it. Well, now I'm suggesting it."

He could take her somewhere quiet and explain the uncomfortable bind he was in, the person he was being asked to interview. *I've tried to get out of it, but Jake wants me to do it. But, I mean, she's living without plumbing and electricity. I won't have anything to say to her. You have no reason to be jealous.*

"All right," she said, setting her wineglass on the coffee table. "There must be an umbrella in one of these boxes."

The television blinked soundlessly: an ad about Toyotas, then another about eHarmony dating service. "Actually." Charles gazed out the window. "It *is* pretty bad out there."

Joanna paused, her hand on the doorknob. "So . . . you *don't* want to go out now?"

He shrugged. He knew he wasn't making sense. He felt like he was losing his mind.

Joanna slapped her hands on her thighs. "Whatever." She walked to the kitchen sink and turned on the faucet. "Oh. I have to go to Maryland next week. My mom's having a biopsy on Tuesday."

Tuesday. The day of his interview with Bronwyn. "Is she all right?"

"I hope so. Probably."

Then he had an idea. "Do you want me to come?"

She looked up from the sink, startled. "What?"

"Do you want me to come?" he repeated. "We could go to Baltimore after your mom has her appointment. Or to D.C."

She blinked. "You've never wanted to come before."

"Okay. Never mind. I just thought I'd ask."

"No, I mean, sure. Come."

"Yeah?"

"Of course."

There. It was a good enough excuse. His mother-in-law was having a biopsy. He needed to be there for moral support. It would get him out of the interview. He could assign someone else to the story. The end.

"Don't expect much," Joanna said over the running water. "We don't have to stay at my mom's house if you don't want to."

"Okay. Whatever you want."

Decision made. He stood there in silence for a while, watching the muted TV, the rain on the windows, assessing the piles of still-sealed boxes. Most of them were marked JOANNA, KITCHEN or JOANNA, BEDROOM or JOANNA, MISC, remnants of her life before him. *Good*, he thought. This was figured out. He was free.

And then, feeling something rise up inside him, he padded down the hall to the first floor full bath, the one they never used. He shut the door.

It was warm in the bathroom. The towels were fresh and dry. The dispenser was full of orange soap, and the shower curtain was printed with bug-eyed fish, maniacal octopi. Charles ripped it back and stepped into the scoured, empty tub. He sank to his knees, spread his legs out, and closed his eyes. The memory pressed at him, begging him to think it through. Even though he didn't want to, even though he might not have to explain it, it wouldn't leave his mind.

The last time Charles had seen Bronwyn was the end of his senior year, at the Swithin award ceremony and banquet. The ceremony, which presented achievement awards in academics and sports, was taking place in his parents' garden. Charles's great-grandfather had held one of the first award banquets there, and a board member had held succeeding banquets at one of their homes ever since.

Charles and Bronwyn sat together with their friends around one of the large, round tables that had been set up in the back garden, sneaking sips of champagne when their parents weren't looking. They were all guaranteed to win something: Nadine the English department's award, Rob a plaque for student government, Bronwyn for art and science, and Charles, well, Charles was pretty sure he was getting the Academic Achievement of the Year. It was a Renaissance-man award, reserved for the senior who excelled in all areas—academics, community service, and activities. The awards committee allegedly kept the winners secret from the board members, but Charles had a feeling his mother knew something. Why else had she asked his father to come home from the office early so he could catch the entire presentation? Why else had she gazed lovingly at Charles while he put on a jacket and tie, telling him she was so proud of all he'd accomplished?

The headmaster, Jerome, stood in front of the rose trellis—they'd long since replaced the one Scott had burned—calling out the sports awards. When he called Scott's name for wrestling, Charles thought it was a joke. It was unheard of for underclassmen to be honored. Scott burst through the crowd, wearing a brown suit that seemed like it had been dug out of some seventies time capsule. Everything about the suit was huge, made for a much larger man, and the pants sagged low on Scott's hips, the same fit as his jeans. He swaggered with irony up to the stage and instead of shaking Jerome's hand, slapped him high five. Jerome looked startled but then smiled nervously. There was a guffaw from the left—their father. He had materialized at the table next to his mother when Charles wasn't watching. Charles suddenly felt anxious and sweaty, astonished that his father was really here and annoyed that Scott had stolen some of his thunder.

Jerome continued with the sports awards and then moved on to academics. One by one Charles's friends rose to claim plaques. The Academic Achievement of the Year was last, and Jerome took a long time winding up to it. Bronwyn squeezed his hand. Charles glanced at his father. He was still there, listening. When Jerome called out Heather Lawrence's name, Charles stood halfway anyway. Bronwyn pulled him down.

Heather Lawrence made her way across the grass. She was in a wheelchair, paralyzed from the waist down from a childhood illness. She was a coxswain for the boys' crew team; the crewmen gently carried her into the boat whenever it was time to practice or race. Charles had a lot of classes with her; Heather diligently turned in papers and gave oral reports from her chair. She'd been accepted at Harvard and Brown, but she was going to Penn to remain close to her family.

Bronwyn dropped Charles's hand and began to clap. How could she not clap? How could any of them not? When Charles glanced at his parents, his mother looked sheepish. More than likely she'd assumed Charles would win, too, forgetting about Heather entirely. His father clapped tepidly, his expression not wavering. From the back of the garden, someone yelled out, "Yeah!" Charles swore it was Scott's voice.

After that, Jerome thanked everyone for coming and the crowd began to disperse. Scott approached Charles's table, his arms across his chest.

"Uh, hi," Schuyler, one of Charles's friends, finally said.

"Hey," Scott answered.

He stared right at Bronwyn, coolly and challengingly. Bronwyn flinched and looked away, and Charles oscillated between the two of them, wondering if he was missing something. Bronwyn ran her tongue over her teeth and stood up. "Excuse me," she said, walking back into the house.

"Are you all right?" Charles called after her.

"I'm fine," Bronwyn said over her shoulder, shooting him a smile.

Charles's other friends, likely sensing the tension, congratulated Scott on his award. Scott blinked, his trance broken. He stared at the plaque in his right hand. "Right," he said, indifferently.

Scott's fingerprints were all over the brass plaque. It would lan-
guish in some cardboard box under his bed, unappreciated. *Ha*, he
no doubt thought. *Dad came home from work just in time to see you
lose . . . again.* Why else had Scott stopped at this table? Charles's gaze
slid over to their parents. Their mother was still sitting at the table, but
their father was gone. Charles could practically hear Scott's thoughts
as he loomed over them, his suit smelling vaguely of mothballs. *You
think you're so great with your fancy friends and your ass-kissing, but I
know how it really is.*

But when Scott met his eye, his face wasn't full of nasty smugness
but of pity. He lingered on Charles for a moment, and then turned toward the house. Rage flooded Charles's body. Smugness he could handle, but pity was reprehensible. After a few shallow breaths, Charles
stood up roughly, bumping his knees against the bottom of the table,
and followed his brother through the side door.

He found Scott standing in the mud room next to the washing machine. The air felt ionized, fraught with another presence, as if someone had just slipped out of the room. "Apologize," Charles boomed.
"Apologize now."

Scott gazed at him warily, exasperatedly. "Apologize for what?"

Charles twitched. Scott stared at him, waiting. Pity crossed his
face again. He threw his shoulders back, waved his hand, and turned
toward the kitchen.

"Come back!" Charles screamed.

He chased Scott into the mud room, spun his brother around, and
pinned him against the utility sink. His insides felt black and curdled.
Lava rose to his throat and spewed out his mouth. "This is all just a
joke to you, isn't it," he said through his teeth. "You don't get what you
have. You should be *grateful*. But instead you act all . . . entitled. Like

you deserve this. But you're a piece of shit. You came from nothing. And you will *be* nothing. You're the joke, don't you see? You're going to end up just like where you came from. Nothing but a *n–n—*"

The word hung on his lips. He reined himself in, holding back, but it was still out there, as good as said, radiating out in toxic, concentric waves. All the pain inside him, all the dark, insecure caverns of his mind illuminated.

Scott didn't flinch. His gaze was eerily neutral. There was a presence behind them, a horrified crowd, a gasp. Charles could smell Bronwyn's perfume. He heard his father's signature, guttural cough. His father had heard every uttered, and almost uttered, word.

Scott had the view of whoever was behind them. His gaze wavered from Charles, and his eyes dimmed. When he refocused on Charles again, things got blurry, and in a split second Charles was on the ground, gasping for air. Scott's face loomed above him, his breath hot on his cheeks. Their father appeared and pulled Scott to his feet. Charles rolled to his side, coughing.

It was amazing how quickly they hushed things up, how Scott was shuttled to one room and Charles to another. He could hear their father shouting and Scott shouting back, but he couldn't make out the words. Charles's mother ran into the house, crying, "What happened? What happened?"

Bronwyn volunteered to take him away for a while. She helped Charles into her car and they snaked down the driveway. Charles crumpled against the seat, repentant. He didn't dare ask Bronwyn if she'd heard what he'd said. The answer, he knew, was yes—she'd been right there.

They drove to the bottom of the hill and parked at the edge of the cornfield. Bronwyn gripped the steering wheel hard. "There's something I have to tell you," she whispered.

Charles kept his chin wedged to his chest. His stomach felt slashed open.

It took Bronwyn a long time to speak. "I think it would be best if we spent some time apart."

"Okay," he answered stonily. He wasn't about to ask why. He didn't need to hear how disgusted she was that he had the capacity to say such things. He didn't want to hear her say, *You deserved it.* "I'm sorry," he mumbled.

There were tears in her eyes. "*I'm* sorry." Which made him feel even worse: What the hell did she have to be sorry for?

She offered to drive him back up the hill to the party, but he said that wouldn't be necessary—he could walk. She took off fast. He never saw her again.

Did Charles really need to revisit that? Did he really need to face someone who obviously detested him enough to not just cut all ties with him but with *every single one* of his friends, too?

And yet, it was tempting. There would be something both edifying and purifying about seeing Bronwyn now. Having Bronwyn say her piece, once and for all. It could be good to know who Charles had been before in order to know who he had become. It could be good to know the damage he might have done.

It was tempting to see her and know she was real, that it had really happened. Because if it truly was her, what she'd done was the same thing Scott had done—take everything she had been given and cast it aside. Maybe there was something to doing that, something Charles didn't yet understand. Maybe her decision had been the right one.

nine

Sylvie didn't even notice the rain until it turned to hail. It pelted on the roof, making harsh, ugly smacks so forceful she thought it might be taking off whole shingles and layers of paint. Just minutes had passed and there was already a small stream in the front yard. Hail bounced off the roof of Scott's car in crazy angles, ricocheting off the metal pole of the basketball hoop Scott still used. She ran around shutting all the windows.

She went to the living room and nestled under a blanket. It was almost midnight, but she was too wide-eyed to sleep. Once again, she went over the day.

It astonished her that Christian's father had been . . . a person—human, capable of complex and contradictory feelings. She often felt this way about people she didn't know. That it was incredible that their inner lives were as complicated as hers was. It reminded her of when Scott was very young and used to play with Legos, dumping the garbage can of blocks on the living room floor and creating entire towns—houses, doctor's offices, gas stations, grocery stores, airports. He would leave the backs of the buildings exposed so he could reach inside and move the people around. Once Sylvie noticed him leaning over the blocks, frantically moving a bunch of the tiny Lego people at once—making a woman get into her car, guiding a spaceman from a gas-station parking lot to the mini-mart, then quickly moving a black-haired man in a fireman suit from the upstairs part of the house to the downstairs to turn on the giant, battery-run windmill. "Why are you moving them all so fast?" Sylvie asked.

"This is how life works," Scott told her matter-of-factly. That was when he still talked to her. When he still answered her questions. "It all happens at once. But I don't have enough hands for all of it. I never know what they want to do next."

Sylvie didn't have enough hands for all of it either. She hadn't expected Christian's father to have another emotion besides anger. She hadn't expected him to look at her, recognize her, and not immediately fly into a rage.

There was pounding on the side door. She stood up, shuffled through the kitchen, and squinted. With all the lights on in here, she could only see her reflection in the side door's window. Her straight, bluntly cut hair was mussed and the corners of her mouth turned down. She looked tired and puffy, a hundred years old.

Scott was on the porch. He was hugging himself tightly, and there was water dripping from the ends of his hair and the tip of his nose. "Oh." Sylvie whipped open the door. There was something embarrassing, or maybe vulnerable, about seeing him so late at night, in her robe and slippers, her makeup washed off.

"I've been knocking for ten minutes," he yelled over the sound of the rain.

She opened the door wider and let him in. His T-shirt hung heavily past his belt and his waterlogged pant legs dragged on the ground. His shoes squished as he walked.

"Damn," he said, fumbling into the laundry room for a towel. "I kept knocking. I saw you on the couch."

"The rain must be too loud. I didn't hear."

Scott rubbed the towel over his sopping hair.

"You should change clothes," Sylvie said. "I'll get you something from upstairs."

He nodded from underneath the towel. Sylvie dashed upstairs to Scott's old bedroom, but his closet was bare. Charles's was empty, too. She paused, considering, and then padded down the hall to her own room.

She and James had separate walk-in closets, and Sylvie hadn't gone into James's side much since he'd died. His suits and shirts still hung in neat lines. His shined shoes, their leather smell so dignified, were in a row on the closet floor. He kept sweaters and T-shirts at the back on shelves. She pulled out an oversize gray sweatshirt and a plain white T-shirt. To her relief they didn't smell like much of anything except detergent. On one of the shelves was a pair of black sweatpants, the tags still on. She pulled them out, too.

She quickly threw on a pair of khaki pants and a navy cashmere cardigan and kicked her slippers into the corner. On her way down the stairs, she paused. It was portentous seeing Scott tonight of all nights. They sometimes went days without interacting. Could he sense where she'd been this afternoon, whom she'd been talking to? Had he come to ask what she thought she'd accomplish by talking to Christian's father? For really, what did going to see him imply? Did it mean she doubted Scott's innocence once and for all?

Back in the living room, there was a puddle of water at Scott's feet. "I think I might take a shower, if that's okay," he said. "I'm freezing."

"Sure," Sylvie said. "Of course."

They eyed each other warily, neither moving. "There's a leak," Scott finally explained. "Right over my bed. My sheets are soaked. And another big one near my bathroom."

Sylvie swiveled around, searching the counter for the house keys. "We should go take a look."

"It's late," Scott said. "I put a bucket under the leaks. No one will come to fix it now anyway." He paused to scratch his nose, staring blankly at a watercolor painting of a bunch of violets on the laundry room wall. "I was going to stay at Lee's. I was waiting for it to stop raining so hard, but . . ."

"Stay in your old room tonight. Until we have it figured out."

He glanced out the window. "I could make it. At least there won't be much traffic."

Am I that horrible to be around? Sylvie thought. "You're welcome to stay here. Really."

"Fine," Scott conceded, rolling his eyes.

She followed Scott upstairs and got him extra towels, as if he was a guest. Because she knew making up his bed would seem overbearing, she pointed out sheets and pillowcases. Scott nodded and then glanced at her. "It was so weird. That ceiling was suddenly like . . ." He extended his arms and made a *boom* sound.

"Well, this rain is sort of . . ." She fluttered her hands, unsure of the word she was looking for. " . . . Angry."

"All of a sudden this water drips on my head. Like that water torture method they use in interrogations."

Sylvie looked away. She wondered if Scott even realized the irony in what he'd just said. "Well," she said. "That certainly doesn't sound pleasant."

Scott paused for a moment, almost smiling at her. He reached out his hand and touched her shoulder. Sylvie stiffened, his touch unfamiliar. He pulled her in, just slightly, and then let go abruptly as though he had suddenly become aware of what his limbs were doing.

A dull ache rippled through her. This tenderness was heartbreakingly ill-timed, too much to bear. She saw the picture of Christian propped up against that tree at Feverview Dwellings. The father leaning over his thighs, wracked with sobs.

Scott turned awkwardly to the bathroom. "Well, thanks for answering the door."

"Of course," Sylvie said quietly. "Sorry I didn't get there sooner."

Then Scott shut the door.

She stood there for a moment, and then gazed down the hall into her bedroom. James's closet gaped open, the light still on. He was so meticulously organized. His ties on a rack, his sweaters neatly folded, his shirts organized by color. She scanned the blazers, searching for the one he'd worn his last day of work. They'd returned his clothes to her, after it was all over. His shirt had been ruined—they'd had to cut it off him—but he hadn't been wearing his blazer when he collapsed, so she'd brought it back to his closet and returned it to its hanger, as if he would still someday return and wear it again.

Then she turned and stared down the hall into James's office. It was just the same as it had been the last time she looked inside this morning. The same generic desk, the same dust on the bookcase, and the same locked filing cabinet, the only place she hadn't yet searched.

Sometimes she wondered if she would've been better off never knowing she had a reason to search at all. For if the door hadn't been left unlocked and open just a few months ago, in the fall, if she hadn't gone inside to dust, maybe she would have never seen it. Their whole lives could have gone by and she might never have found out. Would she have been better for it?

For she hadn't even *suspected*. Yes, they had gone through periods of distance. Yes, there were certain points in his life when James seemed inconsistent, resentful, frustrated. They certainly didn't agree on how to raise their children. But she kept herself busy through their rough patches, and so did he, and lately, with the kids grown up, things had become better between them.

But that day she'd noticed dust on his new, modern desk while she held a feather duster. She innocently cleaned the glass top of his desk and then his bookcase, marveling at the items on the shelves. This was the first time she'd been inside the room for years, probably since James had replaced her grandfather's desk with this new furniture. James had cleaned out all of her grandfather's knickknacks, too—the old sculpture of the gray whale, the small tan-colored globe, the jade paperweight—and added some items of his own: a Lucite plaque congratulating him for helping launch an IPO in 1999, those busts of Laurel and Hardy he oddly found so funny. On the third shelf, she noticed a velvet box; stamped on the lid was the name of a jewelry store that had been out of business for ten years. Sylvie picked up the box and turned it over. Then she opened it.

Inside was a bracelet made of white gold, chunky and modern. A feeling swept through her; she knew right away. The bracelet was an odd choice, surely selected to suit someone's taste. Someone who wasn't her.

She brought it to him at dinner, holding it by its clasp, afraid to touch it fully. She laid it next to his dinner plate and waited. His eyes rested on it. She watched for telltale signs—paling skin, a shaking hand, darting eyes. James simply looked angry. His whole face tightened.

"You went into my office?" he finally said.

"Who did you buy this for?" she asked.

"You went into my office?" he repeated.

She blinked, aggravated. "Yes! I went into your office! Is this why you keep the door locked? Because ... *this* was in there? Who is this for?"

"I told you not to go into my office."

She stared at him, astonished. She pointed at the box. "You bought this at Goebel's. They closed ten years ago."

He said nothing.

"Was this for someone else? Someone ten years ago?"

"Sylvie," he said. And then he hung his head. "It wasn't like that."

Her mouth fell open. Then what *was* it like? "Tell me her name," she demanded, starting to shake.

"It wasn't—"

"*Tell me her name,*" she screamed. "Do you still see her? Do you still think about her? What's she doing now? Is it someone I know?" And then, "Why would you do this? What reason did I ever give you?"

"Sylvie," he pleaded. "Please leave it."

She mined her memories for clues. Ten years ago. Eleven. Twelve. Both kids had been in high school. Charles was getting good grades, dating Bronwyn, and he had all those nice friends. Even Scott seemed steadier, doing so well in wrestling, only an occasional detention here and there. Okay, so things with James weren't at their most romantic. She was harried with all the work she did for Swithin, and he'd just switched to his current employer. Sometimes they were so tired they fell asleep without really talking; sometimes he came home after she was in bed. He'd eaten a lot of dinners with clients, heavy meals with a lot of meat and wine. He'd purchased a membership in a health club right around that time, too, saying that all the other guys at the office went and it was a good place to make connections. Could that have been a cover-up for something more sinister? Was *health club* a code for . . . for what? He'd taken lots of business trips back then, but she couldn't recall where. She thought of the time she'd called her father's hotel in New York. *Are you looking for Teddy?* the woman in his room had asked. She had a thick city accent, a husky smoker's rasp.

Sylvie dug her nails into the kitchen table. "Tell me her name."

A little sound escaped from the back of James's throat. "I can't."

She'd been so blindsided and stricken that she'd fallen ill, spiking a fever that lasted for days. James took time off work. Sometimes she woke and heard him down the hall in his office. The filing-cabinet drawers slid open and closed. She had a feverish dream about him stuffing a woman in the filing cabinet, putting her in ass-first and folding up her legs and then closing the door tight so that only a few locks of hair hung over the cabinet's sides. Sometimes she woke and he was sitting next to her, a look of remorse and concern on his face. *I'm sorry,* he kept mouthing.

When her fever broke, they went out to dinner. He slid a velvet box across the table. It was from a different jeweler, a better one.

"No," she said when she gazed upon the canary-yellow diamond ring. "I can't take this."

"I just want to show you how I feel about you," he said. "I just want you to know."

In the end, she accepted it. Maybe she shouldn't have—it implied that she forgave him. It meant she wouldn't bring it up again. But she felt too breathless to fight. She wanted it to be over, forgotten, and maybe she *could* forget. So she took the ring and slid it on her finger and pretended it was simply a gift, something without subtext.

That was in September. Six months later, in February, James didn't check in from work at 6 p.m. as usual. Sylvie had been annoyed. Was he ignoring her because she'd brought up the affair again the previous night? Was he punishing her? It wasn't funny.

The minutes ticked by. Maybe what she'd said the night before had been a turning point, shoving him over the edge. Maybe he no longer cared about holding things together. Who was he with right now? What was he doing? Her heart pounded. She tried to picture him places. She called his cell phone again and again, but there was no answer. The more time passed, the more her panic spiraled. He *was* out with someone, doing something floridly awful. All of the feelings she'd tried to contain were urgently present. *I thought you said you'd let that go,* James had said to her at the party the night before. But of course she couldn't let it go. How could he not understand that? How could he just brush it off? It altered the whole landscape of her life.

When the phone finally rang, the reality of the situation caught her off guard. A cleaning woman in his office had found James collapsed on the executive bathroom floor. He didn't have his ID on him, and because it was after hours no one knew who he was. Luckily, a doctor in the ER was a friend and had recognized him; he'd sent a nurse to call Sylvie.

At first, she thought it was part of the ruse. Her mind was so fixed in one direction that it was hard to switch gears. She couldn't turn from scorned rage to . . . to this. To panic. Concern. Fear for his life. She kept saying to the nurse, "I'm sorry, *what?*" The nurse had had to repeat what had happened three times, maybe four, before she started to understand.

They'd all rushed to the hospital to be with him. They had to sit in the ER waiting room for the first few hours. Even though it was the middle of the night, the waiting room was crowded, full of screaming babies and sallow-skinned old people and a shoeless, sour-smelling man. Charles sat next to Sylvie, his back straight, his hands folded in his lap. Joanna picked at a loose thread on her sweater until she'd unraveled almost an entire row. Scott slid a pair of padded headphones over his ears and bounced silently to what he called music.

At one point, Scott removed his headphones and asked Sylvie if he could borrow her cell phone. His battery had died, and he wanted to call a friend to see if they were still meeting up tomorrow. Sylvie stared at him. He'd left the music on; she heard a pounding bass through the headphones, someone's voice pattering tonelessly. Could he really think that far ahead? Could he really worry about something as trivial as a social obligation he had to keep? Was this the kind of kid she'd raised, someone who thought his ailing father was an inconvenience? James had bent over backward to be a good father to Scott. He was still bending over backward, even though Scott barely noticed. And this was what he got for it?

Scott noted her look of disgust and raised his hands in surrender. "Jesus. Forget it."

Sylvie couldn't stand to be next to him for one more minute. She stood up, straightened her skirt, and stormed to the vending machine area. She sat in a phone kiosk, picked up the receiver, and listened to the dial tone clang in her ear. She felt like yelling at the operator when she interrupted, demanding that Sylvie insert fifty cents.

Finally, a doctor came and retrieved Sylvie. James had collapsed because of an artery leading to his brain, he explained. The artery had been widening over time, and it had burst. He'd had an aneurysm and was now bleeding quite severely.

They were going to treat the aneurysm by feeding a catheter into a blood vessel in James's groin, slowly pushing it through the aorta, up into the brain's main artery, and creating a clot. They were going to excavate him. They were going to dig a trench.

"Isn't there an easier way?" she asked, mortified. The doctor shook his head and told her that he and his team had talked and evaluated, and this was their best shot at saving him. He handed her a consent form for the surgery. "It's in your hands," he said.

She signed it, practically threw the clipboard back at him, and then said she needed a minute.

The doctor slid the curtain shut. Sylvie peered down at James. He looked so damn old and small. And even though she should have concentrated all her energy on what the doctors were about to do to him and that she might, possibly, lose him, in that moment, the only thing she could think about was what she'd brought up the night before. What he'd done. All she could think about was what the woman's name was. She wanted to shake him awake and ask him.

She hated herself for even thinking it. She hated herself for how numb she was, too—numb to fear, numb to the possibilities. She knew she should be sobbing at his bedside, cooing soothing words to him, making promises for their lives, but her anger pushed those parts of her away. She shoved out of James's curtained-off area and went into the ICU waiting room. It was smaller and more intimate than the vast holding pen of the ER, with a stained-glass window and church pew shoved into the corner, a crucifix of Jesus on the far wall. Scott was lying on the twin bed the hospital put out in case visitors wanted to rest. His head nestled on the flat, dingy pillow.

When Scott saw her, he sat up, laying a copy of *Maxim* on his lap. She stood over him quivering, taking in his enormous, filthy jeans, his headphones, that permanent apathetic look on his face. James might have been an inert, unresponsive receptacle for her anger, but Scott wasn't.

"Did you see Dad?" Scott asked. "Is he okay?"

"You could at least brush those knots out of your hair once in a while," she exploded. "And put on something that covers up all those tattoos. I don't want to be seen with you. You look like a criminal."

And then she whirled around and took the stairs all the way to the main level. In the lobby, nurses pushed heavily pregnant women in wheelchairs. Elderly people dragged their IV poles outside for some fresh morning air. A man, a woman, and two kids pushed by her for the elevator, holding a big bouquet of flowers and smiling. Sylvie smiled back at them as if she wasn't going through what she was going through. As if the person she was visiting was suffering from something minor, too.

Sylvie realized she had been leaning against the upstairs hallway console table for quite some time, clutching a small jade bear sculpture between her hands. Scott bumped around on the other side of the bathroom door, getting ready for a shower. It was silent outside now; the biblical rain must have stopped. She thought of a phrase her grandfather sometimes used to say—*après moi, le deluge*. Some French guy coined it, some great leader. It meant that after he was dead, he didn't care what mess he left behind for his country to clean up. France could be flooded or raided or crumble, and it would be okay with him—it was someone else's problem.

Scott pulled the nozzle to start the shower. Sylvie shut off the hall light and slipped into her room.

ten

It was clear the following day, as though the world had never known rain. Joanna went out into her front yard and looked around. The world had been transformed overnight. It was now green, earthy. The sun threw heat onto her shoulders, and the wind smelled like lilacs. A UPS truck trundled down the street, the brown-suited driver's knees and forearms bare, having shed his wintry long underwear.

Joanna called her mother and told her that Charles would be coming to Maryland, too, something that still surprised and puzzled her. Why did he want to come all of a sudden? Why the sudden interest? He'd never come before. She'd helped Catherine move to Maryland by herself, while Charles was off on some work project. She'd never burdened him to accompany her to Catherine's medical procedures. Part of her was embarrassed to show Charles the poky little house her mother had inherited. It was bad enough bringing him into the split-level in Lionville, although Charles was very diplomatic about it, never remarking about the house one way or another. Another part of her just figured he wasn't very interested in going to Maryland, in getting to know her mother. Which was fine, too. Catherine was a handful; she and Charles didn't need to bond.

But what was wrong with Joanna—didn't she *want* him to come? Her mother was, thank goodness, too distracted to detect anything was off. She'd just spoken to a friend at the sail club, a man named Robert, and was trying to get Joanna to promise that they'd make a trip there the night before the biopsy. "I've told him all about you," Catherine pressed. "I'd like you to meet him."

"Okay, okay," Joanna answered reluctantly, wondering if Catherine and this Robert guy were dating. She'd never considered the idea of her mother having a boyfriend before.

After she hung up, she walked around the house, antsy yet aimless. Her unopened boxes mocked her, a thin layer of dust on each. The packing tape that sealed them shut was beginning to peel away from the cardboard. What did Joanna own that she wasn't using? What if she opened a box and found something unexpected inside, something that had been wiped from her identity? Something that reminded her, maybe, of how wonderful her life used to be? Only, *had* it been?

A few photo albums had been unpacked and were now sitting on a bookshelf. Joanna pulled them down and sat on the couch with the stack in her lap. The spine cracked as she opened the first page of the wedding book. There they were, Joanna in her silk sheath dress that now hung in plastic in the upstairs closet, Charles in a tuxedo with his hair pushed back off his face. They stood in the gazebo in Roderick's backyard, white flowers all around them.

He looked happy, and so did she. Except for that one shaky moment where Joanna's mother ordered her not to screw it up, Joanna really *had* been happy that day. She picked up the other book that showed photos of moments before their marriage. First were pages and pages of the trip they'd taken to Jamaica before they'd gotten engaged. After a series of shots of the dazzling pool and the thatched-roof tiki huts, there was a picture of Joanna and Charles sitting on a hammock, doodling pictures in the guest journal they'd found in their room. Next was a picture of Charles holding a literal log of marijuana, at least a foot of solidly packed weed. A waiter had procured it for them for a pithily small sum of money, maybe forty or fifty dollars. They'd giggled about how easy it had been to get it, how *natural* their butler seemed when presenting it to them, how their families, if they knew, would be horrified that they'd done this. Well, Charles's family. Joanna's mother would probably ask if she could have some.

"Watch, we'll end up in a Jamaican prison," Charles had joked. Back in the real world, he never smoked pot, never even joints that sometimes circulated at parties. But there he did, getting so stoned he could barely move. He was different in Jamaica, not bound to the rules of his life. She was probably different, too.

Next in the album were photos of their first Christmas together, just this past year. They'd been married for three months; Charles's father hadn't died yet. They hadn't moved yet, either; the photos were from Charles's apartment in the city. She'd gotten him a digital SLR camera, and he'd taken countless photos of her that day, holding up every present she'd received. A copy of the *New York Times*, symbolizing the weekend subscription he bought her. A running jacket and matching shorts, both pale pink. And then, one of the last photos, lacy black underwear and a matching bra. Her smile was wobbly, not sure if she should take it seriously or not, as she had considered wearing a sports bra under her wedding gown. While other women pranced around their Jamaican resort in string bikinis, thongs up their asses, Joanna wore a two-piece Speedo with thick straps and a very concealing bottom. It wasn't that she was ashamed of her body; she just wasn't an exhibitionist. Fancy underwear always made her feel like an actor in a bad play. She thought Charles understood this about her.

But maybe there was an implicit message in the gift. Maybe it signified the kind of woman Charles wanted her to be—a sophisticate who craved fancy undergarments, good-smelling soaps, and French perfume. A woman, say, like Mrs. Cox or Mrs. Batten, like the scores of ladies at La Marquette. Made-up even to do their weekly shopping. Preened even when drinking coffee. Not a shoelace untied, not a lash unpainted. Someone who would know how to dress for a dinner party. Someone who would wear a bikini without feeling self-conscious. Someone like Bronwyn.

Was that when things had begun to falter? When Charles had given her that underwear? And was that what was happening—were they *faltering*? She pressed a hand to her forehead. She was forever trying to define things these days. What had seemed so solid before was now so unclear.

The weather was so unseasonably glorious that Charles asked Joanna to meet him in the city to go out to dinner. Joanna took SEPTA in, suddenly feeling giddy and golden. When had she and Charles last gone out to dinner—a *real* dinner, not the local pizza joint or the Chinese place in the strip mall? Maybe it signified a change, all their petty tension washing away.

She got off at Market East and walked to the restaurant in Old City. It was a Friday; the bar was packed and Charles hadn't yet arrived. Joanna flagged down the bartender and ordered a glass of pinot noir, settling into her stool and looking idly around at the dramatic purple curtains against the walls and the chefs that fluttered about in the open kitchen at the back. Other guests flitted around her, ordering drinks, swilling them back, thrusting their fingers into the bowls of mixed nuts at the bar. There were men and women who came straight from work, a couple talking about their apartment in Fishtown, a woman with a daughter of about eleven or twelve, the girl gazing off disinterestedly at the passing cars on the street. Joanna suddenly realized how much she missed Philadelphia. She missed the crowds and the smells and the anonymity. She missed sitting in a bar without everyone staring at her pityingly, wondering why she was alone.

Joanna was almost halfway through her wine when she suddenly saw Charles waving at her from across the bar. *Hey,* he mouthed. He held a palm to the air as if to say, *What are you doing all the way over there?* He was standing with two other people, an almost-empty gin and tonic in his hand. The two people turned and looked, too. It was Nadine and Rob, two of Charles's friends from Swithin who had gotten married. They lived in the city, though Joanna wasn't sure where. Nadine wore bright red lipstick and was clutching a glass of water. She was hugely pregnant, cupping one hand over the base of her belly.

Joanna looked down, gripped with panic, wishing Charles hadn't seen her. She didn't want to talk to Swithin people. Not tonight. She wanted to remain on this side of the bar, safe and alone. But she picked up her glass and walked over.

"How long have you been here?" Charles asked when she reached him. His face was already pink from the gin.

"Um, twenty minutes maybe?" she answered, squeezing in beside him. There were no available stools on this side of the bar. Only Nadine was sitting.

"And you didn't see us? I got here at six. I ran straight into these two. We've been here the whole time."

"You didn't see me, either," Joanna said bitingly, though her words were absorbed by the din of the crowd.

"Well, now that you're here, I can tell the hostess we're ready," Charles said. He considered his old friends. Rob still had his handsome, well-balanced features, but his once-thick, longish hair was starting to thin. Nadine was as pale as ever, even her eyelashes. Her diamond ring kept throwing prismatic shapes all over the room. "You guys must join us," Charles decided.

Nadine waved her hand. "It's okay," she said. "You guys don't live here. Joanna probably came into the city so you could have a nice, romantic dinner by yourselves."

"Nah, we'd love to have you," Charles insisted. "It'll be ages before we see you again. Right, Joanna?"

And then they were all looking at her. Joanna had no control over the muscles of her face. And now that this mood had settled around her, she couldn't just untangle herself from it so fast. She didn't want them joining their table. She didn't want to struggle to make conversation. She thought of her comfy stool across the bar. She thought of her cozy couch at home. She could have stayed there and made pudding, watched television.

"Really," she managed. "I don't mind."

And that was good enough for them. Nadine and Rob followed behind Charles and Joanna to a four-top at the back of the restaurant. Nadine struggled to sit down, Rob spotting her back. Diners at nearby tables glanced over and smiled. They both put their napkins on their laps and said that yes, sparkling water would be lovely. Charles gave Joanna an inquisitive look, a little eyebrow raise that seemed so say, *Is everything okay?* But he should know what wasn't okay, shouldn't he? Joanna smiled at him icily, and then turned back to her glass of wine, swilling back the rest of it fast.

They started talking about Rob's boss—he worked at WXPN, Penn's radio station, doing something for one of the show producers. "He made me babysit this band last week," Rob was saying. "They were about nineteen years old but really sweet, came from some little town in Wales. What they wanted most was to see an authentic Philadelphia crime. They wanted to see guys in low-riders carjacking someone or, like, a shoot-out. They begged me to drive them into the worst neighborhood so we could see some action." He rolled his eyes and then paused. Everyone laughed.

The conversation moved on to another story about a band Rob had dealt with, then to Charles and his job, and then to Nadine and her pregnancy. Around and around and around, though they kept skipping her. Intentionally . . . or by accident? She began to tune them out, watching the sous chefs scramble to and fro, mixing things, adding items to sauce pans, searing pieces of fish.

After the waiter took their orders, Rob looked at Charles. "So how's your mom?"

Joanna snapped to attention. Charles paled. "She's hanging in there."

"Still doing all that stuff at the school?" Nadine asked.

Charles nodded. "Still ruling with an iron fist."

Nadine glanced down at her menu. Rob took a sip of water. Of course they didn't know about what had happened at the school. Not everyone's lives circled around Swithin.

"There's a new headmaster at Swithin, isn't there?" Rob crossed his arms over his chest.

Charles nodded. "Jerome retired."

"He did?" Nadine widened her eyes. "When?"

"At the beginning of this year," Charles said.

"Wonder what the new guy's like," Nadine mused. "Maybe another stamp collector?"

The three of them laughed. No one filled Joanna in on the joke, so she ducked her head and took a hearty sip of wine. A stream of waiters carefully wheeled a tall chocolate cake with a single sparkler candle poking out the top to a nearby table. As they sang *Happy Birthday* to a beautiful older woman in a brown and white poncho, Rob and Charles began to reminisce about their days on the high-school debate team. Their coach, Gregory, would take them to an Indian restaurant in Malvern Friday nights whenever someone had a birthday. Remember the sitar player? Remember the poetry readings? Gregory took them to hear Bill Clinton, then just the governor of Arkansas and the Democratic candidate for president, speak at the University of Pennsylvania.

"Do you think he and Schuyler really had a thing?" Nadine leaned forward on her elbows.

"That never happened." Rob shook his head. "It was just a rumor."

"Really?"

"Yeah, some girls saw them talking and completely misconstrued it," Charles said. "Remember?"

"Huh." Nadine wound a pale strand of hair around her finger. "Greg always had eyes for the girls, though. Definitely Schuyler . . . and Bronwyn, too."

Bronwyn. Joanna curled her toes. Charles breathed in, his face agleam. And just like that, Joanna knew he was going to bring her up. He was seriously going to talk about Bronwyn right now. Her heart pounded with resentment.

"Did you guys ever haze?" she blurted out.

Everyone stopped and looked at her. Charles clapped his mouth closed. He laid the piece of bread he'd been chewing back on his plate.

"What?" Nadine said.

"On the debate team," Joanna explained. Her mouth felt funny, way too large. "Like, for newcomers. Freshmen. Did you ever, like, make them eat toilet paper? Stand outside on a winter day in their underwear?"

"What, like in a frat?" Rob bit off the word *frat* and held it tautly between his front teeth.

"Like bullying?" Nadine said at the same time.

"I guess," Joanna answered.

"We didn't do anything like that," Rob said slowly, looking up at the pagoda-shaped light fixtures, as if trying to remember. "If the newcomers sucked, they didn't debate. If they were good, they did."

"What about on your sports teams?" Joanna asked. "Basketball? Football?"

She could feel Charles's foot pressing down on hers. But when they were first dating, she'd explicitly told him that she didn't like hearing about Bronwyn. It had been part of their early arguments, those first sticking points all couples needed to work through. It had been a difficult thing for her to say that to him, for she'd felt so vulnerable and petty. The conversation was still so clear to her; was it for him?

"We don't have a football team." Nadine said slowly, raising her shoulders.

"Wrestling?" Joanna tried.

"Joanna," Charles growled.

He gave her a private glance. But she wasn't going anywhere dangerous with this. She was just asking questions. "I always knew frats and sororities hazed," Joanna said, turning to Rob and Nadine. "But I've been reading this article that it's sort of prevalent in high-school sports, too."

Nadine shook her head quickly. "Our school isn't really like that."

"Maybe it's more of a public school thing," Rob volunteered sweetly.

They were silent for a while, staring at their empty place settings. Out of the corner of her eye, Joanna saw Charles's finger digging into the surface of the wooden table, as if to carve a groove. His Adam's apple bobbed, and he looked up. "So, Nadine. Are you having a shower?"

Nadine nodded, and then glanced guiltily at Joanna, whom she hadn't invited. Joanna looked down. "It's going to be at my mother's house," Nadine said. "In Wayne. I'll send an e-mail."

"Did you track down Bronwyn again and ask her to it?" Charles asked.

Joanna breathed in sharply. Charles glanced at her, his expression eerily neutral.

"Because you guys were friends, I mean," Charles went on. "Does she even know you're having a baby?"

Nadine shrugged. "I haven't heard from her. I think she's still in Europe."

"I thought it was South Africa," Rob murmured.

Joanna stared hard at Charles's ear, waiting for him to turn back to her and give her some apologetic gesture to explain himself. But Charles took another bite of bread, nodding thoughtfully. By the time he did look over, Joanna's look had wilted into a grimace, not nearly as potent. "What?" Charles snapped quietly. He took a swallow of his drink.

She looked away. "Nothing," she mouthed. And then the waiter arrived with their dinners. Joanna wiped her mouth on her napkin, gave the waiter a forced smile, and took her first bite of her baked chicken and haricots verts.

By dessert, Charles had downed five more gin and tonics. His face was flushed, and he was starting to slur his words. Rob was talking about the Craftsman-style house they'd just bought for a steal in Narberth. Nadine told Charles and Joanna that they should check their birth blog for a weekly progress report. After they hugged, Charles kept the smile pasted on his face for exactly one block. Once they were out of sight, he dropped Joanna's hand and wordlessly passed her the car keys. He staggered to the car, dropping his canvas bag on the sidewalk. "I think there's a bottle of water on the back seat," she instructed. Charles grunted and reached for it. His cheeks flared red.

She started the car and backed out of the space. Charles drained the whole water bottle, sloppily screwing the cap back on when he was finished.

"What was that, back there?" he said as she paused at a traffic light.

"What was what?"

"You know what. *Do you guys haze?*"

"I was just curious."

"Yeah, well, it's probably not the right thing to bring up right now." She sniffed. "It's not like they *know*. They didn't even ask about Scott! They don't even care!"

They'd talked about Nadine's brother, Christopher, and Rob's sister, Camille, and a whole slew of other people who'd gone to that school—and, of course, Sylvie—but not a word about Scott. Joanna couldn't recall a time they'd *ever* talked about him. He was a nonissue, just like she was.

Charles rolled the water bottle between his palms. He lowered the window, then changed his mind and rolled it back up. "I know no one knows."

"Then what is wrong with you? Why did you get so angry?"

"I didn't get angry."

Joanna groaned. "You *did*. And . . ." She took a deep breath, considering if she should really say this. "And you think Scott's guilty. You've made that pretty clear." She peeked at him, almost positive she should've kept her mouth shut.

"Well, yeah. Maybe I do," Charles murmured after a moment.

She waited. They were merging onto I-76 now, the lights watery blurs. "Is it because he's adopted?" she blurted out.

Charles stared at her in horror. "*Jesus*. No."

"I don't mean *you* think that. I just mean . . . is it what other people think? Is that why other people are assuming he's . . ."

"I should hope not."

She pressed the brake. The rain obscured the windshield. They passed a car that had pulled over to the shoulder, its hazard lights blinking. A shapeless man sat in the passenger seat, seemingly just staring out into the inky night. And swish, he was gone.

"Scott beat me up once," Charles said in barely more than a whisper. "In the middle of this party we were having. Like he enjoyed it. It just . . . worries me."

She kept her eyes on the road. So here it was. He was going to tell her about the fight after all. "When was this?" she asked, halfheartedly feigning ignorance.

He shrugged. "Years ago. When we were in high school. A lot of my friends were there. Many people saw it."

"Why?"

"Why what?"

"Why did he beat you up?"

"I don't know."

"He just started beating you up for no reason?"

Charles didn't answer. Joanna felt her pulse against her throat. Headlights streaked down the highway, leaving an imprint on her retinas long after they'd passed. "Why didn't you tell me this before?" she said quietly, trying to control her anger.

"I don't know. It's not something I like to think about much."

He was turned away from her, so Joanna couldn't see his face. She slowed at the turnpike gate, waited for the EZ Pass sensor to detect her car.

"I mean, maybe I deserved it." Charles broke the silence.

"Why would you say that?"

Charles bit his lip, as if considering saying something more. Then he shrugged and slumped down in his seat.

"I wish that headmaster had never called your mom," Joanna muttered. "It's just getting everyone worked up. And it's dredging up things that are irrelevant. I think it's criminal to start this kind of panic over rumors. Like that thing with that Schuyler girl and your debate coach—it's just bored people looking for conspiracy theories, making assumptions before actually getting the facts."

"Sometimes assumptions are right."

"And sometimes they *aren't*."

Charles went quiet, picking at a loose thread on the seat. Joanna breathed in. Her stomach jumped into her heart for just a moment before she spat it out. "Why don't you tell me anything, Charles? Why don't you share anything with me?"

"Huh?"

"Sometimes I feel like I don't know a thing about you. Your friends know much more about you than I do. Your mother knows *way* more. Is it because I didn't go to Swithin?"

"Joanna . . ." He blew out through his nose. "You're being ridiculous."

But now that she'd started she couldn't stop. "Tonight, for example. With your friends. They didn't ask me a thing about myself. They asked about you, they asked about your mom, but they didn't ask about me. And you didn't bring me into the conversation."

"They asked about you!"

Pressure rose up in her chest, higher and higher. "They didn't. And you ignored me around them. I got the impression that you would have preferred it if I hadn't been there at all. It would have been *easier* that way. Just like old times."

He squeezed the empty water bottle so hard that it crinkled. "If you didn't want to have dinner with them, you should have said something."

"And what, look like an asshole? How did you not *realize* I didn't want to have dinner with them? It must have been written all over my face. I thought it was just going to be you and me! I was waiting for you to step in!"

He raised his palms in surrender. "How was I supposed to know that? I'm not a mind reader!" He rolled his neck around, cracking a joint. "So, what, you're pissed off at me for not knowing what you wanted and you bring up the hazing thing in revenge?"

"Is that why you brought up Bronwyn?" she shot back. "Maybe the revenge goes both ways."

He let air seep from his nose. The bottle slipped from between his hands to the floor of the car. "I was just curious if Nadine talked to her. I wasn't trying to hurt you. Not like you deliberately tried to hurt me."

"I did no such thing."

He turned away from her, pressing his head against the window. "Sometimes I think you *want* to hurt me."

She gaped at him. "How could you say that?"

But he didn't retract it. She bit down on her lip. Was *that* what she was doing? But she couldn't; that would mean she was a heartless, sinister person. A saboteur.

She faced front again, put on her turn signal, and got off at the rest stop. Her tires squealed as she pulled into the parking lot.

"What are you doing?" Charles asked.

She didn't answer. The mini-mart attached to the gas station gleamed fluorescently; a clerk lingered behind the counter, surrounded by shelves of cigarettes. Joanna pulled into a space and shoved the gearshift into PARK.

"You *do* hurt me, Charles," she said. "You leave me out of things. And it feels deliberate. And then you ask about Bronwyn in this *voice*, this completely wistful, longing voice, like *she's* the one who's important. Like it's *always* been her. What am I supposed to do? How does that make me look, just sitting there?"

"I didn't use a voice," he said. "And Bronwyn . . ." He trailed off.

She stiffened, on alert. "Bronwyn . . . what?"

Charles shook his head. "Forget it."

"What were you going to say?"

"Nothing."

Joanna's mouth trembled. It was clearly *not* nothing. She glared out at the green highway sign in the distance. A Honda drove into the parking lot. Another Honda was parked next to them. This whole place was full of Hondas, completely unoriginal. This conversation was unoriginal, too; it was probably a conversation every couple had at one point or another, probably even verbatim. A conversation not special in the least.

Joanna gazed at Charles imploringly. Charles winced. "Don't look at me like that."

"Like what?"

"You . . ." He waved his hands in front of his face. "It's like you're so disappointed."

"Disappointed in what?"

"How am I supposed to know? I never know what you want."

There was a thin line of spittle between his top and bottom lips. The turn signal was still on, making an irksome, repetitive *tick-tuh-tick-tuh-tick-tuh*. She *was* disappointed. Of course she was. She'd felt it about their wedding in Roderick's garden, which had been organized long before Joanna came into the picture. She felt it touring old, creaky, dusty Roderick, not nearly as grandiose as in her dreams. She felt it when Sylvie and Charles left Joanna out of family matters, when Charles's Swithin friends ignored her, even when Charles didn't cry at his father's funeral, not one tear, and not even when they went back to their apartment in Philly, instead suggesting that they check out the Jennifer Convertibles store—they were having a sale on sectionals.

She felt it when she assessed what she'd wanted to happen and what had happened instead. Nothing felt right. And then she realized exactly who she sounded like. She realized who she was turning into.

She heaved her door open in one smooth movement and stepped out of the car. It had started to rain again. The night sky was thick with dark clouds, indicating it would probably turn into a deluge.

Charles was out of the car. "Where are you going?"

"Drive yourself home. I'm getting a cab."

"Joanna . . . come on."

She walked across the parking lot and flung open the door to the mini-mart. It was bright and freezing inside. Pop music blared so loudly, the floor vibrated with every bass note. A man wearing a work shirt with his name, *Stewart,* stitched on the breast pocket was checking out the hot dogs. Two teenage boys, both acne-riddled, were staring at the refrigerators, probably waiting to shoplift a few cans of beer. The whole place smelled like a confused mix of coffee and burnt peanuts and bleach.

"Joanna." Charles followed her down the candy aisle. "This is inappropriate."

"Go away," she said, shaking him off. The lone counterperson looked over. The register to her right said OUT OF SERVICE. Next to her was a big box of horoscope scrolls.

Joanna zigzagged through the aisles, passing the mini-bags of chips, the refrigerator cases of soda. Pepsi. Nestea. Fresca. She kept her arms glued to her sides, her shoulders in.

"Will you come back to the car?" Charles protested. "We can talk about it there, okay? We don't need to be in here."

She walked down the row of car maintenance products, motor oil and wiper fluid and air fresheners. Charles let out a frustrated grunt, then turned to the do-it-yourself coffee bar, poured himself a cup of coffee, and brought it to the register. "Hello," he said pleasantly to the counter-woman. After he paid, Charles lingered by the door, sipping his coffee, watching her.

She did another lap of the convenience store, gazing at every item. So she was disappointed. So Charles had his idealized Bronwyn. Joanna had her ideal, too. Someone who hadn't disappointed her. Someone she'd probably never know well enough *to* disappoint her.

She dared to imagine the look on Charles's face if she told him what sometimes went through her mind. The feeling that had coursed through her body the first time she'd seen his brother standing in the kitchen at Roderick, the very first day Charles brought her there. She'd walked into the kitchen before Charles and his mother, and there was

Scott, standing at the fridge. She hadn't anticipated the sultry, desirous heat that rippled through her when he turned those eyes on her, those mysterious, dangerous, heavy-lidded eyes, looking her up and down, looking *inside* her. When she reached out her hand for him to shake, her movements were heavy and dreamlike. She was rendered breathless.

She could tell Charles that whenever they had dinner at his parents' house, she hoped Scott would join them. For Scott would sit there, thrillingly sullen and noncompliant. Sometimes she felt him watching her, his gaze predatory and primal. She had dreams about him, too. In her fantasies, Scott was rough and passionate. It was after those dreams that she woke up facedown on her stomach, her hand between her legs.

She looked at her husband, leaning against the rack of newspapers, drinking his cup of coffee. It was amazing how separate they were. Here she was with this huge, ghastly secret, silent and closed inside her. He had no idea.

An obese man gathered up a few bottles of soda from the counter and trundled out the door. The little TV behind the counter broke for commercials, and a local news teaser came on. "Unknown death at a local Philadelphia school leads to questions," the newscaster announced.

Joanna froze. Charles pivoted, his eyes on the TV.

The newscast's signature music blared. "We have the exclusive," a second newscaster bragged. "Up next."

The fluorescent lights pulsed. The hot dog machine creaked atonally. Joanna walked to Charles and put a hand on his arm. "It's not the boy from Swithin," she said.

Charles didn't move.

"They said a *Philadelphia* school. Swithin is too far out."

A small noise escaped from Charles's throat.

"And, I mean, Swithin wouldn't release this kind of story to the press, right? They'd keep it quiet."

Charles gazed at her, fear in his eyes.

"They *would*," Joanna said.

They had no choice but to stay in the mini-mart to watch the rest of the news. The story came on almost at the end. It was about a boy from an inner-city Philadelphia school, just as Joanna had predicted, gunned down in his neighborhood for what police suspected had to do with drugs. They watched as snapshots of the boy paraded past. There he was opening a Christmas present, then standing with a whole gaggle of other Latino kids, then kissing the cheek of a woman of indeterminate age.

Joanna turned to Charles and put her hand on his waist. They didn't say anything for a long time.

"They want me to interview someone for work next week," Charles croaked. "Like, follow them around all day. They want me to write a story for one of the magazines. A magazine that's advertising this community that lives like the Amish, but at least it's a shot at writing something."

Joanna put a finger to her mouth, not following why he was bringing this up right now.

"It's weird," he went on. "I'm not going to have anything in common with them. They had normal lives before this, like you and me. They live off the land, to build their houses, to get rid of TVs and cars. It's not like we're going to get along."

She searched his face. "But you don't have to be friends with them, do you? You just have to interview them."

"No, you're right. Of course you're right. The thing is, it's on Tuesday. The day of your mom's . . . thing."

"Oh." Joanna raked her hand through her hair. "It's all right if you don't come. It's not a big deal. It's a good thing, like you said. You'll get a writing credit."

Charles picked at the plastic lid to his coffee. "I should just quit instead."

"Quit?"

"I don't have to do it. I don't have to break my commitment to you."

She breathed out. "I go to my mom's all the time. It's not a big deal."

Charles's jaw wobbled.

Joanna cocked her head. "You're serious? You want to quit."

"I don't know. Maybe."

"Why?"

"It's insincere, writing for things I don't believe in. I feel like I lie for a living."

She leaned against the window. "Everyone lies for a living. And anyway, it's a group of people who want to live in log cabins. It's a little weird, but it doesn't seem amoral."

"Maybe it's not just that. I don't feel right about any of it anymore."

"And so then what? Would you look for another job?"

"I don't know."

The air around them felt fraught. She wondered if there was something more he was trying to tell her in all this. She glanced at the television again. The news had moved on to a weather report. Rain for the next few days. Today's sun was a short-lived tease.

She turned back to Charles. "Don't quit your job, okay? Try to have a clear head about this. Do the interview next week, and then we'll figure out your job situation together."

He paused a few moments, and then nodded his head. She rested her head on his shoulder, relieved. "I'm sorry," she whispered.

"*I'm* sorry," Charles said, staring off toward the freezers.

And then they walked out to the car, unlocked it, and Joanna drove home. It ended the argument for the night, deflating the balloon of tension. Because really, after that, there wasn't much more either of them could say.

eleven

They sat on the couch and watched TV, quietly at first. Awkwardly. Then the next day, he said hi. She said hi back. They said nothing after that, but at least they continued watching together. Sometimes he laughed at the jokes on sitcoms. Sometimes she walked into the room and found him watching PBS nature programs—about the mating habits of weasels, about lions on the Serengeti—and was surprised, never knowing he liked these shows. Now when Scott went into his room, he didn't always shut the door. He even joined Sylvie for dinner last night, whereas before he'd just eaten on his own, often standing over the sink, shoving bites into his mouth as fast as he could.

She offered to make him whatever he wanted. Finally he said he wouldn't mind a banana cream pie. It seemed so random—*banana cream pie!* She'd never seen him eat a banana in his life. But after she made the pie, throwing out her first attempt at the crust because it was a bit too soggy, she watched him eat it with pleasure, every forkful a confirmation that she was doing something right. She didn't want to comment on the sudden shift in their dynamic. Scott was like a flighty cat—the slightest thing would send him scurrying back under the desk. And what would she say, anyway? *Gee, isn't this nice? You and I are finally acting like mother and son!* He'd sneer.

She listened to him breathing evenly as he slept in his old bedroom. It was the same thing she did when he was a little boy, hovering over his soft, twisted shape, wondering who he was, what the first eighteen months of his life had been like before she'd come along. Those eighteen months worried her, certainly; there were plenty of things that could happen to a child in that span of time that could affect them for life. Why had his mother given him up, ultimately? Had it been the right thing to do to not ask to know anything about her, beyond that she was healthy and living across the country? Scott was brought to them by plane; Sylvie had stood with James and Charles at the airport gate, her stomach jumping nervously as two adoption coordinators stepped off the Jetway dragging a baby carrier, a fold-up stroller, a bunch of cloth bags, and, finally, a stroller containing Scott. "Oh," Sylvie had cried, clutching her hands at her breastbone when she saw him, those round, shiny eyes, that small dewdrop of a mouth, those fat cheeks. He was such a little *person*, so different than she was. It wasn't the same having him in the house as it had been when Charles was a baby; she never had an intuitive, maternal sense of what he might do next. When he cried and cried, she had no idea what he wanted. Because she wasn't his coauthor, because he hadn't sprung from her, he would always be impenetrable and alien. Sylvie sometimes fretted that there might be a more suitable mother out there for Scott who would understand him instinctively and automatically, bringing him what he needed, instantly hushing him when he sobbed.

When Scott was about seven, he took piano lessons from the same woman Charles did: Rose, an African-American woman who taught out of her home. It didn't take long for Rose to become smitten with Scott and Scott to become smitten with her. While she assigned Charles Chopin and Beethoven pieces, she taught Scott jazz standards,

The Entertainer. "I can tell he'll be a tough one, and I want to make it fun for him," Rose explained to Sylvie. "I want to make sure he keeps coming to lessons." Once, Sylvie arrived to pick Scott up from his lesson a little early and heard the two of them talking in the piano room, giggling and pressing keys. Her heart felt sore; she resented Rose for her easy rapport with Scott. Why couldn't Scott be this way at home with her, his own mother? A year later, Rose announced that she was moving to Georgia to be with her mother, who'd been diagnosed with Alzheimer's. Sylvie taught the boys piano herself for a while, drawing from her ten years of lessons, but Scott immediately lost interest.

And now, standing over his bed, she wished she could look inside his head. Because that was the thing—if Sylvie thought she didn't understand him when he was a toddler or a seven-year-old or even a teenager, he was thick, cinder-block wall to her now. She hadn't realized how good she'd had it, how much he used to let her in. But as she gazed down at him, one side of her wished she could know, truly, what had happened with the wrestlers. But at the same time, knowing for sure scared her. What if he *had* done something? Could she bear to have him under this same roof? Could she ever look at him in the same way again?

She sat outside his room one night, her head pressed up against the door to James's office, wondering if there really was a mythical document inside the filing cabinet that bore the woman's name. She really had nothing to go by except instinct. That and the fact that James had always locked his office, meaning he may have hidden more in there than just the bracelet. Really, she had no idea what James kept in those cabinets—documents about the boys, copies of their car insurance and titles, copies upon copies of things they also kept in a safe deposit box. She wondered which outcome would be worse: going in there and finding some evidence of who the woman might have been, or going in there and finding nothing but old credit card statements, pay stubs, the titles to their homes and cars. *What was better, knowing or not knowing? What would make her suffer less?*

On Friday afternoon, Michael Tayson had called Sylvie and told her that Scott would be meeting with the teachers on Monday. "Just so you know," he said. She asked whom the meeting would be with, but he wouldn't tell her. "Have they gotten the autopsy back?" she asked, but Tayson didn't know that, either. "Sometimes autopsies take a long time" was his answer.

But with a suicide, an autopsy wouldn't. The coroner would find drugs in the boy's system. They would look at his neck and windpipe and know he'd hung himself. They'd pull up his shirt and find an exit wound. Sylvie thought about Warren Givens hunched over his thighs on that bench. She thought of him going through life's simple motions. Buying milk at the store. Turning on the taps to take a shower. Stopping to have his car washed by students raising money for their school's sports team.

Friday was also the day she'd received a follow-up call from Geoff, asking if she was coming to the party he was throwing for his wife's birthday on Monday, the same party he'd mentioned at the board meeting. "It's just a casual thing," he said. "Melinda certainly isn't expecting a gift. And no need to dress up."

Sylvie felt put on the spot. She hadn't been to a party since the very last one she and James had attended together, the day before his aneurysm. Coincidentally that party had been at Geoff's house, too. James hadn't wanted to go, but Sylvie had been annoyed with him and demanded that he go. It was at that party that she'd brought up the nameless woman again, even though Sylvie had promised James she was strong enough to let her go.

If Sylvie went to Geoff's party, she would have to stand in the very same rooms where she and James fought, among many of the same people. And yet she didn't know how to say no, so she told Geoff she'd be delighted. Geoff sounded pleased and surprised, as if he'd expected her to decline.

The longer Scott stayed on her side of the house, the less Sylvie wanted to bring up the task of cleaning out his suite and fixing the leak. For they were making strides; the latticework of their relationship was getting stronger and stronger with every hello they exchanged, every detail she learned about him. If she said something and the leak was fixed, Scott might retreat back to his side of the house and all they'd accomplished would be undone. Who knew what they'd eventually talk about, what they'd eventually admit to one another.

But then Scott walked into the kitchen on Sunday morning and said, "I called a guy to pump out the water. He's coming Monday. Maybe I should show you where it all is in case I'm not here."

Sylvie stood up straighter, shocked. Monday was his meeting. Was that what he was referring to when he said *in case I'm not here?*

The mildewed smell swept around them like a cloak as soon as they opened the door. Some of the water had spilled over the side of the plastic bucket Scott had placed by his bed, leaving a warped puddle on the parquet floor. There was a big yellow stain on the ceiling where all the water had seeped through. Scott had had the sense to pull the mattress off his bed.

Neither of them said anything for a while, looking glumly at the mess. Scott crossed the room and opened his closet. "Oh."

Sylvie walked over, too. All his clothes were damp. There was still a considerable puddle on the closet floor, pooled around Scott's piles and piles of sneakers. When she looked up, there was a second yellowed Rorschach-blot over the metal hanging rod. The leak had turned the plaster soft and rippled.

"Shit," Scott said. He touched an oversize sweatshirt, then another. He kicked the sneakers with his foot.

"The shoes will dry out," Sylvie told him. "And we can wash the clothes."

She lingered on his jeans and T-shirts. Nothing of Scott's looked remotely appropriate to wear, say, to a meeting with teachers. Not that she meant to think about it; it had just crept in there.

She tried not to sweep her eyes around the rest of the apartment, for fear Scott would accuse her of prying into his private space. The television and various stereo components, a network of boxes and devices and consoles below it, most with little green LED windows, seemed unharmed. Scott's speakers did, too; they were arranged around the space, two in the front corners, one in the front middle, and two in the back corners—James had helped him set them up that way for theaterlike surround sound. Sylvie noticed a postcard pinned up to his refrigerator of an African-American girl in a short, tight argyle sweater-vest, her breasts spilling out at the vest's V-neck. The girl wore a minuscule pleated skirt with her kneesocks pulled all the way up, and she had one hand at her ultrared lips. *Shhh.*

"She's very pretty," Sylvie mused, pointing.

Scott followed her gaze and winced.

"Well, I mean, her *face*," Sylvie tried again.

The girl had a soft, round face and maple-colored eyes. Sylvie had always tried to be diplomatic about the girls Scott gravitated toward, pretending not to notice the obvious thing about them, pretending—and often succeeding—that their race didn't matter. She was curious about a lot of things she didn't dare bring up—the science behind the girls he preferred, the mechanics of attraction. Did it come down to rebellion—did he choose girls who were the furthest from her as humanly possible? Or was there some genetic proclivity about all of it that Sylvie would never understand?

"She's got a pretty face," Sylvie repeated. "Though she'd go much further in life if she didn't dress like *that*."

"*Mom*," Scott said, squeezing his eyes shut. And Sylvie laughed as if it was a joke, though it kind of wasn't. There was more implicit in it than she'd intended.

People make assumptions about everything, she wished she could say. Would this situation with the dead boy—the hazing rumors, the coach's supposed role—would it be different if, say, Scott didn't have that tattoo on his calf? If he didn't have that smirking, subversive look on his face whenever he dealt with authority, if he didn't wear street clothes with brightly colored sneakers? If he looked like all the other teachers at Swithin—say, if he looked like Charles—would this be anything?

The world wasn't fair, she wanted to say. All it wants to do is pigeonhole you. It reminded her of what James had said about the miniature birdhouse, which she could see outside Scott's window, high on its post next to James's office. One day not long after they were married and settled, James finished feeding the birds from the window, walked into the upstairs hall and said, "Did you ever notice that all the jays go to one hole, all the starlings go to a different hole, and same with the cardinals and the woodpeckers and the towhees?"

"That's silly," she answered. "Birds don't do that. They go to any spot on the feeder that's open."

He shook his head. "Not this birdfeeder. I've watched them. They never diverge from their spots. It's like they know their place in life and that's that." Then he added, "Seems like an appropriate metaphor for all you Bateses, I should think." When he glanced at her, his eyes felt like knives.

Water dripped into the bucket, drawing her back to reality. Sylvie had to be oversimplifying things. People didn't make accusations purely on how someone looked. But as Scott turned and poured the water that had collected in the bucket into the sink, just as she'd asked, she felt wary. Why wasn't he arguing with her? Did it mean he thought she was right? That he'd thought about the accusations, too, and had maybe even wondered the same things? Was all this getting to him, even though he tried so hard to be cavalier?

Scott turned back to her when he finished. "Come on," he said. "It smells disgusting in here."

They turned and left Scott's apartment, going back into the main house. Sylvie quickly busied herself with the breakfast dishes, wanting a moment away from him to collect her thoughts. Was it possible that she *could* just ask him what had happened with the wrestlers? If she put it in just the right gentle and unbiased way, would Scott tell her the truth?

When she walked into her bedroom a half hour later, Scott was standing at the mirror in her walk-in closet, dressed in a pair of James's pinstripe pants, a white button-down shirt, a gray sweater-vest. He'd even put on a pair of James's shoes, brown and white wing tips.

She ducked behind the door, covering her mouth with her hand. He hadn't seen her. She clenched inside, watching as he pivoted and lowered his chin, examining himself from all angles. Right here, right in this moment, she could ask him. It was possible.

Then Scott caught her reflection in the mirror and jumped. His face tightened. He folded in his shoulders and pulled off the shirt. "I was just fucking around." He kicked off the shoes and socks.

"It's all right," she said earnestly. "Take it. Wear whatever you want." She leaned on the console table to get her balance. "It all looks nice on you."

Scott snorted. "Right."

As he put his hands in the pants pockets, he hitched them up a little, revealing his socks. She pointed. "You put on a brown one and a black one."

Scott leaned over to look. "Huh."

"Your father used to do that, too. Especially when we were first dating. He said it was because he was distracted. Because he was in love."

The words hung in the air for a moment; more personal than anything she'd ever told him. Scott whipped the sweater off his head fast and sniffed. "In love," he muttered under his breath, as if it was a joke.

Sylvie's skin prickled. "Why did you say it like that?"

Scott eyed her. He chewed on his top lip, considering. "Forget it."

The room seemed to drop a few degrees. Sylvie placed her hands on her throat. An alarm in her head went off. Scott *knew*. He knew something about her. Something about James. What James had done.

Maybe she'd known all along. Maybe that was why it had been so easy to direct her anger at him in the hospital the day of James's collapse. How long had Scott known? Months? Years? The moment it happened? Was this why Scott had seemingly stopped speaking to James in high school? Only why would he side against his father? They were so much more alike, after all. He sided with James in everything else.

Scott was still watching her. Rage bubbled up in Sylvie again. She thought about him sitting in the hospital waiting room, bored. She thought about what Charles had said to him at the Swithin banquet all those years ago, the incident he'd referenced on the phone the other day after the headmaster had called. She'd only caught the tail end of it, hearing a few awful words and then seeing both boys on the ground. When she ran inside, horrified that her children were fighting in front of guests, James was already pulling Scott away.

"Did you hear what Charles said?" James said later. "He deserved what he got." Sylvie turned away, saying she didn't want to talk about it. "Oh sure, you don't want to talk about *Charles* doing something wrong," James hissed. "But if Scott had said these things, it would be entirely different."

Sylvie tried to push what she'd heard Charles say to Scott out of her mind as best she could, not wanting to believe that he'd held on to those feelings for *that long*, not wanting to admit that perhaps *she* had perpetuated it. But now as she looked at Scott who *knew* she felt such shame. He'd kept what James had done from her on purpose. He was laughing at her behind her back. He probably thought she deserved it.

"Your father was a good man," she said to Scott now. He was down to his bare chest and boxer shorts now, all those tattoos staring at her. "You shouldn't laugh at him. And . . . and how dare you put me in this position?"

Scott widened his eyes. "What position would that be?"

"Didn't we give you a good life?" she cried. "Didn't we take care of you?"

Scott's forehead wrinkled with contempt. "What the fuck is that supposed to mean?"

She was going mad. It hurt everything inside her, all this ruin. She wanted him to hate her; she wanted him to love her. She wanted him not to know this and hated that he did. And suddenly, the veil over her eyes lifted, and she saw what could have happened in that wrestling locker room. She saw her son capable, culpable. Everything that had been said about him could be true. She felt the slow dam of anger burst free. She gaped at Scott, a stranger, an interloper, a heartbreaker, and then turned away, so overcome with dizziness she could barely stand.

"Please leave," she then said. She stepped out of the doorway so he could pass.

"But—"

"Go," she screamed. "I can't have you in this room right now."

Scott gathered his own clothes in his arms. "I don't even need to be in this *house* right now."

"All right, then."

He pressed his clothes to his chest. His eyes burned coal-black. "This house has always been a fucking prison. A big stone jail."

"I'm sorry you feel that way," she said stiffly. "I'm sorry we made things so *difficult* for you."

And then he turned and stomped past her into his old bedroom. He dropped one of his socks on the way out without noticing. Sylvie didn't call him back to tell him.

twelve

onday morning Joanna felt Charles's lips on her forehead. She listened as he shuffled around the house, pulling the shower curtain back, flushing the toilet, brushing his teeth. She heard him slam the front door, walk down the driveway to get the paper. He climbed back upstairs before he left and loomed in the doorway. "I hope everything goes well in Maryland," he said. "I'll come with you next time, I promise."

She sat up in bed and wished him good luck with his interview tomorrow. When he walked back down the stairs, she flopped back down on the mattress and pulled the covers over her head. She remained in bed until eight, well after he left. When Charles kissed her good-bye, he'd had such a strange look on his face. Or maybe he didn't. Maybe she was imagining it.

She got out of bed, walked to the kitchen, sat down at the island, and dialed his cell. When he didn't pick up, she left a message saying she wanted him to call. She thought about all the things they'd gone through on Friday night. Looking back on it, she'd acted like a crazy person. Whining because his friends weren't—what? Kissing her ass? Picking a fight with him about Bronwyn. Nearly telling him about her crush on his younger brother.

What was she trying to do? What were her actions trying to achieve?

The coffee she made was bitter—she couldn't remember if she rinsed out Charles's grounds or re-filtered them through. She tried Charles's cell again. Voice mail. Same with his work phone. It had caller ID, certainly, and he saw her number coming up every time. *I'm sorry,* she started to text him. She was sorry she was like this, utterly and unchangeably herself, sorry that she was maybe sabotaging this relationship because of a silly fantasy of how reality was *supposed* to be.

When the phone rang, she jumped. The ringer sounded like a siren. She looked at the caller ID. It was a number she didn't recognize from an area code in the middle of the state.

The phone rang again. She lurched for it and picked it up. There was static on the other end, a whooshing sound as if the caller was on a train. "Is Charles there?" a woman asked.

"He's not." Joanna said. "Who's calling?"

"My name is Bronwyn Pembroke," the woman said.

Joanna almost dropped the phone.

But it had to be a cruel coincidence. She was probably someone taking a survey. A telemarketer.

"Can I have him call you back?" Joanna whispered.

"Well, no." The woman sounded dismayed. "I don't . . . I won't really be reachable by this phone. Can you give him a message? I need to change the time that we're meeting tomorrow. It needs to be nine, not ten."

Joanna watched her eyes widen in the hallway mirror. The reflection didn't look like her at all but like some other woman, some person she thought she'd never be. She placed the phone back into the receiver.

The kitchen was apathetically still. All the little charging devices for Joanna's cell phone, digital camera, and laptop blinked red, unfazed. The phone rang again, but she didn't answer. The machine clicked on. Her voice. *Thanks for calling*, and then their phone number. Because out here in the suburbs, you didn't say *the Bates-McAllister residence*. No one told their last names on answering machines for fear of giving too much away. When it beeped, there was only a dial tone.

When the answering machine clicked off, she grabbed the phone again and dialed Charles's office number. Voice mail. She dialed his cell phone. Nothing. She listened to his polite, cheerful voice recite his outgoing message. She waited, considering, and then let the phone slip from her fingers. It landed on the floor and skidded toward the fridge. The operator eventually interrupted, warning that the phone was off the hook, and then that grating, pulsing noise began.

Breathing hard, she ran upstairs, opened Charles's sock drawer and plunged her hands inside, feeling past his socks until she hit the drawer's fiberboard bottom. She didn't know what she was looking for. A picture of Bronwyn? A . . . what, a condom? She ran her hands over his patterned boxers. There was a pair with little dogs on them, a pair with breakfast foods, a pair with paisleys. Finding nothing, she shut the drawer and leaned against it.

A part of her had expected this, and yet she wasn't ready for it at all. Was this why Charles had abruptly canceled on coming to Maryland? Was this what he was doing after his interview of the people in the nudist colony or whatever it was? He'd probably scheduled the interview in the morning and then blocked off the rest of the day for Bronwyn.

She stopped. Maybe there *wasn't* an interview. Maybe the place didn't exist. Maybe it was a test, something she should've seen through. Charles claimed he was staying here because of his job—he'd told her he had something with work that got in the way, and then he'd threatened to quit, and then she said he was being ridiculous. He'd manipulated it around and made it *her* choice. It was positively Machiavellian. *Do the interview*, she'd told him. *We'll figure this out later.* She'd given him permission.

She had to get out of here. She took Charles's suitcase because it was nicer. She threw incongruous things into the bag—heavy sweaters, filmy dresses, high heels, a raincoat. Throwing a toothbrush and soap into a toiletry bag took seconds. After a moment, she decided to take some of his things, too—his expensive moisturizer, his Polo cologne, the book he was reading. Then she stood back, both palms on the top of her head. Her mother would be surprised at how early she would be. She might still be asleep, resting up for her big appointment tomorrow. Joanna would make breakfast and coffee. She wouldn't tell her about this.

The cold outside air made her spasm with shivers. She stood for a moment at the edge of the garage, staring at the houses around her. All the lawns were sickeningly green and even, with the same red flowers in the mulched gardens off the front walks. Why hadn't just one person planted blue flowers, or yellow? Who *lived* in these houses?

Joanna squared her shoulders and hit the unlock button on her car key. The door remained locked. She hit it again. Nothing. "Goddamn it," she whispered, punching every button on the key until the alarm started to sound. The noise was so loud it made her teeth ache. She fumbled with the key chain, desperate for it to stop. Then she noticed movement to her right. Mrs. Batten stood in the middle of her driveway, staring. Her hair was perfectly combed, her trench coat knotted tightly and evenly at her tiny waist, her ballet flats unscuffed. One of her children, the little girl who played in the sandbox, leaned into her, wide-eyed. Joanna hit another button, but the alarm kept blazing. Maybe she needed to try it from a different angle. As she stepped around to the other side of the car, her shoe caught on the lip of concrete between the garage and the driveway. Instantly, her cheek smacked the asphalt. There was a gasp behind her.

Joanna groaned and pushed herself up. Somehow the alarm had stopped. Blood was trickling down her knee. She turned around. Mrs. Batten's eyes were round, but she remained motionless in the driveway, instead of rushing over to see if Joanna was okay.

"What?" Joanna shouted. Her neighbor flinched. "Jesus, *what?*" Joanna said again. Her neighbor's eyes averted downward. She hustled her child into her minivan and slammed the door. Joanna hit the key again and the car unlocked, insufferably easily. Then she sat in the driver's seat without turning on the ignition. If only there was something insulting she could scream out to Batten, safe in the privacy of her car, but the first word she thought of, after *bitch*, was *eggbeater. You bitch, you eggbeater.*

A skunk had sprayed in the middle of the night; even the air inside the car smelled of it. Joanna started the engine. It was only an hour-and-a-half drive to her mother's if she took the highway. She usually avoided I-95, taking the quaint, quiet back roads, but today she didn't feel like lingering. As she drove, she gnashed her teeth, picturing Charles at work, smiling about his meeting tomorrow with Bronwyn. *He was in the clear.* When she came to a traffic light, she noticed where she was. To the left of the intersection was the garden center. To the right was the old stone mansion that had been converted into a bed-and-breakfast. This was the turn to Sylvie's house.

Something inside her flipped. She drummed her fingers on the steering wheel, considering. It was almost 11 a.m. Who knew if Scott would even be there—his meeting at the school was today. Sylvie might answer the door instead, and then what would Joanna say? That she hadn't been paying attention, that she'd inadvertently ended up here?

But she'd asked Scott if he'd come, and he said he would. The words had popped out of Joanna's mouth unwittingly, but maybe she'd meant them.

A car behind her honked. The light had turned green. She jumped, and then put on her turn signal. If Sylvie's car was there, she would turn around and go back. With any luck, Sylvie wouldn't see her.

The houses got bigger and bigger, old converted barns, enormous structures behind fancy iron gates, rolling properties with horse stables. She'd never driven to Roderick without Charles—she'd never felt like she had the right to. She made the turn at the red mailbox and started up the winding driveway. The tires crackled over fallen twigs and branches. The trees didn't have all their leaves in yet; her car was easily visible from the second-floor windows. Sylvie would probably already be on the porch by the time she got to the driveway. She would invite her in, saying what a nice surprise. She wouldn't ask questions. She would make her some tea and probably show her pictures of the vacation house and say nothing, absolutely nothing, pretending that Scott's meeting wasn't today, pretending it wasn't weird Joanna was there without Charles, not at all.

Only, Sylvie's car wasn't in the driveway—just Scott's. Joanna's heart lifted, and for a shining moment, she was so overcome with a mix of emotions she put her fist in her mouth and bit down hard. The decision had been made. This was in the hands of something bigger than she was. She parked behind Scott's car and turned hers off. He probably wouldn't need a very big bag. It would take him five minutes to put things together, nothing like Charles, who took hours to meticulously iron and fold and pack. She ran her tongue over her teeth, considering, and then decided not to consider. Whatever.

She slammed the door. She knocked and waited. A light came on, and there he was, opening the door, smiling, as if he knew she was going to show up here all along.

Part II

thirteen

Joanna, Scott, and Catherine sat in the sail club's dark, square room, smoke swirling above their heads. A plastic swordfish, blood-red crab, and long-armed stingray were snared in a fisherman's net strung up on the far wall. There was a Day-Glo mural of a giant squid next to the nets, the squid's tentacles outstretched wide. Across the bar sat a stringy-haired woman in a faded green tank top that showed off her wrinkled, sun-spotted décolletage.

A large, fleshy-armed man plopped on the stool next to Catherine. He had frizzy gray hair, kind eyes, and a massive beard that looked like a series of gray crayon scribbles. His gray flannel shirt was enormous, and he wore Teva flip-flops with his jeans. "This is Robert," Catherine said, gesturing to him. "You should hear his voice. He could get a record contract."

"Nice to meetcha," Robert said, reaching out his hand. He had a deep, James Earl Jones voice.

Joanna shook hands, barely feeling his skin. Robert held a pitcher of beer in his left hand, seemingly ordered all for himself. "Well, I'll be back later," he said. "You probably have lots to catch up on."

Then he waddled away toward the octopus mural. Catherine watched him go, patting her hair. "Robert is modest, but he really *does* sound just like Tom Petty. It's quite a sight to see."

Joanna tried to smile, though she felt uncomfortable and embarrassed. When her mother pulled into the parking lot of this place, Joanna had thought it was a joke. SAIL CLUB, said the squat, windowless building. It was next to a burrito shack called Viva La Mexico! There was a line of Harleys parked crookedly by the door and a piece of paper posted over the handicapped parking sign that said, SHOES MUST BE WORN AT ALL TIMES. The sign said nothing about shirts.

Inside the close, yeasty-smelling room was a small stage at the front of the bar meant for karaoke. Catherine had marched up to the bar and greeted the sinewy bartender with a big kiss, and a Tom Collins had appeared before her. To say Joanna had been aghast was an understatement. Where was the dockside country club? Where were the aloof men in yachter's caps? Where were the international glitterati? People stood at the pinball machine and dartboard without irony. In the hall to the bathroom was an old cigarette machine, the kind where one had to insert quarters and pull a knob. Joanna wanted to ask her mother why she frequented a place like this, a place so unexpected for her, but she didn't know how to phrase such a question. Maybe her mom *did* have something wrong with her—a brain tumor.

A petite girl in a denim miniskirt was belting out the chorus to *Like a Virgin*. She pranced up and down the narrow bar area, her limbs wobbly and loose. Scott watched her, sipping his Guinness. "She's good."

"Oh, I know," Catherine said. "She sings all the time."

"What do you say?" Scott looked at them. "Should we sing something?"

"*You* sing?" Catherine cried. "I bet you're good. Joanna and I will sing backup."

Scott thought for a moment. "I'll sign us up for something." He winked at them and slid off the stool, strutting to the front of the bar to signal the karaoke MC, who doubled as the bartender. Several women turned and watched Scott walk the length of the bar. Joanna's mother set down her drink and breathed in.

"He looks very handsome today," Catherine remarked. "That was nice of him to come while Charles is away."

Joanna could feel her mother's eyes on her, waiting. When they'd arrived at Catherine's house a few hours earlier, her mother had done a double take in surprise. "Scott, isn't it?" she'd asked, as if she didn't know precisely who he was.

"You haven't forgotten me?" Scott bantered.

"Of course not, of course not," Catherine said, ushering him in. "You look wonderful, darling." She turned to Joanna, beaming with curiosity.

"Charles is out of town," Joanna had explained quickly, loudly. "He had an important writing assignment that came up unexpectedly. Scott was nice enough to keep me company."

Scott glanced at her, startled, but for once he had the good sense not to say anything.

This was the first time Joanna had brought anyone to her mother's new house. Catherine welcomed them in unabashedly, yet another departure from how she used to let Charles reluctantly into their house in Lionville, making excuses for the ragged carpet in the den and the pineapple wallpaper in the kitchen. Just like Sylvie, Catherine had inherited this house scot-free from a relative, her great-aunt Marjorie. There was this house, and then there was Roderick. It was something Joanna always thought about whenever she visited.

Since moving in, Catherine had replaced Marjorie's stuff with the things from her old house in Lionville, the leather furniture, the farmhouse chairs, and the media center that had been such a point of contention between her parents—because of the price, no doubt—when Joanna was a teenager. All of it looked so shabby in the small, square living room with its royal blue carpet and lace curtains. Joanna had never met Great-aunt Marjorie, but she was mystified about who she might have been by the items of hers that still lingered around the house: a one-thousand-piece Eiffel Tower puzzle stacked in the coat closet. A whole drawer full of Hallmark cards featuring a cranky old lady wearing cat-eye glasses and spouting curmudgeonly good tidings. An assortment of Garfield cartoon and joke books on the small, white bookshelf in the upstairs bathroom and stacks of records of pasty-faced crooners Joanna didn't recognize in the moldy basement. And in a cabinet under a bathroom sink, a small, zippered case full of lubricants, edible body gel, even a pair of padded handcuffs. Catherine had been with Joanna when she'd found the case and had seemed just as shocked as Joanna was. They'd left the case under the sink where they'd found it, not sure what to do with it.

Scott had walked right into the house, as comfortable as he was at Roderick. He allowed Catherine to make him a drink. Although he widened his eyes at Catherine's various medications that were lined up on the kitchen counter and piled in the cupboard above the sink, he didn't say anything nasty. He didn't seem appalled to be here, instead sinking onto the couch and accepting a beer. Joanna felt so ambivalent. By this point the high had worn off, and she wasn't sure if bringing him had been a good idea. But then she thought of the phone call from Bronwyn, feeling justified all over again. Moments later her emotions finished their orbit, and she was back to feeling terrified. *What the hell was she doing? What did she want to happen?*

Scott returned to his bar stool. "The bartender says we're sixth in line."

"What did you pick?" Joanna asked.

"It's a surprise." He grinned.

"Great." Catherine rubbed her palms together. She was wearing dark red lipstick, and her hair was its same ash blonde. She was fifty-five, but men often thought she was younger. It had been a theory about why she wasn't 100 percent accepted in their old neighborhood: because all the husbands secretly wanted her and all the wives secretly resented her.

"So did Joanna tell you they're doing a biopsy?" Catherine said to Scott. "My doctor found a lump, and at first I couldn't feel it, but now I think I can." She prodded at the skin right under her arm, not exactly on her boob but close. "The nurse I spoke to on the phone when setting up the appointment told me it was probably nothing and that I shouldn't panic, but they have to say that, don't they? I have this wonderful doctor, though, and when I pressed him, he admitted that based on my age, profile, and condition, it's most likely cancer."

"Cancer." Scott whistled. "*Damn.*"

"My thoughts exactly," Catherine said, and then gazed longingly at her boobs, as if they were already gone.

Joanna flexed and pointed her toes. A gray-haired old seabird across the bar lit a cigarette. Then Catherine leaned into Scott. "So Joanna told me about the trouble at school. With that boy."

Joanna widened her eyes. "I didn't tell her anything," she pleaded to Scott. "Honestly."

"Yes you did." Catherine coolly sipped her drink. "You told me everything."

The neon Budweiser sign across the bar blinked on and off. Joanna aggressively pulled off a chunk of her place mat. It felt satisfying, so she pulled off another. "I'm sorry." She looked at Scott.

Scott shrugged. "It's all right. Whatever."

"So?" Catherine leaned on her elbows. "What were the boys doing to one another?"

"I think we should talk about something else," Joanna said loudly.

Catherine's mouth was a square. "Come on. Like no one has asked him this already?"

Joanna looked away. Everything about her mother was startling her today. The old Catherine, the one she'd finally begun to figure out, wouldn't have asked something so indelicate. Maybe it was the sail club's influence. Maybe it was the case of Marjorie's sex toys under the sink.

The metaphorical elephant had been lingering the whole drive to Maryland. First Scott volunteering to take his car instead of hers, then following Joanna back to her house, then Joanna climbing into his car, and Scott speeding the whole way down I-95 in the passing lane for the pure, aggressive enjoyment of it. The unanswered question hung between them. Had Scott gone to the meeting at Swithin today, or was he missing it by coming with her to Maryland? He'd answered the door dressed in khakis that almost fit. His hair looked different, and after a moment, Joanna realized it was clean. Clearly going to the meeting had crossed his mind. Scott's phone had rung a few times on the drive, and Joanna saw Sylvie's name in the caller ID window. Scott had clapped it shut, expressionless.

Scott gazed across the barroom. There was an empty dartboard directly opposite them, a chalkboard beside it, and a Miller Lite schedule of the University of Maryland football season. Another bartender, a ropy-armed woman with stringy blonde hair that hung in her eyes, yanked down the tap and shoved a smudged beer mug underneath.

"Actually," Scott said in a faraway voice. "No one *has* asked me. You're the first."

Catherine pressed her lips together. "Oh."

Scott looked at Joanna. "Can you believe no one has asked me directly?"

Joanna sat back in her chair. "Well, I . . ." She swallowed. "Yes. I guess I can."

"So were they beating up one another or not?" Catherine goaded.

Scott's face clouded. He took a breath, as if about to speak. Then there was the sound of breaking glass from across the bar. Everyone looked over.

A sausage-biceped man in a sleeveless shirt lunged toward another man in a plaid button-down. "You didn't just say that," the first man said. He had a burly beard that concealed most of his face. "Tell me you didn't say that, you piece of shit."

"*You're* the piece of shit," the plaid-shirted man spat. "You and that bitch you live with."

"Oh dear," Catherine said under her breath. "Not again."

Now the men were shoving each other. One bumped into a stool, sending it flying. More glass broke. The karaoke ceased, and the girl on the stage—as well as everyone else in the bar—turned to stare. The men shouted more, and then the guy in the plaid shirt hit the bearded guy in the jaw. It made a cracking sound, louder than Joanna would have imagined. The bearded man in the sleeveless shirt clutched his face for a moment but quickly began swinging again. He groped for a dart on the dartboard and raised it into the air, his eyes loony and enraged. Everyone on the opposite side of the bar moved out of the way. "Let's just calm down now!" called an anonymous voice. The room began to smell pungently of spilled beer.

"We should get out of here," Scott said. Robert materialized from out of nowhere, quickly whisking Catherine toward the door. As they made a beeline for the exit, Joanna stared at Scott's back. What had he been about to say? A denial? A confession? She wondered, suddenly, how she'd feel about Scott if he actually *did* indirectly abet this boy's death. Would her attraction for him instantly vanish?

They could still hear the shouting from the gravel parking lot. Robert helped Catherine into the back seat and patted the hood in farewell. Joanna swung into the driver's seat. Her ears rang from the loud music. The image of that man's face as he held the dart swam before her eyes. "Are there a lot of fights at that bar?" she asked, feeling out of breath.

Catherine wrapped her leopard-print scarf tight around her neck. "Oh, some, I suppose."

"What are you doing going to a bar like that, anyway?" Joanna cried.

"It could've gotten dangerous," Scott added. "Someone might have had a gun."

Catherine tittered. "A gun? *Please.* Those two boys that were fighting are best friends. They'll be drinking together in a half hour!" She leaned forward and touched their shoulders. "You two are so sweet to care."

Everything was the inverse of what it should be. Joanna rolled the windows down and started to back out of the lot. The night was sticky and unusually warm, and she could smell the salty, swampy Chesapeake a few blocks over. As Joanna peered out into the darkness, she saw the round, glowing eyes of a nocturnal animal staring back at her.

She held its gaze for a moment in silent communion. The animal's eyes shone like silver. A few seconds passed, and then, given an invisible signal, the animal whipped around and disappeared into the darkness.

Even though it was only 9:30 p.m., Catherine went to bed as soon as they got home, saying she needed to rest up for her big appointment. Joanna sat on her mother's tiny screened-in porch drinking a glass of V8, the only nonalcoholic beverage Catherine had in the house. In the distance Joanna heard the steady beeping sound of one of the low bridges rising to let a tall-masted boat through. She could smell the rancid, brackish creek just beyond the trees.

Joanna's phone rang, startling her. It was Charles. She stared at it, her heart thrumming. After the third ring, she answered.

"How's your mom?" he asked.

"She's okay," she answered automatically. She cursed herself for saying it so nicely. What would happen if she continued to feign ignorance about Bronwyn? Would he admit it on his own? Crack under the guilt and come clean?

She looked through the screen door to the house. Scott was standing over the kitchen counter, pouring himself a drink. Probably Dewar's Scotch; it was Catherine's favorite. She hoped he wouldn't come out. She hoped he didn't hear her talking.

"So did someone give you a hot ride to Maryland?" Charles asked.

She sat up, horrified. How could Charles know? "W—what?"

"Because your car is still in the garage. You took the train, right?"

The air left her lungs. *Right.* He was joking. "Yeah. The train. And I called a cab from the house. It was easier than finding parking." She squeezed her eyes shut, hating that she was lying.

"I guess Scott had his meeting today," Charles said.

Joanna watched as Scott turned and shut the cabinet. *Don't come out*, she silently willed, but he swiveled and headed for the screen door. She balled her fist.

"I don't know how it went, though," Charles was saying. "I tried to call Mom, but she was on her way to some party."

"Huh." Scott slid open the door and looked at her. She put a finger to her lips, and he nodded. *You're on the phone. I got it.* But he didn't leave.

"I don't know if she's talked to him, either," Charles was saying. "She probably would've called me if she did."

"Uh-huh," Joanna said. She stared out at the dark backyard. Hank and Carla, the neighbors, kept a parrot's cage on their back porch; she could see its curved shadow. The parrot often babbled when they left it alone, screaming out Hank and Carla's names.

"Are you all right?" Charles asked.

Joanna jumped. "I'm fine. Why?"

"I don't know. You sound . . . not altogether there."

"I'm fine. Just . . . you know. My mom."

"Do you want me to come down there?" Charles asked.

"W–when?"

"Tonight. Tomorrow morning. I don't know."

Her pulse beat so strongly she could feel its steady pace in her fingertips. *Did that mean he'd called Bronwyn and canceled tomorrow's meeting? Or had they met today, and he now had some free time?*

She wound a piece of hair around her finger so tightly that it pulled at her scalp. Scott was sitting on the glider, staring. *Why didn't he just leave? Why couldn't he understand she wanted to be alone?*

"I thought you had your work interview tomorrow," she finally said.

Charles paused. She paused. Neither said anything. She wondered if he knew that she knew. Maybe Bronwyn had called him and said, *We've got to call it off. I called your house and she answered.*

"It's okay," Joanna said when it became clear he wasn't going to say anything more. "I don't need you here. I'm holding up all right."

There was a sigh on his end. "Well, okay then," Charles said.

"I should go," she said quickly. She clapped the phone shut and sat still for a few long moments, a sob building in her chest. She thought the phone might ring again, but it remained silent.

The distant beeping started up again; the boat must be through, and the bridge was coming back down. Joanna stood up, padded into the kitchen, poured out the V8, and replaced it with Dewar's. Then she went back outside and slumped down on a plastic chair. Scott was smoking a cigarette, making the whole screened-in porch smell of it.

"Was that Charles?" he asked after a moment.

"Yes."

The wind knocked the long chimes hanging from the porch roof together. A dog barked a few houses down. Catherine's porch was so small that Joanna and Scott's knees were almost touching.

"So are you going to tell me or not?" Scott said quietly.

She whipped her head up. "Tell you what?"

Scott's face was hidden by the shadows; she could only make out the outline of his jaw, the tips of his hair, and the whites of his eyes. "Where Charles's out-of-town trip has taken him, of course," he said. "Where he was calling from. What he's writing about."

"That just came out. I had to tell her something before she asked."

Scott swirled his glass. She bet he was smirking.

"My mom needs an explanation. Every time she thinks she's got something, I come down here. But she doesn't get that not everyone can just drop everything and come. Charles always has something going on, but she doesn't understand that he just has to work."

Scott moved slightly, shifting his weight to his left side. She listened as he raised his glass to his lips, pulled the liquid to the back of his throat, and swallowed. "So Charles is working."

She wanted to hit him. Why bother answering, if he already had it all figured out? "Of course," she said stiffly.

But then her face started to tremble, first just a little, then a lot. But she wouldn't let herself cry, not here. She swallowed. "Did you know I grew up not that far from you?"

"In Parkesburg?"

"Lionville."

"Right."

She'd never told him this before, so it was curious that he knew this about her. "When I was little, maybe in like third grade, there was a big announcement about the Kimberton Fair. Do you remember the Kimberton Fair?"

"I've heard of it. I've never been."

"I got really excited about this fair. There was going to be an amusement park as part of it, and I thought, *This is going to be great. An amusement park right down the street from my house! I'll go every day. I'll wake up and ride a roller coaster.* There wouldn't be any lines or crowds, it would just be me running free and alone through this enormous park with workers ready to attend to me."

"I think every kid fantasized about that," Scott answered.

Joanna uncrossed her legs and crossed them in the other direction.

"So the fair shows up. I'm so excited I can't sleep the night before opening day. And I get up really early, before the sun is even up, and I run down there. And there's already a line of kids waiting. They'd gotten up earlier than I did. I had no idea how—I mean, I guess they just didn't sleep at all. And so finally someone comes along and lets us all in. There were only five rides, not even a roller coaster. Just a merry-go-round, a Ferris wheel, swings, some lame-ass fun house, and a tilt-a-whirl."

Her voice caught on *whirl*, but she swallowed fast, trying to pass it off as nothing. "I only went that one morning," she said. "I spent the rest of the summer at the pool."

Scott nodded. He bent his knee in and out, making his joint crack.

"I don't know what made me tell you that story," Joanna said. "It has nothing to do with anything."

Scott took another sip of his drink. "Maybe it has to do with a lot of things."

Joanna picked at a loose thread on the knee of her jeans. She should thank him for accompanying her here, and then go inside to her old bedroom and go to sleep. This could still be explained to Charles. She'd come to the house looking for Sylvie, maybe, but Scott had been there instead. She'd been distraught, and he'd offered to come. She just needed some company, someone to take the edge off her mother. It was *hard*, coming down here alone every time.

She was still unmarred, unharmed. She could still look Charles straight in the eye.

Scott's eyes burned into her. Taking a deep breath, she raised her head and stared back. Electricity passed through them. She could almost see it, a blue snap through the air. He knew what she wanted. He had to. He knew what was going on inside her, but he was going to make her work for it. He was going to make her ask.

Hank and Carla's parrot screeched. The same sob rose up inside her. She felt so terrible.

The moment broke, and Scott looked away. Joanna lowered her shoulders and looked down, too, disappointed that he hadn't acted on the moment, then ashamed by her disappointment. She made a tight fist with her hand. "Charles told me about that time you hit him, you know."

Scott stopped rocking. "Oh yeah?"

"Uh-huh. He said you did it for no reason."

The ice rattled in his glass. "Is that what he said?"

"Yes."

"Then he didn't tell you everything."

"What's . . . everything?"

"There was a reason I did that."

"And that would be . . . what?"

He stubbed out his cigarette.

"Come on."

But he stood, not answering, and opened the screen door and walked inside the house. Joanna felt confused. Did that mean something more *had* happened than what Charles had told her? Or was that just what Scott wanted her to think?

Scott opened the freezer; cold, blue light shone against his face. She heard the crack of the ice cube tray, and the clank of the cubes hitting the glass. This was probably just a game for Scott. A mind-fuck.

She stood up, too, and made her way slowly down the hall to the first-floor bedroom that was always set up for her. She would sleep on her old childhood twin bed, its creaky mattress as stiff and loud as the paper liner on an examining table at a doctor's office. Scott, of course, would sleep on the couch.

fourteen

Geoff's house was hidden behind a heavy wrought-iron gate. A video camera watched Sylvie as she idled in the driveway, and she imagined her image being fed by wireless signals to a closed-circuit television. The gate swung open, and she pulled up behind the other cars, parking next to a black Audi. It was very possible she had parked next to this very same black Audi at the last party here, the last one she and James ever attended together.

"Sylvie," Geoff's young wife, Melinda, cried when she reached the door, throwing her arms open. Sylvie stepped in, wrapping her arms around Melinda and feeling the sharp edges of her shoulder blades. "Happy birthday," Sylvie murmured.

"Thanks," Melinda answered. They both stepped back. The only spot of color on Melinda's pale face was her dark red lipstick. "You look lovely," she added to Sylvie.

Sylvie ducked her head and shrugged out of her coat. Melinda swept right over her, her expression not faltering, not giving away that she might know something that Sylvie didn't.

All afternoon Sylvie had tried to get in touch with Scott, eager to hear about the meeting earlier today. He wasn't in the house. He wasn't in his apartment. His phone had been turned off. She hadn't

known where else to call. She even tried looking up the number to
the sneaker shop his friend owned in the city, but she didn't know the
store's name.

She thought someone at Swithin would call her with an update,
but no one did. She had paced the house, trying to imagine what
could have happened. Scott's bed in his old bedroom was unmade,
his clothes strewn about all over the floor. An iPod was on the pillow
along with an overturned magazine about cars. He'd still been living
here the last two nights, but he'd holed up in his bedroom, not speaking to her. *How dare you put me in this position*, she'd said to him. His
face had crumpled with contempt. And now he was punishing her, not
even telling her whether or not he'd gone.

"Drinks are back there," Melinda instructed, pointing. "And . . . oh!
There's Kristen and Bill!" Her face brightened at another couple that
had come in after Sylvie, two younger people Sylvie didn't recognize.

Sylvie picked up a cocktail and looked around the room. The party
was already packed, everyone milling around with drinks in hand, the
caterers weaving through the crowd with big trays of crab puffs and
pot stickers. Geoff stood in the corner surrounded by a bunch of men
in dark suits similar to his own. He caught Sylvie's eye and waved but
didn't come over.

Sylvie had walked this very route of rooms the day before James
had died. Oh, how annoyed she'd been at him at that last party. He'd
agreed to accompany her, but moments before they were supposed to
leave, she found him in his office, fiddling on his computer, wearing a
stained polo shirt.

"We're going to be late," she said. "You need to get dressed."

He didn't move. "I'm not really in the mood tonight. I feel tired.
Maybe you should go by yourself."

Tired. Was that due to the impending aneurysm? Was it an early warning that it was going to happen the next day? But she hadn't known. She'd thought he was being difficult. "You have to come," she said. "You promised." She didn't like navigating parties by herself any more than she had when she was a student at Swithin or a freshman at Swarthmore.

Grumbling, James finally trudged down the stairs and got his coat. As they were getting into the car, he looked at her and said, "I never make you come to *my* business parties if you don't want to. But I guess Swithin's more important, huh?"

James knew it hurt, in the same way all of his little *your*-things, *your*-family, *your*-life-is-more-important-than-mine comments always hurt. Gone was the sweet, agreeable man who revered everything about her family, who said they could keep Roderick intact as long as she liked. And once that wound was open, others opened, too. That night she had started picking on James about how he hadn't gone to dinner at Charles and Joanna's apartment in the city a few nights before. They wanted to show off their Christmas tree, but James had blown them off entirely. "Charles wanted you to come," Sylvie harped. "You could have at least sent him an e-mail saying you weren't coming instead of letting me make the excuse for you."

"I was stuck in meetings until nine that night," he answered. By this time, they were getting out of the car, walking up Geoff's driveway. "What was I supposed to do? *Not* work?"

"Why can't you be kinder to Charles?" Sylvie blurted out. "You know how sensitive he is."

"Sylvie . . ." James raised his hands in protest. "Jesus."

They had reached the door by then. Melinda took their coats just as she had today. As soon as they got away from the throng of guests,

Sylvie picked up on the thread of the fight. "Why don't you care about Charles?" she hissed. "Why don't you ever try?"

"Of course I try," James answered tightly. And then after a moment's thought, "Maybe he doesn't see it. Maybe *you* don't see it. It's like everyone's minds were made up about me and him a long time ago."

Sylvie stepped back. "How can you turn this around and make it his fault? How can you act so blameless about everything?"

James's eyes narrowed, obviously sensing what was coming next. "Jesus," he whispered. "Don't turn this into an argument about *that*."

"How can I not?" she cried. The faceless woman, tall and sophisticated, the kind that wore bold, modern jewelry, pulsed in Sylvie's mind, suddenly present. "How can I not make *everything* an argument about that?"

James's gaze fell to the ring on Sylvie's right hand. *That's why,* his look said. "I'm so tired, Sylvie," he whimpered. "I don't want to be here."

She turned away from him, hurt. Never in a million years did she imagine this would happen to her. Other people, yes. Her mother, yes. But her mother deserved it. Why had James turned to this woman years ago? Because of their rift over the kids? From resentment over Sylvie's unquenchable respect for her grandfather? To get back at the Bates-McAllisters because they didn't give him a job? But how could he still be angry about that? He had succeeded in his own right. He had achieved without her family's help. Wasn't that better?

A hand touched her arm now, and Sylvie turned. Martha Wittig, her fellow board member, was putting the last of a canapé into her mouth, delicately wiping her chin. "Long time no see," she joked. She kissed Sylvie on both cheeks. "Did you see their new painting yet?"

Sylvie blinked, feeling light-headed, her emotions whipping around too fast. "No," she murmured.

Martha looped her arm through Sylvie's and guided her to the left. "Melinda's birthday was just a ruse to get us all here and show the thing off, don't you think?" She led her into the grand living room, which had not one but two fireplaces. "It's not *my* taste, of course. And have you noticed how thin Melinda looks? It's not very becoming. Do you think it's because of all the financial trouble they're in? I hear they're short-selling their Florida house."

Sylvie murmured a noncommittal answer and followed Martha to the enormous canvas that Geoff and his wife had bought at a Sotheby's auction a few weeks ago. The painting was dark and muddy, completely unremarkable, but the throng of people in front of it oohed and ahhed as though they were amazed. Sylvie wondered if, once they were safe in their own cars, they would cut it to pieces, wondering aloud why on earth Geoff had paid so much money for something so ugly.

"Oh, Sylvie!" Martha cried. "Here's someone I want to introduce you to!"

She brought forward a small man with a salt-and-pepper beard and barely any hair on the top of his head. The man was shorter than Sylvie, with the compact physique of a man who cycled the roads near her house, the kind who wore tight spandex shirts and pants and always rode in a pack. He wore pleasant, round glasses and a dark red cashmere sweater instead of a jacket.

"This is Michael Tayson," Martha trilled. "Michael, this is Sylvie Bates-McAllister."

Sylvie's body went limp.

"Nice to meet you," the man said, sticking out his hand. His handshake was almost bone crushing. Everything was moving too fast.

"Ah," Sylvie finally managed to say. "I–I didn't know you were coming."

"I apologize for not being at the board meeting," Michael said, finally drawing his hand away. "My son had the flu, and my wife was on call. She's a neurosurgeon."

Sylvie nodded dumbly. A rushing sound was growing louder and louder in her ears.

"But it's good to finally meet you in person," Michael Tayson added. "I've heard a lot of nice things about you."

"Uh-huh." Sylvie couldn't quite control her mouth. Michael's steadiness was unnerving. It seemed as though he knew a delicious secret, perhaps something about Christian Givens and Scott. It also seemed as if he was gazing straight into Sylvie and decoding her motives. He probably knew she'd sought out Warren Givens. He probably even knew what she suspected about Scott's guilt.

"How was the board meeting?" he asked.

"Great," she managed to answer. "We always get a lot of work done."

"Good," Michael Tayson said. "Glad to hear it."

She looked behind him. Martha had drifted into the other room. The only other people left in the study besides the two of them were a couple Sylvie didn't know, standing very close to the art, talking among themselves. A shiver rocketed through her body. All the other sounds of the party melted away. Her heart chugged at her temples.

"How did it go?" she blurted out. "Scott's meeting with the teachers today. I haven't heard from him. I haven't heard from anyone."

Michael Tayson's smile wilted only a fraction. "I don't think . . ."

"I mean, I'm not concerned, of course. I always thought it was a crazy rumor. But . . . still. Was everything all right?"

"Well, I wasn't part of the meeting. The teachers are formulating an opinion and will report to me in a few days."

Formulating an opinion? What was there to formulate? Scott had gone in and confessed to something horrible or he'd shrugged and said he knew nothing. They'd found something on him or they'd absolved him. Did that really require several days of *formulating?*

"You don't even know if the hazing was happening," Sylvie whispered.

"There were bruises on his body," Michael Tayson stated.

"There were?"

He nodded. "And cuts."

She felt as though someone had punched her. "Where?"

"I don't know. I just heard that there were."

"What is the father saying?" she exclaimed. Her heart was beating inhumanly fast. "The boy's father? What does he think?"

Michael Tayson looked alarmed. The question surprised Sylvie, too. "Does the father believe there was hazing?" Her voice rose higher and higher.

"I can't . . ." He sighed, defeated, and looked toward the large windows that opened out to Geoff's big backyard. "I'm not really sure this is the place to talk about it, Mrs. Bates-McAllister. Maybe we should meet in my office in a few days, when the opinion comes in. This just doesn't seem the right . . ."

"Whatever you know, just say it," Sylvie insisted. "I want to know what's going on. This has been terrible for me."

Michael Tayson's hands formed a steeple. "Look. I don't know anything about the father. I don't know what happened in the meeting. I've turned this over to an independent third party for just these reasons, because I'm too close to it, because the board is too close to it. What I do know is that some of your colleagues on the board are quite concerned. They're afraid this is going to blow up into something much bigger, and they want to extricate themselves from it as much as they can."

A lock of hair fell in Sylvie's eyes, but she was too stunned to brush it away. "The board members know? How?"

He pursed his lips and looked down. *He* had told them.

"But you . . . you said you wouldn't say anything," she whispered.

"It's their right to know. And I said I'd keep the board members out of the meeting with your son and the teachers. I never said anything about keeping it from them entirely."

She ran her hand down the length of her face. Her skin felt numb. "Why haven't they said anything to me about it?"

"They are trying to be discreet, I guess."

The way they'd sat around the meeting the other day, acting oblivious to all of it. The way Martha had sifted through Christian's interests, as if she didn't already know plenty about him. The way they'd patted her hand when she said *stop*, acting sympathetic and sensitive. It was crueler than if they had come right out and told her what they'd heard and that they felt uncomfortable. And the insidious way Martha *fed* her to Michael Tayson just now! Had they been planning an intervention all along?

"Well!" she blurted.

Michael Tayson cleared his throat. "I told you, this isn't the best place to talk about this. But they've come to me with their concerns. They're all worried about this—how this could make the school look, especially since Scott is your son. We have it contained, but as I said, if the autopsy comes back conclusive, if someone else confirms the story about the hazing, if the father takes this to lawyers or to the press, whatever—well, we may need to make some preemptive changes. You want to protect the school's reputation, don't you? This is the school your grandfather re-founded, for God's sake."

"What are you getting at?" she cried.

He stroked his tie. "Your friends would never ask this of you. I'm sure they'll stand by you. But they also defer to me, to do what's best for the school. No one would vote you out, of course, but . . ."

Sylvie laughed. "Are you suggesting I resign?"

A muscle in his cheek twitched.

Sylvie let out a small, ragged breath. "Oh." She pressed her hands together. It felt like she had no nerve endings on her palms—she couldn't feel anything. "Oh. Well."

He shifted his weight, inspecting her carefully. His nostrils flared in and out slowly, calmly. "They're willing to give you a settlement. Your family has been such a part of the school, and they want you to know what you mean to us."

Sylvie widened her eyes. "You're going to *pay me* to leave?"

"Unless, of course, you find a way to resolve this yourself."

"Resolve this myself? How do you expect me to do that?"

He leaned back on his heels. "From what I hear, that's how Swithin works. Plenty of unsavory things are done on behalf of the school's reputation. This isn't the first time your family has had . . . issues. This isn't the first time we've had to do a bit of reconnaissance on some assaults on your family's character."

She looked away. *Your grandfather wasn't the messiah you think he was*, she heard her mother say. She wanted to smack Michael Tayson. She wanted to take his glasses off his squashed little face and smash them between her palms. "So people said things about my grandfather," she spat through her teeth. "What you forget is what he did for Swithin. It wouldn't *be* here if it wasn't for him. Nothing would be here—certainly not *you*. You wouldn't have a job."

Tayson cleared his throat. His cheeks bulged slightly, as if he'd swallowed something unpleasant. "No. I wasn't talking about that."

"What *are* you talking about?"

"Your husband," he stated, uncertainly. "And . . . well, the things people said about the girl."

She stared at him. *The girl.* In the other room someone let out a raucous laugh.

Michael Tayson paled. He placed a palm on his chest. "Oh dear, the board said you were aware of it. They said you knew that they struggled to keep it hushed up. It was a while ago, after all."

Sylvie pressed her hands to the side of her face. "Of course I'm aware," she sputtered, for she could never give him the satisfaction of knowing something she didn't. Her mind scrambled for footing where there was none. What had the board kept from her? What didn't she know? Who was *the girl?*

When she looked at Michael, there was a sickening smile on his face. He *knew* she didn't know. He knew every inch of her ignorance.

People swam past, their smiles craggy and warped. A woman's perfume smelled like sewage to Sylvie. Sylvie fought to remain on her feet. *The girl.* She was waiting for Michael Tayson to relax and touch her arm and tell her that, "Jesus, Mrs. Bates-McAllister, I'm *kidding.* I'm kidding about all of it, about Scott, about the hazing, about you having to leave. They would never do that to you, it's *you*, your family is practically *royalty*, this has nothing to do with you, and it's not even true, anyway. And goodness, the thing with the girl—I'm sorry. There was never a girl. It was a joke, but a mean one. Maybe too mean."

It was coming, wasn't it? It was coming. It had to be.

But Michael Tayson didn't move. His lips were still small, his forehead was still creased, his face was still so serious. Sylvie's throat felt stuffed with cotton. She thought of the pictures her grandfather had showed her of the school after the fire, the black scaffolding, the pile of rubble that remained. *Please don't let me go,* Sylvie had imagined the school crying out, its face crumbling away. *Please help me.*

Michael Tayson's eyes were now full of pity. "I really didn't want to talk about this here. I didn't want to ruin this night. But you should know what they're saying. You would probably have the same concerns if you were in their position, don't you think?" He patted her arm. "Maybe we won't even have to face any of this. Let's hope it just . . . goes away. We're all on your side, Sylvie."

Sylvie. How fast the power could shift. He hadn't even asked, *May I call you Sylvie, Mrs. Bates-McAllister?* He just went ahead and called her whatever he wanted.

It took every ounce of self-control to smile. She took a deep breath and reached for her cocktail, which she'd set on a small table next to the new painting. Three-quarters of the drink was left; it burned her throat going down. She wanted more; her stomach felt like a vast, bottomless bowl.

Michael Tayson watched her, his eyes wide. He was looking at her in that wary way all men looked at unpredictable, emotional women. The same way her father looked at her mother before she said something brash and irrational, the same way James looked at Sylvie in this very house the night before he died, saying, *Don't turn this into an argument about that.*

The girl. It had been a *girl?* A teacher? A *student?* The word meant too many things.

Tayson's ice clinked in his empty glass. If it were her grandfather standing here in Sylvie's place, Sylvie knew just what he would do. Even if someone had just told him all this, he'd take his guest's glass and say, *Can I refresh that for you?* In her grandfather's world, etiquette won the day. Manners were worth their weight in gold.

But Sylvie wasn't her grandfather. She set her empty glass on the sideboard where it would leave a watermark. Then she turned around abruptly and walked out without even saying good-bye.

fifteen

Tuesday morning dawned misty and warm. There were geese on Charles's back lawn, a whole flock of them. He walked around every room of the house, looking at their furniture. He gazed across the street at the silent, identical houses. He noted the property line between his house and his neighbor's, so clearly defined by a crisp line of cut grass on their side, a scruffy tuft of longer grass on his. Then he got into his car.

His heart beat uncomfortably in his throat the whole drive down the turnpike. The seat belt cut into his chest. When he got to the exit, he nearly drove into a lane of oncoming traffic.

He arrived at the Back to the Land site too early, so he pulled into a gas station to kill some time. He went in, bought a cup of coffee, and used the bathroom, shaking out the nerves in his hands. He walked outside again and leaned against his car's hood, looking around. It was just farmland out here. The day was still, sober—a sickly gray. A crow cawed from a tree; a piece of loose metal fence flapped. Across the street was another gas station, much older, all the pumps vacant. A string of frayed, faded flags hung from the eaves of the little mini-mart, probably once announcing a grand opening. After a few moments of staring, Charles's body felt shaky. It was the coffee, probably the wrong thing for him right now. He swirled it in the cup, feeling the liquid slosh back and forth against the sides, and then threw it into a trash can.

The turn to Back to the Land was a pitted gravel road. After about a mile, he came upon a log cabin. It was the visitor's lodge—he knew from all the pamphlets he'd looked through. Residents lived much farther inside the woods, secluded from the highway.

His was the only car in the lot, but there was a light on inside the cabin. Charles wondered how the person inside had gotten here. *Had he or she walked?* Bronwyn was supposed to meet him here, too; *would she also walk?* He gazed into the thick woods. The ground looked soggy and half frozen. The only things he could see in the distance were more trees.

The little *beep* of his car alarm activating was jarring in the stillness. He crunched up the crude gravel path and knocked on the door. "It's open," a woman called. Charles's heart thudded. When he opened the door, he saw a large, older woman at a desk, staring at a computer screen. A phone sat next to her, a fax machine next to that. A fluorescent light shone above her head. Off in the cabin's corner was a bathroom, the door propped slightly open.

Charles breathed out. It was a relief to see technology, as if he'd been away from it for years.

The woman looked up at him. She had short gray hair, downslanted gray eyes, and a straight mouth. "Hi?"

"I'm from Fischer Editorial," Charles said. "We're producing your promotional materials. I'm supposed to meet someone here for an interview. Bronwyn . . . Pembroke. But I'm early."

The woman plucked a Kleenex from a box on the desk and shook her head. "You didn't get her message?"

"Message?"

"She said she was going to call. She wanted to meet you at nine, not ten. Really killed her, having to come down here and use the phone. But it was important she keep her doctor's appointment today. He's making a house call, a last-minute thing."

Charles blinked. He hadn't checked his office voice mail before he left last night; she must have left a message there. Only, if she had, she would have heard his name on his outgoing voice mail message. *This is Charles Bates-McAllister; I'm not available,* et cetera. She might not have left a message at all.

"She was here at nine," the woman went on, turning back to her work. "But she only left a few minutes ago. You might still be able to catch her."

Charles's heart lurched again. So she *had* come. "Which way did she go?"

The woman pointed out the window. "Through those trees there. You'll probably see her. She's not walking too quickly these days, because of how far along she is."

Charles bolted out the door and into the woods, slogging through the soft, murky earth. Far off in the distance, he smelled wood smoke. And then he heard a twig snap. A footstep. He stopped and quieted his breathing. There it was again, ahead of him. He ran a few steps and saw a figure walking quickly down a ravine.

She had dark hair and that same sharp profile. She wore a simple gray dress, a black coat, and black loafers. And she was hugely pregnant. He sucked in his breath, stunned.

"Bronwyn," he called out. It emerged from his lips as not much more than a croak. "Bronwyn," he said, louder.

She stopped and turned and shaded her eyes, looking up the hill.

Charles raised a hand to his mouth. He'd tried to prepare himself for this, for it really being *her*, but his heart still raced, his knees still trembled. Her skin was blotchy, her hair slick. There were rafts of pimples on her chin and her forehead, and her lips were cracked and dry. She met his eyes, first unknowingly, and then her eyebrows sank together. He held up one hand. She squinted, taking a few steps backward.

"Bronwyn," he said, walking down the ravine. The wet ground seeped through his thin loafers, sending a shiver up his spine.

He stopped a few feet from her. Bronwyn's face had gone white. She dropped her hand from her forehead. "Charles?"

He tried to smile. She was now staring at him almost angrily, as if he'd caught her doing something terrible.

"What are you doing here?" she demanded. She placed her hands over her stomach. The gesture seemed vaguely protective.

"I'm the . . . writer. Working on the . . . the magazine. I'm the one interviewing you."

"*You?*"

"I didn't know it would be you. Mirabelle didn't tell me who I was meeting with. But when I saw you here, I . . ."

The words tumbled out of him unwittingly. He didn't know if lying was the right way to play this, but admitting that he'd known seemed so insidious.

Bronwyn blinked. Her eyes were cold and black. Uncomfortable. She picked at her lips with her pinkie finger, a gesture Charles recalled from when they were dating. It was like an old smell, wafting back to him. "They said the writer's name was Charles," she said in a faraway voice. "They didn't give a last name. I didn't ask."

They stood still for a long time. There were no sounds. Charles's gaze fell to her swollen stomach. Her thin, dirt-colored shoes looked as if they were made out of cardboard.

"Do you . . . like this?" He swept his arms around, indicating the woods, the solitude.

Bronwyn nodded meekly. "Yes."

"Is it like . . . camping?"

"A little."

"And you're going to have a baby here?"

"Yes."

"Do you think that's wise?"

"Please," she said quietly, pleadingly.

He paused, grateful she'd stopped him.

She took a breath, composed herself. "This is a little unexpected, Charles."

He placed his hand against a tree trunk, digging his nails into the bark. Her discomfort didn't surprise him. He'd had time to prepare for this, time to gather his emotions, but he would have responded the same way if the situation were reversed, if she had ambushed him. "I'm sorry," he said. "I'll see if I can get another writer to do this. I'll see if we can reschedule."

Bronwyn nodded.

"I mean, it isn't that I don't *want* to see you," he rushed on. "I just . . . I want to do what's best for the magazine."

"The magazine," she repeated.

Behind them, sticks crackled. Charles turned. The woman from the office was standing at the top of the hill. "Winnie?" she called. "You okay?"

"Fine, Laurel," Bronwyn called back, her voice halting.

Sara Shepard

Laurel shrugged, remained for another long moment, and then trudged back into the cabin.

"*Winnie?*" Charles asked when she was gone.

Bronwyn blinked back at him.

"I've never heard anyone call you Winnie before."

She jutted her chin away from him, staring at a spindly tree. Nothing had bloomed out here yet. Everything was still bare. "How do you know, Charles? Have you met everyone who's ever spoken to me?"

Charles opened his mouth, and then shut it fast. "I'm sorry," he said. "It's just . . . this is about the last place I expected to see you. When did you move here?"

"A few months ago. I got married. We lived in LA. But then my dad got sick, so we moved back."

"You lived with your dad when you first moved back?"

"No, Leon and I lived here. We made this decision together. Anyway, Dad has lots of people caring for him. Round-the-clock nurses and stuff. He has Alzheimer's."

All the information hurtled at him too quickly. Leon. Only a few months. And her dad had been sick. Why hadn't they lived in her family's big, beautiful house when they moved back? Why had they chosen this instead? His eyes landed on her stomach again. Her clumsy, handmade dress. One of her fingernails was black.

"I like this," Bronwyn said simply, as if sensing his observations. "I like what I'm doing. I'm happy."

"But you could have been so many things," he blurted out. He had to say it; there was no way he was leaving without saying it. "You could have *become* so much."

She laced her hands over her belly. "What's that supposed to mean?"

"I just mean . . . well, what do your parents think about this?"

"Well, my dad doesn't have much of a grasp on it. And my mom and I don't speak."

"Because of this?"

She paused on him for a long time, as if it was the stupidest question he could ask. "No, Charles. Not because of this. We haven't spoken for a long time."

The tip of her nose was red. He knew, from years of being with her—standing with her out in the cold weather, talking, kissing, arguing, promising things to each other—that her nose wasn't red right now because of the cold. It was because she was upset. He was upsetting her. She led an insulated, pleasant life, and here he was, tramping on it, cheapening it.

"I'll call my boss," he said wearily. "I'm not going to write the story. It's a conflict of interest. They'll send someone else."

"Okay." She pushed a greasy hank of hair out of her face. "Are you going to get in trouble for that?"

"It's fine." He started back up the hill, trying not to trip.

"I heard about your father," she called after him.

Charles stopped but didn't turn. He could just make out the top of his car up the hill. "How?" he asked.

"Laurel? In the office? She sometimes buys the *Inquirer* at the gas station. I was in the office one day, leafing through a paper, and there was your dad's picture."

"Huh."

"But I try not to use the phone, which is why I didn't call. Maybe I should have. I try to be . . . pure about all this, I guess."

Charles gritted his teeth. If Bronwyn were truly pure about all this, she wouldn't have read the newspaper at all. Asceticism was just an excuse. She simply wanted nothing to do with him.

There were crackling noises behind him. It sounded as if Bronwyn was shifting her feet in the dirt. "How did it happen?" she asked.

He turned back to her. "Brain aneurysm," he managed, stiffly. "Hit him from out of nowhere. They tried surgery, but it didn't work. He died on the table."

"Oh my."

"I mean, it would've been worse if he'd lived. He had brain damage. He wouldn't have been able to work or walk or even talk. He signed papers ahead of time, asking not to be kept alive by machines. I don't begrudge him the decision."

Bronwyn nodded. "I'm so sorry."

Charles shrugged. He arched his back and stared at the sky through the emaciated trees. The sun was nowhere to be found. And the air, he noticed, smelled swampy and rotted, like an overflowing septic system.

"And you're married, too," she said.

Joanna came to his mind, fuzzy and far away. "Yeah."

"How long?"

"Nearly a year."

"Do I know her?"

He shook his head, and she smiled, probably figuring as much. He thought about Joanna. She was probably with her mother right now. He thought about the clumsy argument they'd had about Bronwyn, how he'd pretended she wasn't on his mind. He'd kept this interview from her, twisting it around so that it felt like she was making the decision that he come here for him. His stomach roiled with shame.

"I lied," he said.

Bronwyn raised her head. "I'm sorry?"

"I–I knew it was you," he stammered. "I saw your picture in the brochure. And Mirabelle, the woman who came to talk to our firm, she saw me looking and then started talking you up and from there I couldn't stop it. We were writing about you, and that was final—and *I* was going to be the writer. I thought maybe Mirabelle would tell you my name and you'd be okay with it. And at the same time, I didn't want to call and tell you, for fear you'd say no. I thought if you knew it was me coming, you wouldn't show up."

Bronwyn's jaw trembled. "I might not have."

There it was, out in the open. He balled up his fists, feeling something inside him break. "Do you hate me that much? Am I really that terrible? Is what I said why you're doing . . . this?"

Her forehead furrowed. "What are you talking about?"

"I just . . . I just need you to tell me. I need to know if *I* changed you, somehow, saying those awful things I did. Then I'll go."

When Bronwyn still looked puzzled, he took another breath. "Scott has been accused of this . . . thing," he said, even though he hadn't planned to tell her this. It was the *last* thing he'd planned to tell her. "He coaches wrestling now. At Swithin. And he has been accused of something with the boys he coaches. They're saying he might've incited . . . violence . . . among them. Hazing, I guess. Like, he might've encouraged it. And I can't stop thinking that there's some connection between that and what I said that day—the day of the banquet. The last day you and I . . ."

He brushed his hand across his forehead, feeling blown off course. "I deserved Scott hitting me that day for what I said, but maybe he thinks that's a permissible way to handle things—beating up people gets them to listen and change. But I need you to tell me if that's why you left me, if that's why you stopped speaking to me. Because of what

I said. Because you sided with Scott. Because you thought I deserved getting my ass kicked, too. And I want to know if you think that whatever Scott's done now, I'm partly responsible for. I just need to know what you think. I need you to say it out loud."

He felt winded, saying all this. His chest felt like it was on fire.

It took a long time for Bronwyn to speak. "If you think this is funny, it's not."

He dared to look at her face. It was red. She was shaking. "This is a joke," she stated. "Right?"

"No . . ."

"So I'm supposed to believe you just . . . blocked it out."

"Blocked what out?"

"I'm supposed to believe you didn't see it? Or you didn't hear? Or that he didn't tell you?"

"What are you talking about?"

"I'm supposed to believe you really buy that bullshit about Scott? That you didn't come down here to ask me the obvious questions?"

He frowned. "Those *are* my obvious questions."

"I get it, of course," she went on, ignoring him. "I could see you'd want answers right now. But don't play dumb with me about the rumors, Charles. I know you know."

"Rumors?"

She sniffed. "Seriously. Just stop it."

"Huh?"

She lowered her chin and stared at him hard. "You really don't know?"

He shook his head. A crow cawed. Far off, very, very far off, a trunk honked its horn. "Know what?"

"How could you not know?" Bronwyn said.

He shrugged, helpless. His voice started to quiver. "You're freaking me out."

She sighed. "For God's sake, Charles. Do you really think you're the only one who blurts out awful things when they're frustrated or annoyed? You think you're the only one who picks on his younger brother? Who suffers from sibling rivalry? Cut yourself some slack. Sibling rivalry is everywhere. It's even here in the woods. You're not the only one. There's more in this world than just your tiny little life."

"I . . ."

Bronwyn gazed at him warily, her lips parted. "Whatever this thing is that Scott is implicated in, you really think it's because of what you said? Do you really think you have that much power over people's destinies or identities, Charles? And do you really think your brother is that impressionable? Or that *insane?*"

Charles shrugged one shoulder, about to respond, but Bronwyn interrupted, holding up a pointer finger. "Is it possible you want Scott to be guilty, so you can finally be held responsible for the way you felt about him? You *want* to find out something bad about him, don't you? Something that incriminates him. Because that would incriminate you, too. So you're finally rightfully punished."

Charles could feel the sweat under his arms.

She looked at him, her eyes dimming. "I hid from you."

"I know," he said. "Because of what I said to Scott."

"No." She said it loudly, almost a shout. "Not because of what you said to Scott. Jesus. Because of what I thought you *knew.* It's why I told you we shouldn't see each other anymore, Charles. And it's why I cut off ties with all our other friends, too. I thought you saw it, and I figured you'd misunderstand. I thought you'd tell all our friends, too, and they'd side with you."

He started to tremble. "What are you talking about?"

She breathed heavily, and then shook her head. "Forget it."

"Bronwyn . . ."

"Seriously. Let it go." She turned around clumsily, heading away from him. "I didn't leave you because of anything you said. Just . . . that should be enough, right?"

"But . . ."

"It was nice seeing you, Charles. I have to go—I have a doctor's appointment soon. But I wish you all the best. Please tell Mirabelle it's my fault, okay? So they don't blame you. There are plenty of other people here who'd be happy to do an interview. Everyone's great."

A flame rippled through him. "No. You can't leave."

She kept going. He ran down the ravine and caught her cold, fleshy arm. She whirled around, fear flashing across her face. "What aren't you telling me?" Charles demanded.

She shivered. "You don't want to know."

"I do."

Bronwyn wrenched her neck to the side. When she turned her face toward him again, he saw her eyes were glistening. "This is why I never wanted us to run into each other. Because I knew we'd get to this point. I knew it would come up."

"What? What happened?"

She stepped away and lowered her head. Birds sang in the tress. The sun passed behind a cloud, then reemerged.

"I got into a fight with my parents," she said. "They pushed me to be the *best* at everything, and they wouldn't settle if I came in second. It was so easy for them, and they assumed it was easy for me, too. They thought it was what I wanted. So one day, I had this fight with my dad about how he wanted me to go into medicine. I didn't want to, but he said I had to."

Charles frowned. "I thought you wanted to go to medical school. That was all you ever talked about."

Bronwyn stared at him pleadingly. "I didn't, Charles. I never wanted to. I was just . . . his mouthpiece. But that's beside the point. I drove over to your house. Only you were somewhere else . . . doing something with your mom in the basement maybe. But I didn't feel like going to the basement. I didn't feel like talking to your mom. So I sat at the table and waited. And while I was waiting he came in and he just . . . he really *looked* at me. Me, *Bronwyn*. No one else did. Not even you, Charles. I'm sorry but not even you. He asked what was wrong, and it all just poured out of me. And . . . it felt like he really got it."

She paused and took a shaky breath. "We talked, sometimes, after that. Most of the talks weren't about anything important, but we struck up a friendship. He opened up to me, too. He even bought me a Christmas present that last year we were in school, but I said I couldn't accept it—I didn't know how I would explain it. I couldn't tell you because I thought it would just make you uncomfortable. I knew you wouldn't understand."

Charles gaped at her, scrambling to keep up with what she was telling him.

"One time not long before that banquet, we were talking and he leaned in and hugged me. But there was someone in the next room. Someone saw us. I knew in that moment it was going to be miscon-strued. I tried to do damage control, but it was too late for that. I figured you'd hear about it, too, and you'd assume the same things. I wanted to tell you what was going on a million times, but I thought it would hurt you. You guys didn't get along, and there I was, coming in there and disrupting things, taking away some of that attention for myself . . ."

She paused again, shuffling her feet in the slushy ground. "The day of the banquet, I told him that our friendship had to end. But it was hard, I didn't want it to. He didn't want it to either. I didn't mean to, but I leaned over and kissed him. But then you burst into the house, Charles, and I thought you saw us. I *know* some people saw. I thought we were alone, but a group of people came in all of a sudden. Board members, other kids, you. And then you were screaming at Scott, and he pushed you down on the ground and . . . I don't know. I thought it was all a symptom of what you saw. And so I ended it with you. I figured you wanted me to. You *acted* like you did when I told you, just nodding, not even asking why. I didn't blame you for hating me. I didn't blame you for not understanding. I was taking away what was yours."

Charles's head pounded. What she had said began to take shape. He thought about how she always tried to draw Scott in—on the patio, in the halls at school. Sometimes she'd disappear upstairs when she came over to the house for dinner. He'd assumed she was in the bathroom, freshening her makeup, carefully washing her hands . . . but maybe not.

He thought about how Scott hovered over their table at the banquet, staring right at Bronwyn. And when Charles had gone inside after Scott and found him in the laundry room, it had seemed like another person had been in with him moments before. Maybe he'd just missed Scott and Bronwyn's maudlin good-bye. His stomach turned.

"Why?" he whispered.

She blinked. "I know it makes no sense. But it did, back then. It really did."

He stared at her, disgusted. "How could a clandestine relationship with my brother make *sense*?"

Bronwyn blinked rapidly a few times. "Your brother?" she whispered. "Charles, no. *No*. It wasn't Scott."

Charles tilted his head.

"Scott was the one that *saw* us hugging a week before the banquet. He was the one who . . . who read it all wrong." She looked down. "I tried to explain it to him a few times, but he wouldn't listen. He called me terrible names."

Charles's mouth felt dry. "If it wasn't Scott you were with, then . . . who?"

Bronwyn lowered her eyes, ashamed. Charles stepped back, daring to consider the only other possibility it could be. The only other *him*. "*What?*"

She let out a small, animal-like noise.

"You felt like you could . . . *talk* to him?"

"Yes. Kind of."

"What the hell did you talk about?"

"I don't know. School. Pressure. College. My future. The weather."

He clapped his hands on his head. "Why didn't you talk about any of this with *your* parents?"

"You know my parents, Charles. You know you can't talk to them like that."

But that was the thing—Charles didn't know Bronwyn's parents, not really, not intimately. Just as she wasn't supposed to know *his* parents. "I'm supposed to believe this?" he sputtered. "He wasn't . . . *touchy-feely*. He wasn't a *talker*. I'm supposed to believe that you two just had nice little conversations and that there wasn't anything more to it?"

"Charles, I'm sorry. This is why I didn't want to get into it with you. I knew you'd jump to conclusions. Who wouldn't? That's why I ended it. That's why I got out of the picture. I thought you knew already and we would never get past it."

Charles rubbed his eyes. When he took his hands away, Bronwyn was still there, huddled and small. "I still don't understand why you picked *him*."

"He listened. I think . . . well, we both felt out of place, maybe. We both felt a funny kind of angst that sort of . . . matched up."

"Don't act like you know him. Don't talk about his *angst*."

"I'm so sorry," she whispered. "People saw us at the banquet, though, including my mother. She was horrified. Of course she told my father, and my family practically disowned me. They got me out of this area as best they could. Sent me away to Europe every summer. Made sure I was never around your family ever again. Not that it was difficult. You made no effort to contact me."

"I never knew any of this," Charles murmured. "Lots of people saw, but I never had any idea."

"Well, I think my father did a pretty good job keeping it a secret."

"Jesus."

She wrung her hands. After a while she said, "I should have told you a long time ago. But I didn't want to hurt you. In a way, I knew this would feel like more of a betrayal than if it had been . . . sexual. But he told me things about you, Charles. Good things. Do you want me to tell you what he said?"

"No," he shouted. "Absolutely not."

"Okay, okay."

"So did you talk to him again? After the banquet?"

"I saw him only once, kind of recently. It was right when I came back home, a few days before Leon and I moved out to the woods. I ran into him at the mall. When he saw me, his face went white, like he'd seen a ghost. We talked for just a moment before he made an excuse to get away."

"What were you doing at a mall? I thought you were supposed to renounce your possessions."

She sank heavily into one hip. "It wasn't a prearranged thing, Charles. We really met by accident."

He struggled for a breath. "So what did he get you?"

"Sorry?"

"You said he got you a Christmas present our senior year. Did you open it? Do you know what it was?"

She lowered her eyes. "It was a bracelet."

"*Jesus.*"

"No, it wasn't like that. It was . . . sweet." She cupped her hands around her big belly. "Do you know that my parents never got us Christmas gifts? They sent us on *experiences.* They arranged meetings for us with dignitaries and film directors. Yes, I realize I'm being an ungrateful bitch by saying that sometimes that wasn't enough, but sometimes, it *wasn't.* It wasn't what I asked for. Often, it didn't even suit my interests. My parents were so determined that they knew what was right for me, Charles, but you know what? That bracelet was what was right for me. It was picked out for *me.*"

"Am I supposed to feel sorry for you?"

"No, Charles. I know how this sounds. I just . . ."

"Why did I never know this?" he interrupted. "We were together for three years. Why didn't you ever say anything?"

She pressed her lips together, holding in a sob. "It's wasn't something I could really explain. I'm sorry."

He bent over at the waist. Horrible images sifted into his mind. He imagined Bronwyn and his father leaning close in the hallway of his

childhood home, having heart-to-hearts. He pictured his father picking out a bracelet for her, asking the salesclerk to wrap it, presenting it
to her in a stolen moment. He saw Bronwyn telling him that this had
to end, that people wouldn't understand. He tried to envision a look
of turmoil on his father's face, but that was just the thing—he *couldn't*.
He couldn't fathom his father having such deep, powerful, *fatherly*
feelings for anyone, not even Scott. Bronwyn was right—it would have
been easier to swallow this if it had been an advance from a dirty old
man, a sick little grope in a hallway, a forced kiss in the laundry room.
But *this*, something rich, complex, and mature, was unbearable.

The sun suddenly felt bright and sharp, revealing way too much.
He rubbed his hands together. They were still freezing, even though
he was wearing gloves.

Something struck him. He wheeled around at Bronwyn. "How
did you know I was married?"

She blinked, caught off guard. "I . . ."

"I have gloves on. You can't see my fingers. You couldn't see a ring.
Did you just guess?"

She lowered her shoulders. "I called your house yesterday. I didn't
realize it was your house number, but I think your office sent me that
instead of your work number. Your wife answered. I only just put two
and two together now."

"Did you tell her your name?"

"I think I did. Then we got cut off."

Pain shot through his stomach. "I have to go."

"Charles?"

"I have to *go*."

He fumbled blindly up the hill, running so hard for his car that
he couldn't quite stop himself when he reached it, crashing into the

back bumper hard with his hip. He wrenched the door open, smacking it against a tree trunk, not even bothering to check if he'd done any damage.

When he turned the engine on, the radio blared loud through the speakers. He threw the car into reverse and peeled away from the cabin. It felt good to be moving. When he looked in the rearview mirror, he saw that Bronwyn had climbed the hill and was now standing on the edge of the gulley, watching him. By the time he got to the stop sign, three-tenths of a mile away in a perfectly straight, as-the-crow-flies line, he could still see her shape, but she looked featureless and anonymous. He could pretend she was merely some strange, pregnant, country woman. Someone he knew nothing about.

sixteen

Catherine's biopsy had been scheduled for 8 a.m., but because of a few emergencies, they hadn't gotten to her until almost noon. Joanna and Scott sat in an open waiting room, surrounded by other people, and Scott passed the time by quietly making fun of them all. There was Hard Boiled, the man with the bad combover, strands of hair growing just above his ear swept across his entire bald, egg-shaped head. There was Aggressive Word Finder, attacking the puzzle with her pen, making little tears in the oatmeal-colored page. There was an obese woman in an American flag sweatshirt; her ankles were so swollen that Scott burst out laughing every time he looked at her. He made up names for the doctors and nurses based on characters from old cartoons: the hunchbacked, sour-faced nurse was Ram Man; the butch, broad-shouldered woman doctor was She-Ra; and the emaciated surgeon was, of course, Skeletor.

Joanna didn't want to laugh. She still felt prickly about their talk last night, all she felt she'd revealed to Scott. Part of her wanted him to go home. Another part wanted him here, sitting next to her, doing exactly what he was doing. She hated that she felt so torn. She hated that she wasn't taking Charles's calls. It felt like things were slipping through her fingers and she was just *letting* them.

Catherine's surgeon, Dr. Nestor, visited Joanna and Scott at 12:30, informing them that Catherine was resting while they waited for the test results. After Catherine had time to nap but before the results came back, they went in to see her. She was in the bed nearest the door, her ash-blonde hair fanned out on the pillow, the white sheets pulled up to her mid-chest. Something about her appeared undone, like an unfinished painting. There were machines next to her, something monitoring blood pressure and pulse, an IV bag hovering over her shoulder. "The operation went well," Joanna told her. "They were able to remove the cyst. You're going to be fine."

Catherine, still slightly woozy from whatever it was that had knocked her out for the biopsy, scowled. "It's not a cyst. It's *something else*. I can feel it in my blood. I feel diseased."

"Mom, you're okay," Joanna reassured her.

"I'm *not*. I can feel something growing."

Joanna bit down hard on her lip and turned, staring at a poster on how to self-administer a breast exam. When she faced her mother again, Catherine was patting Scott's hand. "Honey," she croaked in a faraway voice, "you're such a sweetheart. Thank you for being here."

Scott ducked his head. "It's no trouble."

She looked at Joanna. "You know, if things get messed up with Charles, just marry this one instead."

"Mom." Joanna felt her face flush in horror. *If things get messed up with Charles.* And Joanna, presumably, was the one doing the messing. She shot Scott an apologetic glance. "Sorry, she's looped from the drugs."

Catherine shook her head. "No I'm not. It's obvious Scott's in love with you. And, honey, you'd still get what you wanted. He's still a Bates-McAllister."

Joanna bristled. *He's still a Bates-McAllister.* The tips of her fingers throbbed. "What are you talking about?" she said quietly.

Catherine's face grew more lucid. She gave Joanna a clever look, then turned to Scott. "She wanted the Bates-McAllisters from the very start, and she got one. I was floored when she told me she and Charles were dating. But she got what she wanted."

So this *was* where she was going. Joanna couldn't breathe. The room instantly became very, very silent. She could feel Scott's eyes on her.

Catherine turned to Scott. "She collected photos of your mom and you boys since she was about eleven years old, you see," she said. "Saved tons of them. Loved your fairy-tale life."

"Mom!" Joanna tried to laugh. Catherine's voice wasn't laced with nastiness; it didn't seem like she had an insidious, ulterior motive for telling Scott this. Maybe Catherine just thought it was a funny story, an amusing little anecdote about Joanna as a girl. Only, it *wasn't*. Of course it wasn't.

Now Scott was staring at Joanna, a befuddled expression on his face. He turned back to Catherine. "A scrapbook, did you say?"

"Uh-huh," Catherine said. "Loved pictures of you all going to parties and benefits. Kept every single one. It was her little dream, to be part of your family."

Scott's gaze swept back to Joanna. He was probably connecting what Catherine was saying with what Joanna had told him last night, her inane story about the Kimberton Fair, how she thought it would be one thing and was disappointed when it turned out to be something different. It was her fairy tale to be part of their family, but their family had let her down.

"Mom," Joanna said weakly. She brushed her hair out of her face. "That's not exactly how it happened, and you know it."

Catherine gave her a patronizing look, "Of course it was! You kept a scrapbook. You idolized them. It's okay, honey. You were young."

Joanna pushed her tongue into the back corner of her cheek. Something deep inside her broke. This had to be corrected. "*You* idolized them," she cried. "You were the one who obsessed over them. You were the one who was disappointed about absolutely *everything* in your life and wished you were someone else."

Catherine blew a raspberry. "What are you talking about? I did no such thing."

Joanna blinked at her. "Mom. You wouldn't shut up about Sylvie Bates-McAllister, hoping that, I don't know, you'd become more like her by osmosis."

She snorted. "Now that's just silly."

Joanna couldn't believe it. Her mother was flat-out denying everything she had been, as though Joanna had dreamed it up. "So then I suppose you were *satisfied* with your life? I suppose you were happy with where we lived, and *belongings* didn't matter. The way people thought about you didn't matter. Do I have that right?"

It didn't even sound like her voice, but the voice of someone older, nastier. "And I suppose you didn't have to go to the hospital every week, either?" she continued. "I suppose you didn't drag me there all the time, making me sit in the little ER waiting room thinking you were dead?"

"There's something wrong with me," Catherine insisted.

"No, there isn't!" Joanna moaned. "One of these days, there might be. And one of these days, it's not going to feel so great."

Catherine shrunk into her pillow. Scott swiveled his head back and forth, tennis match–style, watching them. Joanna pivoted away. "Just . . . don't go saying the Bates-McAllisters were my little obsession," she said. "*You* wanted to trade your life in, not me."

The room was still. No one moved. Then Catherine's blood pressure monitor made a loud, angry quack. A figure appeared in the doorway and cleared his throat. Dr. Nestor wore a surgeon's mask around his neck. He glared at Joanna as though he'd heard every scathing thing Joanna had just said.

"Can I have a word with you?" Dr. Nestor asked Joanna.

"What is it?" Catherine struggled to sit up. "Whatever you can tell her, you can tell me."

"Just a moment, Mrs. Farrow," the doctor said, smiling at her. "You just rest."

Joanna trudged into the hall, her skin cold. It felt as if everyone was staring at her. They were in a *hospital*, for God's sake. Among sick people. People who needed to be uplifted, not yelled at. She kept her eyes trained on the shiny white floor, afraid to look at either the doctor or Scott, who had followed them out.

The doctor walked a few doors down and stopped near an empty wheelchair. "We had to do a special type of procedure to locate Catherine's cyst. But we finally found it and had it surgically removed. It's benign."

Joanna breathed out. "Okay. Thanks."

But then the doctor hesitated.

"When we were removing the tumor, we couldn't help but notice how swollen her liver was." He paused to scratch his nose. "We'll do a scan, but we could tell by touch that it was enlarged. Do you know if your mother's on any medication we might not have recorded in her chart?"

"My mother's on all kinds of medication," she answered.

The doctor's eyebrows knitted together. "She didn't give any prescription information when the nurse took her history."

Joanna swallowed hard. The doctor's eyebrows crept even higher. "Is some of this not prescribed?"

She lowered her head, feeling backed into a corner. She wondered if she'd just stepped into something, if Dr. Nestor was secretly an undercover drug enforcement officer here to bust Catherine and her illegal prescription habit. "Yes," she whispered.

"What does she take?"

Joanna shrugged. "I have no idea."

"Tylenol?"

"Well, sure."

"Vitamin supplements?"

Joanna felt her face twisting helplessly. "I mean, she takes all kinds of things. She had drawers full of . . . of everything."

"Cholesterol medicine, like Lipitor? Does she take anything like Phenobarbital? Does she take a lot of antibiotics? Tetracyclines? Nitrofurantoins?"

"She takes antibiotics whenever she gets a cold," Joanna whispered. She said the other medications he mentioned were familiar, too—she'd seen them strewn around the house. She'd seen all kinds of things lying around the house. Whenever she turned around, Catherine was popping something.

Dr. Nestor stretched out his palms, lowered his eyes, and heaved a centering, Zenlike sigh. "Okay. Let's not panic. We're just testing right now. But . . . the liver, you see, it filters the blood. It filters toxins out of the body, excesses of vitamins or high levels of medications. It processes all of that."

"Okay."

He scratched behind his ear, sheepish. "A damaged liver is . . . blocked. It doesn't clean the blood as well. The more you put into your body, the more clogged it gets. You have noticed that your mother is rather yellow, right?"

Joanna stared at him.

"Her skin," Dr. Nestor spelled out. "Her face. The whites of her eyes. You've noticed that, right?"

Joanna felt helpless. "She wears a lot of makeup."

"Has she talked about any pain? Itching? Feeling bloated?"

"She complains about that, sure. She complains about a lot of things."

The doctor stared at her, pursing his lips judgmentally. Joanna's skin prickled with shame and embarrassment. What kind of asshole marches out here and basically implies that her mother has . . . God knows what? Cirrhosis? Hepatitis? And what kind of doctor makes a patient's child feel shitty and irresponsible, as if she should've noticed her mother's yellowness, listened more carefully to her mother's hysterical complaints, or stopped her from popping her unlimited supply of samples? Whatever had happened was clearly all Catherine's doing—but no, Joanna was to blame. Joanna was the criminal, the enabler.

"It's not serious, is it?" Joanna asked. "I mean, she can be cured, can't she?"

"We won't know anything until we get the screens back," the doctor answered sternly. "It could be mild damage. It could be hepatitis or its autoimmune version, which we can control. On the other end of the spectrum, it could require a transplant."

Joanna's jaw locked. Scott's phone started to ring. He quickly patted his pocket and it stopped.

"But again, let's not get ahead of ourselves," Dr. Nestor said quickly. "I'm just preparing you for everything, okay? We're taking good care of her. Let's just hope for the best." He glanced over his shoulder in the direction of Catherine's room. "I didn't mean to overhear, but maybe you shouldn't be fighting right now. It gets her blood pressure up, stresses her out. My apologies if I've overstepped my bounds, but what she needs right now is you and your husband's support."

A whole beat went by. Joanna and Scott looked at one another. Scott opened his mouth but didn't respond. Joanna shook her head and said, "No, he's not . . ."

But the doctor had already turned around and was walking down the hall. Joanna watched him skirt around a woman with a walker. Scott shifted his weight, and then jingled the change in his pockets.

"Well," he said.

Joanna pushed her purse strap higher on her shoulder and started down the hall. Scott followed. He didn't ask if he should, he just lagged next to her, in step. He fiddled with the strings of his hooded sweat-shirt. His shoes were untied, the laces dragging on the floor. Joanna felt that what she'd just said back in the hospital room had brought on her mother's illness in a fast-acting karmic revenge. If there truly was someone above the clouds controlling the whole world, someone with levers and pulleys and gauges, and if he had seen Joanna behaving like this—and even more, if he'd seen that she was here with *Scott*—surely he had delivered the damage into her mother's liver, like a FedEx of disease.

She stopped at her mother's doorway and peered through the por-tal. Catherine was watching the little television fixed to the end of her bed. All at once it was obvious why her mother looked unfinished: they'd taken off all her makeup, all the mascara, eye shadow, blush, lipstick, eyebrow pencil, everything. They'd scrubbed her clean before the surgery, even though they weren't going anywhere near her face.

Why did they have to do that? Why couldn't they have left her as she was?

The most shocking thing of all was that Catherine did indeed look a little yellow. Certainly not sunburst or raincoat or daffodil yellow, but not quite skin-colored, either.

"Goddamn it," Joanna said through her teeth. All the times she'd accompanied her mom to the ER, all the times the doctors had come out and said it was nothing and her mother had protested later that the doctor was a quack. She *felt* like something was wrong, and so reached into her purse and took God-knows-what blue or pink, white or neon green pill. Joanna had wanted to grab Catherine by the shoulders and say *Would you just stop this? Can't you just be happy?*

So now Catherine was *right?* Well, great. She was right. She got her wish.

Joanna turned from the door and walked back down the hall to the waiting room, past the fake fig tree and the ugly triage nurses. Scott followed. "You don't want to go back in?" he asked.

"No." Joanna marched past the vending machines, the check-in desk, and finally out into the cold air.

She turned her cell phone back on and looked at the screen. She had six new messages. They could have been from Charles, but she didn't feel like listening to them. She dropped the phone back in her pocket.

Scott sat down on a wet bench and lit a cigarette. He took off his jacket and arranged it on the seat. She plopped down on it reluctantly, keeping her elbows close to her sides. He offered her his cigarette, but she waved it away.

"You can go if you want," she said stiffly. "I don't want to burden you with this anymore."

"Go where?"

"Back to her house. I have the keys. Or drive back to your house in Pennsylvania."

"What about you? How would you get back?"

"I could take a cab to the train station in Aberdeen."

Scott took a long drag. "Do you *want* me to go back?"

Pressure was building at her temples. She had no idea what she wanted. The wind picked up, running right through her. She shivered.

"Are you cold?" Scott asked. He cycled his shoulders, starting to shrug off his sweatshirt, too. "I can . . ."

"No," Joanna snapped, waving him off. "I'm fine."

"It's not a big deal." He flicked his cigarette and threw the butt into the street.

"I don't want your sweatshirt, okay?"

Scott stopped. "All right, all right." He bent his knees, turning toward her a little. "I'm sorry, Joanna. About this."

She gave him a warning look.

"You don't think this is your fault, do you? Because of what you said to her in there?"

She dug her nails into her palm.

"She practically *forced* you to say that. She wouldn't have stopped until you did. She probably wanted you to say it."

"Just stop it, okay?" she burst out, not able to contain it anymore.

He sat back. "What?"

"Stop being so nice to me," Joanna said.

Scott blinked. "What do you want me to do, laugh?"

"Yes," Joanna said.

"Jesus Christ." Scott crossed his arms over his chest. "What the hell is wrong with you?"

She let her hair fall around her face. He was still watching her, waiting for an answer, maybe even for her to apologize. She looked up, her body trembling. Then she grabbed the sides of his face and pressed her lips to his. His skin was cold. At first his lips were taut, but then he softened and let her in.

It lasted maybe three seconds before he broke away. "Joanna . . ." he said. Something passed over his face. It was this . . . *look*. A sort of empathetic, understanding, pitying look, as if something in his head had said, *Yes, you know why she's doing this, try not to take it too seriously.* He was so fucking wise, all of a sudden.

She jumped up, shaking her head madly back and forth. "I swear to God, just stop it."

He blinked. "Stop *what?*"

"Stop acting so innocent and *concerned*. Charles isn't on a trip, Scott. You *knew* that. And yet you came anyway. Why do you hang out with me, Scott, if you're not trying to undermine me and Charles in some way? I know you two don't get along. I see how you seek me out, preferring to talk to me over your family. You don't think I see that?"

"What are you—"

"And actually," she interrupted, "maybe your instincts are right. Charles is cheating on me right this very second. Guess who with?" She waited a moment and then spread out her arms. "Bronwyn!"

"Bronwyn?" He cocked his head.

She lowered her shoulders. "Jesus! How many Bronwyns do you know? His old girlfriend!"

Scott's mouth drooped. He placed a finger on his bottom lip. There was a thought in front of him, practically in a cartoonlike fluffy balloon. "So . . . I'm not here because you *asked* me to come," he sounded out. "And I don't hang out with you because . . . I *like* you. Because I think you're cool. No, it's because of some . . . power play to break up you and Charles. To piss off my family. That's the kind of person you think I am."

Joanna laughed. "Well . . . *yes*! I *do* think you're that kind of person! It's the *impression* you give everyone! Your mother, your brother, all your friends . . . even this thing with this boy. I mean, you haven't called your mom to tell her what happened in that meeting yesterday. She's called you and called you, I've seen her name come up on your cell phone, and you haven't even bothered to answer. Did you even go? Did it even matter? What am I supposed to think about you, Scott, given what you portray to the world? Yes, you are *exactly* the type of person who would come here to fuck with your brother. That's what you show the world!"

But as soon as the words fell out of Joanna's mouth, she wasn't sure if she could stand behind them. Scott stood up and shoved his hands in his pockets. His lip trembled. "I guess you got me," he said quietly. He jingled his car keys. "I guess you have it all figured out."

An ambulance screamed up the drive, its lights flashing blue and red. It soared past them to the ER entrance. Joanna shivered. Her lips tasted like his, cigarettes and coffee.

He took a few steps, and then whipped back around. He stared at her, his eyes ablaze. "That kid never wanted to wrestle," he said. "But you know what they do with those scholarship kids? They *make* them do a sport. They make them get a certain GPA and do a certain sport every season. Not every kid wants to do a sport, you know."

Joanna blinked, not daring to move.

"He was coughing," Scott said. "This one day I made him work out until he sat down and started crying. The fucking kid started *crying*."

Joanna widened her eyes. "So . . . there *was* hazing?"

Scott raised his arms. "Would it really matter what answer I gave you? Do you really think anyone gives a shit what *I* say? You said it yourself—people have already made up their minds. People have already decided."

"Maybe I'm wrong."

Scott sniffed and gave her a weary look. "The kid was coughing that last day. It was the kind of cough that didn't even sound real. Should I have taken it seriously? Should I have said something to someone about it, 'Gee, this kid sounds like he's got fucking pneumonia? Gee, do you think maybe we should take this kid to a doctor?' Yeah, maybe I should have. But how would that have made the kid's father look? Some shitty father who doesn't even care that his kid's lungs are failing? It was easier to let someone else deal with it. It was easier to just keep my mouth shut and hope this pansy-ass kid who dresses like a fucking hobbit, who yes, got picked on, got picked on plenty, is just doing it for attention." He wiped hair out of his face. "I kept my mouth shut about it. I've kept my mouth shut about a lot of things, Joanna. Most of it hasn't come to much good. And apparently, most of it makes me look like an asshole."

Joanna shifted from foot to foot, stunned. Scott's eyes were wild. His mouth was craggy and crooked, almost like he was about to cry. He didn't look like himself anymore: tough and impenetrable and mysterious. He looked like a little boy.

She swallowed hard. Everything around her had shifted. "Maybe it's easier to be an asshole, though. Same as it is to . . . to dress up like a hobbit instead of like a normal person. It's a way to hide. People don't expect as much from you. You don't have to try. There's less chance of you disappointing anyone."

He snorted. "So you're making excuses for me now? That's a pretty big reversal, Joanna. Maybe I'm an asshole, the whole way down to my core. Just as you originally thought."

"But maybe I *don't* think that," she said quietly.

He pushed the toe of his shoe into a dirty crack in the sidewalk. "By the way, I swiped a bottle of your mom's pills. Pain meds. She had so many, I figured she wouldn't miss one."

She blinked. There was a stony, unreadable look on his face. She thought of what Charles had said last week—all sneaker shops were fronts for meth labs. "You *did?*"

He put his hands on his hips. "No. But you thought I did. At least for a second? You could see me doing it."

A dry, croaking sound emerged from Joanna's lips. "I . . ."

Scott turned back. "I guess everyone does form impressions," he said over his shoulder. "Maybe it's, like, biological or some shit. Maybe people can't help it."

And then he broke away and started across a patch of grass toward the ER entrance. She remained where she was, bewildered as to what had just happened, simply watching him go.

seventeen

When Sylvie woke up, the roads looked icy. But once she was out of the shower, the thermometer James had hung up outside the kitchen window said it had warmed to almost 30 degrees Fahrenheit. After a while, the sun came out and the ice began to melt. Sylvie poured the remains of her coffee down the drain and looked out the window.

Scott's car still wasn't there. She hadn't heard from him yesterday or today, and he hadn't slept at home. She still had no idea what he'd said in the meeting with the teachers or even if he'd gone. Perhaps he was making himself scarce because he was avoiding the conversation. Perhaps he really did have something to feel guilty about. There were bruises on the boy's body, Tayson had said. Scott was running from this as he avoided everything. Though now it kind of was beside the point.

At 7:30, she knew what she wanted to do. By 7:31, she'd changed her mind. People were talking, yes. Parents were worried, yes. This thing was beginning to break out of its hermetic seal. If Christian's father could somehow be kept at bay, it would just . . . fade away. *Unless, of course, you find a way to resolve this yourself*, Michael Tayson had told her.

And there it was. Without saying it outright, he had given Sylvie her orders. *This is your mess, so clean it up. You know how. It's in your genes, after all.*

It was the way things had always worked, she just now realized. Only up until this point, she'd remained outside of all that. She'd left someone else to take care of those types of problems, the few that had come along. While she pretended that they didn't exist.

If she didn't do anything about this, if she stolidly insisted that the hazing was all a ridiculous rumor and that Scott was blameless, Sylvie risked more and more parents coming to Michael Tayson. She risked more kids talking. And worst, she risked the father taking action, the newspapers being called, court cases starting, the school's name being tarnished, admissions dropping for the next year, and who knew what else.

Doing nothing could cause a domino effect.

On the other hand, she could resign. It was another way to cover it up. Her family was, in essence, responsible for his son's death, and her absence—as well as Scott's—might be justice enough. They could settle out of court on an undisclosed but ridiculously high figure and all would be well.

Resigning, however, would show Scott that she believed the rumors wholeheartedly.

For it *was* what she believed. She didn't want to think it was possible, but she was done being naive. It *could* have happened. She knew what it felt like to have so much pent-up anger inside, rage she had no idea what to do with. It broke her heart to finally realize that Scott could have had something to do with it. He was her son, a boy *she had raised*, so what did that say about her?

And she hated the idea of her resignation sending a message to everyone else at Swithin that she, too, figured Scott was guilty. She could imagine them chuckling, drunk with *Schadenfreude*, over the old Bates family finally getting the comeuppance they'd long deserved.

She went upstairs and looked at James's clothes on the bedroom floor, the ones Scott had tried on a few days ago. She hadn't been able to pick them up. *I should have left a long time ago*, Scott had said. He'd smirked when she'd insisted that James was a good man. *Do you really believe that?* But he couldn't *know*. It certainly couldn't be why he'd wanted nothing to do with James all these years. Perhaps Scott suspected infidelity, but why would it matter to him? Scott had been James's chosen one; why would Scott turn away from him and side with his mother?

The year after Sylvie and James were married, James had brought up burial plots. He said he'd reserved spots for the two of them in the private Protestant cemetery a ten-minute drive from their home. Sylvie had blinked, blindsided. All her life, she'd assumed she would be buried with her grandfather and the other Bateses in the little cemetery near the Swithin grounds. "Yes, but it's not Presbyterian," James argued. Sylvie laughed. "*You're* not Presbyterian." "My family is," he said. "Has been for generations. And that's important to me."

This was also a choosing of sides. The idea of being buried next to her grandfather comforted her, she told him. "You're going to be *dead*," James protested, raising his hands. "It's not like it's going to make a difference." "Ha!" she pointed at him, enraged. "If you were truly Presbyterian, you'd believe in heaven! If you think we're just . . . rotting away down there . . . then why do you care where we are?"

"Look, I just don't want to be buried with your family, all right?" James finally spat out. "It's bad enough I have to live here among your grandfather's things. It's bad enough I have to sit at his *desk* when I'm at home, in his old chair, at his old dinner table. It's bad enough that it feels like he's *judging* me every day of my life—can't we be alone in death?"

He had been building up to that outburst, she knew. It had been welling up inside him for a long time, maybe since that first Thanksgiving with her family. He'd expected something from them, but they hadn't delivered. Maybe he'd thought they'd passed him over, deemed him subpar. Whatever it was, his respect for them had withered away until it was only resentment.

A little piece of Sylvie's heart broke loose. He could hate most of her family for all she cared, but her grandfather? Hadn't Sylvie conveyed how important he'd been in her life? Didn't James understand what a good man he was? "Get your own desk, if it means that much to you," she'd growled. "I didn't realize it mattered so much." "I will," James said. And he did. He'd spent almost $10,000 redecorating that office, replacing her grandfather's gorgeous old desk with that hideous glass thing that didn't match the house in the slightest.

Sylvie obsessed over their argument and what it had revealed. It was the same year that she had decided to run for the Swithin board. If she couldn't be buried there in death, she could be remembered there in life. After she was elected, she filled her days with Swithin goings-on. When she found out she was pregnant, she resolved to emphasize to the baby from a very early age what her grandfather meant to this world. If James didn't understand, then she'd make sure the baby did.

When Charles was born, Sylvie didn't let him out of her sight. She practically didn't let James near him. When James held him, she hovered nervously a few feet away. In the middle of the night, if she woke up and found he wasn't in bed beside her, she fought the urge to spring up and search through the house for him. She felt guilty for those moments—what did she think he was doing, corrupting Charles? Whispering nasty things about her grandfather? *He's your husband,* she kept telling herself, but she felt so protective, as though she was the only one who knew what was best for Charles. She told Charles from an early age, probably before he could really comprehend things, that he was going to Swithin, where Mommy went and that his great-grandfather had rebuilt. James never argued, but after a while, he participated less and less.

It was no wonder Charles had grown up so sensitive and overprotected. It explained, too, why James lost interest in Charles and, on a subconscious level, turned to Scott, who was in no way Sylvie's—a clean break from Bates blood. And perhaps it was why he'd momentarily lost interest in Sylvie.

The worst of it was that after James had died, his lawyer discussed his burial wishes with Sylvie, and in James's will, he had stated that wherever Sylvie wanted them buried was fine with him. She was astonished. After all that, James secretly didn't care? It made her feel even more confused. She'd based the entire shape of their life on an issue that didn't even matter to him. And really, so James wasn't crazy about her family! So he had a chip on his shoulder! Why had she fought it so much? Why hadn't she tried harder to understand where he was coming from?

When she'd stood over James's hospital bed before his surgery, watching his heart monitor spike and trough, she'd felt as cold and alone as when she was a new freshman at Swarthmore, her grandfather just having abandoned her. She looked down at James's bruised face. His eyes were taped shut, and there was a tube stuffed down his throat. Who was to say *she* hadn't caused this aneurysm? He'd said he was tired the night before and didn't want to go to the party, but she'd made him. She'd pushed him; she'd hissed at him; she'd worked him up. Who was to say this wasn't her doing? These feelings only compounded after the operation failed and Sylvie found herself standing over James's cold, inert body again, this time with Charles and Scott by her side. *This is your fault*, a voice prodded her. She vowed not to show the boys what she was thinking or feeling, terrified they would know that she had somehow brought this on.

When she thought of standing over her husband's dead body now, it didn't seem quite real. She hadn't gone through the motions one was supposed to go through standing over a loved one; instead, she'd fixated and obsessed and raged about that woman, that nameless woman, sealing herself off from grief. Sometimes she wondered if the moment had ever happened at all—maybe James wasn't dead but just on a trip somewhere, due home any minute.

A little past 8 a.m., Sylvie stood up from the kitchen table. She sat down at her computer in the study and pulled out a piece of stationery from the drawer. The letter should be handwritten, she decided, with a good pen. She thought of a thousand things she wanted to say, but with her pen poised over the paper, very little came out. She wrote a few sentences, changing them some, crossing out words, adding others. She recopied the letter and put it in an envelope. Before sealing it, she reached into her purse and pulled out her checkbook.

By the time Sylvie pulled into the Feverview Dwellings parking lot, it had started to rain through the fog. The weather was as gloomy as Sylvie felt.

The apartment house's double doors were still and closed. The usual dented cars were in the lot. There were a few dilapidated bikes jutting at odd angles in the bike rack, two of them not even locked up. Pink chalk writing was all over the sidewalk. Sylvie's heart lifted at the sight. At least this was something sweet and childlike, but when she got closer, she saw the marks were drawings of anatomically correct women with breasts and wildly curly pubic hair, and men with penises and overly exaggerated testicles.

Sylvie held her umbrella feebly over her head. Every so often she touched her raincoat's inside right pocket, feeling for the envelope. Christian's little shrine was still there, the same soggy pile by the tree. A door to the complex opened, and out walked Warren, the belt of his trench coat flapping, his face paunchy and pale. There were circles under his eyes, as if he hadn't slept. He carried a white mug. Wisps of steam floated out of the top.

It was as if Sylvie had called up Warren beforehand and told him she was coming, though she hadn't. There was no reason he should be outside in this weather; she'd planned on waiting for him for hours. He trudged to the bench nearest the shrine and sat down. One foot constantly tapped, splashing in a mud puddle. Every once in a while he reached into his pocket and jingled loose change. Sylvie imagined her grandfather standing next to her, witnessing this. *What would he say? Would he appreciate this? Would he see this as the only way to save the school?*

Warren Givens looked up and saw her. He smiled. "Nice day."

She stared at him. He seemed serious. "If you like rain."

"I do." He held out his palms to catch a few drops. "Rain makes everything very clean."

She walked closer to him, her heart pounding. When she was right next to him, she took a deep breath. "I need to talk to you."

"Me?" He thumbed his chest.

The wind picked up, making the empty swings in the park across the courtyard sway. It was as if ghost children were swinging on them, pumping their invisible legs. This was it. This was the time to say it. The time to explain—he deserved an explanation, didn't he? She stared at his threadbare sweater, visible under his coat. His nicotine-stained fingers. His mussed hair. The dirty bandage wrapped around his pointer finger.

She closed her eyes for a moment and imagined Swithin's gym after they'd lost a match. It wasn't hard to picture all the boys in there, disappointed and ashamed. They were combinations of their hard-ass fathers, critical mothers, and absent siblings. They were their doting grandfathers and philandering fathers. They were the sum of the family fights, the missed expectations, the parental disappointments, and the genetics that had crossed and created something not quite ideal. It wasn't hard to imagine getting angry, trying to find an outlet for it.

And then she thought of her grandfather, writing check after check. She'd always believed that each and every check—to workers' families, to build an art studio, to buy new sports equipment, to provide scholarships—was charitable. But what if some of the checks were for bribes, cover-ups, influence? It was easier to consider it than she thought. Backed far enough into a corner, it was easy to consider anything.

Unless you find a way to resolve this yourself, Michael Tayson had said. But what would that achieve? She'd glossed over so much, too much. She couldn't do that to this man. It felt wrong to strike some kind of deal, negotiate some kind of compromise.

Warren's head was cocked, patiently waiting. For the past week or two, he'd probably been walking the rooms of his house, wondering how this might have happened, thinking that this was purely his fault. A part of it probably was his fault—all parents were probably at fault, most of them unknowingly so. *We try hard,* she could tell him.

We take precautions. We think we do everything. We think we send our children to the best schools, our husbands to the best doctors. And yet things still happen.

"My husband died," she blurted out. "Two months ago."

"Goodness. I'm very sorry to hear that," he answered, blinking rapidly.

"I'm not sure I even believe it yet," she said. "He could have lived. *Should* have."

Warren ran his tongue over his teeth, his eyes softening. "It's hard," he said. "I'm not going to lie to you about that. And I'm not going to say some stupid thing people think they should say, either, because that just makes it worse."

Her cheeks burned. He shouldn't be comforting her. It should be the other way around. And yet she couldn't stop.

"I don't have many friends," Sylvie said, her head down. "I . . . I *know* a lot of people. But there aren't many people I can really talk to. I find it hard to connect. I've always envied people who find it easy."

A garbage truck two streets over began to back up, making a high-pitched beeping sound. Sylvie brushed hair out of her face. Warren was still staring at her, puzzled. "My last name is Bates-McAllister," she explained.

His eyes darted back and forth. He put a thumb to his chin.

"You might have heard things," she said. "Things that seem terrible. I'm not asking you to believe them or not believe them. I'm not asking you to do anything."

Warren still looked baffled, but she had to keep going. He deserved exactly this, didn't he? To judge for himself. To make up his own mind. To make this right, if that was what he wanted.

The letter was in her hand. All she had to do was pull it out of her pocket. All that money she knew he could use. But all at once, she knew she couldn't. It wouldn't make things right. It wouldn't make things go away or even serve as any kind of salve. Just like the ring James had given her didn't serve as a salve. She had accepted it, yes, because if she didn't, it would've made things worse. And all she'd wanted was to wipe the slate clean. It wasn't possible, though. It wasn't that easy.

"I have to go," she said, pulling her coat around her, the envelope still tucked inside her pocket. She walked backward fast, accidentally sloshing through an enormous mud puddle, the water seeping through her shoes and socks and straight to the bottoms of her feet. But she also suddenly felt free, as if she'd stepped off a cliff and was now floating through the air. Down, down, down, as delicate as a feather.

eighteen

Charles drove for hours. He drove by landmarks he'd known since he was a child: the old stone house where the family of a childhood friend still lived, the old bowling alley near Swithin, abandoned but not yet torn down, an old thatched-roof play-house where he'd taken Bronwyn to see *The Importance of Being Earnest* in high school. It comforted him to see things that were familiar and unchanged, a reminder of a time when life made a lot more sense.

What Bronwyn had just told him rang in his head. There were so many things to consider. His mother didn't know about it, for one thing. She might have guessed that some sort of transgression had occurred—perhaps it was the reason for the big diamond ring that had randomly shown up a few months ago—but she didn't know it was Bronwyn, that was for sure. For she'd asked Charles about her too recently and much too innocently, *So no one has heard from her? Well, I'm sure she's done well for herself.* She'd even gone so far as saying, once, *I always thought Bronwyn was such a sweet girl. I mean, Joanna is sweet too, of course, but as high-school girlfriends go, she was just so . . . pleasant.*

Charles had tried to call Joanna dozens of times, but her phone went straight to voice mail. *Call me*, he said in each message. *Please pick up.* He feared what had happened, what she had assumed.

He reached a familiar intersection and stopped. Charles knew where he wanted to go—only it scared him. Finally, he coasted up the winding driveway. His mother's car wasn't there; nor was Scott's. This relieved him—he couldn't imagine seeing either of them right now. Not like this.

He gripped the steering wheel, staring at the house. Every day his father walked up those slate steps and through the mudroom door. Every day his father plunged his hand into the stone mailbox and extracted bills, magazines, junk coupon circulars.

We had the same kind of angst, Bronwyn had said. *It matched up.*

We talked about anything. College. My parents. Pressure.

He told me a lot of good things about you, Charles. Do you want to know?

Charles felt for the key in his pocket, opened the side door, walked up the stairs, and stood in the doorway of his father's office. He felt along the wall and turned on the light switch. On the left wall was a line of bookcases that held financial reference books, autobiographies, a bunch of glass plaques he'd been awarded when handling a company's IPO. There was a silver-framed photograph of his mother in a bridal gown next to the plaques. She looked younger than Charles was now, her hair much longer and her body a bit thinner.

Behind the bookshelves was an old bar cart, the kind that he imagined had once been regularly wheeled around office buildings in late afternoons. Cocktail hour. A crystal decanter sat on top, filled with amber-colored liquid. There was one lowball glass beside it, scrubbed clean. In the middle of the room was a big glass-topped desk. There was a Dell laptop closed in the center of the desk. His mother probably hadn't opened it once since he'd been here last. She'd kept this room absolutely untouched, as if it were a museum or a crime scene.

And that was the worst of it—she'd honored his memory. She probably figured he'd had a short-lived tryst with a woman, someone around her age. It would have been easier to swallow that, easier to accept that his father had reached out for someone for purely sexual reasons. As hard as Charles tried, he couldn't stop thinking about his father going into a store and choosing something for Bronwyn, asking the clerk to wrap it carefully. And then presenting it to her—when? Did they meet privately, away from the rest of the family?

No, his mother couldn't know any of that. Charles hadn't known, either. But according to Bronwyn, Scott did. Why hadn't he told anyone about it? Telling seemed like just the kind of thing Scott would do. Did he feel some kind of power, keeping what he'd seen to himself?

Charles wanted to ask his father the same questions he'd asked Bronwyn: Did he really hate Charles that much? Had he sought out Bronwyn as some sort of punishment, because Charles wasn't the son he wanted? Because Charles didn't buy that his dad and Bronwyn truly had anything in common; their relationship couldn't have been out of emotional necessity. It was because of some cruel psychological desire of his father's to hurt the rest of his family. Right?

Charles stood up, scraping his fingernails up and down his arms. Just outside the window, birds flitted in and out of the birdhouse on the post. He walked over to the window and hefted it up. Cold air swirled in. All the birds scattered except for a cardinal who was greedily eating the last scraps of seed from one of the small windows.

The pressure in his stomach broke free. Charles whirled around, picked up a glass paperweight from his father's desk, and hurled it at the birdhouse. He hit the metal post on which it stood. The cardinal fluttered away quickly, the house tipped, the paperweight made a slushy *thud* in the bush below.

The clanging noise resonated through the air for a few hollow seconds. The birdhouse was now tilted about fifteen degrees, seed slowly pouring out of the openings angled toward the ground. Birds rushed to the newly spilled seed on the grass, fighting for scraps. If Charles reached out, he couldn't touch the house anymore. It was suspended out in the yard, unreachable by human hands. After a moment, a bird hovered by the house and finally settled on the top, poking its beak into one of the partitions.

After that, Charles's rage felt wrung out. He tried to picture his father coming into his office right now. His dad had needed a friend so badly that he reached out to *Bronwyn*. A teenage girl. Wasn't his father supposed to be the strong, unwieldy, impeccably *correct* man? That was always how he'd portrayed himself.

If his father walked in right now, Charles might not be so afraid of him anymore.

He shut his eyes and saw Bronwyn standing in the gulley, her stomach round and swollen, her face full of pain. He had dated her for three years, and he hadn't known she was unhappy. He'd envied how interested her parents were in her. She'd made no mention of them being overbearing and impersonal, but she'd turned to *his* father, maybe at random, definitely in desperation. She never told Charles, never told his friends, just ran away from all of them, too afraid to face what she assumed they knew. Charles wondered if maybe there *was* more to the story than what Bronwyn had told him. She'd kissed his dad, she said, and not the other way around. Maybe she had even fallen in love with him, a mixed, confused love that was both sexual and childlike. She was so worried about people thinking they were having an affair because maybe in her mind, they were.

All this time, Charles thought Bronwyn had abandoned him because she thought she was better than he was, and that she'd embarked on the Back to the Land adventure because she was a purer, needless, higher-evolved being. But really, she was running away. She was no better than he was.

Charles turned off the overhead light in the office and shut the door. He was halfway down the stairs when he paused, hearing a shuffle and a creak. Someone was in the kitchen.

"Oh," Scott said when Charles walked into the room. He was standing at the open fridge, peeking at something wrapped in foil on one of the shelves.

"Oh," Charles said in return, freezing in place.

They blinked nervously at each other. Charles couldn't remember the last time they were in the same room together. His brother still had his down parka on. His black ski cap was lying on the kitchen table. He had just arrived here, from wherever he'd been. Something about him looked smaller today. Meeker. And tired, too, all his energy wrung out.

Scott's throat bobbed. He turned back to the fridge, to whatever was wrapped in the foil. "I was looking for turkey," he explained. "But instead, there's this . . . I don't know what the hell it is. *Pâté*, maybe." He sniffed it and made a repulsed face. "I think this has been in here since Great-grandpa lived here. Maybe Great-grandpa *put* it here."

"Great-grandpa," Charles repeated, somewhat idiotically. The word felt foolish in his mouth. They'd never called Charlie Bates *Great-grandpa*, had they? He'd died before they were born; he was too unknown to them to have a nickname. At the same time, Charles knew him so well. Charlie Bates loomed over this house, his picture in almost all of the rooms. He was part of every conversation they had.

Who they were supposed to be. Who they weren't. The differences between them.

Suddenly Charles was unclear about the history he shared with his brother. It all felt jumbled in his head, some of it fact, some of it twisted, opportunistic fiction. He felt so unsure about everyone in his life, too, so heavy with what he now knew about Bronwyn. He needed to get out of this room.

"Anyway," Charles said, letting out a held breath and ducking into the garage.

The room was dark and smelled like oil. He flicked the light on next to the door. There was his father's BMW, silent and shiny. Behind it were cans of paint, shelves of tools, a band saw, some shovels. He spied something folded up in the corner. Charles walked over to it and pulled it out from the cobwebs. It really was the same tent from all those years ago; he remembered the yellow posts.

He bent down and looked at the other shelves. The aluminum staking poles were also there, all tied together with a big purple rubber band meant for vegetables. The carabiners, which locked the posts together, were on the floor underneath the shelf. His father, anal to the end, had even saved the instruction booklet; it was nestled in a ziplock nearby.

Charles gathered everything up and started to carry it to the backyard. It took a few trips. Once there, he laid it all out on a flat piece of grass: the posts, the carabiners, the tent with its exoskeleton, and the vinyl subfloor. He spread the tent out, assembled the poles, and started to stake them, just as the instructions said. When he had all four poles staked, he raised them up so the tent stood and pulled the carabiners around the poles to secure them. Sometimes the instructions didn't make sense, and he had to study the figures for a long time before he understood how to attach all the carabiners and posts together in such a way that the tent would stand on its own, tight and secure. It took him a long time, probably far longer than it had taken his father, but doing it alone, doing it with no one watching, he felt able to make mistakes.

He heard a door slam and jumped. Scott was standing on the back porch, chewing on what looked like a hunk of bread pulled raggedly from a loaf. He carried a backpack over one shoulder. "You mind moving some of the poles?" he said. "They're blocking my car."

"Oh." Charles dropped the tarp and walked toward the driveway.

Scott looked at the tent somewhat blandly, as if he wasn't surprised that Charles was building it. "Do you want any help?"

"That's okay," Charles said, dragging the poles to the grass. And then he waited for Scott to make fun of what he was doing. Scott just kept chewing. He didn't move.

"Yeah, I guess you got it almost up," his brother remarked after a while. "Better than Dad, anyway. He couldn't build for shit."

One of the rods slipped from Charles's hands. "What do you mean?"

Scott stuffed another piece of bread in his mouth. "Dad was pathetic. Acted like he knew what the hell he was doing. He would never admit when something didn't make sense. He was hopeless, though."

"Dad could build things," Charles said weakly. *Couldn't he?*

Scott fiddled with the strap on his bag, looking fraught, like he wanted to say something else. All kinds of possibilities crashed through Charles's mind. A confession about this kid that died. An indication of what he knew about Bronwyn and their father. Maybe he wanted to surge at Charles, hitting him again for what Charles had said years ago. Because even if Bronwyn was right, even if it didn't change him, what Charles said was still the worst thing Charles had ever said to anyone, the worst thing he had ever done.

Charles glanced at the garden, where the old rose trellises had once been, the ones Scott had burned down. As Scott struck the match, he'd looked at Charles with such authority and confidence. He didn't care who his adoptive parents were or what their legacy was. He was in control of his destiny, freer and richer than Charles had ever been.

"Joanna," Scott said. He spun the key around his finger. "Don't fuck that up, man. Okay?"

"Okay . . ." Charles sounded out, baffled.

Scott nodded, seemingly satisfied, and walked to his car, opened his passenger door, and threw his bag inside. "Well, I'm off," he said.

"Off where?"

Scott just grinned. He walked around the car and got in the driver's seat. The car growled to life, the stereo's thunderous bass buzzing.

"Wait," Charles called just as his brother began to back up.

Scott braked, turned down the stereo, and stuck his head out the window.

"I'm sorry," Charles said.

"For what?"

There was a lump the size of a golf ball in Charles's throat, a spicy taste on his tongue. "For . . . the poles," he managed to say. "For blocking your way."

Scott's expression wavered for a moment, as if he'd decoded what Charles really meant. As if they were, for at least a moment, really brothers. "You're cool," he said.

And then he turned up the music again and rolled up the window. The headlights snapped on. Charles shaded his eyes, watching as Scott slung one arm over the back of the passenger seat and maneuvered the wheel so that the car pivoted down the driveway. He backed out the whole way down, navigating the curves through the back window, something Charles had never been able to do. And then he was gone.

Charles stood still for a few minutes, his ear cocked. Scott's engine growled and sputtered the whole way down the road, and Charles was certain he could still hear it even a few miles away. The sound felt imprinted inside him, the same way a bright orange shimmer lingered on his corneas after staring too long at the sun.

Then he turned back to work on the tent. When it finally stood, he stepped back. There it was, a big yellow teepee with a flap for an entrance. He had built it. The wind blew; the tent fluttered but didn't fall.

He ducked down and climbed through the small opening. Once inside, he zipped up the flap, closing himself in. Everything in here looked yellow, from his skin to his fingernails to the face of his watch. He could hear traffic on the street down the hill. When he moved, the mesh beneath him swished. There was a tiny flap in the ceiling that could be unzipped, probably for stargazing. He lay back, putting his arms behind his head, feeling the brittle grass through the thin subfloor. When he looked into the corner, he saw something written on the canvas. *J.M.* James McAllister. His father liked to put his initials on everything.

A sob welled up inside him, coming from somewhere very deep. It got stuck in his throat and then burst out his nose. He turned his head to the side and shook.

He sobbed for a while until he wasn't even sure anymore what he was crying about. He was simply too exhausted to keep this up anymore, to pretend that things were fine. Realizing this made him feel fresh, like he'd just stepped out of a shower. *There.* He was still breathing. His heart was still pumping. The world hadn't ended just because he'd admitted that he wasn't fine, he wasn't fine at all.

He raised his head, realizing something about what Bronwyn had said. Scott had seen their father and Bronwyn hugging a week or so before the banquet, and he'd assumed the worst. At the party, Scott stopped at their table, but Bronwyn went inside first, presumably to talk to his father and explain that they couldn't be friends anymore. Scott followed—why? To intervene?—but Charles interrupted him, venting years of frustration. Scott took Charles's abuse, but for a moment, Charles remembered his brother's eyes dimming, noticing something behind them. All this time, Charles hadn't known what he was looking at, but Scott had seen *them*, his father and Bronwyn.

Instead of letting it play out, instead of letting Charles *see*, Scott had tackled Charles, diverting his attention. Maybe he didn't want Charles's opinion of his father ruined forever. Maybe Scott wanted to protect their father, or Charles, or even their mother, by creating a subterfuge. What if it hadn't been some random act of violence but a noble gesture, a protective measure?

"No," Charles said out loud, his voice hollow and loud inside the little tent. That was bullshit. He didn't want to consider that Scott was actually . . . *perceptive*. It was so much more satisfying to dwell on Scott jumping him, throwing him to the ground in revenge.

He bit down hard on the inside of his cheek. "Right," he said gruffly to himself, imagining that his brother was still here, that he'd climbed into the tent with him. "Nice try. Big noble explanation, twelve years in the making."

Believe what you want, his brother answered. *It's not like I'm looking for thanks or anything.* But it wasn't Scott's normal tone of voice, all biting and sarcastic. He sounded deflated, maybe even sad, just as he'd sounded when he told Charles not to fuck it up with Joanna just now. Charles crossed his arms over his chest, feeling something inside him start to crack. A ball-shaped lump was stuck halfway down his wind-pipe, hard and immobile.

"He was kind of an asshole to me," Charles mumbled aloud.

And what would Scott say? *I know?* Would he smile? Laugh? Or would he look as miserable as Charles felt? *It's not like we had a very decent relationship, either,* he'd maybe say. *It's not like he ever talked to me really. Not like how he talked to her.*

Scott's voice was so real, the words so credible. It was as though he and his brother had really had this conversation once, maybe when very drunk or very sleepy. But when could that have been? When had they really talked? And yet Charles could picture the conversation playing out exactly like this, which made him wonder if these weren't things he'd already known, deep down, without Scott ever having to tell him.

The wind shivered in the trees, sweeping right into the tent. Charles rolled over and felt something in his pocket. His phone. He pulled it out and stared at it, turning it on. The screen bleated with life. He'd turned it off when he went into the house, but now his screen said he had three new messages.

He wondered if at least one of them was from Fischer, asking if he'd completed the interview. Maybe Back to the Land had already called and told them he hadn't, that he'd screeched away from the cabin after only a few minutes of talking to Bronwyn. He listened to the first one. At first, it was just dead noise, the sound of an ambulance. Joanna, probably. She often did this, called him, got his voice mail, and then didn't bother to listen for when the beep came. "Charles?" she said after a moment, and then hung up.

He smiled, daring to be hopeful. He thought about the way Joanna had kissed him on the mouth in that bar two years ago. He thought about the little notebook she kept by her computer entitled *Words I Like*. Inside were a list of words like *anathema, thistle, erstwhile,* written down for no other reason than that she thought they were pretty. He thought of her smooth body lying in the Jamaican sun, and he thought of the worry dolls she'd bought on a college trip to Guatemala. She'd had them lined up on the windowsill of her old apartment, the one she'd lived in when he met her. What had happened to those dolls? She must have had at least fifty, all of them different, but he hadn't seen them in ages. He kind of missed them.

The sun broke from behind a cloud, shining through the tent's yellow skin. The beams of light turned everything golden. Charles lay on his back again, soaking it up. He wasn't in his backyard anymore but in the wilderness, all alone. There was no one around to help him. He was responsible for his food, his shelter. He imagined lying here all night, listening to the deer crash through the woods, shivering under a blanket, experiencing every inch of the bumpy soil. Honestly, camping wasn't for him. It would never be for him. But it was, he understood now, in its own way, beautiful.

nineteen

harles's car was parked crookedly in the driveway, so Sylvie called his name as she walked into the house. No answer. She dropped her bag on the counter and looked around, trying to feel comforted by the familiar. "Charles?" she called again. Nothing. She walked through the living room to the dining room. Everything was still. She went outside and cupped her hands on Scott's apartment windows. Dark.

Figuring he'd gone out for a run, she walked back into the kitchen and absently paced from fridge to table to telephone to island. Her letter to Warren was still in her pocket, along with the check. There was no way she could bring herself to read what she'd written. What had he done after she'd left? Called the police? Reported her to Swithin? Actually, she hoped Warren *did* go to Swithin. He could say she stalked him. He could say she was trying to manipulate him, bribe him. Maybe he'd seen her reach for the letter in her pocket. Maybe he sensed there was a check in the envelope, a check for him. All at once she didn't want to be a part of Swithin any longer. It had mattered so much, but it didn't anymore. It felt like the wrong thing to care about.

She crouched under the telephone table and fed the letter into the paper shredder. Same with the check. The shredder made a whirring noise and deposited the remains into the basin below.

The kitchen was still. A peace came over her, one she hadn't felt in a long time. Smoothing back her hair, she started for the second floor. She could see the key in her mind, sitting on James's desk. It was small and silver with a square top. "Sentry," it said on one side. On the other: "Made in China."

There were conflicting voices in her head. *It doesn't matter.* She would look in the cabinet and find some evidence of the woman, whoever she was . . . and then what? It would open up something she should just let pass. But, on the other hand, she wanted something real, something truthful. A name. Even if it hurt. She was ready.

A glint of light on the landing caught her eye. James's office door was already ajar.

She walked inside. It was chilly in the room. She walked to the window and looked out. There was something in the yard. She leaned her head against the glass, frowning.

It was a tent.

She hurried back downstairs and out the door, certain it was a hallucination—for how could she have missed it when she came inside? But no, it was a tent, big and yellow, fully erected in her backyard. She had no idea when she'd last seen a tent. Its presence here seemed alien, unnerving. And then she saw something dark moving inside. A shadow.

Slowly, she walked toward it. She squatted, her heels immediately sinking in the mud. There was a zipped flap at the front. "Hello?" she said softly.

There was rustling. "Mom?"

More rustling. Then the opening unzipped and Charles stared out at her. He'd taken his shoes off; they were sitting on the tent floor next to him. He was dressed in work clothes, a blue button-down shirt and dark khaki pants. His eyes, cheeks, and the tip of his nose were red. At first she thought it might be windburn, but then she wondered if he'd been crying.

"What are you doing?" she asked. She tapped one of the posts. "Where did you get this?"

"In the garage. It was Dad's."

She blinked, still not understanding.

"I built it," Charles went on. "Do you want to come in?"

She hesitated, the idea of it was not very appealing. The ground was cold, wet, and there was a bitter chill in the air. But she wondered if something in him had broken, just as something in her had. It was probably high time things broke inside all of them. She looked inside the tent again. Everything was an iridescent gold. "I guess I could come in for a minute," she said softly.

Charles moved back so she'd have enough room to crawl in. She climbed into the tent awkwardly, her skirt riding up, her necklace bouncing against her collarbone, her knees instantly cold, separated from the tent's floor by only a thin layer of pantyhose. Charles was lying down, so Sylvie did, too. There was just enough room for them to lie side by side, their arms touching.

For a long time, neither of them said anything. There were a lot of things Sylvie wanted to ask him—why he'd built the tent or why he wasn't at work, for instance—but she sensed that she shouldn't. They lay next to each other in their own separate and walled-off pain, listening to the wind.

"It kind of doesn't feel like we're in our backyard," Sylvie said.

"I know. We could be anywhere."

"And it's cozy, in a way. Sort of like a nest."

"I guess it is," Charles said. "It's pretty crazy that people used to live like this. Not in tents, I mean, but so exposed to the elements. So primitively."

"They were used to it, though," she said. "I guess if you're used to it, it's not such a big deal."

Far off in the distance, someone started up what sounded like a buzz saw. "Why did Dad hate me?" Charles asked.

A shiver ran through her. She sat up halfway. "Honey. He loved you."

"Well, he didn't exactly like me. Is there something I could've done differently? Is there something I should've said? A way I should've looked?"

Her throat was tight. "I don't know if it was as simple as that."

"So you *did* notice it." He watched her for a moment. She neither nodded nor shook her head. "Couldn't you have said something to him? Couldn't you have asked?"

"You don't think I tried? You don't think I agonized over it? That I questioned why he acted the way he did? You don't think it killed me?"

"I . . ." Charles stammered, surprised.

She shut her eyes. It felt like there was a tidal wave brewing deep inside her, beginning to build momentum. What had she harmed, trying to keep the peace? *Après moi, le deluge*, her grandfather said. She didn't know any answers. She wished she did, but she didn't.

"I'm sorry," she said, sighing. "I did try. I did. But no, I didn't try enough. No one did. Don't just blame him, though," she said quietly. "It's my fault, too. Maybe it's mostly my fault. Don't think it's yours."

Charles said nothing in response. Sylvie touched his hand and then leaned her head on his shoulder. His skin was warmer than hers.

"I'm sorry," he said.

"For what?"

He looked away, maybe guilty. A crack formed in her brain. *Could he know, too? About this girl, as Tayson had called her?*

But, no. It hadn't been a girl. She couldn't believe that. Tayson had heard a rumor and took a gamble. It worked on Sylvie, too. He'd hit her in her softest, weakest spot, exactly where he needed to in order to get her to act.

She waited for Charles to say something, but all he did was shake his head. "You have nothing to be sorry for," she said. And then she moved onto her hands and knees. "I think I'm going to go inside now."

"Okay." Charles unzipped the tent flap for her. She crawled out, stood up, and assessed herself. Her skirt was wrinkled. Individual blades of grass were imprinted on her knees. She peered in at Charles, who was sitting cross-legged.

"Are you going to stay in there?"

"For a while, if that's okay."

"Of course it's okay."

She turned and opened the front door. Retraced her steps up the stairs, walking under her grandfather's portrait, coming to a stop outside James's office. She took a deep breath and walked across the room.

The key slid easily into the filing cabinet lock. She heard a release and the drawer opened. A dull, metallic sound echoed throughout the room.

There was a single paper clip at the bottom of the drawer. Rusted. A bit bent. Nothing else.

She pulled the next drawer open. It, too, was empty. And so was the next. She reached to the very back, but there was only cold metal. She stood back and pushed her hand through her hair, letting out a defeated laugh through her nose.

All this time, fearing an empty drawer.

She sank down on his office chair. What James had done was an indelible part of her now; she would have to live with it. So it had blind-sided her; so she hadn't seen it coming. So James hadn't seemed like the type of man who would ever do such a thing. The point was that it *had* happened, and there was nothing she could do to change that. He had made a mistake; a lot of people did. People she loved, people she thought would never make mistakes. That was the only conclusion she could come to, the only way she could really come to terms with it.

The sun outside broke free from a cloud, sending a carpet of gold across James's desk. Sylvie was sitting at just the right angle to notice a gleaming hair next to his old computer. She bent down. It was a gray hair, short and coarse. His.

A sob welled up in her throat. It felt like it was the only tangible, organic thing left of him. Not the ring he gave her, not the clothes in his closet, only this single, tenuous hair. Her heart clenched. She'd spent so much time fixating on *the woman*, maybe as shelter from the fact that he was really gone. And he *was* gone. He would not come downstairs to talk to her ever again. He would not sit next to her when she was sick, putting cold washcloths on her forehead. She wouldn't hear the noises of him moving around, getting ready for work, swearing as he bumped around in the clumsy, woozy morning. She had stood over him in his last few hours alive, cursing what he'd done, and after he died, she'd stared down at him, too numb to think. And that was all there was. She wouldn't get any more time with him. She'd squandered what she had.

After a while, she looked down into the backyard. The tent loomed, silent and cheerful, next to the exact same brick patio that had been there when Sylvie was a girl. And there were the exact same flowerbeds, too, and the same gazebo and pool that no one used but they'd never replaced with something else. That old decking. That old blue diving board. The DNA from her grandfather's feet was probably all over that diving board, as well as skin from his hands on the edges of the pool and the metal ladder and the long-handled device that skimmed the bugs from the surface.

Sylvie supposed she could imagine that the Charles inside the tent wasn't a troubled adult but still a little boy. Both he and Scott could still be little boys, and things could still turn out differently for them, more like what she'd envisioned. She supposed she could even imagine that *she* was a little girl, too. This office was still her grandfather's, and the tent down there was hers. And she wondered if that was what she'd been doing all this time, living in this big, broken house, working so hard to keep things exactly the same. She wondered if, deep down, she hoped time wasn't a straight line but could loop back on itself, letting her start over.

She turned away from the window and walked downstairs to the kitchen. Taking a long time to consider, she decided to make herself a tuna sandwich on rye bread, mixing the tuna and the mayo and putting in pieces of celery and red onion. And she put on classical music, something from her own collection, not her grandfather's old records, and she sat down at the kitchen table and ate. She tried as hard as she could to enjoy every bite.

twenty

Catherine spent the rest of the afternoon and the early evening in the hands of doctors, heavily drugged. They did an ultrasound of her liver, then a small biopsy. They were running tests for hepatitis and cancer. Joanna went from thinking this was a cruel joke to knowing it was some manifestation of karma to feeling numb all over, all in the span of three or four seconds. Finally, when she was in the waiting room, reading the same pregnancy magazine for the third time, Dr. Nestor called her aside and told Joanna the news was good—her mother had cirrhosis.

"That's *good?*" Joanna exclaimed.

It was good because it was manageable, he said. But she would have to quit drinking immediately. One drink, and she could be dead. She'd have to begin taking a whole host of pills, ones that were actually prescribed for her, and nothing else. But in a few days, she could actually go home.

Joanna sat in her mother's room, waiting for her to wake up. The most entertaining things in the room were her mother's monitors, the gentle, subtle changes of her pulse rate and blood pressure, the amount of oxygen present in her blood. Catherine's face was still free of makeup, and she looked both younger and so much older concurrently.

Then her mother opened her eyes. "Hi," Joanna said.

Catherine made little smacking noises with her lips and tentatively touched the tube that fed oxygen into her nose. "Jesus. I must look awful."

"You look fine."

She stared up at the ceiling, placing her hands over her sternum again. "Well," she breathed. They looked at each other for a moment. Catherine sighed dramatically. "They're telling me I took too many pills."

"Yes."

"And my liver's shot. It's going to kill me, I bet."

"The doctor actually said it could be managed."

"Mark my words. These doctors don't know anything."

Joanna looked away. A little smile curled on Catherine's lips. "You think I'm overreacting."

"I don't know." She counted three long breaths. "I'm sorry for what I said before," she said. "I shouldn't have gotten you worked up."

Her mother shifted, not answering. "So, where's Scott?"

"I don't know. I think he left." On a trip outside, she'd noticed Scott's car wasn't in the parking lot. She'd tried not to think about their conversation very much; it made her feel too gloomy and ashamed. Where had he gone? Back to Pennsylvania? He'd seemed so *changed* after what she said to him, as if she'd opened his eyes to how he truly appeared.

"Did you have a fight?" Catherine asked.

"No." Joanna let out an exclamation point of a snort. "Scott and I aren't close enough to have a fight."

"You seem pretty close."

She flexed her calf muscles. She had to say something. "Contrary to how it seemed, I would *not* want to marry him. Any old Bates-McAllister won't do."

Catherine pressed her lips together sternly.

"Is that why you said that stuff about me and him? And about the photos of his family? Making it sound like I was some kind of crazy, obsessed teenager? Because you thought he was in love with me?"

"I didn't tell him you were *obsessed*." Catherine crossed her arms.

"I heard that very word come out of your mouth."

Catherine weakly crossed her arms over her chest. "I didn't mean *obsessed*, necessarily. Enamored. Entranced."

"But *you* weren't enamored and entranced? I just . . . dreamed all that up?"

"Well." Catherine flicked her hair over her shoulder. "I don't know. I mean, I was going through all kinds of things, Joanna. It was a long time ago."

Joanna stared at the front walkway. The black plastic bag in the trash can was empty, and it flapped in the wind against the can's mesh sides. A couple passed, their heads down, their faces somber. No one looked happy at hospitals.

She picked at a string on her sweater. "I think Charles is having an affair," she admitted, bracing herself.

Her mother's sheets rustled.

"With his old girlfriend. The girl he dated in high school."

"Are you sure?"

She couldn't meet her mother's eye. "I talked to her on the phone before I came here. She was telling me where they were going to meet. Either she's really ballsy or she thought I was the cleaning lady."

"It could've been a misunderstanding. Did you confront him about it? Ask him if that's what he was doing? I figure he must've called you since you've been here, right?"

Joanna watched several nurses rush down the hall. "He did call. But I didn't ask him, no."

"Why?"

"He would've denied it."

Catherine struggled to sit up. "So, what, you talked to him on the phone and pretended it hadn't happened?"

Joanna gazed out the window. The sky was an ashy gray. A man with a walker hobbled down the sidewalk. "She's better for him, probably. They come from the same background. They both went to Swithin."

"So?"

Joanna looked at her helplessly.

Catherine's lips were tautly pressed together. "What the hell is wrong with you?"

"I know, I went and ruined it. Look at all I was given, everything we ever wanted, and I've messed it all up."

It was hard to contain the bitterness she felt. But Catherine was squinting at her, lost. Joanna sighed. "You said that at my wedding."

"What? I *didn't*."

"Yeah. You did."

"Well, surely I meant—" Catherine trailed off abruptly, pressing her lips together and shifting her eyes to the right. Realization seemed to slowly trickle into her, reminding Joanna of red food-coloring dye dropped into a water glass, the molecules gradually dispersing and turning the water pink. Catherine's throat bobbed as she swallowed. "Well," she said, touching her neck. She looked out the window, then at her hands. "I just meant . . . I didn't want you to ruin the day by dwelling on the negative. I could tell you were. I could see you looking around, scowling at *something* that was wrong. The apple doesn't fall very far from the tree, I guess."

Joanna flinched, amazed at her mother's self-introspection. But she didn't believe Catherine for a second. Surely this explanation was fabricated, once Catherine realized the harshness of what she'd said. "You never thought I deserved Charles. You were horrified when I told you we were dating, as if it was unnatural or something."

Catherine sighed and shut her eyes. A nurse at the desk just outside her room let out a cawing laugh. A doctor ran past the door at a full gallop. "Look," Catherine said. "I spent a long time around those people. I don't know what they deserved or who deserved them. I tried so hard, but they didn't want me. I couldn't help but be bitter and hate them a little. Of course, once I moved here, I realized it wasn't even about them, specifically. It was just about belonging *somewhere*. I've found that here."

Joanna sniffed. "The sail club?"

"That's right."

Joanna breathed out. It felt like she'd been holding something in for years. She looked around the room, from the monitors to the gray-green walls to the flecks in the linoleum to her mother's feet, stumps beneath the blanket. "What was so *wrong* with your life, Mom?"

Catherine thought for a while, as if no one had ever asked that question. Finally she cleared her throat. "One day, when you were about ten, your dad just wasn't there anymore." Catherine kept her eyes on her blankets. "For years he adored me. He *defined* me. Because he watched everything I did like it mattered. And then . . . he just . . . checked out. I thought you understood that. You were there. You watched it happen."

"I was ten."

"I thought . . . I don't know. I thought you understood."

"Why would I understand that?"

Catherine sighed, shaking her head. "When you were a baby, you were very clumsy," she said in a faraway voice. "You used to fall all the time. And then I would pick you up all worried, and you'd be crying and I'd sit you on the couch and give you a little piece of a banana and after a while you were okay. But then, this one day, you were playing outside by yourself, and you tripped over something and landed face-first. It wasn't a bad fall but the kind of thing you'd normally get upset about. Only this time you just looked around and then picked yourself up. You didn't cry. The next time you fell around me, I got it. There was always this pause after you fell, where you'd look at me, waiting to see what my face would do. It didn't mean anything if you were alone; it was how *I* responded to it that made you respond to it, too. It was the damnedest thing."

More doctors hurried down the hall. Joanna crossed her arms over her chest, not knowing where this was going.

"We all just rely on everyone else's reaction, don't we?" Catherine said. "When I fall over, I look around to see if people are going to get all crazy. And once your dad left, maybe I looked around for you. Because if no one sees what I do, it doesn't mean anything. It wouldn't have been real if you hadn't been there with me to see it."

"So it's like that tree falls in the forest question?"

Catherine smiled questioningly.

"You know, that philosophical question: If a tree falls in the forest and no one hears it, does it make a sound?"

Catherine cocked her head. "Why, I don't know! *Does* it?"

Her voice had a wondrous quality to it, as if this was a catchy song she was hearing for the first time. It seemed implausible—irreverent, almost—that her mother had hit upon the idea completely on her own. "Come on," Joanna said. "You've heard that. Everyone has."

Catherine shook her head, still smiling.

"Well, that's what you're saying," Joanna said. "And you're saying a tree doesn't make a sound if there's no one around to hear it. And what we feel or do doesn't matter if there's no one around to witness it. When we're all alone, it's almost as if we don't exist. We have no identity."

Catherine nodded. "We're all just big sponges. The only thing that matters is how other people see what we're going through."

Joanna shrugged. "Yeah. Maybe."

They were silent for a while. Joanna leaned against the wall. Her throat tickled. She was suddenly horribly aware she was about to cry and ducked her head. An ambulance drifted past outside. Her mother's monitors fluttered and squeaked. Joanna thought about what Catherine had just said about her father, how he'd abruptly left her so long ago. It could explain why Catherine developed all those medical problems. In her backward way, it was her attempt to bring his attention back to her, but it hadn't worked. Joanna was the one who coddled her. Joanna was the one who sat and waited and worried and gave her mother what she needed. Her father was long gone.

She suddenly wondered what her father was doing in Maine, where he now lived. They'd barely spoken at her wedding. He'd shown up, walked her down the aisle, but then she'd barely seen him at the reception. He and her mother didn't sit together, and if he'd tried to find her to say good-bye, he hadn't succeeded. But she remembered feeling relieved that he hadn't stayed longer—the more Catherine drank, the feistier she got, and she would have picked a fight with him, right in front of the Bates-McAllisters.

She excused a lot of her dad's absences this way, not really examining if those were really his intentions. She couldn't even recall the last time they'd had an actual conversation. Probably about three years ago; he'd been driving south for a business trip and stopped off to see her for lunch, picking somewhere cheap and close to the turnpike. He paid for their club sandwiches with an American Express corporate card and talked a lot about a mystery book on tape he'd been listening to during the drive.

She should have asked him why he'd been the way he'd been. Why he'd stopped accompanying Catherine to the hospital, how the responsibility had always fallen on Joanna. And why, that day of her eleventh birthday party, when Catherine declared she felt sick, her father had been so adamant about removing Joanna from the situation and taking her and her friends for pizza. "You're doing the right thing," he'd said to Joanna as they got out of the car at the pizza parlor. "We need to break this cycle." Joanna tried to believe him. She wanted to think he was doing this for her because it was her birthday. But what if it was to undermine Catherine, too?

When Joanna had arrived home from the pizza parlor later that evening, her friends rushing to the Nintendo in the basement, she noticed a light in her mother's bedroom and went upstairs. Her mother was lying facedown on her bed, curled up in a ball. Her eyes were closed, and she didn't seem to sense Joanna was there. She didn't look ill, just *alone*. As if there was no one in the world who wanted her.

It made Joanna crumple up inside. She couldn't bear to see her mother like that, so lost and without purpose. And so she'd swallowed her frustration. It was the only thing she could do. She collected the photos of the Bates-McAllisters, turning to them for respite. They were removed from Joanna's world, eternally as perfect as their pictures.

She thought about what she'd said to Scott a few hours ago. And how he'd stormed away, upset. It was no different than the way anyone would have reacted. Scott was the last bastion of the Bates-McAllister mystique, an impenetrable, unknowable person that she could mold to her whims and desires. But Scott was the same as she was—as anyone was—with the same emotions, secrets, and demons.

Realizing this made her feel woozy and weak-kneed. It made her feel childish, too, for being so naive as to think that Scott would be any different. And for being so blind as to assume that Charles would be exactly what she'd created in her mind. Maybe she was the one who lived in the bubble, not Charles and his family, not Catherine with her diseases and her panic. Joanna was so set on people being one way and one way only, her brain practically locked when someone did something unexpected. Of course she was disappointed—she had nowhere to go *but* disappointment. But it didn't mean the disappointment was bad.

"That tree that fell over," Catherine piped up. "It has to make a sound, doesn't it? Everything makes a sound, whether we're there or not."

"I don't know. I guess it's up to everyone individually."

"And this is a common question you've heard before?"

"A popular philosophical question, yes."

Her mother patted her hand. "You should go back home. You should go home and talk to him, figure this out."

Joanna shrugged. "I don't know."

"You think this ex-girlfriend is better for him? That's the worst excuse I've ever heard. It just sounds like you're scared."

"I'm not scared."

Catherine grabbed Joanna's wrist hard. "Did you marry this man because *I* wanted you to? Because of those silly pictures in the newspaper?"

She thought for a moment. Maybe at first she did. But there was more to it now, too. "No," she answered honestly.

"Do you really want to end things with him?"

She looked away. "I don't know."

"Come on."

Joanna bit down on her lip. She had no idea what the right choice was. She had no idea how things would play out. No one did.

"Just answer," Catherine encouraged. "Say the first thing that comes to mind."

Joanna's mouth wobbled. Her mother's nails dug into her skin. "No," she whispered. "I don't want things to end."

Catherine released her grip. "There you go."

"It's not as easy as that."

"With Charles, maybe it is."

Joanna snorted. "You don't really know Charles, Mom."

Catherine turned her head from side to side. "Charles called me once. Back in December. You'd been married for a few months. He asked me what you'd like for Christmas."

Joanna lifted her hands from the bed.

"I told him that I had no idea what you'd like for Christmas and that he probably had a much better idea of what to get you than I did. But he was persistent. He asked me what *I* would have wanted for Christmas my first year of marriage. 'My marriage didn't work out,' I reminded him. And he said, 'Well, pretend that it had.'"

Joanna stared at her. Charles hadn't told her any of this. "He got me lingerie," she said.

Catherine's eyes lit up. "That's what I *told* him to get you! I wanted your father to get me fancy lingerie for our first Christmas together. It sounded so sexy. Not that he did. He got me a vacuum."

But it wasn't what I wanted, Joanna wanted to protest. Charles didn't know her at all. And instead of asking his mother, who was no doubt an expert at choosing the right gifts for everyone, he'd called Catherine.

"Isn't that funny," Joanna said in a faraway voice. A heavy gloom came over her suddenly, and every cell in her body felt immensely tired. When had people become so confusing? When had things suddenly shifted from Joanna knowing everything to knowing absolutely nothing?

She sat on the edge of Catherine's bed for a while longer. Catherine turned on the television and flipped around until they found a reality show about four very wealthy women living in Southern California. The show featured a lot of shots that panned over the women's mansions, their jewelry collections, their cars, their asses, and the two of them watched silently for at least three minutes until there was a commercial break. Catherine was leaning forward a little, taking it all in. Joanna could see her mind at work. Even if Catherine had discovered that status would never fulfill her, her hunger for it hadn't abated. It probably never would, not entirely.

The following day, after the doctors started Catherine on proper medicine and scared the shit out of her some more about how if she drank one more drop, she'd go into liver failure, and after Robert arrived at Catherine's bedside, looking concerned—it was obvious, Joanna realized, that he was in love with her—and after Catherine told Joanna she should go back home now, Joanna would gather her things and drive back up I-95.

She would call Charles's cell phone on the drive and tell him she was coming home. He would sound relieved and say *That's good.* He would also say that something happened while she was away. Something he needed to talk to her about. Joanna would clench her stomach and wish they could just bypass all this, but then she would say she needed to talk to him about some things, too. *Okay*, he would say. There would be a twinge to his voice, a worried desperation she'd never heard before. She would wonder, after hanging up, whether he knew *she* knew. She would wonder, too, if he knew she'd brought Scott along, all the things she'd said to Scott, even that she'd kissed him. It seemed doubtful Scott would have told him, but anything was possible.

She would turn into their development and pull into her garage. She would drop her bags in the foyer. The house would be dark and empty. Outside the sky would be gray, rain imminent. She'd hesitate a moment, then turn back for the door. She would walk to the end of the block, and then take a left. Her footsteps would ring out on the cold slick pavement. All the houses she would pass would have cars in the garages and lights shining in the windows until she would turn on Spirit.

The huge, empty houses loomed. All the driveways slanted at the exact same angle. The first one on the block was the very same model as her house, the Commonwealth. Except this one was bare and dark, its windows unadorned.

Joanna would walk up the front steps. At first she would intend to just ring the doorbell to see if it worked or to see if that, too, had fallen into disrepair. But then her hand would touch the doorknob, and it would feel loose. The Realtor's lockbox would clunk against the doorframe. The door would swing open eagerly.

The house would still smell like paint and new carpet. There would be the same little archway into the dining room as was in her house, the same light fixtures. She would open a closet to find a bare shelf, empty space. No life here. No happiness, no sadness. Just emptiness.

The kitchen countertops would be covered in a fine layer of dust. Instead of a table in the breakfast nook, there would be raw square footage. Every sound she would make would echo off the bare walls and vaulted ceilings, nothing to absorb it. She would walk upstairs. The rooms were without beds or bureaus. She would continue into the bedroom where she and Charles slept. The day they'd moved into their own version of this house, after the movers left, Charles had urged her upstairs and tossed her down on the bed. He'd tickled her, too, saying all good houses needed to be christened with its first tickling. She writhed around, blissfully aware that she could make whatever sounds she wanted—there were no downstairs neighbors to complain. *We are now adults*, she'd thought. But she had so much further to go. There was so much she didn't know about herself and even more she didn't know about Charles. They were strangers to each other, assumptions upon assumptions. It might take years for them to peel down to who they really were.

A car door would slam outside. Joanna would freeze in the empty upstairs hallway. There would be lights in the driveway. She'd rush down the steps, her heart pounding, remembering the rumors about the kids using the houses to grow cannabis. There would be a figure at the front door, peering through the window. Joanna would search for somewhere to hide. She'd consider slipping out a window. Before she could do anything, the front door would open.

"Ahem."

Mariel Batten would be wearing a down-filled coat with a furry hood and black leather gloves. She would be brandishing her car key at her sternum, pointing it toward Joanna like a weapon.

"Oh," Joanna would say, stepping back.

"What are you *doing* here?" Mrs. Batten would say, eyes wide, making a slightly ugly face.

Joanna would blink. "I just . . . wanted to see it."

"It looks exactly like everyone else's house." Mrs. Batten sounded exasperated.

But Joanna wouldn't be sure about that. It did . . . and yet it didn't. She was happy for how much it didn't. "What are *you* doing here?" she'd say next.

"It's my night for neighborhood watch," Mariel Batten would explain. "I thought you were some tweaked-out kid or something."

"I'm sorry," Joanna would stammer, diffident. "I didn't think the door would open. But I got kind of . . . curious. I wanted to see what it looked like in here."

Batten would step into the foyer and look around at all the emptiness, all the white walls. "It's really different in here." But it wasn't different. It was the same layout as both their houses, the same dimensions and plaster and floorboards. But Joanna would know what she meant.

Mrs. Batten would shove her hands into her pockets and glare at Joanna. "There are kids that sometimes try to break into these and vandalize them. It's really dangerous."

"I guess I didn't think about that."

In the dim light, Mrs. Batten would look younger and less polished, with purple circles under her eyes and a big stain on her zip-up hooded sweatshirt. "Well, you should have. This world is crazy."

And then Joanna would turn back to the lonely, empty rooms. "All these houses, just sitting here," she'd say dolefully, looking around again. "Doesn't seem like it's going to change, either."

"Don't say that," Mrs. Batten would say. "They'll sell."

Batten would give her a ride back up the street in her minivan. The passenger seat would be littered with toy trucks and dolls, and when she would turn on the stereo, a sing-along tape would blare. A bunch of kids would be singing "Row, Row, Row Your Boat" in a round, encouraging the listeners to join in. Batten would make no effort to turn it off. After a moment, very subtly, her lips would begin to move, singing along. *Row, row, row your boat, gently down the stream.* Absently, tiredly, automatically. *Merrily, merrily, merrily, merrily, life is but a dream.*

"Thank you," Joanna would say when Batten pulled into her driveway.

Batten would stiffen. "I'd be a failure at neighborhood watch if I made you walk."

But Joanna wasn't thanking her for the ride. Not entirely, anyway.

Joanna's house would smell like a vanilla plug-in candle and Tide and something much more primal, a mix of her and Charles's skin and hair and secretions. There would be clutter on the mantel and cooking apparatus on the kitchen counter. Desks and chairs and beds in the bedrooms, clothes in their closets, piles of mail on the front table, unpacked boxes in the living room. Pausing at a window, she'd see Batten's master bedroom light go off, a bathroom light snap on. She'd meant what she said in the empty house. People would live in those houses eventually. Nothing would stay the same forever.

She'd approach the piles of boxes, hands on her hips. JOANNA, APARTMENT, they said. They contained only things, knickknacks and lamps and books, nothing more symbolic than that. Things that might have rightful places around this new house, on tables and windowsills and shelves. She would find the yellow box cutter in the drawer in the kitchen and extend the blade. And one by one she would slice open each box, all eight of them. The packing tape would split in two. The cardboard flaps would flop free. Dust would emerge from the boxes, surely collected from her old apartment and the storage unit and the moving truck and this house, too.

It would be enough for the night just to open them and then stand back. And she would think about the invisible dust as it floated into the air, carried by the currents inside the house, exploring every room, joining and combining and spreading and settling somewhere new. And she would realize, standing there, that this thing with her and Charles, this trouble, it was a crack, but it wasn't a break. Just like everything else, it too would pass.

twenty-one

The first few nights after Scott left, Sylvie thought he was just staying with friends in the city. But his mail began to pile up. A UPS box remained on his doorstep until she finally brought it inside and, after enough time, opened it. Inside was a pair of yellow high-top Nikes wrapped in butcher paper. She set them at his place at the table, side by side next to his plate.

When Sylvie dared to enter her son's empty suite, she was astonished to find it clean. It was as if he'd used a toothbrush to scrape off every bit of grime. Everything was put away. The floors were vacuumed. His bed was made. She ran her finger along the dust-free television, disappointed. She wanted to see it tumultuous and grungy, the way he'd lived. It didn't even smell like him. It looked like a rental, a hotel room.

Sometimes she sat at the kitchen table and wrote him letters, though she had nowhere to send them. They were mostly filled with platitudes. *I hope you're okay. We're thinking about you.* And, as time went on, *Maybe you haven't heard what happened. You can have your job back, if you want it.*

Once, she drank too much red wine and wrote him a letter that said, over and over, how sorry she was, how this was never how she imagined things would turn out, how if she could rewind everything and do it all again, she would. She would do anything for him. She would change what needed changing. The letter remained on the table until the next morning; when she woke up, she found Charles in the kitchen, having stopped over to check on her. Their eyes met, and Charles turned away. He had read it. She didn't blame him. After that, he and Joanna began coming over more often, mostly for dinners, but sometimes after dinner, just to watch TV.

The house wasn't the same without him. For years Sylvie had been cringing at the loud booms from the television, the speedy, guttural music from the stereo, the people that showed up in the middle of the night. She'd pressed her fingernails into her palm, hating his puerile ways, certain her neighbors, distant as they were, would hear the sounds and cringe. But now she felt like slapping the silence.

She could hear every breath she took. Every swallow. She hated the noises of her chewing. She heard the mailman's truck at the bottom of the hill and sometimes even the cows mooing in the pasture a half-mile away. Some sounds scared her—creaks, ghostly footsteps, an anonymous crash whose origin she never identified. One night she tried sleeping with her biggest Wüsthof knife under her pillow, but she worried that she might roll over in the night and inadvertently stab herself.

She thought about getting a dog.

The day after she talked to Christian's father at Feverview Dwellings, she wrote her official Swithin board resignation. After the board received it, several members called to ask what on earth had come over her. They all acted so meticulously neutral. They feigned puzzlement when Sylvie told them she wanted to do other things for a while. Travel. Volunteer. Go back to school. She played her part, politely not impugning any of them, not saying, *I know you wanted me to do exactly this. You can't fool me.* Only Martha tipped her hand—*Is this because of that boy's death, Sylvie? We knew that would blow over. We knew you and your son weren't involved. Was someone saying he was? Who would say something like that?*

A week later, Sylvie was walking around her favorite gardening store, staring at the violets in their paper tubs, the fledgling trees held up by posts, the soft, massive bags of soil stacked in the corner. Someone tugged her arm. It was a Swithin teacher, though Sylvie couldn't place her. "Angela Curtis," the woman reminded her. "I teach art."

Angela had been part of the committee that was supposed to meet with Scott. *Supposed.* "I guess you know he didn't show up," Angela said, shrugging. "It was a moot point by then, of course, since the medical examiner had turned in her report that day."

"The autopsy came back?" Sylvie exclaimed. No one had told her.

Angela pressed her hand to her mouth, surprised that Sylvie didn't know. She probably didn't know Sylvie had resigned from the board, either. "You should probably talk to Michael Tayson about this." She backpedaled and rushed away.

In the end Sylvie didn't need to ask anyone about the autopsy; the results came out in the newspaper the following day, splashed across the front page of the local section. *Another MRSA infection claims private school boy, fifteen.* There was Christian's school picture with his joker green hair. And the caption underneath: "Deadly Methicillin-Resistant Staphylococcus Aureus bacteria, or MRSA, infect more than 90,000 Americans each year."

The bacteria could be carried by healthy people, said the article, living in their skin or in their noses. The coroner guessed that the bacteria had entered an open wound on Christian's skin and traveled into the bloodstream, lodging in his lungs. There were sores on his stomach, the coroner said, which was most likely the entry point. This kind of infection was common in sports teams, especially when they shared equipment and mats that weren't regularly washed. The article mentioned the health department and the Swithin school board. There was a quote from Geoff, vowing that the board hadn't been aware of this tragic oversight and that the school was now doing everything possible to prevent further MRSA outbreaks. The school would be closed for two days while a commercial cleaning service came in and scoured the place from top to bottom.

Sylvie stared at the article for a long time. According to what both the story and Angela said, the autopsy results had been released the day of Scott's meeting. That was the day of Geoff's party, too. The day Tayson had cornered her and accused her and told her that she should *make it go away*. And yet, they'd kept it from her. They'd let her think what she wanted to think, for if she knew the truth, she would never have sought out Warren Givens. Perhaps Tayson had hoped that Sylvie was so terrified Mr. Givens was going to point fingers at Scott, she would blindly hand him a check. All the while, Mr. Givens, who was aware of the autopsy results full well by then, would assume that Sylvie, the chairman of the board, was compensating him for the MRSA infection Christian had contracted at Swithin, that the money was reparation for his loss. Maybe Tayson had thought Sylvie would just thrust a check at Mr. Givens, too mortified to get into details. Well, he was almost right—she practically *had* done that. She certainly hadn't wanted to rehash the accusations, which meant Mr. Givens would have had no opportunity to explain where she had it wrong.

It had almost happened that way. Tayson had almost tricked both of them.

"You could sue," Charles said to her when she explained what had happened. "They manipulated you. You could oust Tayson and get your job back."

Though Sylvie considered it for a moment, she realized she didn't want her job anymore. Not *that* job, not in its current iteration. Too much was lost.

But if Scott didn't have anything to do with this, why *hadn't* he gone to the meeting? She brought it up once to Joanna and Charles. What did Scott think he knew about the wrestling boys that, eventually, made him leave town? *Was* there hazing? Why would he have just taken off like that otherwise? Joanna had poked at her dinner for a while, and then said, "Maybe he just *wanted* us to think there was something else to the story about the boys and the wrestling team, and that was why he was running away. Instead of, you know, just picking up and leaving because he simply didn't want to be here."

At first, Sylvie threw out that possibility—people didn't do that. But she wondered what would hurt worse—knowing that Scott had abetted in something or realizing that Scott just wanted nothing to do with them anymore. The first option carried disappointment and shame, but the second carried personal guilt. There might have been more *she* could have done to keep him here. It startled her when she realized which option she preferred to believe.

Resigning from the board stopped her life abruptly. Suddenly there were no meetings. No obligatory parties. Other things halted, too—they decided not to go on a family vacation to Cape May, and Charles and Joanna began tentatively planning a trip of their own to Saint Lucia. Charles had put down a deposit on a six-night stay in a seaside bungalow there; he would be able to write off some of it as expenses, he explained, because he was working on a story for the *Philadelphia Inquirer* about a Pulitzer Prize–winning author's vacation home also on the island. It's a start, he said. At least it's a writing clip. After he quit his job—he didn't get into why, only that he wasn't cut out for advertising—Charles followed an *Inquirer* editor around until he paid attention to him, even crashing an office party he knew the editor was attending. It could have been a disaster, Charles told Sylvie, but I think the guy was kind of proud of me. I think it showed him I was serious.

When Charles came over for dinner, Joanna sometimes called in the middle—she was often in Maryland, visiting her recuperating mother and her mother's new boyfriend, Robert. Charles and Joanna had decided to move back to Philadelphia, putting their house up for sale. While they waited for it to sell, they met with Philadelphia Realtors, looking at different apartments, comparing square footage, pet policies, and twenty-four-hour doormen.

One weekend in mid-June, Charles decided to join Joanna in Maryland. Before he left, he kept asking Sylvie if she'd be all right. Did she need anything from the store? Should he bring her some DVDs to watch? Could she call a neighbor if something happened? Stop it, Sylvie kept telling him. I'll be fine. I'm used to being alone.

She drove to his house and saw him off, needlessly helping him pack his car and lock up his house. Before Charles got into his car, he gave her a long, contemplative look. "There's something we need to talk about one of these days."

"What?" she asked.

He rattled the keys in his hand. "It's nothing I want to get into right now. It's just . . . we need to have a long talk."

She watched as he backed out of the driveway and started down the street. Was it a reference to the girl? *Did* Charles know? If he did, did *she* want to know? It seemed better just to let it go.

As his car disappeared around the corner, a fist formed in her chest. A weekend was forty-eight hours long, which seemed like an eternity. But there were plenty of things to do. Cleaning and organizing, preparing elaborate dinners, re-reading her grandfather's marked-up copy of *Anna Karenina*. Dismantling that tent in the yard—it was still there from when Charles had built it a few months ago. Sometimes she peered inside the tent, searching out James's initials on the canvas. She kept telling herself she'd sleep in it on a warm night, but so far she hadn't.

She got back into her car. First she drove to Swithin. There it was, still standing without her. The flag flapped from the flagpole, no longer half-mast. One of the landscapers was hunched over the bushes, pruning. Another was on a riding mower. Sometimes they had camps here in the summer, but she didn't see any children in the fields. Sylvie had tried her best not to inquire about how the school had weathered the MRSA news, but she could guess the repercussions. Parents had very likely thrown a fit, horrified that an institution they paid so much money to send their children to could be so negligent. It was possible some had pulled their kids out. It was possible other students had contracted little MRSA pustules on their skin, too—it was highly contagious, the article said—and that their parents had demanded the school pay for their medical treatment. Enrollment might be down for next year. In the fall certain colleges might overlook Swithin applicants. The board would have to answer a lot of questions, for they'd recorded every meeting, the software on Martha's husband's computer translating their conversations verbatim, the tapes immediately going into the school's files. An investigation would uncover that there was even discussion about purchasing new sports equipment at the last meeting—Sylvie remembered it well—and the board had laughingly glossed over it.

Sylvie thought she'd feel some satisfaction that Tayson and the others were under the microscope, but her insides just felt scooped out and raw. She felt sorry for the school, festering with so many germs, cruelly neglected. It had happened under her watch, after all. This was the only thing she was responsible for, and she had blown it. She felt sorry for Scott having to go through this for something that had nothing to do with him, too. She even felt a little sorry for herself. She couldn't help it.

She could only idle at the school for a few minutes before it became too much to bear. After that, because she didn't want to go home yet, she drove out to Kimberton, which was above the turnpike. It was simply somewhere to go, a place that had no emotional ties to any part of her life. The houses there were small and crooked, many with green carpet on the porch steps and lacy curtains in the windows. There were still corner bars and a tiny, family-run grocery store, though a Wal-Mart also loomed on the hill just outside the town. She'd brought her camera, and she walked around a little park taking pictures of kids on swings, people's dogs, a couple sitting on a park bench. No one told her to stop or insisted she was being intrusive. *What a sweet, lonely lady*, their smiles said. Maybe they even threw in *old*—Sylvie suddenly felt the weight of her years. She wore a string of pearls around her neck, which probably made her look older than fifty-eight. And she wore nylons under her skirt even though they made her legs and crotch sweat. She'd dressed this way for years, but suddenly it seemed so burdensome. Ducking into the park's public restroom, she unclasped the pearls from her neck and dropped them in her purse. She peeled off the nylons and stuffed them into the trash can.

There was a little pavilion at the bottom of the hill decorated with white bunting and streamers. A Madonna song was playing, and a couple of guys in suits loitered under the awning. At first she thought it was just a party, but then she saw a girl in a long, lacy white dress fidgeting with flowers. The inside of the pavilion was lined with chairs. All the men were tattooed up and down their arms, and all the women wore strappy dresses and lots of necklaces. Makeup prevailed on both sexes. A few people had brought dogs, fat golden retrievers with bandannas around their necks, a little papillon with feather-duster ears. The Madonna song continued, and finally the girl in the lacy white dress looped her arm around an older, hippie-ish man with a white beard—her father, Sylvie presumed. They started wedding marching down the aisle.

Sylvie took a picture. She couldn't help it. The groom was sitting on a picnic table at the front of the pavilion. There was an officiant in a long, tie-dyed gown, reading from a ragged piece of lined paper. Sylvie took a picture of a baby in only a diaper, sitting next to his long-haired parents. She took another picture of the beaming father, giving the bride a big kiss. The newly married couple proceeded out to another Madonna song—that peppy one during that phase where she was into yoga—pumping their fists and grinning. Everyone clapped. When the couple saw Sylvie and her camera, they walked right up to her. She backed away, feeling like an invader.

"Can we see?" the groom asked. He was more lithe than his new wife, with thinning brown hair and square glasses. "We didn't hire a photographer."

Both leaned over the viewfinder. The bride nodded, pleased. "I'm Samara." She thrust her hand out. Her nails were painted blue.

"Sylvie."

"Do you want to come to our reception?"

Sylvie shook her head fast. "I'm not really a photographer."

"No, as a guest. You don't have to take pictures if you don't want to."

Sylvie fluttered her hands, scrambling for some excuse.

"His mom's a chef," the girl insisted, pointing to her new husband. "She did all the food. We have a bluegrass band coming. And there are cupcakes."

The reception was in a barn even farther out in the country. Early-summer crickets were chirping, and there were a few goats and chickens wandering around. Most of the guests took off their shoes and walked around in the dirt. One old man didn't leave the dance floor once. In the middle of a polka, he suddenly dropped to his knees, crawling around on the floor. Sylvie tensed, wondering if he'd had a stroke. Then the news rippled through the barn—Paul had lost his teeth again. Soon everyone was crawling on the dance floor, looking for Paul's teeth. The polka kept playing. People laughed. No one seemed concerned about germs. Dangers like MRSA seemed very far away. A little girl found the dentures under a table, apparently kicked there by some overzealous dancer. She raised them above her head, running into the middle of the dance floor. The toothless man picked her up and spun her around. He wiped off the teeth and popped them back into his mouth. Sylvie found herself smiling, laughing along with everyone else. And then in the next second, she became very aware of what she was doing. It was as though as soon as she'd peeled those nylons off her legs, something had altered in her. Here she was taking pictures of Paul and his newly found teeth. Here she was eating an extra cupcake and drinking a third glass of wine.

When Charles arrived home from Maryland, Sylvie told him her weekend had been quiet and without incident. Later she asked a boy who lived down the road to show her how to upload the photos to a server so that Samara and her new husband, Chris, could view them. A few days after she e-mailed them off, her phone rang. A woman introduced herself as Tabitha Wyler, a wedding photographer. "I'm an acquaintance of Samara Johnson," she explained. "Samara showed me the pictures you took of their wedding."

"It was just for fun," Sylvie said quickly. She wondered if she'd broken some sort of photographer code—maybe they had unions and she'd stolen a legitimate worker's business. Then Tabitha cleared her throat and asked if Sylvie wanted to do it for *more* than fun. "You're good," she said. "Maybe you'd like to work for me."

She needed an assistant, she explained, someone to help with the set-up shots, an extra pair of hands at the receptions. Most of the jobs were smaller affairs in Phoenixville and Elverson, Spring City and Gap and even Lancaster. "Most aren't high-end," Tabitha added. "I won't be able to pay you much."

"That's fine," Sylvie said fast.

The day before her first job, Sylvie was so nervous she sweated profusely through two T-shirts and kept dropping things. She fretted over her equipment. What if her camera stopped working? What if every picture she took turned out black and overexposed?

"They're digital," Charles reminded her when he came over—she'd told him by then about this increasingly foolish-sounding endeavor she'd gotten herself into. He pointed at the back of the camera. "You'll be able to see exactly what you do in the little screen. But you knew that already."

"Do you realize I've *never* had a proper job?" she cried.

Charles aimed the camera's viewfinder at the back garden and snapped a picture of Joanna, who was standing near the pool, seemingly admiring the diving board. "Did I tell you I found the cleaning lady who found Dad?" Charles said after a moment.

Sylvie stood up straighter, caught off guard. "What?"

"I ran into the guard from Dad's office who called the ambulance at this bar down the street. He told me where the cleaning lady was—she's working in another building. I tried to look for her after Dad died, but no one would tell me where she was."

"You *did?*" Sylvie asked. He had never told her this.

Charles ducked his head, shrugging it off. "So we went to her building, and the guard pointed her out to me. She was just coming through the lobby at the exact time we came through the double doors—it was like, I don't know, fate. I was going to say something to her, but I didn't. She had a kind face, though. Caring."

"Well," Sylvie said uncomfortably. "Imagine that."

But it seemed to pacify something in Charles. Even though he would never get into it, even though he might not have been able to define it for himself, she finally was assured that he had felt great depths for his father. "She seemed caring," Charles repeated.

Sylvie took a deep breath and took photos at her first wedding job. She and Tabitha, a round, chatty woman who immediately put Sylvie at ease, took pictures of the wedding at the family's farm, in a pumpkin patch. And she did more after that. Weddings that were simple lunches in people's backyards. Ones that were traditional, where the family prayed before the meal and the bride wore white without irony. There was one that was more like a sorority party, the eleven bridesmaids climbing into an enormous white limo, posing for pictures with little plastic shot glasses raised, all of them smoking cigarettes and fixing one another's hair. At a few weddings she photographed, the wedded couple didn't seem very happy, the marriage quite possibly forced. Those were always the hardest to do; when sorting through their images, she wished she knew how to use Photoshop. If she could create smiles on their faces, maybe they'd change their minds and decide to be happy.

The weddings got to her. She cried as the bride walked down the aisle with her father; she encouraged single girls to rush to the front and catch the bouquet. She found herself wishing that she and James had had a traditional wedding instead of going off to Italy and getting married there alone, estranging their families even more. She sometimes felt such strong pangs for James that she had to duck into the bathroom and press her forehead against the cool, tiled walls. Sometimes she penned letters to James in her head, explaining her new job. She wondered what James would think of her if he suddenly walked back into her life, robustly alive. Would he think she'd changed? Would he recognize her?

And what would Scott say, if, or when, he came back? She hoped he would think she'd changed. She wondered if some of these changes she'd made were with him in mind.

After the sixth or seventh wedding she worked, she woke up and realized that the heaviness in the base of her stomach had lifted. She folded James's old clothes and sent them to the Salvation Army. She bought new sheets and pillows for her bed. She drove to Philadelphia and walked to Jeweler's Row, dropping her ring onto the counter of the first store she came upon. The jeweler, a large Hasidic man, used a loupe to check the color and the carat weight and called everyone else on the street trying to come up with an accurate price. She enjoyed the anonymity of it. No one gawked at her, asking why she was getting rid of something so large and pretty.

Then she went into James's old office and put all his books in boxes. She called an antiques dealer to appraise James's desk and bookshelves—a mid-century designer had made them, so they were probably worth some money. When the dealer walked into the house, his eyes boggled at her grandfather's items, the furniture in the living room and the oil paintings on the walls. It wasn't the first time someone had done this; Sylvie could practically see him making calculations in his head, already counting the money. She'd always balked at selling anything of her grandfather's, but something in her slowly began to turn. She called an appraiser named Florence, who had known her parents and had helped Sylvie sell off some of their furnishings when both of them died. Florence wandered around the house, making notes in a book, pressing her pencil eraser to her lips. She ran her fingers over his books and paintings. She opened drawers in the kitchen and smiled at their old dishes and silverware. There was no point in moving all of this stuff out of the house and breaking up what was here, Florence concluded. It all was worth more together, an encapsulated life.

"It is amazing how preserved this place is," Florence said with a sigh when Sylvie saw her out. "Your grandfather would be very proud."

After Florence left, Sylvie sat in the empty living room with the lights off, feeling almost as though she was saying her good-byes now. As she heaved another sigh, she sensed a presence behind her and turned. The light shimmered and shifted, and suddenly he was there, really there, all cigar smoke and mustache and twinkling eyes.

"Hello, Charlie Roderick," Sylvie whispered. He lingered there, light waves and ozone, watching her. Tears came to her eyes. It had been so long since she'd said his name out loud. She hoped he thought she'd done the right thing. She hoped he would forgive her, too. But before she could ask him, he was gone.

Sylvie saw the same wedding industry people again and again—Frankie-the-DJ, who line-danced with the crowd, Hattie-the-florist who drove a big van painted yellow and black like a bumblebee, the same string quartet, made up of three Asian women and a tall, reedy black man who always wore three-piece suits. He waved at her every time he saw her, and finally, at a fire-hall wedding in Elverson, Sylvie waved back. His name was Desmond, and he lived in Villanova. His wife had died fifteen years ago of pancreatic cancer, and he'd been alone ever since. His voice was just what she expected—deep and resonant. Years ago she would've shied away from Desmond, wary of his upright self-composure. But that felt like a long time ago. The first time Sylvie danced with Desmond, at the end of one of the weddings when the band was playing their last song, she fully understood how different she'd become.

Sometimes Christian and Warren snuck into her thoughts. By the time Labor Day rolled around, she'd almost let that go, too. She hadn't expected to work a wedding that long weekend, but Tabitha called her and said that a photographer needed an emergency appendectomy, and a bride who was getting married this evening had just called in a panic. Can you run out and get film for me, Tabitha pleaded—she liked to use both film and digital.

Sylvie threw on some clothes and got into the car. She didn't go to the camera store she usually frequented, whose owners she'd gotten to know, but to the photo shop next to the new Target that had sprung up near her house.

Inside, the shop smelled like developing chemicals. Sylvie waited in line, gazing blankly out the window at the families going into Target. "Oh," said the person in front of her in line. "Well, hello."

It took a moment before she realized the man was talking to her. She turned and then pressed her fingers to her throat. Warren Givens didn't look nearly as ragged as she remembered. His hair was combed, his face had more color to it, and he was wearing a clean, snazzy green Windbreaker and crisp dark jeans. "H–hi," she stammered, her chest seized with apprehension. She hadn't seen him since the MRSA news broke. Since she'd resigned.

"How are you?" Warren asked. His eyes were still that watery blue.

One of his front teeth was gray, maybe dead. The overhead lights beat down on her head. "Listen," she started, shuffling through the possibilities of how she could broach the subject. *I'm so sorry about what happened.* Or, *I hope the school took care of you.* Or, *I want you to know I have nothing to do with that place anymore. It's just terrible that it happened.*

But before she could say anything, Warren interrupted. "So you hear about the new management?"

She blinked. New management . . . where? Here in this little photo shop?

"They're doing landscaping and everything," he went on. "Cleaning up that park. Finally, right? Making that playground actually safe for kids." He gave her a weary smile. "My five-year-old grandson fell off the monkey bars in that playground. I turned my back for one minute and he was flat on the ground. Broke his back, can you imagine? They were worried he'd be paralyzed. Bitch of a thing. But he's okay now. He dodged a bullet, so to speak . . . gonna be fine."

Sylvie frowned, scrambling to understand. Warren had a grandson as well as a son? Did that mean Christian had a much older brother or sister, perhaps? There had been so little information about the Givens family.

The salesman behind the counter reappeared with a thick packet. "Verona?"

Warren Givens raised one finger and stepped to the counter. He was hunched over, signing his name on a receipt. Sylvie crept forward, even more puzzled. She peeked at the name on the packet of film. *Sam Verona*, it said. The handwriting was clear and round with little margin for mistake.

Sam Verona?

He palmed the packet of photos and smiled at her. "Pictures of my grandson," he announced. "He's in rehab. He *loves* rehab. Best friends with everyone. Helps the clown make balloon animals." He opened the flap and pulled one out. A chubby-cheeked kid with blond curls sat on a hospital bed, a spongy brace around his neck. He had a gap-toothed smile.

"How long will he have to be in rehab?" Sylvie asked.

"Oh, a couple of months. Pretty soon it'll be outpatient."

"He's beautiful," Sylvie said with a sigh. "I'm glad he's okay."

"You said it." He put his wallet in his back pocket. "What did you say your name was again?"

"Sylvie," she said. "Sylvie Bates-McAllister."

"Right," Sam said. "And I'm Sam Verona. Well, see you around, Sylvie. Maybe on the benches, huh?"

She nodded, everything moving much too fast. One second later, the photo shop bells were ringing and he was out the door. A few seconds after that, he was stepping off the curb and crossing to his car.

It was a white car, a car she was pretty sure she recognized from the Feverview Dwellings parking lot.

It should have occurred to her, really. She'd never asked his name, and when she'd given him her name at the apartment complex, he hadn't shown any recognition. Nor had she ever seen a picture of Christian's real father, whoever he was. This man had stumbled out of the apartment complex and put his head in his hands, and she'd assumed that the world was very small, that everything was connected. But this man, Sam, was crying about something else. About his injured grandchild, maybe, and some misguided guilt he felt for it. Or maybe he was upset about something else. His life could include a wide range of things to grieve over, just as it could encompass a vast range of things to be happy about.

Christian's father had an apartment at Feverview Dwellings, too, and yet he'd never made himself known. It was possible he'd passed her as she and the man she thought was him were talking. But he'd grieved differently, in a way she hadn't anticipated. His whole life was probably wildly different from what she pictured.

Something else struck her. *Did you hear?* Sam asked. *We have new management. They're going to landscape and everything.*

We have new management. He thought she lived at Feverview Dwellings. She'd been *there*, after all, and who loiters around a place like that? She glanced down at herself, alarmed. Did she look as though she lived there? Hadn't he noticed the label on her purse, the kidskin leather of her gloves, the quality of her shoes, her ring? And yet he must not have. He'd only seen her proximity. He had misjudged her just as she had misjudged him. She pressed her hand to her forehead. And then she smiled.

The wedding she and Tabitha were photographing was in Philadelphia in a big clipper-ship restaurant that sat in the Delaware

River harbor. When Sylvie climbed aboard, she realized she'd once been here with James a long time ago, back when the boys were still in high school. She fought to remember the mood of the dinner, but she couldn't recall a single thing they'd talked about, a single thing they'd eaten. It was possible James had been seeing the woman back then. It was possible he had already bought that bracelet for her. He could already have been carrying the secret around by then, doing everything he could so that she would never find out.

She loved him, despite all of it. That was real love, she supposed—overlooking even what was ugly. But it made her sad, too, to realize that the ugliness was there. The blinders were off her now, and she couldn't put them back on no matter how badly she wanted to. Some days, she really wanted to. Some days, she didn't feel better off. She didn't feel cleaner, purer, wiser; instead it felt like she was constantly standing naked in a raw, whipping wind. She envied her past self, purposeful, oblivious, and naive. But she also felt a battle-worn trueness that hadn't been there before. She felt like she could really do things now. Really change things. Even things she'd thought she'd never dare.

One side of the boat was pitched down slightly. The tables on that side were bolted down, the legs cut to uneven lengths so they'd be level. The ceremony was to take place in front of a mural of a bearded Poseidon holding a trident. The same string quartet was setting up shop on the slanty side of the room, and there was Desmond. His face lit up when he saw Sylvie, and she waved. She decided she would tell him about Sam Verona. And about what had happened, and who she thought Sam had been, and even the letter she'd written to him, the letter she'd never given him. It was crazy—she barely knew anything about Desmond except for the broad, sweeping things everyone told strangers about their lives when they first meet—but she knew she'd tell him anyway, and weather whatever response he had.

There was commotion in the lobby; the wedding party began to file in. The groom walked down the aisle to the Poseidon mural. He was older than she was—maybe James's age, around seventy. As he got closer, she saw there was a small hearing aid in his ear. The groom noticed the camera around her neck and came over. "Thanks for helping us out at such short notice," he exhaled, grasping her hand. "We thought we were stuck."

The bride walked alone down the aisle. She had shoulder-length white hair. Her drop-waist dress hit at the knee, and she wore ivory pumps. When she saw the man she was marrying, tears came to her eyes. She waved at him giddily, as if she was a kid on a merry-go-round and had just rounded past her parents. They exchanged rings and kissed, then hugged their respective children, six in all.

Not long ago, Sylvie might've thought the ecstatic, hopeful looks on the couple's faces were impractical. Why go through all that trouble to get married at that age? It's not as if they were naive teens. But now, she was sympathetic to their exuberance. It was kind of beautiful how regenerative optimism was, how people could hurl themselves headlong into the same situations again and again.

Felicia and Graham, the bride and groom, got up for their first dance. His big, craggy hands clutched her waist, and they both took small, careful steps. They smiled into each other, delighted. It was a look Sylvie had seen on so many other faces this summer—the look that said this day set the tone for their entire marriage and that every day henceforth would be as beautiful as this one. They didn't bother worrying about the curveballs life would throw at them, the difficult decisions they'd have to make, or even the disappointments. Right now, those things didn't exist.

Sylvie crouched down and took another picture. And she silently said the same thing she always said to all the couples she'd met. *Keep holding on to that,* she told them. *Keep holding on and don't let go.*

Epilogue

He almost drove by the exit at first. The sign for it was smaller than he remembered. The toll booths were meager and hokey, the lanes separated by staggered orange construction cones. There was a steakhouse on the corner now instead of the old Applebee's. The sign for the Gray Horse Inn that hosted art shows and served Mother's Day brunch had gotten larger, now featuring curly, old-timey script. There were leaves on the trees now, not just buds but fat, summery foliage. He had missed the beginning of spring, the floral scents in the air, everyone opening their windows for the first time, the appearance of bees in the garden. He'd missed summer, fall, and winter, too, looping back to late spring. It was an unusually humid day. When he shifted his legs on the seats, there was a thin sheen of sweat on the leather.

When he came to the turnoff to the house, he realized he couldn't go there. Not yet. So he checked into the motel down the road, a one-story complex he'd driven past countless times. He expected alarm bells to go off as soon as he set foot back here. He expected the motel proprietor to beam broadly and say, "Why, hey there, boy! Where've you been?" What would he reply? Would he grin back and answer, sheepishly, "I took a little adventure"? Would he tell him why?

As it turned out, Scott didn't recognize the guy behind the motel desk. His face wasn't one he'd passed at the grocery store or nodded at while stopped at a traffic light. He'd never seen the man in the aisles at Pep Boys. The man handed Scott a flat, credit card–shaped room key impersonally and turned back to his baseball game on a little black-and-white TV. There was a Phillies pennant hanging behind the desk, a tribute to their World Series win last year. As Scott walked to his room, he wondered if he was still a Phillies fan. Or were the Diamondbacks now officially his team? Maybe the Diamondbacks had always technically been his team—in Arizona, when people asked him where he was from, he always said, "Here." It was, he figured, the truest answer.

When he got to the motel room, he slung his bag on the table, took off his shoes, and lay down on the bed. The ceiling was roughly plastered, looking like thick globs of cottage cheese. Outside, birds twittered. They sounded different from the Arizona birds, but the same, too. And the wind brushing through the trees was the same, the cars swishing down the roads. Somehow, he'd expected things to be different. He'd expected the world to fall down as soon as he crossed state lines.

It had all started when his apartment got that leak. He'd been staying in his mother's side of the house for a couple of days when he woke up in his childhood bedroom, drenched with sweat. It happened sometimes. He was never able to fall back to sleep when it did, so he'd gotten up and padded around the upstairs, looking into his brother's old room, the shared bathroom, and then, finally, his father's office.

A key had been sitting on the desk. There was only one thing in the room that had a lock. Why he unlocked the drawer, he wasn't sure. How he'd known what would be inside wasn't clear to him. There had been one folder, lying flat at the metal bottom. It was unmarked. Scott had picked it up and opened it. Inside were a few documents from the Family Service adoption agency in Tucson, Arizona.

They had never shown him these papers, though he'd searched for them for years. Although he'd asked details about his birth mother, where she was from, what she was like, nothing was ever explained. He'd had a whole two years of his life elsewhere, and it was infuriating that he didn't remember a single thing about it. His mother told Scott when he was very young that she didn't really know whom he'd come from, only that *they* had stepped in, *they* had adopted him. His parents told him that his mommy was white and his daddy was black—which was *special*—but after Scott brought up that a friend at school had whispered that Scott's great-grandfather banned black children from Swithin, all talk about his birth parents ceased. His mother veered away from the topic whenever it came up; his father made vague hand motions and told Scott that it wasn't worth dwelling on things like that.

Scott *did* dwell. How could he not? How was he supposed to swallow this and just *be* one of them when he knew he wasn't? They were doing this on purpose, he figured, hiding it from him for precisely the reasons only Charles had had the balls to suggest, because he was *different*, and being different wasn't good. *Fine*, he'd thought. Let them really see how different he was. He'd show them all.

The adoption papers in the filing cabinet didn't say much. There were prints of his hands and feet, a record of his birth weight and length and date. Names were blacked out, but there was the adoption agency's address and phone number. It was in Tucson, Arizona. He had been born at the University Medical Center on Campbell Avenue.

It had been as good a time as any to leave. He barely remembered that drive across the country, a frantic, scattered four days of highways and sad, generic motels, maxing out his credit card, throwing his cell phone, which kept ringing, out the window at one point, watching it disappear in the side mirror. When he got to Tucson, he checked into the cheapest hotel he could find, bought a map, found his way to the adoption agency, and explained who he was. The woman working there, an overweight lady in her thirties who spoke in broken, accented English, said that his adoption file had been closed—there was no way he could find out any more information about the people who had given him up.

"I'm sorry," she said, giving him a watery smile.

"But I drove across the country for this," Scott protested.

"I'm sorry" was all she replied, in honeyed tones.

He turned away, stepping out into the impenetrable heat. Tucson, Arizona. Never did he imagine he was from somewhere like here. Detroit, maybe. South Central. Not that Tucson wasn't tough, but it seemed slow, lazy, stupefied by the sun. He stared at the sun-baked stucco on the outside of the adoption agency building. Across the street, a leathery-skinned man was fiddling with the tire of his car. He tried to picture growing up here, living here, never knowing of his life in that big, spooky house with that great-grandfather he was in no way related to bearing down on him every time he walked up the stairs.

Over the next few days he went to the adoption agency again

and again, begging for answers. The obsession with knowing metastasized in his head. It was the only way, he decided, that he would truly understand who he *was*. But it was always that same padded woman, always that same dim smile, always the same *I'm sorry*. Once, he threw a balled-up napkin at her, furious. Another time, he fought with the locked door to the agency's bathroom until the person on the inside came out, hands raised in surrender, as if Scott was robbing him. It was an old man, a suspicious wet dribble on the front of his khaki pants. "I'm sorry," the man said over and over. His eyes looked enormous behind his glasses. "It's all yours. I'm sorry." As the complex's security guard escorted Scott out of the agency, telling him he was never allowed to set foot there again, Scott felt sticky with shame.

This was all his parents' fault, he decided, for hiding the truth from him. For his mother wanting him to be part of their world but always making him feel separate. For his father never encouraging him to look beyond working on cars or beating up kids in wrestling to something loftier and more challenging. For both of them turning the other cheek at his miserable report cards, for nodding mutely when he said he wanted to quit piano lessons, all the while forcing Charles to play, smacking his wrists if he didn't practice. For never telling Scott to move out of their house, for so completely sheltering him from the world.

And why? Was it because of some long-seeded, pent-up guilt? Some fist-curling, hair-pulling agony they felt for all the dirty looks and thoughts they'd had about people of different races, people of different means? What flowed out of Charles's mouth that day of the party all those years ago didn't surprise Scott in the slightest—it was what he'd imagined they thought all along. Except they weren't saying it, of course. They were suppressing it as best they could. They had been so politically correct with him, tripping over their feet trying to make him feel equal, merely pigeonholing him more.

Or maybe they hadn't pushed him because they'd known he wouldn't be able to take it. Maybe they'd lost faith in him long before he'd had the chance to prove anything. Maybe that was part of the pigeonhole, too. They knew Charles's background and thus could pinpoint his potential, but with Scott? Who the hell knew? Just let him do whatever the hell he wants.

Didn't we give you a good life? his mother had said to him. *Didn't we take care of you?*

And then there was that kid, Christian. Scott knew his name all too well now, called up his name at lightning speed, whereas before it sometimes took him a moment, only identifying him by the nickname he'd given him in his head, *Phantom*, because of the way he lurked around the locker room, because of the way he slipped soundlessly into warm-up before practice, because of his pancake-white face and that burlap thing he wore as a jacket and the way he chattered to himself, freaking out the other boys. He wasn't a nice kid. Oh they twisted that after he died. He was a son of a bitch, sniggering remarks about the other kids loud enough for them to hear, precisely diagnosing their worst insecurities: one boy's bubble ass, another boy's stutter. Scott even heard Christian's snarky, slithery, Jack Nicholson–timbre voice cackle about the puny size of a certain kid's cock, the biggest, burliest kid on the team, the one who made disparaging remarks about homos at every turn. It was surgical, the way Christian did it. A precise, deadly talent.

And no wonder the kid got shit for it. As time went on, though, Scott came to realize that Christian wanted to provoke them. He wanted to catch hell for it. After practice one day, Scott caught him alone and grabbed his arm. Christian's face got stone hard and opaque. There were a lot of things Scott wanted to say to him. Scott knew why he was doing it. He might not know the specifics—a shitty home life, an absent father, an overworked mother, beatings, molestation, somehow landing in this school, always feeling unwanted and never knowing his place—but Christian had a good eye for insecurities because he had so many of his own. Scott wanted to tell the kid that he didn't have to be like this, and the more he was, the worse it would be. The thicker the shell, the darker the days, the more miserable the life until he would wake up and have no idea who he fucking *was* anymore. He wanted to bestow dadlike wisdom to him, really get through to him that it *didn't have to be like this*. But all he could say was, "Watch it, bro. Got it?" And Christian had stared at him, dead-eyed, and hissed, "Whatever, white boy. Go drive your Lexus." And then he turned around and sauntered out.

A few days later, Scott saw some of the boys in the practice room, huddled in a circle, Christian in the middle. It was probably where someone got the idea they were hazing—there was a fraternal ritual to it, each boy taking an orderly turn to throw a punch. And yeah, Scott looked away. He felt no emotions about it, either. His apathy formed a hard and waxy crust around him, like the outer shell of a beetle. Fuck that kid. Let him learn the hard way. He deserved it.

In Arizona, after the guard shoved Scott out of the agency, fury snapped off his body like lightning. He hated that he'd walked away from that kid. He hated what he'd somehow become. He sank to the ground and slammed his fist into the concrete sidewalk, again and again, blood rising on his knuckles. He did it until it hurt, and then cradled his damaged fist in his lap, watching the blood pool.

Next door to the adoption agency was another office, some sort of nonprofit for immigrant services. A blade-thin woman pushed out that office's door and noticed him, sitting there, bleeding, his arms around his jack-knifed knees. "Oh my goodness," she said, rushing over. "What happened?"

Scott didn't answer. She crouched down. Her lipstick was glossy and over-applied. Under her arm were a bunch of papers in a manila folder. Scott's mouth felt dry. The Arizona desert had sucked all the words from him. He could hear his heart sloshing in his ears. All the breath seemed to leave him, and spots formed in front of his eyes.

When he woke up, he was lying on an uncomfortable couch. The room was very cold; the woman who had been standing over him outside was now sitting behind a gray, metal desk, watching him carefully. She sighed with relief as he took in a breath. "I think you had a panic attack," she said. "My brother used to get them. I'm Veronica, by the way."

She let Scott lie there for a moment and get his bearings, bringing him a sip of water from a paper cone. After a while, she gestured toward where the adoption agency was and asked if he had been turned down. "Yes," he answered.

She clucked her tongue. "Their rules," she said. "The way I see it, whoever wants a child should get one."

He blinked, startled. "No, I *am* the child," he said.

At that, Veronica said she was finished with work for the day. She took him by the hand and brought him back to her apartment, which was only a few blocks away. It was the bottom unit of a sunburst-yellow stucco building, the railings chipped, the walkways crumbling, the landscaping tattered and weedy. The apartment was small but clean, with cheerful striped curtains in the windows. She got him some tea, and then sat down next to him on the couch and asked him to tell her what had happened. Scott did. And when he was finished, he asked what he should do. "Keep going back to that agency," she said. 'They'll eventually tell you, if you want to know."

"They kicked me out."

"I'll go for you, if you want."

Because he didn't want to touch any more of the money he'd withdrawn from his trust—he didn't want his family to trace him here—Scott got a job cleaning a dog daycare center in the university section of town to pay for his tiny one-room apartment. Veronica, who slept over a lot, pestered the adoption agency again and again, but it never came to anything. Still, she kept trying.

A year passed, a whole year in Arizona—the excruciating heat leading to brain-melting heat, leading to God-fearing thunderstorms, leading to thick humidity. There were about two weeks of pleasant weather, and then the cycle repeated again. Veronica was originally from Phoenix. She told him about her job helping undocumented workers find work and medical care and housing. She told Scott stories of how those people trekked through the desert for six days just to reach the United States, some of them falling behind, some of them getting lost, many of them dying of dehydration. "All to get here," she said. "All to get to this country and have what we all take for granted."

Scott hadn't meant to fall in love with her; he hadn't meant to fall in love with anyone. And yet, maybe he'd fallen in love with her the very first moment she'd squatted down on that hot pavement and put her arms around him. Maybe he'd fallen for her for listen-ing.

But he should have known. He should have known the day was going to come. He was lying in Veronica's bed, the sheets wrapped around him, the fan pointed at his head. Veronica emerged from the bathroom holding something plastic between her fingers. There had been a big smile on her face when she held the pink wand aloft. Her happiness had been the most shocking part of it all.

After she told him, he sat up in bed. "I'm not going to be able to give you what you want," he said. "I can't be the person you need for this."

"Oh, now," she said, perching next to him. "You're just scared. I called my family. You should call yours."

"Call *mine?*" he repeated. He shook his head. He expected her, of all people, to understand. "I can't do that. I can't do *this.*"

Her face fell. She set the wand on the nightstand. "Why not?"

"Because . . . I can't. I can't do anything."

She blew a raspberry at him. "Of course you can. Do you think I just go around sleeping with anybody? Do you think I would've even *come* to you if I thought you wouldn't have been able to handle this?"

He stared at her. It was then he realized that in her eyes, he had actually seemed capable. Powerful. Up to the challenge. It wasn't something he was used to.

He stood up and thrust his legs into his jeans. "I have to go."

"What?" she cried.

"I just need some time."

"Can you talk to me about it?"

But he wasn't sure he could explain it if he tried, only that it felt like there was a pressure inside him, a blinking red light ready to detonate. Escaping seemed like the only option. He kept his phone off, not wanting to answer her calls. He would disappear. She would never hear from him again.

At first, he didn't know where he was going. On the road, his fingers gripping the wheel, the car stinking of his sweat, he screamed when people cut him off. He smoked cigarettes down to the nub and immediately lit new ones. A child stuck her tongue out at him as a minivan passed, and he felt the urge to run the car off the road.

And then, all of the anger seeped out of him, a slow leak from a tire. Was it really the worst thing that someone believed in him? Was it really the smartest thing to *run* from her? He thought about what Joanna had said more than a year ago, that acting like an asshole was easier because people had fewer expectations of him. It *was* what he was doing. It was what that spook kid had done, too.

And then he began to wonder what his brother was doing. And his mother, knocking around in that big house, passing under that picture of Charlie Roderick Bates. He wondered what his apartment had been converted into, and if the same rusty patio furniture was on the back deck, and if his mother was planting the exact same configuration of flowers in the garden, re-creating her childhood anew every spring. It wasn't with nostalgia that he thought about this, not at first, but more with weary guilt. All this time, he'd told himself that they probably weren't wondering about him, or if they were, it was in a tight-assed, bitter sort of way—*look what we did for him, and this is how he repays us, the piece of shit.* But all of a sudden, he wondered if they weren't as cruel as he thought. And he wanted to see that house. See if it matched up to the house in his memory and his dreams, so everything would make sense again.

T hey *had* expected more from him, though. That was what Scott
    also began to realize, driving back to the East Coast. That was
the thought that had begun to trickle in uninvited. It was in the secret
his father had made him keep. It was in the silence he'd made him
promise to fulfill.

His father had found him the day Scott had seen them together,
after Bronwyn had left. "It's not what you think," he'd tried to explain.

But Scott knew what he saw. There had been the silence in the
room, serious and intimate. There had been their expressions when
they turned and saw him standing there, for he'd been too stunned
to slip away unnoticed.

"Please," his father said, crouching down next to Scott's bed,
curling his finger tight around the wooden bedpost. Scott's room
had been filthy, boxers strewn everywhere, drawers flung open, rotting food in the trash can, but his father hadn't complained. He
probably hadn't noticed the mess at all. "You can't tell anyone about
this," he said. "It's not something I can explain. You'll do that for
me, won't you?"

In the end, Scott didn't do it to please his father. He told him
as much, too. He did it because there seemed nothing worse than
his mother finding *this* out. His brother, too. He wiped it from his
memory, pretending he'd never seen it and it hadn't happened. But
it forced him to wipe away his father, too.

You can have any of your father's clothes, his mother had said.
And, *he was a good man*. She didn't know. She had never known.
And that was partly because of him. His brother had never known
it about Bronwyn, either—although he wondered if Charles had

finally found out, the day Scott left home. Joanna had suggested they were meeting, and then there was the look on Charles's face when Scott crossed his path at the house. The look that the rug had been pulled out from under him. Everything he thought was true was suddenly suspect.

There were countless times Scott wondered if he should have just said something, if it was worse that he was keeping it quiet, if perhaps *this* was why he was given all he'd been given—all the leeway, the suite, the car, the spending money. Then again, he'd willingly taken it. He'd willingly been a part of his father's lie, though he didn't have to. He could have left a long time ago. Just like he could have sloughed off the identity they'd pinned on him, from whatever guidelines and whatever sources, so early on. They assumed what they assumed about him partly because he'd let them. Partly because it was easier to. But he might have had a choice.

Roderick was only a few miles away from the motel, so after Scott took a shower, changed, and watched a few hours' worth of crap television, he finally felt that he was ready to go. It would be a trial run, he decided, a drive-by. He got into the car and started the engine. Every inch of the road was familiar, every leaf on the trees. When he rounded the turn toward his house, he held his breath. The trees blurred past. There was the farm with the split-rail fence and the endlessly identical white woolen sheep. There was the little red house set precariously close to the road, the one Scott and Charles used to joke about in the back of the car that would get mowed in half if a car accidentally swerved into it. And then, the light hitting the tops of the trees, the road curving just so, and there was the big black mailbox.

Except there was a gate at the end of the driveway now. A big metal gate that was ajar but that had a large lock dangling from a hinge. There was a sign on the gate, too. RODERICK. EST. 1922. TOURS AVAILABLE.

Also on the sign was a list of hours of operation, 10 A.M.–5 P.M. ON WEEKDAYS AND 12 P.M.–4 P.M. ON SATURDAYS, CLOSED SUN-DAYS. Scott's brain was so scrambled for a moment that he couldn't recall what day it was, and when he looked at the glowing num-bers of the clock on the dashboard—4:23—he wasn't sure if it was morning or afternoon. And then he wondered if he was on a differ-ent road entirely, in front of a different house, another house also coincidentally named Roderick.

When he heard a tap on his window, he jumped and looked over. It was a woman he didn't recognize, with blonde hair and a long face. She bent over halfway, smiling toothily into the car. Her mouth moved, saying something Scott couldn't hear. He rolled down the window. "What was that?" he said.

"Are you here for a tour?" she asked. "I was just closing up. We close officially in about a half hour."

He blinked at her. "People tour this place?"

She smiled cheerfully. "It was just added to the Pennsylvania registry of historical homes. This house is very significant to the area. Gorgeous gardens. A lot of priceless antiques. A real treasure."

She had cupped her hand over the lip of his window. He could smell her floral perfume. She didn't recognize who he was. She had no idea what it meant that he was here. She probably knew nothing about this house beyond its facts and figures, the types of flowers in the gardens, the craftsmen of the furniture in the living room, the artists of the paintings on the walls. She was probably just a bored

Main Line wife, busying herself with something she considered culturally significant.

Headlights appeared in the rearview mirror, a car wanting to get around. Scott looked at the woman. "It's okay," he said after a moment. "Another time, maybe."

She smiled and raised a finger in the air. "Here," she said, reaching into her cardigan pocket. She pulled out a long, thin pamphlet and passed it through the open window. "This'll give you an idea of what's inside."

"Thanks," Scott said, barely feeling the pamphlet between his fingers. And then he cut the wheel left to turn back onto the road. He drove back to the motel, parked the car, and walked up the metal steps to his room. He slipped off his shoes and turned on the television, settling down on the bed, his arms straight at his sides, his feet pointed to the ceiling. The AC was on too high, and the tip of his nose felt cold. Shivers ran up and down his spine.

He should have asked the woman how this house had been turned over to the registry. Why had his mother done it? Where did she go? Where *could* she go? All Scott's life his mother hadn't as much as replaced a dish . . . and now she was gone? It gave him an odd, prickly sensation that almost bordered on panic. All the time he'd spent wondering about how his family was getting on without him, it had never occurred to him that they might *change*. They'd always been so static, so unwilling to deviate an inch one way or another. Scott wasn't sure he'd ever been so surprised in his life. It made him sit up, swing his legs over the bed, and put his hands on his knees, smiling vacantly toward the carpet, utterly mystified. *This house is a prison*, he'd told his mother the last time he'd seen her. *A great stone jail*. Maybe in the end, she agreed with him. Maybe he didn't understand her as much as he thought he did. What he saw of her was his projection, not exactly the truth.

The pamphlet for the house sat on the little wooden table by the window, and he was able to reach for it without getting off the bed. *Roderick*, said the cover. *Historic Pennsylvania Home.* And there was his house. There was his front yard where he and his dad had carved their names into one of the sycamore tree trunks. There was his bedroom window. There was the roundabout driveway where he'd parked his car. Inside, he saw that sad old kitchen, that fussy dining room, the chandelier above the entranceway. That crazy grand staircase that seemed better suited for a Southern plantation house. The stained-glass windows and the old four-poster beds in every bedroom and the window seats and the secret passageway that led from the guest bedroom down to the kitchen, probably once meant for servants. Scott used to play in that secret staircase, which wasn't really a secret at all, as his parents knew full well it was there, but they pretended it was his and only his. Once, he wrote a message that said *SOS, I am from another planet, who are you?* and left it on the stairs, hoping someone—Charles, especially—would find it and write back. Every day he checked. He even hinted to his brother that there was something strange on the staircase, but Charles never took the bait, never cared. A few days later, a new slip of paper appeared, lifting Scott's heart. *My name is Mom*, said the message. *Welcome, extraterrestrial! Would you like to come for dinner? We feed all kinds from all planets.*

Scott leafed through every page of the pamphlet until he got to the very back, which listed the phone number, hours of operation, and showed a picture of the house's gift shop. And to his astonishment—although he realized just a few seconds later that he shouldn't be surprised at all, for it made complete sense—the gift shop was where his apartment used to be. They'd cleaned up the water damage, smoothed the splintering wood floor, and ripped up the kitchenette, and now there were small tables of books, T-shirts, stickers, and other knickknacks. Squinting at the inset photos of the featured items for sale, the things sold in the gift shop had no significance to the house at all. Little animal finger puppets for kids. A heavy ceramic frog paperweight. A book of Pennsylvania Dutch recipes.

It wasn't really his house anymore. It wasn't really any of theirs, and maybe it never had been.

He hugged his knees to his chest and then looked at his cell phone. When he moved to Tucson, he'd changed over his number to one with a 520 area code, but he'd keyed in all his contacts from his old phone from Pennsylvania, including everyone in his family. Even though he'd staunchly told himself that he wanted nothing to do with them, some part of his brain told him to keep their numbers safe. Maybe his mother hadn't changed her cell phone number. Maybe his brother lived in that same development. There were ways of finding them.

A car rumbled past outside. The air smelled like sweet, Pennsylvania spring, a sharp contrast to the dusty, gritty, baked smell that permeated Tucson. But he liked it there. He liked it a lot. It felt like an epiphany, admitting that. It felt like the first time he'd conceded to liking anything.

The cell phone's interior light glowed a dull, ice-pop blue. He scrolled through his contact numbers and pressed SEND. As he listened to the phone ringing, he felt lighter and lighter, a balloon rising higher into the sky. There were lots of things he liked. There were a lot of things left to do. It was possible that if he pestered the adoption agency enough, they would tell him something. It was possible that he could be what Veronica wanted him to be. At least he could try for her.

He could bring Veronica back here, walk her through the historical house, pretending he was a tourist, and show her the map of the life he'd once lived. The table where they'd eaten meals together. The backyard where so many parties had been held. The garage where he and his father worked on cars. His brother's room, which he'd sat outside of sometimes when he was small, listening, hoping for an invitation inside. The chair in which his mother sat in his room when she read him stories before bed.

The phone rang, and then there was a *click*. "Scott?" Veronica asked, in lieu of hello. "Is that you?"

He pressed the phone close to his face, feeling its inert, mechanical warmth. "Yes," he answered. "It's me."

Acknowledgments

Many thanks to the early readers of this book: Cari Luna, Colleen McGarry, and my mother, Mindy Shepard. The business of writing is so difficult, but you make it much less solitary. Much appreciation to Cathryn Summerhayes, Andy McNicol, and Anais Borja at William Morris for their many read-throughs and insight. And I would be lost without the brilliant support of Carrie Kania, Jennifer Hart, and Amanda Kain at HarperCollins, and especially my editor, Maya Ziv. They keep me going, they're always my champion, and they've given me such fantastic support. I feel so fortunate to have them on my team.

Thanks to Doug and Fran Wilkens for opening their house to us, where much of this novel was completed. And, finally, much love to Joel, for still being here, for being okay, for getting through this year. I don't know what I'd do without you.

S ara Shepard graduated from NYU and has an MFA from Brooklyn College. The author of the bestselling young adult series *Pretty Little Liars* and *The Lying Game*, as well as the adult novel *The Visibles*, she currently lives outside Philadelphia with her husband and dogs.